CEDAR MILL COMM LIBRARY
12505 NW CORNELL RD
PORTLAND, OR 97229
(503) 644-0043

WITHDRAWN
CEDAR MILL LIBRARY

D0049264

THE
TRIUMPHANT

Lesley Livingston

RAZORBILL

RAZORBILL

An Imprint of Penguin Random House LLC
New York

First published in the United States of America by Razorbill,
an imprint of Penguin Random House LLC, 2019

Copyright © 2019 Lesley Livingston

RAZORBILL & colophon is a registered trademark
of Penguin Random House LLC.

Visit us online at penguinrandomhouse.com

Penguin Random House supports copyright. Copyright fuels
creativity, encourages diverse voices, promotes free speech, and creates
a vibrant culture. Thank you for buying an authorized edition of this book
and for complying with copyright laws by not reproducing, scanning,
or distributing any part of it in any form without permission. You are
supporting writers and allowing Penguin Random House to continue
to publish books for every reader.

LIBRARY OF CONGRESS CATALOGING-IN-PUBLICATION DATA IS AVAILABLE.
ISBN 9780451480682

Printed in the United States of America

1 3 5 7 9 10 8 6 4 2

Interior design: Eric Ford

This is a work of fiction. Names, characters, places, and incidents
either are the product of the author's imagination or are used fictitiously,
and any resemblance to actual persons, living or dead, businesses,
companies, events, or locales is entirely coincidental.

For the women in my life: warriors, gladiators, sisters, queens.

I

"URI . . . VINCIRI . . ."

Standing with my eyes shaded against the brightness of the rising sun, I could hear the sacred gladiatorial oath I'd spoken beneath the light of the Huntress Moon whispering like a strange, secret song in my ears.

"Verberari . . . ferroque necari . . ."

I blinked and looked around, glancing over at Elka, who stood beside me in the practice yard, eyes closed, murmuring the oath.

"What are you doing?"

"Hm?" She opened one eye and peered at me.

"What are you doing?" I repeated.

"Just going over the oath," she said. " 'I will endure to be burned . . . to be bound . . . to be beaten . . .' "

" 'And to be killed by the sword,' " I finished for her. "Yes. I know. I took it too, remember?"

"Right. Nothing in there about flying."

Ah, I thought. *So that's what this is about.*

"It's *not* flying," I said. "Think of it more as . . . uh, leaping large?"

"Imagine you're a stone!" Quintus called encouragingly to Elka from the stands beyond the barrier fence. "A great, heavy stone flung from a catapult, flying over an enemy rampart—"

He broke off abruptly when Elka turned a glare on him that made me think she was, instead, imagining herself as the gorgon Medusa, turning *him* to stone. Quint had recently joined the Roman legion corps of engineers, and as a consequence, his speech was freshly littered with animated talk of siege engines and bank-and-ditch enclosures. It made him hard to understand at the best of times, but in this case, he did have a point.

So did Elka.

There was *no* mention of flying in the oath.

And yet, in spite of that particular omission, Kore and Thalassa—the Ludus Achillea's two Cretan-born recruits—were still determined to make us do just that. Fly. Even if only for a moment . . . and right over the horns of an angry bull.

The two of them had first proposed we add the ancient art of bull-leaping to our collective skill set in the mess hall one afternoon. A sullen, steady rain had fallen for three days straight, making it impossible to practice in the yard without drowning in mud, and we were all restless.

"I'm bored," Damya had sighed gustily.

"Don't mope," Ajani had consoled her. "The sun will shine again one day. And then you can go back to hacking things to bits."

"That's just it." Damya shook her head. "I can hack things to bits with my eyes closed and both hands tied behind my back. I need a new challenge."

To be fair, she wasn't the only one.

It had been several months since we'd won back the ludus from our rival academy, the Ludus Amazona, and driven their master—and my own personal nightmare— Pontius Aquila into disgrace. The popularity of our fighters in subsequent matches had, unsurprisingly, risen dramatically from an already high point. The mob had gone wild for us. But that was months ago. And now . . . well, the mob was the mob. "Fickle" was perhaps the politest word I could conjure.

Now, when any of us stepped into the arena, there was a noticeable lull. If we weren't leading a rebellion through the streets, it seemed, the plebs weren't quite as interested. Neither were we. Our routines had become polished, precise . . . predictable. We needed something to spice up the act, as it were.

Hence Kore's suggestion of death-defying acrobatic leaps.

Through the air.

Over bulls.

Flying . . .

"Sounds like a bad idea to me," Damya had said at the time, shaking her head. "If the gods had meant for us to fly, they would have given us wings. Remember what-was-his-name? With the wax and feathers?"

"You mean Icarus?" Thalassa frowned across the table at her, reaching for an olive from a clay dish and popping it into her mouth. "Don't be silly. The gods didn't give Icarus his wings, his father Daedalus did. So he could fly away from imprisonment."

"Right," Damya snorted. "And look how well that worked out for him."

"It didn't work out well at all," Thalassa explained patiently, either ignoring or having missed the sarcasm. "In his arrogance, Icarus flew too close to the sun and the heat melted the wax that held his wings together. He fell to his death in the sea and was mourned by sirens. It's a warning. For men who think of themselves as gods. They all fall, eventually."

"Yes," Kore said, elbowing her sharply. "But *we're* not doing that. No falling. We just need to find a willing bull and build a springboard that will fling one of us up into the air, high enough to avoid its horns."

Discussion grew animated at that point. I grinned and sat back, watching my ludus sisters argue and lob bread rolls at each other, and realized, at some point, that Kore and Thalassa had actually convinced them all that introducing Cretan bull-leaping into our ludus routines was the way to go. A real guaranteed crowd-pleaser. I shook my head, thinking that it would, at the very least, keep my ludus mates occupied and out of trouble for a little while.

Then I realized that *someone* had volunteered *me* to make the first attempt.

Seven days later, and I was down on one knee in the practice arena, tying my sandal laces and tucking them in tightly so there was no chance of me tripping over them.

"I can't believe you did that."

"What?" I looked up at where Elka stood glowering murderously down at me.

"Volunteered me," she said.

"You mean after *you* volunteered *me*?" I blinked at her innocently.

"That's different." She shook her head, her tight blonde braids swinging. "You're always flinging yourself about on chariot poles and leaping off ships' masts. You're a natural."

I grinned at her. "If I can survive it, you can survive it. And then you can kill me later." I stood and rolled the tightness out of my shoulders. "If we survive . . ."

I stood and looked over to the middle of the practice ring where Kore and Thalassa were setting up their Cretan contraption. The design was based on the ones they used in the bull rings of Knossos, and they'd worked on the thing with Quint, the mighty legion engineer, for the better part of the past week. That morning, they'd dragged it proudly out of the workshop and across the sand with a flourish.

"It's . . . uh . . . a plank?" Gratia had tilted her head this way and that, looking at the thing.

It was pretty much exactly that. A plank. Only balanced on a fulcrum and secured in a frame and . . . there were ropes. And winches, maybe? I really didn't understand the workings of it. I only knew that, once my foot hit one end, that would activate what Quint called the "torsion mechanism" and the thing would fling me up and— theoretically—*over* my arena adversary.

A cantankerous cart ox named Tempest.

The closest thing we could get to an actual Cretan bull.

The air that morning had a bite to it that nipped at the exposed skin of my arms and legs, making me wish I'd worn my heavier tunic. But I also didn't want anything weighing me down. The sonorous bellowing coming from the causeway leading to the practice pitch sounded like a mournful war horn.

"I still think we should try this without the bull first," I said.

"*Ja,*" Elka agreed heartily. "Or maybe just say we did, call it a day, and head to the baths—"

"How are we supposed to tell if you can actually clear the bull with your jump if you don't actually have a bull there to clear?" Vorya asked.

Vorya was pragmatic, but she was also Varini and a fatalist—even *more* of a fatalist than Elka—so I didn't trust her opinion on the matter. Also, she wasn't the one jumping.

"And besides," she continued with a decidedly fatalistic shrug, "if it doesn't work, this way you'll probably die quickly and avoid the shame of failure."

I could never tell if she was joking or not.

Elka and I waited, pacing the arena stands in nervous anticipation, as they finished the springboard setup and brought out the ox. He looked much larger that day, out in the middle of the practice arena, than he did in his stall. With *much* larger, sharper horns. We'd tied ropes around both of his horns so that some of the girls—in this case, our Amazon sisters Kallista and Selene, and Ceto and Lysa, our two newest recruits to the ludus, both with farm backgrounds—could hold his head immobile. Tempest clearly wasn't happy about the encumbrances, though, and he snorted and bellowed. As I threw a leg over the barrier and dropped down into the arena, he fixed a baleful glare on me and pawed at the sand with one great hoof.

"I think he likes you," Elka said dryly, landing beside me.

"You better hope he likes *you*," I said. "You're going first."

That was the moment when Elka fell silent.

And started reciting the gladiatorial oath.

After enough shouted encouragement from Quint, Elka finally rounded on him and shouted back, "Call me a stone one more time, Quintus! I *dare* you!"

His mouth snapped shut, and a silence rippling with anticipation descended on the pitch. Elka snorted a breath out through her nostrils—not unlike a bull herself—and turned toward the springboard. She took a hard run at it, arms and legs pumping, and hit the target spot with both feet. The board mechanism triggered and launched her up and forward through the air, just as promised!

Elka sailed over the beast—perfectly framed in the curve of his horns—arms stretched out in front of her like she was swimming through the air. She flew clear over Tempest's withers and past his angrily swishing tail to land on her hands, tucking into a neat shoulder roll. She tumbled twice and was back up on her feet with a sprightly bounce, a look of surprise and utter delight on her face.

"I did it!" she yelped, punching her fists in the air. "I *flew*!"

An elated roar went up from our watching comrades, and I breathed a sigh of relief—for her *and* me—and waited with slightly less trepidation for Quint and Kore to reset the whole arrangement. The girls holding Tempest pulled tight on their ropes. I gathered my focus and steadied my breathing. Then I launched into a run.

My feet hit the springboard square on target, and it launched me into the arc of a perfect forward dive—just like it had Elka—only *this* time, Tempest was having none of it. The great, nasty monster threw his huge head up and to one side, knocking me cartwheeling through the air with one of his horns and flinging Kallista and the others about like dolls tied on the ends of strings. I hit the ground hard and bounced until I hit the barrier. I heard shouts from the stands and lifted my head to see the girls getting dragged across the sand by the ropes meant to hold Tempest immobile. He shook his head, yanking three of the four ropes from their hands. Kallista was the only one to hang on—barely—and she staggered to her feet as the angry beast turned his attention toward me. Selene, along with Ceto and Lysa, scampered to safety as Kallista ran to an iron ring set into the stone wall and looped the rope through, pulling it tight in the hopes of giving me a chance to escape.

Which it did . . .

But it also made her the only target left in range, and Tempest wasn't about to let her slip past. Kallista ducked down behind a low wooden wall, making herself as small as she could as Tempest battered at the barrier with his horns, snorting fury and bellowing his rage. The planks splintered and bowed inward. They wouldn't protect Kallista for very long.

Suddenly, I heard the voice of our ludus fight master ring out across the sands. "Ajani!" Kronos shouted. "*Shoot that monster!*"

Out of the corner of my eye, I saw Ajani nock an arrow to her bow.

"No!" I cried. "Ajani—no! Don't shoot!"

She hesitated.

"I'll solve this!" I called, not taking my focus off the animal in front of me.

Ajani lowered her bow, reluctant—as I knew she would be—to kill a poor, dumb beast that was only acting according to his nature. Kronos would be angry, but Ajani and I could face the consequences of his wrath together—once I managed to get out of the arena. I also simply couldn't resign myself to matching wits with a farm animal—and losing. Surely I was smarter than some grumpy old bovine.

I flung my arms wide and whistled to get Tempest's attention again.

I called out, "Kallista . . . let go of the rope!"

"If I do that, there'll be nothing stopping him," she answered, gritting her teeth as Tempest drove one of his horns all the way through the wood plank barrier, right next to her head. "He'll just come for you—aiiy!" She yelped as he shouldered the barrier and tore one of the support posts right out of the ground.

"That's the idea!" I shouted back. "Trust me—let go! Elka, throw me a towel and get to the stands above the gate!"

Without question, Elka wadded up one of the practice towels and, from where she stood in the stands, lobbed it at me. Then she ran between the benches, heading for the gate at the far end of the arena. I unwound the towel and held it unfurled in front of me. The ox had poor eyesight and swung his head from side to side trying to get a better look at me—a fresh target for his formidable horns. I'd once seen my father's cattle master get the attention of the young bulls in the herd that way. They reacted to the movement.

"Come on, you great, smelly thing . . ."

Once he'd locked his senses on to me, I called out, "Kallista . . . walk. Slowly. Don't run . . . just get out of the ring by the shortest path."

She was light on her feet and over the wall in a blink. That left just me and Tempest. I waved the towel in front of me as I backed toward the gate. When I was right in front of the archway, Elka directly above me, I snapped the towel through the air, let it go, and swung my arms up, leaping high into the air as Tempest lowered his head and charged right at me, horns gleaming. With a cry of effort, Elka caught me by both my wrists and hung on with all her strength as I swung my legs up and Tempest thundered past, a handsbreadth beneath me, through the archway. I let go of Elka's hands and dropped to the ground, running to swing the heavy gate shut. I slammed the bar through the brackets and collapsed against it, gasping in relief, and heard Tempest's confused lowing.

We'd already closed the grate on the other side of the entrance, setting up the tunnel between as a kind of gated enclosure, and the stable boy we'd coerced into helping us with Tempest in the first place was standing by with bundles of new hay and clover to feed the beast through the grate. Tempest's tantrums only ever lasted until he was given something sweet to eat. Then he was docile as a lamb and the boy could lead him peacefully back to his stall.

No harm done. Except, perhaps, to my pride . . .

Vorya slapped me on the shoulder as she passed and said, "Only a little shame. And you didn't even die. I'm impressed."

I shook my head as she walked off, whistling. But then I saw Kronos waiting for me, arms crossed over his broad chest, and I felt my neck muscles tighten. I expected him to be furious and had already resigned myself to the prospect of being relegated to laundry duty for a month.

But when I staggered over to him and sank down on a bench to catch my wind and hear my punishment, all he said was, "You want my advice? You girls need to practice the acrobatics first, Fallon. Master them. *Then* add in the livestock. Ask any fledgling leaving the nest: Flying's hard enough, even when nothing else is trying to knock you out of the sky."

II

ELKA SIGHED AS she settled onto the bench across from me in the massage room in the ludus baths. I nodded to one of the two attendants as she chose an oil infused with geranium for me. I lay facedown on my own bench, letting the heat and her hands work the tension from my neck and back, while skillfully avoiding the bruises I'd collected during my failed leap that morning. I felt like a lump of bread dough being punched into shape and readied for the oven.

"I miss the days when all we had to worry about was beating the living tar out of each other," Elka said, her words muffled by the towel under her head that squished the side of her face. "Don't you?"

"You are slightly easier to reason with than a bull, it's true," I said.

"And you smell better than one." Elka grinned. "Most days."

"If only the mob was content with just us."

"Bah." Elka waved away the notion with a languid hand. "The Romans and their make-believe. I wonder how they'd react if they came face-to-face with real war inside the walls of their precious city."

"Why do you think all the houses here have such stout doors?" I snorted. "They'd hide in their wine cellars and drink until the danger had passed."

After a very short while, a gentle snore drifted from Elka's lips. I closed my own eyes and tried to relax, but it wasn't as easy for me—or for most people, really— as it seemed to be for her. Elka was the only person I knew who could doze on a stone bench in an arena full of screaming multitudes and wake moments later, refreshed and ready for her bout. I envied her blithe nature sometimes.

My mind rebelled against such blissful oblivion and, instead, mulled over the nature of the people we worked our bodies so hard to entertain. My comment to Elka had been glib and self-congratulatory, of course, and we both knew it. Any tribe of men had its share of cowards, I thought. Rome was simply fortunate enough to have an army and soldiers to do its fighting for it—with a brilliant general at its head: Gaius Julius Caesar.

But I knew well that there were those in Rome who had already declared war on Caesar. A secret war, waged by power-hungry men like Cai's father. Like Pontius Aquila. Men who made dark bargains with dangerous factions and darker gods, and who would stop at nothing to bring Rome's conquering hero to his knees. And I didn't think we'd seen the last of them.

It was an uncomfortable thought that sometimes kept me awake long into the night, never mind on the massage bench. I'd confided my worries to Sorcha on one or two occasions, but my sister seemed convinced that Aquila was no longer a threat, not to us or to the Ludus Achillea or to Caesar. I fervently hoped she was right. Certainly, the Sons of Dis had troubled us no more since we'd retaken the ludus. And, of course, Senator Varro lay cold and moldering on a marble slab in the Varro family vault, a permanent resident of Rome's finest necropolis.

Cai had seen to it that he'd been interred alongside his beloved wife in a quiet ceremony. Dignified, honorable, with most of the mourners never really knowing the true circumstances of Decimus Fulvius Varro's demise. They only knew that his son, Caius Antonius Varro, had been responsible—and had been conspicuously absent from the rites as a result. Of course, had he attended, they would have very likely buried *him* in the ground that day too.

"Too hard?" the masseuse asked suddenly, easing up the pressure she'd been applying to a particularly stubborn spot on my left shoulder.

I shook my head no and felt her work her thumbs deeper into the spot. The tears seeping out from under my lashes had nothing to do with a muscle knot.

Caesar, of course, *had* learned the full truth about Senator Varro's death. And his reaction to the situation had served to remind me that even the heroic service of a loyal officer in his legions was secondary to him when it came to the business of politics. It was a hard lesson for me, but a much harder one for Cai. The memory of that day washed over me as I lay on the bench, almost as if it had been stored in the muscles the masseuse focused on, working loose the knots there and setting the memories free.

A few months after we had triumphed over Pontius Aquila and regained the Ludus Achillea, Caesar had returned to Rome with victories of his own. There'd been a decisive battle in Hispania at a place called Munda—one that Cai, had he still been with Caesar on the campaign, would have doubtless fought in—waged against Caesar's own folk. Being Caesar, of course, he won. But also, being Caesar, that didn't necessarily mean his success would be met with laurels and lavish praise upon his return.

I suppose, then, it shouldn't have been that much of a surprise that the great general—once again appointed dictator—might be in some incarnation of a foul mood on the day when I received a summons to appear before him at his estate on the west bank of the Tiber. He'd once again taken up residence there and was presumably busy reacquainting himself with his friends in Rome and his wife, Calpurnia.

After the messenger arrived at the ludus with the imperative that I was to present myself to Caesar that very afternoon, I barely had time to change out of my practice gear and make myself presentable before being bundled into the enclosed carriage and driven down the Via Clodia, south toward Rome. As we approached the city, I drew aside the curtains on the carriage window, just enough to be able to see the sunlight sparkling off the red-tiled roofs and gleaming marble walls of the buildings seemingly piled one upon the other up the sides of the seven hills. It was a sight that always filled me with conflicting emotions. In the same way that Caesar himself did. I'd spent a good deal of my life growing up wishing a fate worse than death upon the man responsible—I'd always thought, at least—for the death of my sister. I still blamed him for a lot of other things, but that one truth of my childhood had proven false. Her loss, yes. But not her death. And I'd found her again. In the days since, we'd become more than sisters. A team. A force to be reckoned with. Everything, I'd thought, was finally going so well. With the ludus, my friends, Cai . . .

The carriage turned west, toward the stone bridge that spanned the River Tiber, and I pulled the curtains shut again, leaning back on the cushioned seat and trying not to wonder what it was that Caesar had in store for me. When the driver slowed to a stop in front of the sweeping front terrace that graced the entrance to Caesar's villa and opened the door to let me out, I discovered that Cai had been summoned too.

We met in the fragrant main courtyard of the sprawling villa and barely had time to greet each other before one of Caesar's praetorian guards was marching us through the airy, light-filled corridors on our way to Caesar's scriptorium.

"Come," he barked impatiently when we were announced. "Sit."

Without looking up, he waved a hand at the low, back-less chairs off to one side of the desk where he sat behind fortifications built of stacked tablets and scrolls, fever-ishly writing on a sheet of vellum. The stylus in his hand made a scratching noise across the surface of the scraped-thin sheepskin, and Caesar's secretary—a portly, serious-faced man who was probably Macedonian, by the look of him—stood waiting to receive the missive from Caesar's hand.

Together, Cai and I crossed the polished marble floor—me trying to make as little noise as possible—and sat. I glanced sideways at Cai, but his gaze was focused on the far wall in front of us, on a tapestry that hung above Caesar's head, a scene of warring gods and goddesses. I vaguely remembered the tale as I'd been told it: a story of familial bloodshed in which the children of immortals rose up to dethrone their parents and make themselves gods. The central image of the tapestry was of Jupiter overthrow-ing his own Titan father and casting him into the under-world realm of Tartarus.

I folded my hands in my lap and waited, staring up at the divine conflict frozen forever in the woven patterns of the gleaming silken threads. An uncomfortable chill crawled across my skin as I was reminded of my own time spent in a place named after that horrid prison. Tartarus. Once we'd retaken the ludus, Sorcha had ordered the squat, ugly stone structure to be demolished. It was torn down and the stones repurposed, the dank subterranean cells filled in, and a garden planted there in its place.

She'd given me the black iron key, heavy and clawlike, when I'd asked her for it. When she wanted to know why, I could only answer, "Because I want to remember. I never want to forget any of the things that have happened to me. Any of the places I've been, or the things that I've done. No matter how horrible. That key is as much me as the oath lamp that you gave me and Nyx shattered. As real as my swords and as much a part of me, both broken and whole."

My sister had tilted her head and looked at me for a long moment. Then, without another word, she laid the key across my palm and turned back to watch the yoked team of oxen strain and start forward, pulling the doors of Tartarus right off their hinges.

After that, I'd spent my days in a haze of tentative happiness, soaking in the small joys of long practice, dreamless sleep, good food and company, and the unfurling of the new small wings of my soul that would one day beat strong enough to carry me all the way to freedom. It had never even occurred to me I'd be making that flight alone.

Then the summons had come.

At first, I was elated. When he finally turned his attention on us where we sat patiently waiting, Caesar congratulated both of us for our valor in retaking the Ludus Achillea. He had his secretary present us both with gifts of money and brooches fashioned in the shape of gilded laurel branches.

But then . . .

"*Discharged*," Caesar said for a second time, visibly reining in his patience at having to repeat himself when we both expressed our lack of understanding. "Be glad, Caius Varro, it's not dishonorably."

Somewhere outside the cool, bright colonnaded room where Caesar had received us that day a bird sang, its voice trilling carelessly and joyfully as it called for its mate. It was the only other sound as I sat, staring openmouthed at the most powerful man in the world as he pronounced the words that decommissioned Cai from his position as an officer in the Roman legions.

For the crime of saving my life.

Cai sat like a stone beside me, his face gone rigid and pale.

"You can't do that!" I protested, my own voice drowning out the birdsong.

The glare Caesar turned on me told me that of course he could—and *would*—do anything he damned well pleased. I closed my mouth and bit the inside of my cheek to stay silent. Argument from me would only make it worse for Cai. After a long, fraught silence, Caesar relented a bit. He sighed and pushed himself to standing, waving his servants out of the room and closing the door behind them. Now it was just the three of us—Caesar, Cai, and me—and two of Caesar's praetorian guards, who might as well have been statues in the room and who, I knew, were loyal to Caesar to the gates of death and beyond.

Cai had been loyal too, I thought.

"I don't question your actions, Caius," Caesar said in a quiet, measured tone. "In fact, I applaud them. Of course." He stalked over to a table that held goblets and a small amphora and poured us each a measure of wine. "You saved my ludus and my honor. I know you didn't do it for me. Either of you—"

"My lord—"

"Dear girl . . ." He held up a hand, forestalling my protest. "I *know* why you did it. The fact that you rendered me invaluable service at the same time, well, let us consider that a happy coincidence. I know what was in your heart, and I commend you for your bravery and your loyalty to your . . . what is it the plebs are calling *my* gladiatrices now? 'Victrix and her war band'? Charming, really . . ."

The corner of his mouth quirked upward and he laughed a little, shaking his head. But then his expression grew serious again.

"I owe your sister, Achillea, a great deal as well," he continued. "But I also see now that I have done her a disservice. You two are from a world, Fallon, that values honor over everything else. Rome is not that world. I see now that your sister has yet to fully comprehend that, in spite of her laudable efforts to assimilate."

"I'm not sure I understand."

"*Trust*, my dear." Caesar shook his head, a wan half smile on his face. "A noble, useless, frequently terminal affliction of your people. Achillea *trusted* Thalestris. She allowed her greatest enemy to get close enough to stab her in the back, Fallon. That's what blind trust does."

"I still don't understand. What does any of that have to do with Cai?"

Caesar sighed gustily. "Because—ironically enough—you're both going to have to trust that, in this case, what I've done is for the best. For you."

"I do understand," Cai said, and rose to his feet to face his general. "I knew I wouldn't be able to stay in the legions after . . . after what I did. I am honored that you saw fit to deliver the decree yourself."

Caesar looked at him, silent for a moment, then said, "That's not all, Cai."

"Sir?"

"I want you to report within three days to the Ludus Flaminius."

"For what purpose?"

"To train. For the games . . . Gladiator Varro."

It must have been the discipline instilled in Cai by the legions—which Caesar had only moments ago unceremoniously thrown him out of—that kept Cai standing there, at attention, unmoving and unprotesting. I had no such training. Instead, my undisciplined Cantii emotions came roaring to the surface and I shot to my feet and lurched toward Caesar, only to be stopped cold by the iron grip of Cai's hand clamped around my upper arm, holding me there immobile. He turned to me.

"Whatever you are about to say in protest, Fallon . . ." His hazel gaze was hard and cool as marble. "Don't. I will fight my own battles when I find them. There isn't one here." He turned back to Caesar, who watched our exchange in silence, and nodded once, curtly. "I'll be there tomorrow, sir."

"Good." Caesar returned the nod, a little less curtly.

Then his gaze flicked over to my face, and his eyes glimmered with the same veiled emotion I'd seen there on more than one occasion when he looked at me. I knew, somehow, that he was thinking of his dead daughter, Julia, in that moment. I wondered, not for the first time, exactly what it was in me that reminded him of her. I knew that she'd died when Caesar had been across the sea, making war upon my own folk—the tribes of the Island of the Mighty—but I didn't know much more than that. Maybe she'd just argued a lot with her father. Not many other people did that. Cai certainly wasn't doing it now, and I didn't understand why.

Caesar decided in that moment to try to explain himself—something else that didn't happen very often.

"You see, my dear?" he said. "Caius sees what I'm doing, and he trusts me. Because what I'm trying to do is keep him safe. I did not lie when I said I owed you both a debt of gratitude, and I am a man who pays his debts. And takes care of his friends to the best of his abilities."

"You're keeping him safe by sending him into the arena?" I asked. Having a rather good deal of experience in that same circumstance, I was skeptical.

Caesar's eyebrows climbed up his high forehead. "You don't trust that Caius can handle himself just as well as you?"

I felt my face go red. "Of course not! I—"

"Understand this, Fallon." Caesar took a sip of his wine before continuing. "And you understand too, Cai. You are in far greater danger walking the streets of Rome than you will be within the walls of a ludus. *My* ludus."

Cai nodded. "I understand."

"I don't," I said. "Not really."

"What Pontius Aquila did," Caesar explained, "he did with extreme cleverness, Fallon. Because he was in possession of Sorcha's will—with, of course, Thalestris's addendum selling him the Ludus Achillea and its assets and chattels *and* because Thalestris is now dead and unable to offer contrary accounting of the transaction—he's given his actions the appearance of legitimacy. His story, which he's widely recounted, is that he was safeguarding the ludus for me upon my eventual return. He blames the dead Amazon for misleading him about the circumstances of the Lady Achillea's absence—and supposed death— that night. Everything else, he claims, is simply a dreadful misunderstanding. There is, of course, no one to refute that, and insofar as he has *graciously* returned ownership of the academy now that his perfidy has proven unsuccessful . . . well." Caesar shrugged. "In the eyes of the senate, a goodly portion of whom are secretly in league—or at least share sympathies—with the Tribune, he is exonerated. A laughingstock to the mob, perhaps, but a man of honorable actions among his peers."

I felt my blood simmering hotly in my veins at the thought of Pontius Aquila suffering no consequences for his evils. I don't know that I'd really been expecting that he would. Hoped, yes—fervently so—but I was growing inured to the casual corruption of Roman high society. It flowed through the city's elite like the River Styx: hidden deep underground, thick and stinking, with a current that would pull even the best of men down to a drowning death if they lost footing on its banks.

"Caius, on the other hand," Caesar continued, "is not so lucky. In the eyes of the senate—and the people—he is guilty of patricide. There is no greater affront to a true Roman. Compounding that heinous crime is the fact that Decimus Fulvius Varro was one of the wealthiest and most influential senators in all of Rome. A decorated war hero. A man who was loved by all." He took another sip from his cup. "A man who hated *me*. Oh, not publicly, not loudly, but vehemently . . . and for many years."

I gaped at Caesar. "You knew this?"

Caesar nodded. "And could do nothing."

"But you trusted Cai."

"I did. I still do." He turned and gazed up at the tapestry, at Jupiter lifting his father, Saturn, above his head, ready to cast him down. "The father is not the son."

"No," Cai said softly, staring up at the image. "He isn't . . ."

"I will hold your father's estate and assets in trust," Caesar continued, "until such time as it is safe for you to reclaim your inheritance. In the meantime, all I can ask of you is to forgive me for that necessity."

"No need for forgiveness, my lord," Cai said, with a brief bow of his head. "Only thanks."

"You're welcome." Caesar stood. "Now go. Fight well. And, for the love of the gods, Caius . . . *survive*."

Something about the tone of Caesar's voice raised the hackles on the back my neck. *Yes, Cai,* I thought, *for the love of the gods—yours* and *mine—survive.*

As we made our way through the enclosed courtyard toward the main doors of the villa, we passed a man sitting on a bench at the edge of a cascading fountain. Cai nodded briefly without breaking his stride.

"The legions will be the poorer without you," the man called after us.

Cai halted in his tracks, and together we turned to address the man, who sat carving a pear with a small, sharp knife.

"Damned shame," he said, popping a slice of fruit into his mouth and licking the blade. "Really. Sorry to hear about it, Decurion Varro."

"*Citizen* Varro, General Antony," Cai said, and turned a tight grin on the man. "Or Gladiator Varro, if you please."

Antony, I thought. *That's Marcus Antonius.*

Of course, I'd heard of Caesar's close friend and pro-tégé—the brilliant general and notorious philanderer—everyone had. Most of what I knew of the man was through what Antonia, my sister gladiatrix, had told me. She was a distant relation of his, born out of wedlock to a third cousin of the sprawling Antonine clan and treated worse than a kitchen slave growing up. When she was old enough, Antonia had decided to take her chances begging on the streets of Rome before finding her way to the ludus. She'd never met her infamous cousin face-to-face, she said, but she'd been under the same roof enough times to have surmised that the actual character of the man bore out the rumors.

He was, by her account, a cad. He was also, by everyone else's account, a genius soldier and cunning strategist. I took the few moments he stood speaking to Cai to study Antony's features. He was handsome in a way that was almost pretty, except for his mouth, which was thin-lipped and looked apt to shift from an expression of warmth to one of mockery with little effort. He wore coral-studded wristbands of silver and a richly embroidered cloak that hung in deep russet folds gathered over his left arm. His hair was dark and thick and carefully curled. I tried to picture him in a soldier's gear, but my mind wouldn't bend to the image. Still, I suspected it would be a mistake to underestimate the man. When he shifted the drape of his cloak, I noticed he also had a plain—and, from the look of the grip, well-used—short sword strapped to his waist.

"Ah, yes," Antony said with a grin. "*Gladiator* Varro. Well. You were an inspired fighter in the field. I'll be sure to cheer you on at your first bout in the arena."

"From the sounds of things, you may be the only one." Cai shrugged. "The only time the mob appreciates a disgraced hero is when they can disgrace him all the more. I won't be showered in laurel sheaves, I don't think. But I thank you."

"Don't thank me." Antony laughed and tossed the core of the pear he'd eaten into the nearby shrubbery. "I'll cheer for you because you'll win. You'll have to. And when you do, the mob will forget all about what you did. It's that easy to turn them in the other direction, Varro. Trust me."

Cai *didn't* trust him. I could see that in his eyes, plainly. In the back of my mind, I wondered why Caesar *did.*

Cai smiled and nodded politely, and it was only then that Antony seemed to notice me, standing there at Cai's side. His gaze shifted and flicked over me, head to foot, with profound disinterest. At first. Until the moment he was about to turn away—and then something sparked behind his eyes, and he blinked. And smiled.

"Am I right in guessing that *you* are Caesar's pet project?" he asked, turning his full attention on me. "The girl gladiator?"

Out of the corner of my eye, I saw Cai wince.

"I am Fallon ferch Virico, General Antony," I replied. "They call me Victrix in the arena. And, yes, I suppose I am Caesar's pet project." I tilted my head and smiled sweetly. "One of them, at least. I hear he has others."

Cai's wince turned to a grin that he swiftly hid behind his hand.

Marc Antony's eyes flashed hotly for an instant. But then his smile widened, baring a row of straight white teeth. "I'm afraid, Victrix, that I've missed your performances to date on the sands," he said, and stood, reaching to take my hand and bending low over it. "That is, I can plainly see, a deficiency on my part. One I hope to have the opportunity to remedy."

"I hope so too, my lord," I said. "There are many fine fighters at the Ludus Achillea—even if we are, as you say, 'girl' gladiators. I think we might surprise you."

"I think you might at that," he said.

He lapsed into silence, and Cai stepped forward to excuse us. Antony waved a languid hand in a kind of dismissal, and we continued on toward where a carriage waited to take me back to the ludus and Cai back into the city. I could feel Marc Antony's gaze between my shoulder blades as we walked away.

Once we were inside the covered carriage and on the road, with the sound of wheels and hooves loud in our ears as we clattered over the stone bridge, I shed whatever composure I'd managed to keep up to that point and vented my full fury over the sheer injustice of Cai's fate. He let me rage for far longer than I probably deserved. When he finally spoke, the look on his face brought me instantly to a stuttering halt.

"Fallon." His voice was quiet. But it was as hard as I'd ever heard from him. "I understand that you are grieved for me because you think what Caesar has decreed as my fate is a harsh one."

I swallowed my fiery indignation and clenched my hands into knots. "Isn't it?" I asked.

He laughed. A bitter bark of derision. "Without Caesar's intervention," he said, "I would have faced the full penalty of a very particular Roman law. It's called *poena cuellei*, and it's reserved for those citizens who are found guilty of the murder of a parent. Personally, I'll take my chances against even the most brutal gladiator in the arena."

"Rather than . . . ?"

He raised an eyebrow at me and said dryly, "Rather than submitting myself to getting sewn up in a leather sack full of venomous snakes and thrown into the Tiber."

I blinked at him, dumbstruck.

The carriage rumbled on, and we sat there silently.

I knew that Romans worshipped their ancestry. That their fathers and mothers were almost as gods to them. And I knew that Cai had adored his father. That is, right up until the moment when he'd put a sword through the elder Varro's guts. To save *my* life. I could remember with shocking clarity the moment when Cai had thrust the blade between his father's ribs. Right to the hilt, without hesitation. I remembered Varro's face, how he had reached for his son . . . and I remembered what Cai had said: "*You have no son,*" he told his father. "*I renounce you, and your name, and your blood. I will not perform the rites for you, old man. I will not put coins for the Ferryman on your eyes. You go to Hades with no issue, no legacy, and no hope to ever walk the fields of Elysium beside my mother's shade.*"

We hadn't really had an opportunity—or maybe it was that we had avoided the opportunity—to talk about what had happened. But that moment in the carriage I suddenly realized the full import of what Cai had done. What he'd said. He had, in essence, laid a curse upon his father. The man who'd raised him, loved him, taught him how to be a soldier and a man. And then betrayed everything Cai had grown to believe in.

And that had forced Cai to betray everything his people believed in.

"If it weren't for me," I said, "none of this ever would have happened—"

"No." He stopped me again with the sharpness of his tone. "Don't."

After a long silence, he sighed and reached for my hand.

"What do you think would have happened if I'd never found out who—*what*—my father really was, Fallon?" Cai asked me. "If I'd never uncovered the gorgon lurking beneath the mask? What do you think might have happened to me? To my soul? He wanted nothing more than for me to follow in his footsteps."

I shook my head. "But you wouldn't have."

"I don't know that. I can't say that with any certainty at all."

"I can. You are the most honorable man I've ever known. And you were my enemy on the day I first met you."

"And I was a different man *until* the day I met you." His eyes searched my face, looking for something . . . I wasn't sure what. But he smiled and said, "Fallon, I'm—I was—a soldier. I obeyed orders. I did what I was told. It took someone like you crashing headlong into my life to make me see that being a good soldier isn't necessarily the same as being a good man. You made me want to be an individual. I never had the will to be that on my own without you. I was my father's son and I was Caesar's instrument and now I am neither. But I am . . . well, I am my *own*, I suppose. And I am yours." He laughed a little. "If you still want me."

"Oh, Cai . . ."

The carriage slowed to a stop, and he pushed aside the curtain. I looked past him to see we had arrived outside the gates of the Varro estate. The legacy Cai would have to wait to inherit, if he could survive long enough. I vowed silently then that, if I had to *will* him to live through the trials he would have to face at the Ludus Flaminius, I would sacrifice my soul to the Morrigan to do it. Because Cai had been given a chance for life. In spite of the decrees of his barbaric Roman laws, he would live in the wake of his father's death. But he would bear the burden of guilt for that for the rest of his life.

That was Caesar's punishment.

And that was Caesar's mercy.

III

I SEEMED TO be collecting goddesses, I thought, as I nodded to the sentry on the wall and slipped out through the main gate of the Ludus Achillea, into the darkness of the night beyond. Or, perhaps, they were collecting me.

The sword that bumped against my hip as I walked was marked with the triple-raven knot, a symbol of my own goddess, the Morrigan, who had in her wisdom seen fit to send me so far from home to seek my destiny. In my hand I carried a lamp, a replacement for the delicate glass one I'd first received on the night I'd taken my gladiatorial oath beneath the light of a Huntress Moon. This one was rather less fragile, made of bronze and inscribed with the image of the Roman battle goddess Minerva. Around my neck, I wore a silver chain. Hanging from that chain was a pendant fashioned in the shape of yet another goddess: Sekhemet, who bore the head of a lioness and made war upon the enemies of Aegypt. Cleopatra, the queen of

Aegypt herself, had given me the charm, and I treasured it. I treasured all of them.

But that night, the pendant lay cold on my breastbone. The new lamp felt heavy in my hand, and the sword on my left hip needed its twin hanging from my right to balance it as I walked. But that blade had been shattered. Broken in two in a fight against the girl whose grave I walked to visit that night.

The moon hung like a scythe in the sky, a slender, gleaming sickle, paler almost than the stars. But my new lamp cast enough light to keep me from stumbling over a tumbled grave marker that had succumbed to age and weather and lay on the ground just inside the low stone wall of the little necropolis. The moment I stepped through the archway into the enclosure, the night breeze died to stillness and the stars seemed to wink at me more brightly. I made my way through the cluster of tombs and statues devoted to departed Romans, most of them from families from the nearby estates that dotted the lush countryside around Lake Sabatinus.

At the far end of the graveyard, there was an enclosure set apart from the rest. There were no ostentatious marble crypts raised over the graves of those who slept in this place. No statues. Just simple stone markers set in the earth. I paused when I found the patch of earth that still bore ghost-faint traces of gray ash—from the funeral pyre that had blazed there months ago. I walked around until I stood between it and another grave: the one I'd first been brought out to stand witness at—along with all the other girls who would become my ludus sisters—for the interment of a gladiatrix I'd never known. It seemed an eternity since that night, the very first night I spent at the Ludus Achillea. Long before I discovered that the hooded woman who'd led the funeral rites was my sister. Before I'd known that I would one day have many more sisters. Before I'd killed the sister that lay in the dark earth now beneath my sandaled feet.

I sank down to sit on the damp, chilly ground and set my lamp beside the grave marker so I could read the name carved there. It was written in Greek, which I'd only just begun to learn, but of course I knew it was hers.

"Hello, Nyx," I said.

This night was the first time I'd come to visit since we'd burned her body and buried her ashes with her weapons and worldly goods. I brought a small jug and two cups, and I sat for a moment, listening to the mournful fall of a nightingale's song, before I pulled the stopper and poured out two measures of good dark Briton beer. *Not* wine. I would never again drink wine with Nyx— not even with her dead and buried—not after the party where she'd given me mandrake-spiked wine to drink. But it would have been rude to come empty-handed. I poured half of Nyx's measure out onto her grave and set the cup down, watching as the thirsty earth swallowed the libation. Then I took a sip from my own cup and sighed.

"I drink to my enemy," I murmured, repeating words I'd heard many times in the great feast hall back in Durovernum. "I raise my cup in peace and the hope that when we meet again, we shall be as friends."

It was an old ritual, one of the oldest of the Cantii, and I'd seen my father enact it many times. Never at a graveside, of course. He, I'm sure, had no idea where most of the bodies of the men he'd killed in battle were buried. But he would speak those words every year on the anniversaries of the battles he'd fought. He would speak them softly to the dark air. To the shades that haunted him.

I wondered, if I said the words right, would Nyx's shade be inclined to be friendly toward me? The notion almost made me choke on my beer.

Not in this life, I thought, *or the next.*

Or any of the others after that.

"This is stupid," I sighed. "We won't be friends. We won't ever meet in the Land of the Blessed Dead. I don't even know where your shade wanders now . . ."

Nyx was Greek, born in the back alleys of a place called Athens and raised as a petty thief by a gang of cutpurses. Caught and sold as a slave, she'd been shipped to Rome and auctioned off in the Forum. And my sister, Sorcha, new-made as the "Lady Achillea" and given a ludus to run by Caesar when her own career in the arena had ended, had seen something in Nyx. A flicker of obstinate spirit, a bloody-minded resilience, some angry spark that refused to be extinguished . . . I don't know what, exactly. But that was how Nyx had found her way to the ludus.

She'd never really known much love in her life. That I *did* know. And so when she'd finally found someone to adore, someone to idolize and make proud—someone like Sorcha—Nyx had devoted herself to that cause. And all she'd had to do was hone and shape and harden all of the rage that had been building inside for her whole life and turn herself into a weapon. And she'd done it so well that it had earned her a place of honor in the ludus. Her new home. Her world.

My unexpected intrusion into that world had not gone over well.

I took a sip of the dark, bitter beer and shook my head. "I fear for you, Nyx," I said. "There was nothing but hate in your heart when you died. I saw it in your eyes. And I'm truly sorry I was the cause of so much of it."

I would have petitioned Nyx's gods to take away that hate from her in death if only I knew who her gods even were. I thought about it for a moment, swallowing another mouthful from my cup. What did I know of Greek gods?

All I knew was that the Romans worshipped virtually the same pantheon, only with different names. Were they really interchangeable, I wondered? The divine beings who, in spite of their own wars and ruins and tangled relationships, did their best to guide us mortals through our muddled and messy lives? I'd even heard Caesar call *my* own gods by Roman names. Was Lugh really Mercury in another guise? Were the Morrigan and Minerva sisters, or cousins, or one and the same? Maybe my Blessed Lands and Nyx's Elysium, Elka's Valhöll, and Neferet's Aaru were all the same thing. Or maybe they were lands whose borders touched . . . blurred, like traveling through a mist from field to forest. Whatever the case, I didn't think it would necessarily do to ask the Morrigan to watch over Nyx in the afterlife. But maybe I could find a deity a little closer to entreat.

To that end, I thought about the coming morning. Sorcha had invited me to attend a ceremony at Caesar's temple of Venus Genetrix with her in the city, during which he would dedicate certain treasures to the goddess: spoils of war, including a breastplate—a magnificent piece of armor dec-orated with river pearls—seized in his Britannia campaign. Sorcha and I were the only ones who knew that it had once belonged to *her*. In her mind, I think she'd framed it as a kind of honor, but I wasn't so sure. Apart from the dedica-tion, I saw nothing interesting about a bunch of priestesses standing around chanting and fogging the air with incense, and I still hadn't made up my mind whether or not I'd go.

But . . . Venus was the Roman goddess of love—Nyx's Greek fellows called her Aphrodite—and so maybe she was a goddess worth making the acquaintance of. I already had a surfeit of war goddesses. I smiled to myself and decided that, the next day, I *would* go to the temple, and I would offer up a prayer to Venus that she might put love in the heart of my dead enemy.

"My tribe believes it's never a good idea to drink alone."

The voice in the darkness startled me from my reverie, and I looked up to see Elka standing there. I hadn't even heard her approach. She hunkered down beside me and pulled a wineskin out of a sack she had slung over her shoulder.

"Leaves you far too vulnerable to malevolent spirits," she said.

"I'm not alone," I said, tilting my cup at the ground in front of me. "I'm visiting a friend."

"Well then, so am I."

I snorted. "You hated Nyx."

"So did you." Elka grinned and twisted the stopper out of the wineskin.

"To be fair," I said, "she did try to kill me."

"On several occasions, *ja*." Elka tilted her head and poured a stream of dark liquid down her throat, wiping her mouth with the back of one hand. "It's not an uncommon reaction, little fox. I remember trying it myself once or twice."

"If you'd really tried to kill me," I said, "*you'd* be the one sitting here drinking alone. And *I'd* be the pile of ashes lying under all that dirt."

"Pff." She waved away the notion. "It would have been a rash decision. After all, I never would have made it this far without you."

"Of course you would have."

Elka raised a pale eyebrow in my direction. "Don't underestimate your ability to kindle the fires of determination in those around you, my friend."

I laughed. "That doesn't really sound like a compliment."

She grinned and took another pull from the wineskin she'd brought for the occasion. "More a statement of fact," she said, then changed the subject before I had a chance to argue or backhand a compliment in return. "How's Cai?"

I sighed and took a drink of my own. "Performing in two days' time."

"I know *that*. Quint and I are going together into the city to watch the games. That's why I asked." She glanced at me sideways. "I meant how *is* he?"

"I honestly don't know." I shrugged, avoiding her inquisitive stare. I hadn't had any contact with Cai since he'd reported to the Ludus Flaminius. "He won't see me. He won't even *write* to me. I've sent messages, letters, but they all come back with the seals unbroken. I'm seriously thinking of visiting the ludus and demanding a visitation with Cai from the *lanista* himself. He's been courting Sorcha's favor for months now, after all. Wants to arrange a joint spectacle."

"What better draw than a disgraced hero of the legions?" Elka shook her head. "Cai's more *infamia* now than you and I ever were."

"And it's all my fault."

"It's *his father's* fault." Elka's voice turned stern. "No one else's. Least of all yours."

"Then why won't Cai even see me?"

"Maybe he needs to win in the arena first," she mused. "Think about it. From respected decurion to reviled gladiator is a far way to fall."

"You're talking to an ex-princess," I snorted. "It's not as if he has something to prove to me, Elka."

"Maybe he has something to prove to himself."

She reached over and picked up the little beer jug I'd brought, pouring out the last of the liquid into both my cup and Nyx's.

"Wait." I turned to blink at her. "Did you say you're going to the games with *Quintus*?"

She grinned, and if only the moon were a little brighter, I suspected I might have seen a blush tint her pale cheeks. "Are *you* going?" she asked, neatly deflecting the conversation again, back toward the subject of Cai's upcoming contest.

If I was already in the city to attend the dedication of Caesar's temple, I thought, it seemed a waste not to stay the extra day to see Cai's match . . .

"Yes." I nodded and drained my drink. "Yes, I am."

Whether Cai wanted me to or not.

As we stood to leave and make our way back to the ludus together, I paused in front of another patch of ground, a plot set a little ways from the resting places of the Ludus Achillea gladiatrices, marked not with a stone but a newly planted yew bush. I pulled one of the empty cups from my bag and scooped up some of the earth, dark but flecked with ash, like Nyx's. If I ever left this place, I thought, I would not want to leave what remained of Aeddan's soul— whatever there was of him that had not found its way to the Blessed Isles and his brother, Maelgwyn Ironhand— there to languish alone. This way I could take a piece of his spirit with me. He deserved that, at least.

I stood with a sigh and gazed out over the little necropolis.

There might have been one more grave there that was the result of the night we retook the ludus, but Kallista and Selene and their Amazon sisters had requested of Sorcha that they deal with Thalestris themselves. Sorcha had agreed, and they'd taken her body, tightly wrapped in a plain linen shroud, and disappeared from the ludus into the surrounding countryside. They were gone for two days, and when they returned, they never spoke of it. But whether they burned her or buried her or left her beneath the sky for her bones to be scattered by the Morrigan's ravens and wolves, I didn't care. For what she'd done to Sorcha, it would serve for Thalestris's spirit to wander lost forever. And if it made me cruel to think such a thing . . . then I had her, in part, to thank for teaching me such cruelty.

IV

THE MORNING OF the temple dedication dawned clear and soft, the sky in the east veiled with a sheer curtain of blush-tinted clouds that vanished with the rising of the sun. Italia, I'd learned, never really got cold. Not like Prydain. The relatively mild winter had begun to fade, but the nights and early mornings still bore a distinct and often biting chill. We'd left the ludus well before sunrise and had dressed accordingly—both for the weather and the occasion—but as the sun climbed higher into the sky, the cool spring breezes that reminded me of home curled up in the hollows of the hills like cats and went to sleep for the day. I shifted the *palla* I wore, like all the other proper Roman ladies in the crowd gathering in front of the temple steps, and pushed it back off my forehead, shrugging uncomfortably beneath the heavy hang of soft folds that draped over my shoulders and arms.

"This is ridiculous," I muttered. "I feel like a swaddled babe."

"If you can learn to wear boiled leather and bronze, you can learn to wear that," Sorcha said, a glint of amusement in her eyes as she reached to tug the material back up over my hair.

Easy for her, I thought. She'd had years more practice.

As we approached the temple at the far end of the Forum, I glanced sideways at my sister, wondering what she was thinking. Her expression, as usual, gave away almost nothing of what she felt. I sometimes wished I had that kind of control over my emotions. Ahead of us, six tall men draped in saffron-dyed tunics carried poles that held aloft a litter bearing the offerings that were to be enshrined in the temple, including the armor my sister had been wearing on the battlefield when she'd made her bargain with Caesar and saved our father's life.

To the other side of Sorcha, Charon walked along with us. He'd offered to accompany us and then take Sorcha back to the Ludus Achillea while I stayed on to attend the games with Elka and Quintus tomorrow. The slave master—well, *ex*–slave master, really—had become something of a fixture at the ludus. Over the months since we'd reclaimed the academy, after Charon had been so instrumental in helping us do that and saving Sorcha's life in the process, he'd given up that particular aspect of his business. The only "acquisitions" Charon made these days were the infrequent purchases of likely gladiatrix candidates.

Charon had been in Prydain—Britannia—with Caesar during his campaigns to conquer the Island of the Mighty, offering his slaver's expertise. He'd been there the night my father was captured. The night Sorcha had surrendered her sword at Caesar's feet in exchange for Virico's freedom. And he was here now, offering his sun-browned arm to her as we ascended the steps to the temple with its eight marble pillars gleaming in the morning sun.

Once inside, Charon stepped back and took up a place at my side as Rome's elite shuffled about, arranging themselves for the best vantage point. He glanced at me and offered a wan grin, likely guessing what I was thinking in that moment.

"If you'd told my ten-year-old self that this day was in my future," I muttered, "I would have cut your tongue out for lying. And maybe burned it for sorcery."

Because when I was ten, my sister was dead. And Caesar was my greatest enemy. Now? Neither of those things was true anymore. Charon put a hand on my shoulder, and I sighed. Life was far too complicated, I thought, and there were far too many paths for my feet to tread.

And not just *mine*, it seemed.

Flutes and drums began to play, and the priestesses of Venus filed out onto the dais with their incense and offerings. They bore sheaves of flowers and baskets of fruit . . . and I was astonished to see that I knew one of them. Her long dark hair was unbound and fell forward, obscuring her face as she knelt to place her basket at the feet of a statue of the goddess, but I'd already recognized Kassandra, the girl I'd first met in a slave cage in the middle of Gaul. The last time I'd seen her, she'd been working in a brothel that catered to a mostly patrician class of patrons in the city. As she stood and turned, her eyes met mine and she blinked, as surprised to see me there as I was to see her. A small smile flickered at the edges of her mouth, and she gave me a little nod of greeting. Then she went to stand with the other priestesses, leaving me to wonder how her radical change of profession had come about.

It was strange. I'd actually been thinking about her over the last few weeks—about how she'd risked her own safety to try to warn Cai about his father—and I'd been meaning to pay her a visit. As music ended and the high priestess of the temple stepped forward, I decided I would try to speak with Kass after the ceremony. In the meantime, I resigned myself to suffering through the next hour or two of invocations and singing and incense wafting up my nose, all of it making me want to do nothing more than either nap or sneeze.

I envied Elka her decision to stay back at the townhouse.

In truth, I don't remember much about the actual dedication ceremony. Perhaps because of everything that happened after, or maybe it was because I simply didn't understand Romans and their gods. I do remember a few details: Caesar, wearing a laurel wreath on his brow, standing on the dais. His wife, Calpurnia, was at his side and looking as if she'd rather be anywhere else in that moment. I suppose I could hardly blame her. There were three statues in the temple. One, of course, of the goddess Venus. One of Caesar. And one, rendered in bronze and leafed in shimmering gold, of Cleopatra. Caesar's paramour. I nudged Sorcha and nodded at the effigy. She bit her lip and gave me a wide-eyed glance that told me *she* didn't fully understand Romans either.

When, finally, the thing was done and Rome's elite filtered back out into the sunlight where the plebs mingled and milled, I told Sorcha I would catch up with her later and stayed back, waiting to see if Kassandra would appear. Eventually she did, trailing behind a group of priestesses who drifted like wraiths out from beneath the temple portico and down the steps, blending into the crowds below enjoying the festival that had blossomed in the streets surrounding the temple, with food and drink stalls unfurling canopies like leaves and merchants selling wares from carts and baskets.

I hurried to catch up with Kass, tugging on the sleeve of her *stola*.

She glanced over her shoulder without stopping, but when she realized who it was, she spun and reached for my hands, a genuine smile lighting her face. "Fallon!" she exclaimed, drawing me into a hug. "I'm so glad to see you . . ."

I hugged her back, feeling how thin she was beneath her robes. When she pushed me back to arm's length, I saw that the shadows beneath her warm brown eyes were still as deep as the last time I saw her. But there was no mistaking the happiness in her expression at the sight of me.

"It's been so long—and I was so worried," she said. "We heard such stories of the ludus and Aquila. And you!" Her glance darted around the bustling street. "Of Varro . . ."

"I know." I smiled and shook my head. "It was . . . well. A lot has happened. But everything is fine now. I mean, better. Much better. Mostly." I didn't know if she knew what had happened to Cai. I still wasn't sure if Kass had—then or now—feelings for him. Although I suspected that, even if she had, the fact that she was a priestess now would render the issue moot.

"What are you doing here?" she asked, slipping her arm in mine as we walked away from the temple to find a space in the street that wasn't so crowded. "I never suspected you as a devotee of Venus." She grinned. "Minerva, yes, but . . ."

I grinned back. "My sister is here on Caesar's invitation."

"Ah. Of course."

"I just decided to come along too." I shrugged and glanced over my shoulder at the temple. "Mostly because I wanted to talk to your goddess."

"Oh!" She blinked at me. "You did?"

I nodded. "She seems like she's probably a bit busy right now, though. But I wanted to ask her to take care of a . . . friend."

"I see."

"How would you go about asking your goddess to do such a thing?"

"Well . . ." Her expression turned priestess-serious. "If this *friend* means a great deal to you, perhaps I could sacrifice a dove or—"

"No!" I exclaimed, recoiling from the thought of any living thing spilling blood because of Nyx ever again. "I mean, I wouldn't want to waste a perfectly good dove. Not for this."

Kassandra bit her lip and looked like she was trying to keep from laughing.

"What?"

"I think I might have misunderstood," she said, something close to a giggle in her voice. "I though you wanted me to propitiate the goddess on behalf of you and Cai."

"Cai?" I blinked at her. "But why . . ."

"She's the goddess of *love*, Fallon."

"Oh . . . Oh!"

She tilted her head and looked at me, frowning. "Aren't you and he . . . I mean, aren't you together?"

"We're trying to be." I sighed. "The rest of the world keeps getting in the way."

"Ah." Her frown shifted to a sympathetic smile. "I heard about what happened—with his father and Cai's . . . disgrace. But I also know the truth of why it happened. And being a gladiator isn't a dishonor to my mind."

"Nor mine," I said wryly.

She smiled and squeezed my hand. "*Keep* trying to be together, Fallon. A man like Caius Varro isn't one you're likely to come across more than once in this lifetime."

We continued our slow stroll through the market stalls, the crowds streaming past us on either side. "What are *you* doing at the temple, Kassandra?" I asked. "I mean—that is to say . . ."

"It's all right," she said, shoulders lifting in a shrug that was almost a shiver. "Life in the House of Venus wasn't agreeing with me so very well. But my mistress there was a good woman, in spite of her trade, and she thought the *temple* of Venus might suit me better."

"Last time I saw you," I said, hesitantly, "you told me of bad dreams."

Dreams were the province of the druiddyn in my tribe, and talk of them usually made me—and any good Celt worth the name, really—wary. I wasn't sure if the same was true of Rome and Romans.

Kass was silent for a moment before she answered, and I wondered if I'd offended her. But then she said, "Not *dreams* so much as . . ." There was that shiver-shrug again. "It's . . . not important."

I looked at her, wondering, as we passed a particularly tawdry market stall selling erotic talismans and cheap *defixio*—thin strips of tin carved with either a spell or a curse purchased by the desperate and the lovelorn, which would then be left on the altar of Venus as a votive offering.

Kass rolled her eyes and sighed.

"Sometimes," she said, lowering her voice as the woman behind the stall eyed Kass's priestess garb with a narrow gaze, "my dreams . . . they come to pass. If it keeps happening, the high priestess has said she might have me trained as a sibyl." At my puzzled expression, she explained, "A soothsayer."

"Ah!" I exclaimed, understanding. "We have those in my tribe—men and women—only we call them druids. My father's druid, Olun, once told him that I would follow in the footsteps of my sister. For a long time, we'd both taken that to mean that I would die on a battlefield." I shook my head. "Little did either of us know just how right his auguries were. Just not in the way we thought they were."

Kass had lapsed into a strange silence beside me.

"It's a position of great honor," I said, trying my best to be encouraging. "The druiddyn are revered. And only a *little* frightening. They get the best seat at the council fire and are always served meat and mead first. At times they—"

I heard a soft gasp and looked over to see Kassandra staring down at her feet, an expression of horror on her face. I followed her gaze and saw that the cobbles beneath her delicate beaded sandals shone slick and crimson. The channels between the stones were red rivulets—it was like gazing down over a miniature hellish landscape carved by streams of blood. Startled, I rocked back a step and spun around to see who it was that had been murdered and lay emptying out their veins into the street . . .

Only to see that, in the chaos of the crowds, someone had overturned a wine stand. Shattered amphorae lay scattered on the ground, leaking rich red wine, and a vendor stood loudly lamenting the loss of his finest Mamertine vintage.

Wine. Not blood. I started to laugh in flustered relief.

"It's all right, Kass," I said. "It's just—"

Her eerie wail stopped the words in my mouth.

I turned to see that Kassandra had gone ghost-pale and rigid. Her eyes were wide and white-rimmed, staring into the middle distance over my shoulder. I glanced behind me and saw that Caesar had finally left the temple and his procession was approaching. The crowd lining the street stood at least ten deep between us and the gilded chariot where he rode. A phalanx of praetorian guards with their gleaming armor and crimson-plumed helmets surrounded Caesar, faces uniformly stern.

As Caesar's chariot rolled past, I caught a blur of motion out of the corner of my eye. I turned to see Kassandra throw off her palla and lunge through the teeming crowd, her long dark hair streaming behind her as she squeezed through the guard perimeter, hands outstretched to grasp the side of Caesar's chariot.

"Caesar!" she cried. "Mars comes for you, great lord!"

The guards reacted on pure instinct, and I heard the rasp of swords being drawn, even as I scrambled after my friend. As the crowd parted with cries of surprise and alarm, I dove between two matronly women, shouldered aside a young man swathed in a choking cloud of scented oils, and missed grabbing Kass's shoulder by a fingersbreadth.

The praetorian didn't miss.

His big, meaty hand clamped down brutally on her bare arm, and he plucked her from the chariot like a fisherman prying a limpet from the keel of his boat—with great difficulty. Kass clung to the chariot rail with surprising strength and tenacity. Long enough for Caesar to notice he had an unexpected passenger. I was close enough to see the barest flicker of recognition in his eyes before the guard hauled Kass back and Caesar turned away, his face once more impassive, expressionless as one of his statues, and the chariot moved on.

Behind the chariot, Calpurnia rode in a garlanded cart with some of her women, and I caught a glimpse of her face as she passed. Her eyes were wide and fixed on Kassandra, and her mouth was drawn in a tight, fearful line. Beside me on the ground, beneath the praetorian's knee, Kass thrashed and cried out, screaming words I couldn't understand over the commotion, still reaching in the direction of the departing chariot as the guard lifted his sword.

"No!" I cried, and stepped over her, reaching to catch his wrist and straining to ward off the blow. The press of the crowd hadn't allowed him to get any kind of momentum into his backswing, and so I was able to block his arm, barely. Beneath the brim of his helmet, I saw his brow crease in anger and his eyes focus on my face. The snarl twisting his lips faltered and faded, and I felt some of the tension leave his arm as he frowned down at me.

"Victrix?" the guard said.

I nodded frantically in relief—he must have recognized me as Caesar's creature—and said, "Yes . . . *yes*! And this is my friend—she's not well, please don't hurt her . . . She's a priestess in the temple!"

He backed off, appearing to suddenly notice the pale yellow stola she wore. I reached for Kassandra, who seemed utterly unaware that I was even standing over her in that moment. There were flecks of foam at the corners of her mouth, and her pupils were so wide her eyes looked black. Her skin was ashen, pale as alabaster, and the veins in her temples and at the sides of her neck shone purple beneath. Her gaze was still fixed upon Caesar's back.

"Beware the war god Mars, Caesar!" she cried, her voice cracking, skirling upward like the warning shriek of a songbird when an eagle attacks its nest. "He will have blood for blood . . . *for Rome!*"

"What in the name of Hades is she on about?" the guard barked at me. "Is that some kind of threat?"

But Kass had subsided into muttering and shaking her head. Her plain, pretty face was twisted in anguish. "So many blades . . . so much blood . . ."

I gathered her close to me, my arm around her shoulders, and tried to help her stand, but she was dead weight. It felt as if she had lost control of her body . . . and maybe, I thought, her mind. I remembered back to the days when we'd been in hiding after escaping the ludus and Pontius Aquila. Kassandra had sought out Cai to tell him of his father's treachery. He hadn't believed her, and she'd refused to divulge the secret to anyone else. All I'd known at that time was that she'd been distraught, telling me of the terrible dreams she'd been having: dreams of blood and fire, and the republic in turmoil.

At the time, Kassandra had been more than just a brothel slave. She'd been an informant for Caesar, gathering secrets from her elite clientele that she would then pass on to the consul. Pillow talk—gossip, boasts, rumors, and lies, mostly—but every now and then something true, useful, or devastating. A dangerous, wearying business on top of the everyday perils she'd negotiated in her "real" work. I'd seen the effects it had had on her. I looked down into her pale, drawn face and wondered if I was seeing them now.

"Kass," I murmured into her ear. "You have to stand up. Help me get you somewhere safe . . ."

The praetorian guard took momentary pity on her and helped haul Kass to her feet. I draped her arm across my shoulders and thanked him as he frowned and turned away, sheathing his gladius and hurrying to join back up with Caesar's procession. I breathed a sigh of relief and hurried Kass off the main street, finding a little courtyard in front of a run-down *taberna* where I could sit her down.

"A cup of wine," I told the keeper when he approached us, eyeing Kass warily. "And bread." I reached into the little purse at my belt and pulled out a coin, slapping it down on the table and ignoring his scowl. "White wine— *not* red!" I called after him as he disappeared through the taberna doors.

The color was slowly returning to Kass's cheeks, and her eyes had lost their cloudy, unfocused aspect. She groaned and put a hand to her head. When the wine arrived, she took a small sip and made a face, pushing the cup away.

At least I knew by her distaste that she'd come back to her senses—I could smell the cheap mustiness of the drink from where I sat.

"Fallon?" She blinked up at me. "Where . . ."

"You fainted," I said. "During the procession."

She frowned, peering at me, and then closed her eyes with a sigh. "I did it again, didn't I? What did I say this time?"

I wasn't sure I wanted to tell her. Mostly because I hadn't really understood her ravings myself. "Something about blades and blood and a war god. Coming for Caesar . . ."

I thought she might faint again.

"Fallon . . . you have to tell him." She gripped my arm, but there was not strength in her fingers. "You have to warn Caesar!"

"Warn him about what?"

"I . . ." The frustration was palpable in her voice as she bleated, "I don't *know*!"

"That's not going to go over very well with him—"

"I only know he's in danger."

"He's always in danger," I said. "That's what comes of making war with the world, Kass."

In truth, I was feeling rather less than charitably inclined toward the great and noble general those days. My thoughts turned toward Cai and the arena where I would have to watch him risk his life on the morrow. But the bleak hopelessness in Kass's eyes made me nod and promise.

"I'll try," I said. "The next time I get the chance to speak with Caesar, I'll tell him to beware."

Kass's gaze had drifted over my shoulder, and she raised the cup to her lips absently, murmuring, "No . . . no you won't. No one will. And it wouldn't matter if you did . . ." Then she laughed a little, a sound like a wild animal, lost and afraid, and said, "My mother named me well, Fallon. Too well."

V

I NEVER DID get the chance to ask Kassandra what she meant. I tossed and turned in my bed that night. When I finally did fall asleep, it seemed as though some of her propensity for nightmares had rubbed off. I found myself dream-wandering through the fragrant confines of Sorcha's private garden back at the Ludus Achillea. I was faintly aware that I'd been there before, bathed in the same haze of moonlight, staring up at the statue of Minerva, the Roman goddess of war. The first time the statue had turned out to be my sister, dressed for battle beneath a cloak of iron feathers. This time I had trouble making out the features of the face beneath the brim of a helmet. I peered up at the shadowy figure as the moonlight grew brighter, redder . . .

I gasped and stumbled back when I saw that the face beneath the helmet belonged to Pontius Aquila. The Collector. My great enemy.

"Fallon . . ." His lips didn't move, but his voice whisper-echoed in my ears. "Won't you join my collection?"

He shifted aside the heavy black cloak he wore, and there, at his feet, I saw Tanis—once a student of the ludus, a talented archer, a sister gladiatrix . . . a girl I had betrayed and left behind. She knelt at his feet, soaked with rain and mud, looking just as she had the night we'd escaped from the ludus and I'd been forced to leave her behind. The mud on her cheeks was streaked with tear tracks, but she was smiling.

"Yes, Fallon," she said. "Join us. We have a cage ready just for you . . ."

The scene shifted, and I found myself back in my cell in Tartarus. Pontius Aquila stood, smiling on the other side of the bars, holding a silver feather—the symbol of his twisted order, the Sons of Dis.

I woke up crying out denial in the darkness of my town-house bedroom.

I was preoccupied enough with my nightmare the next morning that Elka had to stop me from stepping out into the path of an oncoming ox cart as we made our way through the center of town toward the Campus Martius, where we would meet up with Quintus.

I stumbled over the hem of my stola, shrugging off Elka's hands, and made a pretense of my preoccupation being less about bad dreams and more about my mode of dress—which, in all fairness, was a distraction in itself. I had been allowed to stay behind in Rome and attend Cai's gladiatorial performance on one condition: that I continue to dress like a proper female and leave my sword belt behind. Sorcha had insisted I start appreciating the civilized nature of Roman society and stop looking over my shoulder for daggers hidden beneath cloaks all the time.

"Swaddled again like a babe," I grumbled, tugging at the material tangling around my legs as I walked. "And yet? I've never felt so naked while wearing so many clothes . . ."

"You should have strapped a knife to your thigh under your stola," Elka said breezily, "like I did."

"Ha. Sorcha would have known at a glance," I said.

Elka cast an eye at me. "You're probably right," she said. "You're never so awkward as when you're traveling unequipped. You look a bit like a newborn foal that hasn't quite figured out its legs yet."

"Marvelous."

"I still don't know why she insisted. You think all these fine Roman ladies are weaponless?" Elka grinned, gesturing at the butterfly-bright array of women chatting and laughing as they made their way in twos and threes toward the gates of the Campus Martius. "Most of them wear hairpins longer and sharper than my dagger," she said.

I knew, of course, that we were in little danger. Not with Kronos, the senior fight manager from the ludus, looming large behind us as we walked. He had accompanied us into the city and was heading off on Sorcha's business as soon as he handed us over to Quint . . .

Who looked as though he'd taken extra care polishing his armor that day.

"Oh my," I said, suddenly spotting him from a distance. "He's very shiny."

Elka pretended not to notice when he saw us and waved.

I bit my lip to keep from grinning as he shouldered his way through the crowds to get to us and resolved not to tease Elka. Too much. In truth, I was happy for her, even as I felt a little bit like I was intruding on their outing. But Elka had protested repeatedly (and a bit too loudly) that she was really only interested in watching the games—and maybe picking up a new spear technique or two. I decided to just enjoy myself and let the anticipation of seeing Cai again carry my mood.

The games that day were held in the Theatrum Pompeii on the Campus Martius, on the northwest edge of the capital. It was a much smaller venue than the Circus Maximus, where I'd fought during Caesar's Quadruple Triumphs, but it was still an impressive structure. Tiered stone seating rose in steps that curved like the sides of a bowl up around a raked-smooth, sandy half circle. The theater was the first of its kind in the city and mostly used for dramatic presentations. As I understood it, it had been commissioned by a man named Gnaeus Pompeius Magnus—Pompey the Great—a great friend of Caesar's, and a greater rival. Pompey had been assassinated two years before I'd arrived in Rome, at the behest of Cleopatra's brother Ptolemy, the Aegyptian boy king with whom she'd been at war. Ptolemy, so the tale went, had thought to curry favor with Caesar by sending him Pompey's severed head. The effect had been exactly the opposite, with Caesar enraged and disgusted by the gesture. Things had gone rather poorly for Ptolemy after that. Caesar had sided with Cleopatra, and so Cleopatra had, of course, won.

In recent weeks, the queen had been a live-in guest of the Ludus Achillea, visiting my sister while the great love of her life attended temple dedications and other public functions with his dour—but nonetheless proper aristocratic *Roman*—wife. Cleopatra wasn't happy about the situation she found herself in, but she was also pragmatic about it. Before coming to the ludus, she'd sent her young son—hers and Caesar's—back to Alexandria, telling Sorcha it was so he could begin a proper Aegyptian education, but I wondered if that was the whole truth. Public opinion of Cleopatra had never climbed up out of the roadside gutters, and public opinion on Caesar's civil wars swung wildly from week to week. Depending, it seemed to me, on the weather and the wind and however much a wine jug sold for in the marketplace.

To say the mob was not fickle was to never have encountered the mob. It was the very essence of the gladiatorial games. The reason for their existence: *public opinion*. Which could be a very dangerous thing. And not just for upstart Aegyptian queens.

I already knew, walking into the theater beside Elka and Quint, that public opinion was heavily stacked against a certain ex-decurion-turned-gladiator. I could hear snatches of horridly gleeful speculation and saw the wagers being traded back and forth. The odds seemed to overwhelmingly

favor Cai's impending bloody demise. I wondered if anyone in the crowd would have kept that opinion to themselves if they'd known who I was. But I also couldn't blame
the plebs for not recognizing me—or even Elka, for that
matter—dressed as we were, as Sorcha had mandated, in
our stolas and pallas.

But we certainly weren't the only ones who were unrec-
ognizable that day.

I don't know what I was expecting, but it was star-
tling to see Cai out of uniform, dressed in the gear and
attire of a gladiator. He stood over by the Flaminian dugout adjusting the fit of his leather wrist bracers and, once
I realized it was him, I couldn't take my eyes off him. Cai
had let his hair grow out from the military cut he'd always
worn. It brushed the sides of his face, just above his jawline, which stood out sharply, accentuated by the stubble
that shadowed his cheeks and chin. I'd never seen Cai
unshaven before. He wore no breastplate, no tunic, just a
short leather-strap battle kilt and a broad leather belt that
protected his abdomen but left his chest and arms bare. A
bronze helmet lay on the bench beside him, fashioned to
look like it sported two curving ram's horns, one on either
side. He turned to pick up his sword belt, and I saw the
scars on his shoulder—three jagged parallel lines made by
the claws of the bear that had attacked him in Hispania,
when he'd been on campaign with Caesar—gleaming pale
against the sun-browned skin that slid over the contours of
his lean, muscled frame.

He looked nothing like the decurion I knew.

There was something . . . *primal* about him. Something barely leashed inside his soul, straining to break the bonds of his training. His discipline. I shivered beneath my palla, remembering what Senator Varro had said to him in the moments before Cai had buried his sword in his father's chest. *"You even fight like one of them,"* Varro had sneered at his only son. *"Like a filthy gladiator. A real legion officer would be ashamed."*

I knew those words had burned into Cai's heart like a brand. But looking at him in that moment, I suspected they'd also kindled to life a flame that burned deep within him. The fire of a warrior, not just a soldier. He lifted his helmet, settling it on his head, and drew his blades, and I imagined him painted with woad beneath a thundercloud sky, fighting shoulder to shoulder with me alongside the bravest and wildest of the Cantii warriors. A treasured member of the royal war band . . .

A moment of outlandish daydream, maybe, but a nice one.

I shook my head to clear away the reverie. There was no woad, no thunderclouds. No war band. Cai stood beneath the pale, bright Roman sun, his skin unmarked by paint, waiting to fight for the pleasure of the crowd. I watched as he rolled the tightness from his shoulders, noticing that he seemed to have regained some of the weight he'd lost recovering from his injuries. The too-lean look that had been there on our journey to and from Corsica had disappeared, and I was glad of it. At least he looked healthy enough to fight. And I had faith in Cai's fighting abilities, having tested them myself on more than one occasion.

For his first contest that day, Cai was slated to fight against an opponent who was kitted out as a *murmillo* fighter, and I winced at the no doubt intended irony. In recreation spectacles, murmillo were typically cast in the role of the hero and uniformed in such a way as to mimic the glorious legions of the mighty Republic. Cai, on the other hand—and the sight of it instantly made my heart beat faster in my chest—wore *dimachaerus* gear. Like me. Only, where I wielded two short, straight-bladed swords, Cai had opted to use a pair of *sica* as his weapons of choice. Sica were longer, curved, and better to use to get around the edges of the *scutum*. A smart choice.

The *cornua* sounded their mournful, strident notes.

The combatants stepped toward each other.

"What's the theme of the day?" Elka asked.

I squinted at the painted board at the far end of the arena detailing the particulars of the dramatic representation we were about to watch, working out the meaning of the words one at a time. One *letter* at a time, really. I'd been neglecting my reading lessons of late.

"Something about Rome's gallant—and, of course, triumphant—struggles," I replied, "against the . . . the barbarous hordes from the four corners of the world."

Elka's subsequent eyeroll was almost an audible thing.

I grinned and kept reading. "The first round of contests will consist of four duels fought . . . uh . . ."

"Simultaneously," Quint helped me out. "It means at the same time."

"Right." I nodded, tucking the unfamiliar word away into my growing store of Latin and peering at the board. "Simultaneously. The winners of those contests will go on to fight in two pairs. And those winners will then fight each other for the prize."

At least, that was how it was supposed to go. And it was painfully obvious which combatant was expected to win in each matchup. Four legionnaire-like murmillo fighters—the "heroes"—all squaring off against a variety of the other classes—the "villains."

The first round followed the prescribed format, as expected.

The fights were well-matched, the combatants mostly evenly skilled. One gladiator—a *thraex*—fell to a sword thrust to the upper thigh and would likely need a good deal of stitching to close him up again. Another, a *retiarius*, dropped to his knees after a showy, frenzied bout that ended with both his net and his trident torn from his hands. Clearly the crowd's favorite whipping post, he left the sands with a wave of his hand and was showered in a flurry of cheerful catcalls. The third combatant fared rather worse and had to be helped back into the tunnel after being knocked senseless from a vicious blow to the head.

That left only Cai and his opponent engaged.

The two adversaries danced, bobbing and weaving in a circle around each other, probing for weaknesses, feinting, attacking, defending, and backing off to circle again.

The murmillo fighter was competent, but more inclined to brutishness rather than finesse. He had a thick, bull-ish neck and bulging arms and thighs. He was shorter than Cai, but he must have outweighed him by fifteen or twenty *libra*. The heavy bronze plates studding the leather belt that girdled his waist protected his vitals from Cai's longer reach and curved blades whenever he managed to snake round the edges of the scutum, but the sica had still hit the mark early on and more than once. The man's shield-arm shoulder and biceps were running blood from several long, shallow cuts.

Cai had remained, to that point, unscathed as far as I could tell. Still, it was almost unbearable sitting up there in the stands watching him fight. I felt my hands clench-ing and unclenching every time he flexed his fingers on the hilts of his swords. My muscles tensing with his blocks and blows . . .

A solid strike from his opponent's shield sent Cai stag-gering across the sands, drawing a roar of approval. The crowd was clearly on the side of the murmillo fighter. Decurion Caius Antonius Varro might have been widely known as the dashing young legion officer who'd so gal-lantly celebrated my triumph as Victrix with a passionate kiss before the whole of the Circus Maximus, but Cai the Gladiator was nothing but a patricide—a murderer and a pariah—and, oh, how loudly they howled for his spec-tacular death. Of course, the thing about the Roman mob was this: You could be guilty of a crime without a trial, without evidence, with vastly mitigating circumstances . . .

but to be innocent? You only had to prove yourself *worth* something.

Entertainment, as Caesar had so shrewdly surmised, was worth a great deal. And the mob would reap a marvelous return on the coins they'd paid out to enter the theater that day. The tide of bloodlust was running high and hectic. The other three bouts had been perfunctory, serviceable, and over too soon. But Cai's fight was getting interesting. *Entertaining.*

The murmillo was getting tired. The weight of hefting around not only his shield but his own considerable bulk had him running with sweat. The point of his gladius kept dipping carelessly, and the bottom of the murmillo's shield angled too sharply in toward his center line—only a handsbreadth, maybe two . . .

I took a sharp breath in and leaned forward, rigid with anticipation.

"*Ja!*" Elka exclaimed fiercely when she saw the same opening.

Does Cai see? I wondered, my heart in my throat.

He answered suddenly—and with a definitive *yes*—ducking low and lunging in a diving arc with both sica darting out in front of him like flicking serpents' tongues. As Cai scrambled past his adversary, the points of his curved blades tagged the murmillo again—this time on the back of his legs, below his armored kilt. Blood splashed from a wound behind the gladiator's knee on his right leg, while the shin guard on his left dangled loose, flopping from the single strap left holding it on.

"*That's* it!" Quint punched the air with his fist. "Take the bastard down!"

Cai spun and delivered a sharp kick to the outside of the murmillo's now-unprotected left knee, and he crumpled and hit the ground in a cloud of dust, blood pooling on the sand beneath him. The injuries were precise and purposefully not career-ending, but any weight the gladiator tried to put on his injured right leg that day would just send him back down in a heap. The bout was over.

Cai stepped back from his fallen opponent and glared defiantly up at the crowd in the stands. I shouted a Cantii victory cry, and Elka put her fingers to her lips and whistled loudly. Quint hollered with savage joy. I didn't care that we three seemed to be the only ones in the entire place cheering Cai on. He'd won his bout, and that was all that mattered. He could walk out of the arena that day with his head held high and live to fight another day.

At least, he could have—if it was a fair fight.

It wasn't.

The murmillo wasn't getting back up onto his feet anytime soon, but *he* wasn't the problem. As Cai turned away from the downed man and moved to take his place with the other bout winners, a retiarius fighter with a full face shield and an arm covered in vibrant blue tattoos stepped up out of the dugout and walked into the middle of the arena. He dropped into a ready crouch facing Cai.

The crowd murmured in confusion . . . and then the other bout winners stepped up beside the tattooed retiarius, fanning out in a half circle against Cai.

"Quint?" I asked, not taking my eyes from the ring. "What's going on?"

"I'm . . . not sure," he murmured.

I saw Cai's fists go white-knuckled on his swords as he tightened his grip, and I glanced over at the games masters. There were two of them officiating that day, and they stood near the *vomitorium*—the tunnel entrance to the arena— roster tablets in their hands. Backs turned to the combatants.

They're going to let this happen, I thought. They were going to stand by and let the other gladiators gang up on Cai and do nothing.

I heard Quint swear under his breath and felt Elka go stiff with tension beside me. That tension seemed to ripple through the watching mob as they realized what was about to happen. Three against one. Against the rules. Before I could stop myself, I was rising to my feet. But Quint reached across Elka and clamped a hand around my arm, stopping me before I could do anything foolish. I looked over at him, and he shook his head.

"No, lass," he said, his brow darkening with an angry frown as he looked back at Cai and the gladiators circling him like hungry curs. "This is his fight alone. It has to be."

I knew that. I knew Quint was right.

But then it was four against one. Then five . . .

Other fighters from the benches where the fresh gladiators waited for the next round stepped up into the ring to join the ones already standing there, ranged in a loose circle facing Cai. Maybe they had scores to settle, maybe they'd been paid, or maybe they just thought it would be fun. But there was no way Cai could win. He would be slaughtered where he stood, overwhelmed by sheer numbers.

The crowd went utterly still with gruesome anticipation.

From the corner of my eye, I could see the jackal-men—the arena attendants who wore dog-headed masks and dragged the bodies of fallen fighters from the sand with corpse hooks—milling about. Preparing.

Then the tattooed retiarius uttered a brief shout and swung his net toward Cai, snapping his wrist so that the weighted hemp ropes whipped viciously through the air. Cai dodged back a step, and the net whistled past his face. The other gladiators shifted and moved to flank him, and I felt myself rising up off my seat again and saw that even Quint was leaning forward like he was about to leap into the arena. But then, suddenly, there was a flurry of activity and another gladiator vaulted up from the trenches into the ring. He, too, was kitted out murmillo-style. One of the designated "heroes" of the arena.

Six against one, I thought, despairing.

But as he strode across the sand, the gladiator reached up and lifted off his murmillo helmet, dropping it to the ground behind him. Beneath his helmet, his hair was shaved on the sides, hanging in long bunches of thin coppery-hued braids from the top of his head down his neck. All over his torso he bore a multitude of scars—both fresh and long-faded—and he positioned himself beside Cai.

Facing the other gladiators.

He and Cai nodded briefly at each other and then, without warning, rushed forward, swords cutting the air before them, flashing sunlight like fire. The other gladiators clearly weren't expecting even a slight evening of the odds. But *two* against five was a vastly different situation than *one* against five. Together, they swept through the line of their opponents, and the man unlucky enough to find himself at the center of that line dropped to the ground as they passed, bleeding from wounds on both sides of his body.

That left four others.

They split into two pairs as Cai and his newfound partner went back-to-back. Not so sure of themselves with their fellow lying, writhing on the ground, howling in pain, the four murmillo backed off, circling warily while the audience jeered and urged them on to attack. In truth, if all four had rushed Cai and his partner at once, that likely would have ended it. But it also, very likely, would have ended at least one of them. And they knew it.

Their betrayal of the rules of the arena meant that this was no longer just a fight. It was a fight to the death. Cai was a soldier before he was a gladiator. He was very used to that. And something about the man with the copper braids—whether it was his scars or his bearing—told me he was too. The mood of the crowd was balanced on a blade's edge and about to turn ugly. But Cai was patient. He could afford to be. The crowd wasn't nearly so sanguine.

"Get on with it, cowards!" someone in the stands yelled, and threw a half-eaten fowl leg at the combatants.

A swelling chorus of jeers from the mob prompted two of the murmillo fighters to attack Cai's partner at once. But with their shoulders jammed up against each other, Cai must have felt the copper-braided man drop into a sudden crouch and, without hesitation, he spun in a circle, slashing with both his blades at full extension over his partner's head. Cai's left blade caught one of the attackers on the side of his neck. The crowd gasped in horrified delight as the man dropped to the ground. Blood spurted in a fountain from between his fingers as he clutched at his throat . . . and then he was still.

Cai's partner sprang up the moment Cai's blades whistled past his head, and he dispatched the other attacking fighter with a short thrust through the gap in his armor where it buckled at the shoulder. A nonlethal blow that would likely still end the man's gladiatorial career. Just not his life.

Carrying through with the momentum of his spin, Cai lunged for one of the other pair, his blades circling up and across on the diagonal. His target was fast, though. A step back and a low dodge and his own sword flashed wickedly. And suddenly there was blood. The slice across Cai's upper arm was clean—from the point of the man's blade—but deep enough to render Cai's arm useless for the moment. His right blade flew from shock-numb fingers, cartwheeling through the air and far beyond his reach.

But his *left* blade . . .

Cai lurched forward and buried a finger's length of that blade in his attacker's thigh.

With an animal squeal of pain, the man dropped to the ground.

Now Cai had only the tattooed retiarius left to face. And *he* looked much less sure of himself than he had when he'd first stepped out onto the sand. Cai glanced at the copper-braided man, who grinned at Cai and stepped back, gesturing for Cai that the retiarius was all his to take care of. Cai nodded curtly and, plucking up his fallen blade, sank into a wary stance. Then he waited, patient as a hunting cat eyeing its prey from a distance. That, I thought, was legion training. The kind of training that tempers passion and rashness in a fight. The retiarius had no such training.

When the crowd again demanded action, he took it as a cue.

Lunging forward, the net in his hand blooming outward in a circle before him, he aimed at Cai's legs to trip him up. With a single fluid motion, Cai stepped to one side and brought the sica in his left hand down in a diagonal slash aimed *not* at his opponent but at the net. The sica hooked through the strands, tangling in the knotted rope, and the crowd hissed savagely at what they saw as Cai's mistake. But I knew what he was doing. With a ferocious heave, Cai yanked the retiarius forward and off balance.

Half the crowd cheered Cai's audacious bravery and the other half booed and hissed, cried foul, and howled for his blood. In a desperate move, the retiarius thrust his trident straight out in front of him, as if to brace for a fall, and Cai thrust the blade in his right hand between the sharpened tines, twisting so that the gladiator's entire torso was wide open, undefended. But with both his blades employed elsewhere, Cai was weaponless. Although certainly not without options. He backed off a single step and delivered a thunderous kick to the retiarius, right below his collarbone. The man fell face-first to the sand, gasping for breath, winded and helpless.

The crowd went momentarily silent, stunned at the abrupt turnaround of what had promised to be the brutal slaughter of the patricide Varro. I held my breath, watching to see if there were any more stirrings in the gladiator trenches.

Cai yanked his weapons free and stood there with his shoulders hunched, breath heaving in his chest and slick with sweat. His right arm was painted in a red sleeve of blood from his wound. Turning in a slow circle with his teeth bared, he was like a cornered bear about to be set upon by the wolf pack.

And I couldn't help him.

Or maybe I could.

I remembered my fight in Caesar's Triumphs and how the crowd had gone wild when Cai had leaped into the arena to sweep me into an embrace. The passions of the arena mob were extravagantly theatrical, but I knew well their sympathies could swing like a pendulum in a whirl-wind, given the right push.

A murmuring in the stands all around me began to grow . . .

I reached up and stripped off the silver armband that circled my left bicep and unwound the filmy silken scarf from around my throat, glad suddenly that I'd decided— that Sorcha had *forced* me—to dress like an actual Roman lady that day.

I knotted a corner of the scarf around the armband and cried out, "Ave, gladiator! Ave!" in my loudest voice to get his attention. As his head swung toward me, I lobbed the armband through the air into the center of the arena, shout-ing, "Bravely done!"

The sunlight glittered off the silver trinket, and the scarf fluttered like a victory pennant as it flew. Cai's eyes went wide, and he thrust out his sword, neatly catching the sil-ver armband on the tip of his blade. It chimed like a bell, and he spun his other sword in his hand and sheathed it on his hip. Then he plucked the bauble from his blade and thrust it high over his head. A handful of the women in the audience near me laughed and clapped with delight.

And then, they began to cheer.

From blood-mad to lovestruck in a moment.

They cheered even louder when Cai reached up to remove his helmet and his hazel eyes locked with mine . . . and he slowly lowered the silver circle to his lips and kissed it. The look on his face was enough to make *my* heart turn over, and the rest of the female contingent of the crowd clearly seemed to feel the same way. The delighted shriek that went up was near deafening, and a young patrician woman sitting directly in front of me looked as though she might actually swoon.

Win the crowd, my old mentor Arviragus had once told me. *Win their love.*

Easy enough for Cai, I thought. *He already has mine.*

And to think I'd wanted to kill him when we'd first met.

Now he had his first—resounding—victory as a gladiator. All he had to do was court the mob, let them get to know him, and all would be well. Then, I thought, he'd be the darling of Rome, Caesar's man again, and we could finally be together outside of the arena. What I didn't realize—what I'd refused repeatedly to acknowledge—was what Kassandra had once warned me of. That the world outside the arena was far more treacherous than the world inside could ever be.

VI

THE LUDUS FLAMINIUS was a very different place from the gladiatorial academy I was used to. Quint had been reluctant to take me there after the games that day, but I'd insisted, and so he'd escorted me to the gates of the compound, where he and Elka told me they would wait for me until after I'd spoken to Cai. The notoriety I'd garnered for myself as Caesar's Victrix took care of getting me through the gates.

It was unfair of me, maybe.

Cai had, after all, made it pretty clear—by way of all the letters returned to me unopened—that he didn't want to see me. But now that I had presented myself in person to the ludus, he couldn't actually refuse. Not without consequence. Gladiators, especially ones who weren't in the trade of their own free will, were beholden to the wishes of their lanistas. And there wasn't a lanista in Rome who would deny a wealthy patrician lady—or, in this case, Caesar's own favorite barbarian-princess-turned-gladiatrix—an encounter with one of their stable. They would drag them out of their cells by the ear, if need be. So what I was doing was really just an abuse of an already abusive system. And I wasn't leaving Rome without having spoken to Cai.

But as I descended the steps into the gladiator barracks, I began to understand Quint's reluctance to bring me there. I started to seriously question my already questionable decision. The Flaminian facility was nothing like the Ludus Achillea. On the surface, it seemed relatively benign, with several group training pitches and a handful of smaller dueling enclosures. A utilitarian compound, with serviceable—if spartan—baths and mess halls, an infirmary, and a smithy. A chariot training circuit and stables and, beyond that, a burial ground.

I had noticed as we walked that there didn't seem to be any aboveground accommodations for the gladiators. Instead, it seemed that all the fighters were housed in subterranean cells—the kind I'd seen reserved for slaves and criminals and prisoners of war at other ludi. The catacombs wound deep beneath the ludus compound with its austere mess hall and practice facilities, and they reminded me uncomfortably of the chambers beneath the Domus Corvinus. Or my prison cell in Tartarus. I shivered at the thought and pulled the palla I wore up higher on my shoulders.

The trainer who'd led me down into those lower depths gave me a glance that was almost apologetic, gesturing me forward at the bottom of a stone stairway. The vaulted ceiling of the main corridor disappeared into the shadows above our heads, and our footsteps echoed on the stones beneath our feet as we passed the gaping maws of the cells, barred with iron—barriers that did nothing to keep hostile glances from raking over me like claws as I passed.

A rank atmosphere of brutality fogged the air, thicker than all the ghosts of blood and sweat and fear lingering there, more acrid than the smoke from the guttering torches on the walls. My heart hammered in my ears, but it didn't block out the sound of the foul catcalls and jeers slung in my direction from all sides. I kept my expression stony and my eyes fixed in front of me. I'd heard worse hurled at me from the stands in the arena, and slowly the voices faded into a muted cacophony. Most of them. One voice did not.

A voice speaking in the language of my home said: "Princess . . ."

I froze in my tracks and turned my head slowly to see a man—a young man wrapped in a long tattered blanket, like a cloak, for warmth against the dank chill—staring at me with a burning intensity that lit up his red-rimmed eyes.

Ignoring my trainer escort's warning glance, I took a few steps toward the cell and asked, "Do I know you?"

"No, princess." The young man shook his head, a humorless grin on his lips. "No reason you should. I was only one of your father's loyal warriors since I was old enough to hold a shield."

"You're . . . Cantii?" I asked, frowning.

"You're surprised." He snorted derisively and shook his head. "Then again, you've been gone a long way from home a long while. The memory fades, one imagines. But I remember *you*. I remember the very night you disappeared from Durovernum."

"What is your name?"

He paused for a long moment, then pulled himself up to stand straight and looked me in the eye. "I'm Yoreth," he said. "Of the royal war band of King Virico Lugotorix."

He was one of my father's elite? I felt a rush of shame that I didn't remember the man. What had Rome done to me that I should forget such a thing?

"What are you doing here?" I asked.

"What does it look like?" he snapped. Then he sighed and shook his head, offering up a wan, apologetic smile. "Forgive me. This place is murder to a man's better nature. Please excuse my bad manners."

I nodded. "Of course. If you'll excuse my bad memory. Please . . . what news of home? How did you find yourself here, in this place?"

He paused for a moment, as if reluctant to tell me, and then said, "The Coritani have been raiding the Catuvellaun lands this past year."

"That's nothing new," I said.

The Coritani were one of the more aggressive tribes on the Island of the Mighty. Raiding against the Catuvellauni—and any of the other tribes they fancied to bother, including my own—was like breathing to them. It would have alarmed me more to hear that they'd given up the practice.

But Yoreth shook his head. "Not like this. Raiding for cattle, sure enough, that's to be expected. But burning whole villages? Killing most of the men and carrying off the women?"

His words felt like cold fingers wrapping around my heart. The Coritani were a hard and warlike people, but I'd never heard of them being so bold. Or so brutal. Things, it seemed, had changed on the Island of the Mighty. And what of my father, I wondered . . .

"The Catuvellauni called on us for aid," Yoreth continued. "Your noble father, Virico, sent his warriors."

I waited. "And . . . ?"

He shrugged and looked away. "And some of us, well . . . maybe we don't fight with the same fires the Morrigan once kindled in our warrior breasts. Maybe, instead, we go down in the mud and are taken prisoner. And maybe . . . the filthy Coritani clap us in chains and sell us to the slavers." His gaze shifted back to me then, and there was bitterness there. "Maybe they bring us here. To this place."

I felt those icy fingers tightening around my heart, remembering in a sudden, vivid flash the night I'd been taken by Charon's men . . . and all the horrid days after on the way to Rome to be sold. I swallowed thickly and said, "I'm sorry for your misfortunes. I do know something of what that's like."

His gaze drifted bleakly over me, head to foot. "Clearly," he said.

My jaw clenched at the note of judgment in his tone. But I had to admit, it was hard to blame the man. Because, of course, I was dressed entirely like a proper Roman lady that day. There was nothing about the way I looked that was of the daughter of the Cantii king. In truth, I was surprised he'd even recognized me.

"Your pardon, Victrix," the ludus trainer who escorted me said, stepping forward. "Scum like this don't know how to act around a lady." He slammed his staff against the bars, narrowly missing the man's fingers. "Back off, cur," he ordered in a blandly threatening tone. "Or I'll have you training with the *bestiarii*. As bait."

He gestured for me to follow him, and I nodded, turning my back on the man in the cell. As I walked away, I heard him say, "You may not remember where you come from, princess. But your new friends do. The Romans have not forgotten Prydain. One day they will return there. One day soon."

I felt a chill along my spine, but I kept walking. I was there to see Cai. Not a disgraced warrior who, from his own account, had lost heart in the heat of battle and turned coward only to become captive. Yoreth would have plenty of opportunities to redeem himself—and his honor—in the arena.

At the end of the row of slave cells, the trainer unlocked a door and harangued its occupant until, finally, Cai stepped out over the threshold. He blinked in the uncertain light and then, when he saw me standing there, his eyes went wide. There was a fresh linen bandage wound around his arm, and I could see the outline of stiches beneath. In that respect, at least, the Ludus Flaminius took care of their gladiators. Of course they did. Even superficial wounds left untended could be deadly, and a dead gladiator was a wasted investment.

Before either of us could say anything, the trainer had pulled the door shut and was ordering Cai to move.

"Did you hear me, Varro?" he snapped. "Get going! Lady wants a session with you, and that's what she's going to get. Move!"

I followed close behind the trainer as he prodded Cai in the back with his staff, knowing I would be instantly lost if I didn't keep up. The place was like a rabbit warren. If all the rabbits living there were actually wolves.

We were led to one of the small training yards used for individual sparring sessions. I suspected, judging by the trainer's demeanor, they were also frequented by wealthy Roman dilettantes wanting to play-fight at being gladiators with the real thing—and wealthy Roman matrons who wanted the play without the fighting. I felt my cheeks grow red as the ludus trainer left us there alone, glancing first at me and then at Cai, and muttering, "No accounting for taste . . ." as he left.

And then suddenly, we were alone. I stood there, awkward and unsure, wondering if I hadn't made a mistake in coming there. I waited for Cai to say something. Anything.

"Thank you," Cai said finally, his voice strangely hollow. "For saving me."

Saving him? I thought. *I* was the reason he was in that arena in the first place. I shook my head. "I didn't," I said. "You won that fight. Even after they cheated, you won. The token was just—"

"That's not what I meant."

"Then what . . . ?"

A pair of ludus guards stalked past our enclosure, pausing to look through the archway at us. Cai cast a flat glare in their direction and then wandered over to a rack of practice gear. He plucked up a pair of wooden gladii, tossing them to me. I caught them out of the air without thinking and waited while he chose a second pair for himself. Once he had, he walked back over to take up a ready stance in front of me. I shrugged off my palla and matched it, mirroring him, barely even needing to think about it.

The guards moved on. Sparring was one thing, I supposed, but if I'd been expecting anything else from one of their fighters—like one of those other rich Roman ladies— I suspect I would have likely had to pay for it. Or for the privilege of passing the time unobserved, at least.

"I've had a lot of time to do a lot of thinking in this place, Fallon," Cai said, and made a thrust toward my right shoulder with his left blade that I blocked easily and responded to with a diagonal slash. "I've thought about how I came to be here . . ." he continued, evading my slash and returning to a guarded stance, "and why."

I lowered my weapons. "Cai, I'm so sorry—"

"No!" He shook his head adamantly. "Oh, gods, Fallon. No. *You* have nothing to be sorry for."

I was at a loss for words in that moment, not really understanding what he was talking about. Cai lifted his blades again, gesturing me to lead with an attack. I shrugged the tension out of my shoulders and, without bothering to ready my stance, launched into an overhead double-strike. Cai narrowly evaded, misreading my strike point, but compensated neatly and ducked past the blow, twisting to come back at me with a slash to my left flank. His reach was longer than mine, and I had to jump a few awkward steps to the side before sinking back into a defensive crouch. I spun my right blade in my hand.

"Are you going to tell me what, exactly, you mean by that?" I asked, getting back to our conversation as he took a horizontal swipe at me.

He nodded and, while we cycled through a series of side-to-side blows and parries that struck splinters from the edges of our wooden blades, he did his best to explain. "What I mean is . . . all my life, I've never really questioned anything," he said. "Not my father, not Caesar, not the Republic or what it means to conquer other lands . . . not enough."

We disengaged for a moment, circling each other.

"Do you remember the first time we talked?" he continued. "On the ship?"

I nodded. Of course I remembered. We'd been attacked by pirates sailing the Mare Nostrum and almost died, and then Cai had, among other things, criticized my fighting technique and then compared me first to a weed and then a wildflower. Not exactly words of wooing . . .

Cai shook his head ruefully at the memory of the conversation.

"I said you didn't act like a slave," he said. "How arrogant of me. How presumptuous. The lordly son of a senator, a decurion who'd never not been free—not for an instant—and there you were, the daughter of a king with an iron collar around your neck. You should have thrown me over the side."

"It's not as if you *knew* I was the daughter of a king," I said.

"I should have. You stood there cloaked in dignity like an empress. I'd already seen you fight like an Amazon. I should have known you were destined to be a queen one day."

I didn't quite remember it that way. Especially not the dignity part, and truthfully, I'd grown leaps as a fighter since that day. Nor was it very likely that I'd ever amount to any kind of queen . . .

We fought on, and I saw a sliver of an opening as Cai dragged a step. I thrust my swords at his right shoulder, and his came up to block them with bone-jarring force. Our weapons locked up, and we strained against each other, our faces almost close enough for us to kiss over the crossed blades.

"Why are you punishing yourself for the way you were raised, Cai?" I asked, panting with the exertion. "It's not your fault—"

"It *is*," he said through gritted teeth. "I have a mind, Fallon, and a heart . . . and I've already lived two decades of my life without actually bothering much to use either. Not until I met you." His clear hazel eyes flashed at me, sparking with a kindled fierceness. "If I'd ever stopped to think about who my father really was, about what I was really doing in the service of the Republic . . . I might have been able to—"

"What?"

"Do something. Something to help. Not hurt."

"The way you've helped me?" I asked as I shifted my stance and tried to break the lockup. "Helped the girls at the ludus?"

"I'm glad of that," he said, pushing back. "It's a start. But it's only a start. And I had to take the life of my father to do it."

"Cai—"

With a heave of his shoulders, he thrust me back and disengaged.

"He deserved it." He shook his head. "I know. No argument there. But there are always consequences, even with the noblest of intentions. This place?" He waved a sword at the high, bleak walls surrounding us. "This is *my* consequence. I accept it as my fate, Fallon. At least . . .

well, at least until I can find—or *fight*—my way to a better one."

"Or die trying?" I asked.

He nodded. "Although I'd rather not. I'd rather just be with you."

He grinned at me and held out his hand for my practice blades. We were both sweating and breathing a little heavy, but it had felt good to spar with him again. I handed over my blades, nodding at the bandage on his arm where spots of blood had appeared.

"You might've pulled a stitch or two," I said.

He shrugged. "I'll live."

I reached up to touch his cheek. Carefully, though, because there were deep bruises on the side of Cai's face that were fading to yellow at the edges.

"You didn't get those in the arena today," I said.

"No. I didn't get them in the arena at all."

I frowned up at him. "Where?"

"The mess hall." He shrugged and racked the blades, fetching two small, rough linen towels from a stack on a wooden shelf so we could wipe the sweat from our faces. "The baths. The corridors . . . Ex-legion soldiers aren't exactly the paragons of popularity among a crowd of ex-Gaulish warriors."

I felt my blood begin to boil again at the injustice of it. What Cai had done to help me had also been in the service of Caesar. And Caesar had rewarded him by throwing him ignominiously out of the legions and into the pits of the Ludus Flaminius to fend for himself—a stag surrounded by a pack of wolves whose daily routine was to face off against each other on the sparring pitch.

"I suppose that's part of what's got me thinking about my destiny too," Cai continued. "And why the Fates saw fit to give me *this* particular bit of perspective."

I was about to tell him exactly what I thought of his Fates and his ludus-mates, but closed my mouth when he reached for me. I stepped toward him, and we clasped hands, the familiar feel of his rough, calloused palms sending a shiver through me, and I suddenly felt like maybe I wouldn't mind so much being one of those wealthy Roman ladies who didn't come to the Ludus Flaminius to *fight* with the gladiators.

There was less than a breath separating us, and I reached up to pull his bruised, beautiful face gently down toward mine. It was strange, being able to tangle my fingers in Cai's hair for the first time, instead of just being able to brush my hands over the short, bristly military cut. And the stubble that was closer to being a beard on his chin and jaw was softer than I expected. But his lips were just the same as I remembered, firm and soft at once, pressed hungrily against mine as if we could make up all the lost months in that moment if we just never let go of each other.

I wonder if we would have, if we hadn't heard a loud throat-clearing coming from the enclosure archway. Cai released his hold on me. Visibly gathering his patience by taking a slow breath in, he turned toward the young man who stood there. His reddish-brown hair was tied back in thin braids, and he had his arms crossed over his broad, scarred chest. He looked only mildly apologetic for the interruption.

"Sorry," he said, lifting one shoulder. "Just passing by and thought you might want to know the ludus guards are on their way back. Me, I couldn't care less, but they'll be wanting a privacy fee if they find you two, uh, thusly engaged. And their rates are nothing short of exorbitant."

Cai sighed and nodded at the other man. "Thank you . . . again."

I recognized the man. He was the one who'd stepped up to Cai's side in the arena. He grinned at me, his gaze sharpening. "Aren't you . . ."

"Fallon," I said. "And yes. Thank you for the warning."

"Fallon, or is it . . . Victrix?" he asked. Then he pushed away from the wall he was leaning on and walked toward us, stopping a few paces away to nod his head in a little bow to me. "Pleased to make your acquaintance, lady."

I smiled and shook my head. "I'm no more a lady than either of you two are lords. We're all just gladiators, after all."

"Fallon, this is Acheron," Cai said before the other man could argue with my assessment. "You, uh, knew his brother."

I looked at Cai. "Who . . . ?"

"Ixion."

I felt the blood drain from my face. Ixion had been one of Pontius Aquila's men. A thuggish brute who'd thoroughly enjoyed imprisoning me in Tartarus, the abyssal prison cell at the Ludus Achillea. He'd enjoyed it rather less when I'd escaped and cut his throat so that I could rescue my sister gladiatrices.

Acheron was staring at me. "You knew my brother?" he asked. And then lifted a hand before I could answer. "Of course you did. I can see you did."

I nodded. "He . . . used to be a fight trainer at my ludus. When I first arrived there." All of which was true. Sorcha had dismissed him soon after, though, for being far too rough with the girls, and that was how he'd wound up working for Aquila—in a position where he could give free rein to his sadistic side.

"What did he do to you?" Acheron asked.

I blinked at him. "Why would you think—"

"Ixion does something to everyone he meets. Trust me. I know. Except . . ." His gaze narrowed as he looked at me and he tilted his head. "Huh. I get the impression that *you*, maybe, did something to *him*."

I don't know what, exactly, he'd seen in my face in that moment. But I wasn't about to tell him that I'd killed his brother. I kept my mouth shut and said nothing.

"Never mind," Acheron said with a shrug. "Whatever it was, I'm sure he deserved it. I'm also sure he probably deserves worse. It'll happen one day. One day, my dear brother will cross paths with someone he can't beat into submission. I only want to be there when it happens, just to see the look of surprise on his great, ugly face."

Acheron would be forever disappointed in that wish, I thought, because I had been that someone. I turned away from him, back to where Cai was looking at me, his expression veiled. I'd never told him explicitly that I'd been the one to kill Ixion that night; for all he knew, that task had been accomplished by Aeddan, not me, as we'd attempted to escape.

He knows now, *of course,* I thought. *Just by looking at me.*

Cai had gotten very good at reading my thoughts. But I was saved any further scrutiny by the ludus guards, returning on their rounds and grunting for their gladiator charges to move along back to their cells. My visit, it seemed, was at an end.

"We have to go," Cai said, reluctance heavy in his voice. "They don't give us much time to eat, and then it's back to the practice pitch until dusk."

"And then?"

"Then they lock us all back up again," he said.

I looked at Acheron, wondering why he'd been roaming free. "Do they lock you up too?" I asked.

"At night, yeah," he said with a shrug. "I get a bit of free rein during the days fetching and carrying and delivering messages—I'm the lanista's dogsbody, really—mostly because I've been here so long they think I wouldn't know what to do with myself if I ever managed to escape and run away."

"Are *any* of the gladiators here free to come and go as they please?" I asked, thinking of my own situation and wondering just how lucky we were to have Sorcha as our lanista.

"Nah, not here." Acheron shook his head, grinning. "That elite stuff's only for the ludi that don't take things seriously. The lads of the Ludus Flaminius win more than any other academy in Rome because we don't have a choice. It's the only way out of here. The only way other than the jackal-men and their hooks, that is. We're a pack of thieves, murderers, slaves, and captives," Acheron laughed. "One big happy family . . ." Then he grinned at Cai and winked at me. "See you around, Victrix," he said with a wave before jogging back toward the archway and disappearing into the darkness of the corridor beyond.

I watched him go. "He's different," I said. "Not like Ixion at all." Although I did wonder what transgression it was that had landed Acheron in the Ludus Flaminius in the first place.

Cai shrugged. "Not all gladiators are treacherous thugs."

"Cai—"

"It was a *joke*, Fallon." He smiled wanly.

"I *know* that." I slapped my palm against his chest. "I was only going to say that I'd like to come see you again."

He looked at me strangely then, tilting his head, the shadow of uncertainty in his eyes. "I'm surprised you came to see me at all," he said. "I didn't think you wanted anything more to do with me."

"What?" I blinked at him, not understanding. After all the letters I'd sent to him that he'd returned to me unopened, I thought he—

"Varro!" One of the ludus guards had returned, an angry frown on his brow and his fingers twitching on the leather grip of a spiked, nasty-looking flail whip he carried. "Get your mangy, murdering arse back to your cell—*now*— or I'll see your rations cut for a week!"

The amount of sheer silent will I had to dredge up from the depths of my soul in order for me not to step forward and proclaim my identity—as Caesar's own Victrix—to the man almost made me dizzy. But Quint had been right, back at the theatrum, when he'd said that this wasn't my fight. This wasn't my consequence. It was Cai's. And I had to trust that he'd survive it. For as long as he needed to before the opportunity presented itself and he could once more be free.

Cai walked toward the guard, his gait unhurried, and stopped right in front of him. "I will remember you, Balba," he said. "I will be free of this place one day, but I will remember."

"Remember this, scum," was Balba's ill-considered reply, as he thrashed his flail at Cai, who threw up his arm and caught the brunt of the spiked leather thongs on his wrist bracer.

Two thin lines of blood appeared higher up on Cai's forearm, but he didn't even flinch. He just turned to me and said, "Lady Victrix," with a nod and a glint in his eye. Then he shook off the flail and stalked past Balba the guard, whose eyes had gone wide as soon as heard how Cai had addressed me. I bit my lip, stifling a grin. Cai clearly didn't disdain using my notoriety in the same way I did. It might have been his battle to fight, but he clearly didn't mind me helping out along the way. I watched as he disappeared through the archway, and then I walked toward the guard myself.

"Balba, is it?" I asked him.

He nodded, having gone a bit pale in such close proximity to Caesar's darling of the sands. Caesar, who also owned the Ludus Flaminius and, by default, all those within its stark stone walls.

"I have a good memory too, Balba," I said sweetly, remembering the bruises on Cai's face—which he'd more than likely received in full view of guards like this one. "And I should like to remember you to my lord Caesar as a good and faithful servant. I'm certain he'll be interested to hear how well you're taking care of his valuable gladiators."

"As well as can be, Lady Victrix," he said, the muscles of his thick neck working as he swallowed nervously.

"That's good to know."

"I serve at the pleasure of Caesar, lady."

I nodded as I continued past him and out into the corridor beyond.

Don't we all? I thought.

VII

WHEN ELKA AND I finally returned to the townhouse later that day, we discovered an invitation waiting for us. Kronos had received the messenger and relayed his message, written on a fine scroll of papyrus. A party was being held that very evening at the house of Octavia of the Julii, a niece of Caesar's. Apparently our attendance at the games that afternoon had not gone unnoticed. Tossing my arm ring into the arena might have had something to do with it, I suspected.

"Well, that's gone and done it," Elka sighed after Kronos finished reading us the details of the invitation.

Summons was more like it. The Julii women were renowned hostesses, and to receive a much sought-after invitation to one of their parties meant that Roman society had taken an interest in you. For good or ill. At any rate, I couldn't say no. Not and have Sorcha forgive me anytime that century.

"You do remember what happened last time you and I went to one of these things, *ja*?" Elka asked later, as we were getting ready to go.

"Vaguely," I muttered, grimacing, as I fiddled with the fastening on the silver belt around my waist. Even trying to remember the details of *that* night—the night at the Domus Corvinus—gave me the stirrings of a headache.

"Maybe stick to goat's milk tonight for drink," she said dryly. "And try to stay inconspicuous . . ."

I turned to blink at Elka, who'd brushed out her long blonde hair—usually tied back in braids—and stood swathed in pale blue. She looked like a goddess who'd decided to descend from Olympus to dally with the mortals for an evening. And she'd admonished *me* to blend in?

You first, I thought as we hurried down to the townhouse courtyard where a carriage waited to take us to one of the wealthiest districts in the city. Once we'd arrived and made our way inside the opulent confines of the Julii-owned domus, I realized that neither of us was going to accomplish anything even close to blending in.

For the first little while, I stood around, nervous and out of place and trying not to be. There was a trio of Aegyptian musicians performing in one corner, and I found myself mesmerized by both the look and sound of them. The women were dressed identically—which was to say that they were hardly dressed at all—and wore perfumed wax cones on their heads that slowly melted with the heat and dripped down over their lithe bodies, covering them in a fragrant, glistening sheen. They played strange and wonderful instruments—a lyre, a sistrum, and a handheld drum that was played with a short stick and reminded me of the war drums my father's warriors would carry to battle. I concentrated on the music and tried to ignore how utterly out of my element I felt.

Elka was better at hiding her apprehension than me, largely because there was a lavish abundance of food laid out on tables all the way around the circumference of the atrium. She simply kept busy by moving from dish to dish to fill her little plate with one delicacy after the other until we'd made it halfway around the room.

For my part, I'd taken her advice and stuck with a goblet of goat's milk flavored with lavender and honey. It was sweet and delicious, but I suddenly wished for something stronger when I saw a familiar head of dark curls moving through the crowd in my direction. Marc Antony broke away from the milling crowd and reached for my free hand.

"Victrix!" he exclaimed as if we were old friends, bending his head so he could brush my knuckles with his lips. "So glad you got my invitation."

"*Your* invitation?" I gaped at him. "I thought it came from—"

"Octavia?" He grinned. "Oh, well, it's her party, certainly. I merely offered my services when it came to the matter of procuring entertainment."

"Oh. Well . . ." I looked around the room. "The musicians are excellent. But that doesn't explain why you sent *us* an invitation." I nodded to Elka, who stood at my side, chewing on a honey-glazed fig and openly staring at Antony curiously.

"Music without dancing is so boring, don't you think?" His grin widened, but there was a glint in his eye that spoke of cold calculation. Then he stepped aside, gesturing to a table in an alcove beside the musicians, where an assortment of weapons had been laid out. "Would you and your lovely friend . . . dance for our guests, Lady Victrix?"

Dance. Cai had once asked me to "dance" with him. Of course I'd said yes then, but here? At a banquet? I was suddenly, uncomfortably, reminded of Pontius Aquila's twisted *munera*. Of Ajax and Aeddan fighting to the death in front of a crowd of glittering socialites. Of what happened after . . .

Antony must have seen my sudden apprehension—even if he couldn't guess where it sprang from—and his grin softened to a winsome smile. "For *fun*, my dear," he said. "Nothing serious. Nothing . . . dangerous. Just a display of your talents. I'm supremely confident you and your companion can provide a demonstration without actually causing any bodily harm to each other?" He lowered his voice. "I quite frankly don't care if you cut up a spectator or two in the process. These people are all so tedious . . ."

I looked at Elka. "Well?"

She shrugged. "I could use the exercise. The food's all a bit rich . . ."

Then she tossed the plate of figs and cheeses she'd been sampling to Antony. He fumbled to catch it and managed not to drop any of the delicacies to the floor. I followed her over to the display, where the two of us went about the business of assessing the weapons arrayed there with detached professionalism. They were all of a decent quality, if a bit showy for my tastes, but I picked a pair of swords half a hand shorter than the ones I was used to, and with broader blades, but well-balanced. Elka, of course, was drawn immediately to a slender spear that bore a blade on each end.

"You know," Antony was saying as we made our choices, "the story of how you two fought together on the day you were sold in the Forum is nearly the stuff of legend now."

"Is it?"

He nodded. "Where d'you think I came up with this idea?"

In truth, I just assumed he'd heard of the kinds of munera that occurred at other parties. I suppose I suspected him of having attended some of them.

"Two beautiful maidens," Antony waxed poetic, raising his voice enough so that the crowd who'd begun to gather around us could hear, "chained together by iron and fate . . ."

More like chained together by iron and a mutual desire to not be killed by a pair of angry Alesian brigands bent on revenge. I turned away from Antony and rolled my eyes at Elka. She grinned back at me and tested the edge of her spear blade with her thumb. Not so sharp that you could shave with it, but sharp enough that I didn't want it anywhere near me.

"Well," I said, "we don't have any leg irons, and I've run a bit short on fate this evening, but . . ." I looked around and noticed the long, pretty scarf embroidered with gold and silver thread draped around Lady Octavia's neck. "If I may?" I asked, gesturing to it.

She blinked at me and then smiled, greatly amused by the whole proceedings and happy to participate.

"I promise to return it unscathed," I said. Then I turned to Antony. "Would you be so kind, Lord Antony, as to bind my left ankle to Elka's right?"

"My absolute pleasure," he murmured.

I ignored the lascivious grin as he plucked the scarf from my fingertips and knelt between us. Elka, for her part, bestowed a glare upon him that warned he'd best keep his hands where she could see them while he tied the knots.

The idea was that, bound together this way, we couldn't retreat too far from each other. Making it more of a challenge for us while, at the same time, providing a bit of a safety margin for the guests watching in a circle around us. Because, regardless of Antony's opinions of them, I had no real burning desire to hack the flesh of a drunken party-goer, accidentally or not.

I gestured to the musicians to play. Back at the ludus, we sometimes trained with Kronos or one of the other masters beating out a tempo on a post. It *was* almost like dancing, and Elka and I, bored one afternoon and wanting to try something new, had worked out a routine of my blades against her spear. It started with a drill that alternated horizontal and vertical strikes from me—my blows coming from above and below, then switching to side to side—and Elka blocking them with her staff. The sequence complete, we'd switch it up and she would come at me, staff whirling, and I would defend with my swords. It was a fun exercise and one that kept us both on our toes.

But it wasn't something we'd ever done with a crowd watching, and maybe that's what made the difference that night. Because once we'd begun to warm up to the ebb and flow of the sequences, I noticed the look in Elka's eyes shifting, starting to resemble the expression she only ever got when she was in the arena. Not the practice ring.

And I'm not so certain I didn't have the exact same look. The one that meant you were so focused on the fight, the rest of the world disappeared. There was only winning. Because beyond that . . . there was only losing. And neither of us was going to lose.

Elka spun deftly on her tethered right leg, hopping over the taut rope of the scarf with her left leg as she did so and winding up for a vicious horizontal slash with her spear held at its greatest extension, which well surpassed how far I could go to evade it. And since I couldn't fly—no Cretan springboards that night—I dropped flat onto my back and rolled instead. But the marble floor was cold and unforgiving and I jammed my elbow hard, sending a flare of shooting pain down into my hand.

I lost my grip on one of my blades and scrambled to retrieve it with numb, prickling fingers. Elka saw my distress and took advantage of it, slapping the flat of the spear blade down between me and my blade and only missing my hand by a hairsbreadth. I felt a surge of red heat crash like a wave behind my eyes and kicked out with my free leg. Elka went down heavily as her knee went sideways from the blow, and suddenly we were both on our hands and knees.

I lunged for my dropped sword and bounced back up onto my feet, yanking hard on the scarf tether and pulling her off balance. With a snarl, she righted herself and slashed through the air, underhand. Her spear's blade sliced clean through the delicate length of silk that bound us together. The sudden lack of tension sent me staggering backward. Elka lunged, nearly impaling me as I twisted frantically away, and—suddenly blind-angry—I lashed out in retaliation with a double cross-body strike that I didn't even think to pull. We were both fighting beyond the limits of control and practice sequences in that moment. The tempo of the drums had increased until it was like a thunderstorm in my ears.

And we were fighting in the arena.

With a cry torn from deep in my chest I spun, my blades flashing up in a whirling overhead arc, and brought them crashing down . . . onto the very center of Elka's spear. Held at a perfect angle to block and hold me there. We strained against each other, matched, balanced, in a perfect lockup. If either of us shifted even minutely to break it, *that* fighter would lose.

And neither one of us was going to lose.

"Yield," I ground out between clenched teeth.

Elka mirrored my grimace. "You first, little fox," she said.

And then, all of a sudden, it was as if our private arena vanished and the party crowd faded back into existence, surrounding us, holding their collective breath. I blinked at Elka and realized that the battle rage had faded, not just from my eyes but hers too.

The corner of her mouth twitched upward.

"Together then," I said.

A silent count of three . . . and we both dropped our weapons, which clattered to the floor. I stepped back, limbs tingling from the exertion . . . and was horrified to see that there was a gaping tear in Elka's stola—right across her abdomen—and two thin crimson lines, beading blood.

When I could tear my gaze from what I'd done, I saw that Elka was staring at the left side of *my* rib cage, where my stola was just as torn . . . and I sported a single gash. A bit deeper, a bit bloodier. Both could have been killing wounds—hers and mine—if we'd put only a fraction more effort into it.

No one else seemed to notice, though. Between us, the ragged edges of Octavia's torn scarf trailed from our ankles along the polished marble floor. I reached down to pull the knot free and, wincing, glanced over to where Caesar's niece stood, rapt. For a moment she was frozen, wide-eyed . . . and then she started to clap wildly.

Elka and I exchanged a relieved glance.

The rest of the place erupted in wine-fueled applause and delighted laughter. I couldn't help thinking how

Aeddan had killed Ajax the gladiator at a dinner party just like this one. Only *not* just like this one. Because—at that dinner party—if he hadn't, Ajax would have killed him.

Elka and I bowed ourselves politely out of the room as coins were traded for wagers won and lost on the contest. A slave ran to fetch us bandages and a basin to wash away the blood. Without saying much, we helped each other dress our wounds and redrape our stolas to cover as much of the damage as we could and then headed back out to the main room.

Elka went to fetch us wine.

"I owe you a scarf, Lady Octavia," I said when she came over to me.

"Don't be silly." She waved away the matter. "I have a hundred of the things. I owe *you* an apology."

"I don't understand."

She slipped an arm through mine and drew me out into the courtyard, where the air was soft and perfumed and the stars overhead were like bright eyes winking down at us. "I thought my uncle Gaius was being ridiculous," she said, "when he told me all those years ago that he was going to put girls in the arena."

"Did you not think women strong enough?" I asked. "Or brave enough?"

She laughed. "Not exactly," she said, shaking her head. "I suppose I didn't think we were *honest* enough."

"Honest?"

"I suppose you'd have to have been born into a Roman high house to understand what I mean," she said. "It's just that . . . the women in my family? We've *always* fought. And strategized and mobilized and waged secret battles that have won and lost whole empires. But with words. With well-spent money. Behind closed doors and in whispers, using weapons that are . . . well . . . just as sharp as yours, perhaps, but not as clean. For all the violence of the way *you* fight, it seems less vicious, somehow."

I wondered about that. If Octavia would feel the same way if she knew just how close I'd come to actually hurting my best friend just then. But I kept those thoughts to myself. From the way she made it sound, an equestrian Roman woman wouldn't think twice about having a friend assassinated if circumstances warranted it. Maybe that was the real difference: whether or not you held the knife yourself when you did your killing.

"I just wanted to tell you that I understand now what Uncle Gaius saw in you," she said.

I glanced around at the glittering contingent of partygoers. "I'm not sure *this* is exactly what he saw in me, lady," I said, grinning ruefully. Then I glanced down and lifted an edge of my gown marred with a spot of blood. "*This*, maybe . . ."

Octavia smiled at me and reached to tuck the bit of fabric artfully into my belt, hiding the stain. "Well," she said. "Even though this isn't precisely the life my uncle—or you, if you'd been given a say—would have chosen, I still think you should be very proud."

"Thank you, lady," I said, with a deferential nod.

She excused herself then, and I went to go find Elka so I could apologize. Because, in spite of what Octavia had said, I *didn't* feel very proud in that moment.

I found Elka near a fountain in the courtyard, gazing up into the star-strewn night, lost in a moment of contemplation. And, as I expected, my dear Varini friend refused to accept the apology.

"I keep telling you. You've been wanting to kill me ever since the moment we met," she said with a languid eyeroll. "Admit it."

"Was that the same moment that you've been wanting to kill *me* ever since?" I asked.

"Probably the moment right after." She shrugged. "I do think I started it."

"You really did."

We grinned and punched each other's shoulders, but then Elka grew serious for a moment. "I was just thinking," she said, a faint frown creasing her brow. "It changes you, doesn't it?"

"What do you mean?"

"The blood on your hands. On *our* hands. The fact that we've ended lives. In and out of the arena, justified or . . . not. I suppose. The fact that this"—she waved at the space in the room where we'd just fought—"becomes so ingrained that it's no longer second nature. It's *first*. We fought for the right to fight. And now what?"

"Are you saying you want to leave the ludus?" I asked her, feeling a small, cold knot tighten in my stomach.

I needn't have worried. Elka cocked an eyebrow at me.

"And leave you to fend for yourself?" she said with a snort. "I wouldn't be able to live with the guilt."

A wave of actual relief washed over me. We sat, perching together on the edge of the marble fountain and cheerfully insulting each other for a few more moments until a man dressed in a purple-striped senatorial toga made his way toward us, listing like a ship in rough seas, with a cup of wine in one hand and a silver pitcher, sloshing liquid onto his sandals, in the other. The wine had flushed his cheeks and forehead crimson, and his watery brown eyes had a glassy sheen. His bleary gaze drifted from me to Elka and back to me again, and he leaned forward, reeking of wine and sour spices.

"Are there any more like you back home?" he said, an avaricious leer twisting his features, enunciating his words as if he thought we might be so barbarous as to barely be able to understand Latin. "Perhaps Caesar should mount another expedition to your wild island home and bring us back a whole bevy of beauties the likes of you . . ."

I did my best to ignore him, staring instead into the middle distance of the courtyard over the senator's shoulder, and let Elka answer for me.

"You wouldn't want that," she said airily. "Where *she* comes from, the men are prettier than the women and have longer hair. You might find yourself courting a strapping Cantii lad by accident."

I stifled a grin as the man's leer collapsed into a befuddled expression and he shrugged his drooping toga back up his shoulder. Then he turned and, with ponderous dignity, wandered back inside the domus to look for easier pickings elsewhere. I watched him go, shaking my head. Of course, Elka had a point. The men of Prydain were notably peacocks—dressing themselves in fine, flamboyant clothes, embellished with gold and silver adornments. I remembered too, with a fond, faded sadness, Maelgwyn Ironhand, the boy I'd once loved, with his beautiful face and long black hair and deep eyes . . .

But then I remembered something else. I remembered Yoreth the gladiator's words from the day before, at the Ludus Flaminius: "*You may not remember where you come from, princess,*" he said. "*But your new friends do. The Romans have not forgotten Prydain. One day they will return there. One day soon.*"

I shivered at the thought. But suddenly, my shiver turned to a shudder of outright horror. In the shadows beneath a cluster of manicured olive trees, I caught sight of a familiar profile in the midst of a small crowd of party guests—the dark eyes and severe, hawkish nose of Pontius Aquila. I must have gasped audibly, because suddenly Elka was shaking me by the shoulder, turning me to face her.

"What's the matter with you?" she demanded. "You look like you've seen a ghost. Is it your wound—"

"A-Aquila . . . he—" I stammered "H-he's here!"

"What? Where?" Her head swiveled around, eyes scanning every face. When she turned back to me, her frown had deepened. "I don't see him anywhere."

"There!" I pushed past her, pointing to where I'd seen that hated, unmistakable visage. "He's right . . ." But he wasn't. There was no one now beneath those trees. Just a statue of the goddess Juno, smiling blandly, a stone pomegranate held in one hand. "I saw him!" I said. "I . . ."

Elka shook her head. "You're jumping at shadows."

"I'm—"

"Still not over what happened with that maniac." She offered me a small, sympathetic smile. "Not really."

Sympathy from Elka, I thought. *I must be in dire shape.* But I still craned my head, looking at every single group of revelers standing or sitting anywhere in view.

"Not that I would ever blame you," Elka continued. "I don't think any of the girls from the ludus are over it, but you have more cause than the rest of us."

"I'm fine."

"Well, no. You're not, but . . ."

I glared at her, but she just shrugged.

"My room at the townhouse is right next to yours, remember?" she said. "I heard your nightmare through the wall, little fox."

"I . . ." I shook my head, muttering, "It was just a dream."

"Here's hoping." She reached out a hand to pat my shoulder.

"I don't believe in dreams, Elka." I rolled my eyes at her. "I'm not Kassandra."

"Who's a Kassandra, now?" Marc Antony asked, navigating his way carefully between a pair of stone urns overflowing with fragrant blooms, three goblets balanced between his long fingers. He offered us two and lifted the third in a toast. "To your continued robust health," he said. "Wonderful performance, ladies."

"Thank you, Lord Antony," I said, taking a sip.

"You're most welcome." He grinned his customary grin. "So . . . who's a Kassandra, then? Did someone bet a fortune on your bout coming up a draw? I, for one, wagered on *you*, my dear." He winked at Elka.

"*A* Kassandra?" I blinked at him, confused. "Forgive me, I'm not certain I understand you."

"No, no," he said with a wave and a long sip of his wine. "You must forgive *me*—I forget that you're not exactly from around these parts and the stories of your people are not the stories of mine. You see, in the old tales 'Kassandra' was the name of a seeress." He looked back and forth from me to Elka, who was gazing at him blankly. "You know—a soothsayer. Only she was cursed by the gods so that no one ever believed her. She could see the future but remained powerless to change it. Poor old thing." He smirked, clearly far more amused by the mythical Kassandra's plight than sympathetic.

Elka shook her head in bemusement. "And I thought the gods of *my* folk had a twisted sense of humor," she said.

Antony laughed and saluted her, drifting back toward the torchlit terrace when a friend hailed him.

"Come on," Elka sighed. "I'm going to get more food. Maybe no one else will dare talk to us if I've got a cheese knife in my hand . . ."

She gestured for me to follow her and I nodded, but my steps faltered and I lagged behind, lingering in the garden. I couldn't stop thinking about Kass—the one I knew, not the one from Antony's legend.

"*My mother named me well,*" she'd said.

The night now felt to me as if it had developed a deep chill, and my gaze kept searching the shadowed corners of the courtyard. Not a soul in sight who even remotely resembled Aquila. Maybe Elka was right. Maybe I was letting my imagination run away with me.

Or maybe, a voice whispered in my mind, *you should tell Marc Antony of Kassandra's warning words to Caesar.*

But just then I heard Elka calling to me—a bit frantically. I hurried to join her, just in case she really was about to stab another guest. The evening wore on, and I never did get the chance to speak to Antony again. I would come to regret that missed opportunity.

Sooner than I would have ever imagined possible.

VIII

"*WHERE* ARE YOU going?" Elka asked for the third time that morning, as we were packing up to return home to the Ludus Achillea with Quintus as our escort.

"To find Caesar," I answered—for the third time that morning—as I shook the folds from my light traveling cloak and laid it out beside her on the couch where she sat.

She shook her head, nimble fingers weaving her pale blonde hair back into the long, tight braids she was used to wearing. "Kronos will have your hide if he finds out you went wandering about the city on your own," she said. "*You're* still a slave, you know. *And* a woman."

"I'm well aware of both those things."

"Right." She stood, still braiding. "I'm coming with you."

"No." I put a hand on her shoulder. "You don't need to get in trouble too. Not that I'm going to either. Look. Just . . . stay here and wait for Quint. I won't be long, and

we'll be on the road back to the ludus before Kronos con-
cludes his business in the city. He won't even know I went
out."

She gave me a disapproving look.

"The senate meets today, and I won't have another
chance to speak to him," I reasoned. "It's a perfect opportunity, don't you think?"

"No." Elka rolled a sardonic eye at me. "What I think
is that a senate meeting isn't exactly like the tribal coun-
cils around the chieftain's fire back home. I don't think
you can just raise your drinking horn above your head
and be allowed to speak your piece to the thane. I don't
even think these Romans sit around a fire for their meet-
ings. Or drink at them." She flipped the finished braid
over her shoulder. "It's uncivilized."

"But it's also my only option." I sat down on a little
folding stool and tugged my boots on, wrapping the laces
around my calves. "The Ludus Flaminius is a nightmare.
And I only need a moment of Caesar's time. I'll offer to
buy Cai's contract, if I have to."

"Because that worked out so well when he offered to
do the same for you."

"Yes, I know." I huffed a frustrated sigh and stood.
"I overreacted. But now that I know what he was really
trying to do at the time, don't you think I—"

"Just go." Elka held up her hands, realizing it was
utterly fruitless to try to convince me not to go. "Hurry
there and hurry back. I'll stall Quintus when he gets
here."

"You're a true friend." I hugged her, and she plucked my cloak up off the couch she'd been sitting on, holding it out to me.

"I'm an idiot," she said. "And so are you. Just . . . *hurry*. The sooner we get out of Rome, the better."

"What? Why do you say that?" I asked.

And yet, even as the words left my mouth, I suddenly wondered why I wasn't feeling the same way she was. Why had the streets and buildings and temples of Rome ceased to feel so strange and unwelcoming to me as they had before? Was it just that I was getting used to the place? Where was my yearning for green, whispering shadows beneath trees?

What am I becoming?

Elka jolted me out of my sudden bout of internal turmoil with her customary pragmatism.

"The gutters," she said as if it were completely obvious. "It's spring, and they smell even worse after the heavy rains. The sooner we leave, the less stench up my delicate nostrils." She waved a hand daintily in front of her face.

I laughed. "I suppose something about you had to be delicate."

I took my cloak from her and swung it over my head, settling it on my shoulders and fastening the round brooch pin at my throat. Sorcha's directives notwithstanding, I was dressed that day for travel, in my suede leggings and tunic. When I caught a glimpse of myself in the bronze wall mirror, I felt instantly better. *Not so Roman after all,*

I thought. Sorcha could wear the palla for us both. And I doubted Caesar would mind at all.

Once I left the townhouse, I began to breathe a little freer and discovered I was finding it easier each time I was in the city to find my way around. *Even without a spectral Gaulish chieftain to guide me through the streets*, I thought, wincing a bit at the memory of that wild, delirious ride as I passed the narrow laneway that led to the house where Arviragus had been imprisoned. I wondered if Caesar had been told of his old enemy's "death" yet—from excess drink, of course. I hoped that Junius, the gruff old soldier assigned as Arviragus's guard, had been convincing in his lie. It couldn't have been that hard. Anyone who'd seen the Gaulish chieftain in recent years likely would have believed such a story without question.

The truth was something else entirely. The last I'd heard of him, Arviragus was relishing his freedom on the island of Corsica. Kallista's fellow Amazons had accepted him into their tribe, rescinding their threat to kill him if any of the girls who'd joined us to retake the ludus failed to return home. In fact, some of them had returned to Corsica. I understood why.

Rome—as Elka had so recently reminded me—wasn't for everyone.

The sky over the city that day was overcast and promising more rain, with banks of tumbled, dark gray clouds lowering on the distant hills in the east. I hitched my cloak up and tugged the cowl forward around my face, just another body swimming in the flow of people trundling up and down the city streets like salmon in a stream, all of us just struggling to get to where we were going. But after the previous night's affair—where I'd been stared at openly by Antony and Octavia's rich friends like I was some sort of exotic sea creature delicacy—I found myself reveling in the anonymity of the crowd.

I walked north along the twisting streets, dodging ox carts and slave-borne curtained litters, until I reached the Campus Martius. The Theatrum Pompeii—the same venue where Cai had so recently won his first gladiatorial victory—had an attached structure called a *curia* that was used sometimes as a meeting place for the senate. I'd learned from Kronos that it was where Caesar and the other senators would gather to discuss the affairs of the Republic that day. It wasn't yet midday when I arrived, and I didn't want to seem as if I were loitering— unwanted attention from the city's patrolling *vigiles* was the last thing I needed—so, instead, I strolled over to the theater itself.

There weren't supposed to be any games scheduled for that day, and so I couldn't quite understand why I could see through the colonnade to where a group of gladiators was standing about inside the theater vomitorium, but I craned my neck to see if Cai was one of them. He wasn't. I didn't recognize any of the men, to be truthful, but I certainly noticed how very many weapons they carried and how tense they seemed. They weren't equipped for arena fighting, though. They wore no heavy armor or padding, and there wasn't a single net or trident or spear among them. Just knives and swords. Close-quarters weaponry. Not one of them even bore a shield, so there was no identifying them by ludus markings.

But ludus *colors* . . . that was another thing.

I realized then that, beneath a variety of light armor and molded leather, all of the men were dressed in identical black tunics. The gladiator uniform of Pontius Aquila's Ludus Saturnus. Those men were sworn to the Sons of Dis. My stomach clenched in a tight knot, and the day went even colder all around me. I already knew that after his disgrace, Aquila had been desperate for money. For the last several months, I'd kept one ear half-cocked listening for any news of him, and so I knew that he'd been forced to sell half of his stake in his Ludus Saturnus. I struggled now to remember just who it was that he'd sold it to, and a name floated to the surface of my memory—a young senator named Marcus Junius Brutus. I'd seen him sitting in the elite seats at the Circus Maximus on a few occasions but had never met him in person and knew little of the man beyond his status as a politician. I suppose that the fact that I'd never heard anything ill spoken about him was notable as far as politicians went.

The gladiators likely belonged to him, I thought. Not Aquila. And the Theatrum Pompeii was a place where gladiatorial games were presented. So there was no reason to wonder at the presence of his gladiators. And no reason to worry. They were probably just using the facility for practice.

I was, as Elka said, jumping at shadows. I shook my head, angry with myself for letting Pontius Aquila occupy so much space in the vault of my skull—*still*—and turned my back on the gathering of men. I went, instead, over to the nearby market stalls to browse the food and wares and distract myself until the senate members began to gather.

The markets of Rome were one of the things that reminded me of home. Some of the food smells and many of the colors and textures of the fabrics on display were unfamiliar, but the cheerful noise and the bustling chaos—men and women haggling, and children running wild between the stalls—were exactly the same. I lingered over bolts of bright linen and strings of amber and glass beads. I settled on a honeycake. Then the senators began to arrive, drifting through the streets in pairs and groups, all serious faces and superior airs, ignoring—and, it seemed, mostly ignored by—the plebs. That was something I was learning. The common folk of Rome seemed to think the senate was mostly something to be tolerated rather than lauded. Had my kingly father gone about comporting himself the way these men did, I thought, his head would have been off and nailed to a doorpost in short order. Instead, Virico had treated chieftains and freemen alike with courtesy and familiarity and had remained king because of it. But in Rome, power and status ruled. Harshly.

By the time I'd finished my honeycake, the assembly had grown. I'd never seen so many purple-striped togas gathered together in one place. The portico of the

Theatrum Pompeii was swarming with senators, clustered and milling about like a flock of agitated geese as
Caesar appeared and climbed the stone steps. I watched
as they waved scrolls and tablets at him to try to get his
attention, treading on the hems of each other's garments
and tripping all over themselves.

I had never understood the Roman mode of dress,
and that scene did nothing to change my mind as to its
practicality. How in the world was a man—even a soldier and an athlete like Caesar—supposed to be able to
move wrapped up in all that wool with swathes of the
stuff draped over one arm? The chiefs of Prydain would
never dress so foolishly as to limit their mobility to such
an extent *and* take away the usefulness of a limb. They
would never leave themselves so vulnerable to attack.

Caesar would have done well to learn from his foreign
adversaries. Because the other thing about the toga was
this: All those folds of cloth made ideal hiding places for
knives.

As I shouldered my way through the packed market
crowd, I kept my gaze focused on where Caesar stood
beneath the shadows of the portico, a head taller than
most of his fellows. As I drew nearer to the theater, I could
hear the faint, muted clamor of arguing voices. A senatorial squabble that suddenly spiked sharply when one voice
rose heatedly above all the others. I saw Caesar turn to
address the man behind him, and there was anger written
plainly on his face. But his expression shifted suddenly to
shock.

Caesar took a stumbling step forward, his body rigid, spine arching like a drawn bow. Something was terribly wrong. Half the senatorial crowd shrank back. The other half surged forward. Caesar staggered out from the shadows, into a beam of sunlight. And when he opened his mouth, gouts of blood spewed from his lips, staining the front of his snow-white robes.

I felt my whole body tense as if I was in the arena or on the battlefield. There was a moment of stillness as Caesar reached out, grasping handfuls of air . . . and then a group of men charged him like a pack of jackals on a wounded lion. There were dozens of assailants. Dagger blades flashed and descended, blood flew, spattering the gleaming marble columns of the theater portico. With a furious roar, Caesar threw off his attackers and lurched forward, his toga stained crimson. For a moment, I thought he was free of them, but his sandals slipped in his own blood, flowing in a stream down the stone steps, and he crashed heavily to one knee.

I don't know if I cried out loud then or if the sound of my denial thundered only inside my own skull. The din in the marketplace was such that no one—not a slave or a citizen—had even noticed the violence in their midst. No one but me . . . And then I saw Caesar lift his head, and for an instant it seemed as if his pain-clouded gaze found me where I still stood, half-hidden behind a textile stall, gaping in horror. I glanced around wildly, wondering where Caesar's bodyguards were. But, of course, why would Caesar need his praetorians that day, surrounded as he was by his great good friends, the senators of the Republic?

One of those friends—a broad-shouldered man with close-cropped black hair who I recognized as Marcus Junius Brutus—stepped up behind Caesar, and I saw one last knife blade descend. Caesar threw his hands in the air, his fingers spread wide like the talons of one of his eagles . . . and then he fell forward.

The murder itself was over in mere moments.

The consequences would ripple down through the days and years to come.

What followed next was simply sheer, unbridled terror.

A matron carrying a basket of olives suddenly seemed to notice the blood, and the body of the man it poured from. She screamed, her skirling shriek piercing clean through the general, muddling chaos of the streets, and suddenly there seemed to be some sort of collective realization of what had actually just happened. As her wail died on the fitful breeze, everyone turned to stare first at the woman where she stood, one hand to her mouth, the other pointing, stiff-armed . . . and then at Gaius Julius Caesar, tangled in his bloody, purple-striped senator's robes, as his body slowly rolled down the steps. It came to a stop at the bottom, one arm flung out, as if in supplication, toward the crowd.

Men started shouting, women began to wail, the sounds of grief mingled with outrage, and a thick, cloying fog of fear descended. If Caesar's assassins had been expecting a triumphant rejoicing in the wake of their heinous act, they had seriously misjudged the citizens of the Republic. Instead, the very air all around me suddenly felt like it did in the moments before a terrible storm—dangerous, deadly even . . . something that wordlessly warned "seek shelter."

People started running, hiding, and tripping over themselves, knocking over baskets and displays in the market. Food sellers and wine merchants ducked and scrambled to gather up their wares before the chaos turned into outright rioting in the streets. They needn't have worried. The city itself would soon be silent and empty, windows shuttered like the eyes of a corpse, doors barred against the coming storm.

The crowd of senators—those who were Optimates and those who were Populares alike—began to melt away as they scurried like rats in all directions. I saw Brutus pelting toward the vomitorium entrance to the theatrum, where he and three or four of his fellow conspirators were swiftly surrounded and swallowed up by the crowd of black-clad gladiators I'd seen earlier.

That explains it, I thought, stunned.

Those gladiators had been there, waiting, in case the assassination—and *that* was exactly what it was, an assassination—went badly. It hadn't been a sudden, unexpected brawl nor a heated disagreement gone wrong. No. The thing I had just witnessed was the end result of a calculated plan to murder Caesar. To remove—permanently—the man who'd only just been decreed

Rome's dictator for life, and the planning for it went deep. It had to have. As deep as the catacombs beneath Pontius Aquila's Domus Corvinus.

And where, exactly, I wondered, was Aquila?

And what was I to do now?

I watched helplessly as the Saturnus gladiators hurried Brutus and a few of the others away before most of the citizenry had even really figured out what had happened. On the other side of the square, a burst of shouting wrenched my attention from the macabre scene, and I looked to see a group of men grappling with each other. Some I recognized as Caesar's praetorian guard, who—if their uniformly stricken expressions were anything to go by—had most likely been lured away from their master by trickery. I'd heard once that the praetorian guards, on the day they were sworn into service, took a vow not to outlive their lord. If that was true, there might be more dead bodies in the streets before sunset.

In the midst of the guard, I recognized Marc Antony, surrounded by a cluster of his friends, some of whom I recalled seeing at Octavia's party. Was it only the night before? Suddenly it seemed to me as if years had passed since I woke up that morning. Antony had the look of a man who hadn't yet been to bed, and his mouth was a gaping hole, howling denial and Caesar's name. Everything had happened so fast, and there was still a small cluster of assassins remaining, gathered in the portico shadows— shoulders heaving, knives weeping blood—and Antony's face went rigid with fury at the sight of them. If he'd been able to reach them in that moment, I think he would have torn those men apart with his bare hands. But between them and Antony was the madness of the crowd.

Havoc crashed over them like a rogue wave as the crowd bolted in their direction, and Antony's friends clustered around him, clutching him frantically by the shoulders and arms, to drag him forcibly away. It seemed almost as if he wasn't even aware they did so. As he went, his gaze was fixed on the lifeless body of Caesar as if it had been hammered there with nails.

In only moments, the crowded marketplace was almost entirely deserted, everyone else fled and gone. But my feet were rooted as an oak tree to the ground. All I could do was stand there, shuddering, the breath strangling in my throat, staring at the body of the man who had—whether I'd wanted him to or not—been an integral part of my life since I was a child.

Even from that distance, I thought I could see the pale gleam of one of Caesar's ribs showing through a gaping wound. There was so much blood. I didn't think I'd ever seen so much blood outside of a body before. It painted the theater steps and the cobblestones below . . . just like the spilled wine that had sent Kassandra into a frenzy of augury on the day of the temple dedication.

"*Mars comes for you*," she had warned Caesar.

And then it struck me: According to the Roman calendar, it was the middle of March, the month named after that bloodthirsty deity. Mars, the god of war. And all of

Caesar's civil wars, all of the strife within the Republic, had gathered like a thunderhead that very day and rained down steel and fury upon his head.

And betrayal.

Treachery.

Kassandra had been right all along.

There was a part of me that whispered I should be dancing and giving thanks to the Morrigan for his death. To see the tyrant conqueror toppled from his pedestal and shattered to pieces should have filled me with a savage joy. It didn't. It took me a moment to realize there were tears on my cheeks.

I *wept* for Caesar.

Suddenly angry—with myself for mourning or with him for having the audacity to die like that, I didn't honestly know—I wiped the tears from my face and looked around the now-deserted square, waiting to see who would come to take the body away. But no one did. No one came near. And so, with the streets so completely emptied of all life, I was the only one there to witness Pontius Aquila as he stepped out from behind a pillar on the portico above the bloodstained steps.

I froze, my heart hammering in my throat.

Aquila glanced left and right and, not seeing anyone there to watch him, hurried down to where Caesar's body lay lifeless in a slowly spreading pool of crimson. I watched him hesitate a moment. Then he drew a long-bladed dagger from the folds of his toga. A large garnet shone in the pommel of the hilt, red as blood, but the blade itself was unsullied with murder and gleamed in the sunlight. It did not remain stainless long. I couldn't bring myself to move as Aquila knelt beside Caesar's still-warm corpse and dipped the blade in his blood.

A memento for the Collector? I wondered. A sort of sick keepsake?

Or maybe it was something even more sinister. Perhaps it was some kind of dark offering to his god of death . . .

I was suddenly very glad of the market stall screen, hung with colorful woven shawls, that hid me from his eyes—and for the heavy stillness of the air that kept them from blowing aside in a breeze. I held my own breath as he stood and, casting one long, laden glance back at the body of the man he'd so despised, hurried away south, toward where the River Tiber curved in a wide bend before heading west to the Mare Nostrum.

As he disappeared from view, I heard the sound of running feet, and it was as if the spell that had held me there was suddenly broken. I turned and, searching desperately for a place to hide, sprinted blindly toward the open gates of the now-empty vomitorium of the theatrum. The shadows of the stone tunnel engulfed me in chill darkness for a moment, and then I burst out into the arena . . . and found myself surrounded by a half dozen gladiator practice dummies arranged in a semicircle and crudely decorated with the chalk paint used for the announcement boards in the arena. The Saturnus gladiators must have gotten restless waiting for their masters to commit murder, I thought, and so they amused themselves with a bit of play-fighting. The dummies were all thoroughly hacked to bits. They were also made up to look like females. And I knew, by the double wooden blades bound to its arms, which one was supposed to be *me*.

A cold rush of fear went up my spine.

"Sweet Morrigan . . ." I murmured as I stood, rooted to the sands.

A second dummy had one eye painted solid black with a red line running vertically through it, like a scar.

Sorcha . . .

But the one figure that had been subjected to the most brutal attacks—the one that still had weapons buried in it, bristling from head and torso—had been made to look as though it had eyes painted in dark rings of Aegyptian-style kohl.

"Cleopatra," I murmured, backing away.

Then I spun on my heel and ran back toward the tunnel, head down . . . and slammed into the armored breastplate of a legion soldier. My heart almost leaped out of my chest in fear, and I uttered a strangled cry.

"Fallon!"

The legionnaire reached out and grabbed me by the shoulders, and it took me far too long to realize that it was Quintus. Elka was about four steps behind him, hurrying down the tunnel to catch up, her pale complexion flushed from exertion.

"Thank the gods!" she exclaimed. "We were coming to find you and—"

"He's dead!" I blurted. "Elka, Quint . . . Caesar is—"

"I know." Quint's face beneath the brim of the helmet he wore was grim and gray. His usually bright eyes had gone flinty. "The whole city knows by now."

"Where are the vigiles?" I asked. "The constables? Why aren't they abroad in the streets to keep order?"

"For whom?" Quint asked. "Caesar's dead. Caesar's friends are in hiding. And Caesar's enemies had *better* be." He glanced up at the sky, to where the sun had hidden his face behind a thick pall of overcast. "I give it three hours—maybe less—before Rome starts to tear herself in two . . ."

He trailed off as Elka brushed past him into the arena, her steps faltering as her gaze took in the sight of the defaced dummies. She walked up to one on the end that bore long, straw-pale ropes draped over its head like braids. I hadn't even noticed that one, but it was clear who it was meant to represent. When Elka looked back at me, I saw that her face had gone white.

"Sons of Dis," I said. "I saw them earlier."

She looked back at the figures—her gaze fixing bleakly on the mangled one with the kohl-heavy eyes—and I saw her come to the same conclusion that I had: It was common knowledge that Cleopatra held court on the shores of Lake Sabatinus, consorting with the gladiatrices of the Ludus Achillea. Pontius Aquila could kill two hated birds with one stone . . . more than two. A whole flock.

"We have to get back to the ludus," she said. "We have to warn them. The lanista and the queen—"

"We won't be going anywhere," Quint interrupted her, "unless we make it to the Porta Flaminia on the north wall before they close the gates of the city and we're trapped inside with all of this madness. Let's go."

He reached out and took Elka by the wrist, and together we ran through the tunnel and back out into the street. But Quint's mention of the gate had knocked some of the sense back into my head.

"Wait!" I stopped and glanced over my shoulder. Toward the walls of the Ludus Flaminius where they rose up, high and topped with jagged stone, just beyond the theatrum.

"Fallon—"

"I'm not leaving the city without Cai."

As fearful as I was for Cleopatra and my sister—*all* my sisters at the ludus—there was no earthly way I would forsake Cai in the midst of the gathering storm. Had I said anyone else's name, I suspect Quint might have just thrown me into the back of a cart and spirited me out of the city regardless of my protests. As it was, he exchanged a glance with Elka, who gave him one of her stoic Varini shrugs. She knew I wouldn't leave. And, really, I think she already knew he wouldn't either. It was Cai—his friend too—and Quint wasn't the type to ever abandon his friend. If I knew anything about him after what we'd all been through together, it was that.

He put up his hands. "All right," he said, pulling off his helmet and raking fingers over his military-short hair.

"All right. But we have to do this fast. There's no telling what will happen in the next few hours."

"Is it really going to be that bad in the city?" Elka asked, frowning. "Leaders die every day."

"Caesar wasn't just a leader to most of these people." Quint shook his head, his expression mystified, as if he couldn't quite believe that the man he spoke of was actually gone. "He was a *god*. For good or ill. And he was the only thing—the only man—capable of keeping that pack of vultures who call themselves senators from shredding not just the city but the whole of the Republic to pieces like a felled deer carcass."

"What do you honestly think is going to happen, Quintus?" I asked quietly.

The look in his eyes as he turned to me made my blood run cold.

"Honestly, Fallon?" he said, putting his helmet back on and tightening the chinstrap. "I don't know. But I can tell you this: Whatever it is, I'd much rather watch from a good long distance. Atop a good high hill . . . surrounded by a good stout fence."

IX

WHEN WE REACHED the Ludus Flaminius, the lanista himself was at the gate along with three of his men, hastening to haul the heavy doors shut. Quint shouted for them to stop.

"Away with you!" the lanista shouted back. "Seek shelter elsewhere. This is no place to—"

"I know exactly what this place is." Quint stalked up to him and gestured back at me, saying, "and I suggest you let this lady in through your gates. We've business with one of your gladiators. You'd best let us conduct it in peace, and then we'll be on our way."

The lanista's gaze narrowed, his eyes darting back and forth between me and Quint. I pushed the hood of my cloak back off my face. I saw a spark of recognition flare and knew the ludus master remembered me. Of course he did. I was Victrix, and I was Caesar's. At least, I *had* been . . .

"Why should I do any such thing?" the lanista asked Quint mulishly.

"Because if you don't," I answered, stepping forward and mustering a shrug that I hoped was half as glacial as one of Elka's, "then we might be inclined to spread word that Caesar's assassins are holed up right here in your ludus. Let's see how well you handle a bloodthirsty mob when they're pounding on your gates instead of sitting in the arena stands."

The lanista's angular features went ash pale, and in only moments, the gates of the ludus were groaning back open just enough to let the three of us squeeze through. Once inside, I stepped up to him and held out my hand.

"Give me the key that will open Caius Varro's cell," I said.

"I can't do that!"

"Why not?"

"Because that man is the property of—"

"Of Caesar?" I tilted my head and waited for him to work that one through.

"I . . . uh."

"The key."

When he hesitated still, I grabbed a fistful of his tunic, ignoring his men, who seemed utterly at a loss as to what to do. Without another word, the lanista reached into the scrip hanging from his belt and withdrew a ring of keys, handing them to me by the one that would open the doors in Cai's barracks block. I nodded and, together with Quint and Elka, started off in that direction. Before we reached the stone archway that led down into those dreadful catacombs, I turned and called to the lanista.

"None of these men belong to anyone anymore," I said. "Not even you, lanista. If I were you, I'd consider a career change. And soon. You won't have much time before the carrion crows come circling to pick over Caesar's leavings."

As I said those words, I could feel them echoing in my own bones. What was true for the gladiators of the Ludus Flaminius was just as true for me. I had been the only gladiatrix left that Caesar had still owned. Now Caesar was dead. I was truly free. And the weight of my freedom hung from my shoulders like a cloak of lead feathers.

Three steps inside the mouth of the tunnel that led down to the slave quarters and it may as well have been middle night. The darkness and dank air pressed against my skin, and the torches set in iron sconces on the wall gave off more smoke and pitch stink than actual light.

"Jupiter's beard," Quint swore as we descended. "If I'd known it was this bad in this place, I would have petitioned Caesar myself to let Cai out. What a rat hole."

"I think it's cozy," Elka muttered, her lip curling as an actual rat scurried out of the darkness and disappeared into more darkness.

It didn't take me long to locate the corridor where Cai's cell was, and I was almost running by the time I found it, the sound of my boot soles slapping on the damp stone floors echoing off the seeping walls.

"Here!" I called to Quint and Elka. "He's down this way—"

"Fallon?" I heard Cai's voice call out and saw a hand reaching between the bars of one of the cell doors.

"Cai!" I sprinted the rest of the way. When I reached him, I clutched at his fingers before letting go to fumble with the lanista's key ring.

"What in Hades are you doing here?" he asked me, his eyes wide. Obviously the news of Caesar's demise hadn't yet filtered down into the lower depths of the ludus. In the uncertain light from the torches, the deep shadows carved on his face beneath cheek and brow gave him a haunted look. "Fallon—what's happened?"

For a moment, I could only stare at him, unable to utter the stark, horrible truth. Finally, I managed to stammer, "C-Caesar . . ."

Cai drew back from the bars of his cell, dread in his eyes, as if he knew what I was about to say. He shook his head, echoing back the name. "Caesar."

"He'd dead, Cai," I said. "Murdered."

"Who was it?" he asked, his voice like cold iron.

"Who *wasn't* it?" Quint answered for me as he and Elka caught up.

"Senators," I said, suddenly remembering the keys I held in my hand and grasping for the one that would open the door to Cai's cell. "Dozens of them—all with daggers—a conspiracy . . . they cut him to pieces on the steps of the theater, in plain sight and bright daylight."

Cai looked back and forth from me to Quint and then, after a long moment, turned his back on us and walked toward the deeper darkness at the back of his cell, fists clenched like stones.

His father, I thought. *He's thinking of his father and the hatred he bore for Caesar.* It was a hatred the elder Varro and men like him—men like Pontius Aquila—had sown and nurtured and carefully cultivated among their peers for years.

"So they finally worked up the guts to do it," Cai spat, disgust in his voice.

It didn't even matter to him that Caesar was the reason he was in that dismal, lightless hole, fighting daily for his life. Even after his time at the Ludus Flaminius, Cai bore his commander no ill will. And now he never would. Caesar was dead.

"There was no courage in what they did," I said.

Cai shook his head. "I didn't say courage."

"You're right about that," Quint agreed. "Both of you. More like they finally managed to cobble together a plan. And not a very good one either. They had luck or the love of their black god Dis on their side, that was all. As I understand it, Antony would have been there in another minute with Caesar's praetorian guard and they could have stopped the whole bloody clot of them. Brutus, Cassius, Casca . . . bastards all."

"And who else?" Cai's eyes narrowed.

"Too many to name," I said as I found the right key, finally, and jammed it into the heavy iron lock. "But . . . I saw

Aquila. He was there, with a knife. Only he . . . he wasn't one of the killers—he was there, but hiding. Hanging back until all the others had fled. And then . . . he . . . he knelt beside the body and dipped his dagger blade in the pool of Caesar's blood."

I felt my stomach roil, and I couldn't go on. The image of Aquila hovering ghoulishly over the body—like a carrion crow on a spent battlefield—was just too fresh and horrid.

"Filthy coward," Cai said, as I swung the cell door open and he ducked his head, stepping over the threshold. "It must have been like watching a dream come to life for him. He's hated Caesar since the day they first met, and he's been prodding men like Cassius and Casca—all those who held a grudge against Caesar, real or imagined—toward this for years." He shook his head and looked at Quint. "But Brutus . . ."

"Yeah. No small surprise there," Quint said.

Suddenly Caesar's words to me—about Sorcha and the perils of blind loyalty—came roaring back like a cruel jest. I remembered how he'd said it had been a mistake for her to trust Thalestris, her primus pilus at the academy and most loyal friend. Or so she'd thought, right up until Thalestris's complete betrayal.

"*Trust,*" Caesar had opined to me on the matter. "*A noble, useless, frequently terminal affliction of your people, my dear. Achillea* trusted *Thalestris. She allowed her greatest enemy to get close enough to stab her in the back, Fallon. That's what blind trust does.*"

And yet, for all *his* wisdom, Caesar had fallen victim to that same affliction. In the most literal fashion possible. The irony was almost too much to bear—along with the grief. But that would have to wait. I told Cai about what I'd seen in the theatrum and the implicit threat it posed from the Sons of Dis to the queen. To our friends . . .

"I have to get home," I said, trying to quell the surge of panic that crawled up from the pit of my stomach again at the thought. "Back to the ludus. I—"

"I know." Cai gripped my shoulder. "And I'm coming with you."

"Of course you are," Elka said, glancing from Cai to Quint. "You both are. Now can we please get out of this place? That rat followed us down here, and now he's staring at me."

We started back the way we came. It hadn't occurred to me—to any of us—to keep our voices down, and so all of the other gladiators in earshot had their faces jammed up against the bars of their cell doors as we passed, expressions ranging from elation to fear to mild curiosity. For them, a regime change might spell either catastrophe or just business as usual. I kept my gaze focused in front of me. They weren't my concern. I had my own folk to worry about.

"Hey!" one of them hailed me as I approached. "Girl!" He thrust an arm out between the bars of his locked cell door, his grasping hand spread wide and reaching, fingers like claws. *"Princess!"*

That made me stop in my tracks. I turned and peered into the darkness and saw that it was the man I'd spoken

to the first time I'd visited Cai in this awful place. Yoreth.
A member of my very own tribe—a warrior in my father
Virico's royal Cantii war band.

"It's me," he said. "Remember?"

"Yoreth . . ."

"Yoreth, yes." He nodded vigorously. "The key, yeah?"
He reached for me again. "Give me the key . . ."

I blinked, my eyes focusing on his arm. On the ser-
pent tattoo that spiraled up from his wrist all the way past
his elbow, knotting and coiling in twisted, familiar patterns. I'd seen those marks before. Whatever—*who*ever—
else he was, Yoreth was also the retiarius fighter from the
Theatrum Pompeii. He'd worn a helmet that day with a
full face visor but, looking at him now, I recognized his tattoos. Yoreth was the one who'd led the other gladiators in
the fight against Cai.

The one who'd almost killed him.

So he was treacherous—and that, in itself, was enough
to make me extremely disinclined to help him—but Yoreth
had done more than just dishonor a fellow gladiator. Yoreth
was a liar. And it was his tattoo that told me both of those
tales. I looked up from his arm into his eyes then, with the
bars of the cell door between us.

"Princess . . ." he said again.

I moved to stand in front of his door, the ring of iron
keys hanging loosely from my fingertips. He looked at me
and flashed what I'm sure he thought was a persuasive
smile. In the cell next to him, I saw Acheron, the gladiator

who had—unlike Yoreth—fought at Cai's side. He stood there, leaning against his door with his arms crossed over his chest, relaxed but watchful, and he nodded when I looked at him, but said nothing. I glanced back and forth between the two men for a moment and then plucked up the key from the ring that fit into the cell door locks.

"That's a good lass," Yoreth said, his grin broadening. He pulled his arm back through the bars. "Your father would be proud . . ."

"My father," I said. "Whose royal war band you were a part of."

He nodded vigorously.

He'd said he remembered me. That he remembered the night I disappeared from Durovernum. There had been a feast that night. Chiefs and their warriors from the Four Tribes gathered to celebrate their alliances . . . But there had been men from other tribes as well at that feast. Men of Gaul, men of the west, men of the north . . . even Coritani men, sent there to foster peace between our tribes that never lasted more than a day past the feasting. Yoreth *was* from the Island of the Mighty. There was no doubt in my mind about *that*.

I unlocked Acheron's door and turned away to rejoin my waiting friends.

"Princess!" Yoreth called, a frantic note to his voice.

I paused and looked at him over my shoulder. "Fallon," I said. "My name is Fallon ferch Virico, and you would know that if you knew me. I *don't* know you."

"I swear—"

"My father's war band has numbered half a hundred men and women of our tribe, give or take, ever since I was a child and my sister Sorcha led those warriors into battle against the Romans," I said in a low, dangerous hiss. "I might not have known all their names, but I knew their faces. They were Cantii. My tribe. My family."

I dropped the key ring to the dirt floor, well out of reach of Yoreth's grasp.

"And I know a Coritani tattoo when I see one."

X

BACK OUT IN the main—decidedly deserted—courtyard of the ludus, the day was still overcast. The sky a dull, mournful gray, and the air strangely muffled. We crossed to the small door set in the stone wall beside the larger gates. Quint tugged back the slide-bar lock and opened it just far enough so that he could stick his head out.

"What's going on?" Cai asked.

Quint ducked back inside. "Not a thing," he said. "It's quiet as a necropolis out there. Every window and door shut up tight."

"It won't stay like that for long," Cai said.

"No," Quint agreed. "It won't. I give it until dusk. Then? Rome is going to burn."

"We need to go. Now." I glanced over my shoulder and was a little surprised to see that Acheron was still with us.

"I'd like to join you, Victrix," he said. Then he nodded at Cai. "If you and Varro here don't mind."

"You don't have to—"

He put up a hand to stop me. "I'm in your debt."

"No. You're not." I shook my head. "You stood by Cai in the arena. You don't owe us anything beyond that. And staying with us could . . ."

"Could present certain, uh, difficulties," Cai finished for me. "Dangers."

Acheron grinned. "All the more reason then," he said. "Not like I have anywhere pressing to be, after all. And you'll maybe need another sword, yeah, to help with those difficulties? Speaking of which . . ."

He jogged over to a weapons shed and, after a few moments, jogged back with a pair of serviceable gladii— one of which he handed to Cai. Cai nodded thanks and shoved it through the plain leather belt he wore.

I hadn't thought to equip myself that day, but, as usual, Elka was thinking for us both. She pulled not one but two long daggers from sheaths concealed behind her back, under her cloak, and handed one to me. I gave her a small smile of thanks. Then, together, we stepped out into the deserted street. In the distance, I heard men shouting and the faint wail of women's voices, but it all sounded miles away. Cai and Acheron took point, walking ahead of me and Elka, with Quint bringing up the rear.

"Walk quickly," Cai said. "But don't run. Heads up, eyes everywhere, blades at the ready."

After two uneventful blocks, he waved for us to hang back while he and Acheron went to scout a few streets ahead of us. In the brief lull, Elka turned to me, her gaze flickering with wary curiosity.

"Back in the ludus," she said. "With that gladiator . . ."

When she trailed off, I waited. Then: "What about it?"

She shrugged. "I just don't think I've ever seen you quite so . . ."

"Vindictive?" I asked.

"*Ja*. I guess that's the word." She looked at me sideways, as if trying to fit a new piece of glass into a mosaic. One that didn't really seem to fit. "Do your folk really hate his folk that much?"

"Truthfully?" I shook my head. "Meriel was Coritani."

"She saved your life," Elka said. "All our lives, probably."

"She did. And that's a debt I can never repay," I said, feeling a deep ache in the center of my chest, like it had only just happened. "For her sake if nothing else, I could have forgiven Yoreth his tribe. I could even have forgiven him the lie about belonging to my father's war band— dishonorable as it was."

Elka's frown deepened. "What then?"

I checked around the corner of the building where we stood to see if Cai had reappeared from scouting. The street was empty still. "Do you remember the first gladiator that turned against Cai in the arena yesterday?" I asked.

"Ahh . . ." The uncertainty and confusion cleared from Elka's blue eyes before I even had to clarify further. "One and the same?"

I nodded. "I recognized the tattoo on his arm."

At that, she laughed. "Poor idiot thing!" she said. "All that 'kindred tribal' nonsense to win your sympathies and he never even had a chance!"

She wasn't wrong. Coritani, Catuvellauni, Gaul, or Greek. I honestly couldn't have cared less where and who Yoreth had come from. But he'd put Caius Varro's life at risk. And for *that*?

Yoreth could rot.

In that moment, Cai and Acheron returned from scouting ahead and Quint appeared from behind. They all had the same thing to report. Nothing. We could have walked through the streets of Rome whistling and no one would have called the tune. Because no one was there to hear it. Even the beggars and the prostitutes had gone to ground. There wasn't so much as a cutpurse to be seen. It was eerie. Ominous.

We hurried unchallenged and unchecked in a tight group through the winding streets. We kept to the shadows and the alleys between buildings as much as possible. Because as much as it seemed like it, we *weren't* the only living souls left in an empty city. And sooner or later . . .

Sooner, it was.

I hissed and drew back into the mouth of the alley, waving frantically for Cai and the others to stay behind me.

At a glance, I'd counted nine of them—black tunics and thick-muscled builds honed on the arena sands, all of them bristling with weapons. It was the same bunch of gladiators that had spirited Brutus and his fellow conspirators away from the Theatrum Pompeii in the moments after the assassination.

"Brutus and Aquila's thugs," I whispered. "They're heavily armed and outnumber us. We have to find another way."

"There is no other way." Cai eased his way around the corner just far enough to see our impediment. "That's the road that leads to the Porta Flaminia just beyond the temple of Vulcan—the building with the red pillars—and it's the only one. If we try to make it to another gate out of the city, we'll be at least another hour."

"What do we do now?" Elka asked.

Cai heaved a frustrated breath "We're going to have to—"

"Go," Acheron said, stepping forward. "I'll lead them in the other direction and then double back."

I shook my head. "No. Acheron, you don't—"

"*You* gave me my freedom," he said, holding up a hand to forestall my objections. "You didn't have to turn that key. You could have left me there with the others, but you didn't. And that's not something I'm likely to forget. My dear old mother used to say that one should always take the chance in life to pay back a done deed in kind, Victrix. Let me do this."

"There's too many of them to fight on your own."

"Don't worry," he said, bending down to check that the laces on his sandals were tightly tied. "I've no burning death wish—especially not now I'm free. Trust me. I know these streets well. I'll be careful, but I'll give them a reason to chase me."

Cai and I exchanged a glance, and then he turned and held out his arm. Acheron clasped his wrist. "Meet us just outside the Flaminian Gate," he said. "We'll wait. But we won't wait long."

"You won't have to. Stay here until I draw them off, and then go."

"How in Hades is he going to draw them into a chase?" Quint wondered.

He didn't have to wonder long. Moments after he'd bolted from the alley, we heard Acheron screaming, "Murderers! Assassins! Caesar's blood drips from your blades! Citizens—come quick! I've found them!"

And then we heard distant swearing and a barked shout of response: "Catch that idiot and shut him up! He'll bring the whole city down on us!"

Then the sound of running feet—hobnailed sandals and leather soles slapping on cobbles—fading into the distance, as Acheron led them on a merry chase away from the Porta Flaminia. After a lengthy silence, I peered cautiously around the corner. The Sons of Dis were gone. The gates stood open in the distance. The road beyond would take us away from Rome. And the Morrigan alone knew if I would ever see the inside of these city walls again.

Outside the gates of the Porta Flaminia, there was a line of picketed, saddled horses left unattended at a legion posting station. Normally reserved for army couriers on official business, the fact that they'd been left there for the taking was a clear indicator of the chaos to come. About half the legions were loyal to Caesar, half—maybe more, maybe less—to the Optimate faction he'd been warring against. If the army command chain didn't receive a clear directive from the generals or the senate—and soon—the Republic really did stand in danger of tearing itself apart. But the untended horses were, at the least, a blessing for us. We mounted up and were on the verge of heading north toward the Via Clodia when Acheron came pelting through the gates. Alone. Unfollowed, as far as I could tell.

He was flushed and gasping for breath but actually seemed to be enjoying himself. I wondered how long he'd really been locked up in the Ludus Flaminius. It seemed that, to him, breathing free air—even while being chased by murderous thugs—was a rare and glorious gift from the gods.

It made me glad of my decision to free him from his ludus cell.

"Told you . . . I could lose them . . ." he huffed. "Led them back . . . toward the center of town. And straight into the beginnings of an angry mob . . . They'll be lucky to get free of that lot with arms and legs still attached."

Quint frowned. "A mob?"

Acheron nodded, straightening up. "It's starting. The hornets in the nest are beginning to buzz. Saw a few vigiles poking about too."

"But you're sure you lost them all," I said. "The gladiators."

"Yeah." He wiped his forearm across his brow and took the reins of the horse Cai had kept waiting for him. "They're none too bright. Had 'em running in circles . . ." As he grabbed the saddle pommel to hoist himself up, something shiny fell from his tunic, chiming metallically on the ground.

I stared at the thing in horror as Acheron bent to retrieve it.

"One of them dropped this," he said, and held up a slender feather, wrought in pure silver, with an edge sharp as a dagger blade. It gleamed in the dull gray afternoon light and struck instant terror in my heart.

"Throw it away," I said, recoiling as if the thing was cursed. It probably was. "Get rid of it, *now*."

Acheron looked back and forth between me and Cai in confusion. I felt the scar on my arm—the one Pontius Aquila had carved with just such a feather—blaze with phantom pain.

"It's a symbol of the Sons of Dis," Cai said, his lip curling in an angry sneer. "Used in their twisted rites."

"Those were—wait. They actually *exist*?" Acheron gaped at him. "The Sons of Dis? I thought they were a myth—"

"Get *rid* of it," I snapped. The image of the defiled practice dummies from the theatrum was still horribly fresh in my mind. A myth? No. The Sons of Dis were terrifyingly real. Prowling the streets of Rome . . . hunting.

"Uh. Could I maybe just . . . tuck it away?" Acheron slid the feather into a fold of his tunic. "I mean, it's *pure* silver, and I left my last purse of winnings back in my cell . . ."

"Fine." I took a deep breath and told myself to relax. It wasn't as if the feather would magically lead them to us here outside the city walls. It didn't need to. They already knew, ultimately, where to find us. "Just . . . keep the damned thing out of my sight."

"Of course, Victrix," he said, nodding in my direction. "And my apologies. I would never mean to upset you."

"It's all right," I said, and tried to muster a smile. "And you can call me Fallon, Acheron."

"Of course."

"Now let's get out of here."

I put my heels to my horse, and we galloped away from the city as the sun began his slow descent into the west. The moon would rise that night on a world without Caesar.

The Ludus Achillea sentries had seen the dust of our rapid approach miles out from their posts up on the wall and were waiting for us, no doubt wondering what in the world the matter was.

"Open the gate!" I shouted as soon as I thought they would hear me over the pounding of our horses' hooves on the dirt road.

I saw one of them disappear, and then the massive wood-and-iron doors swung ponderously open just before we reached them. We thundered through, into the courtyard, and I pulled my mount up to a rearing stop, leaping from his back and calling to Cai and the others over my shoulder.

"Close it and set the bar," I said. "Tell the watch to keep a keen eye out. I'll go find Sorcha . . ."

I burst through the doors of Sorcha's house, calling for her, but the place seemed empty. I rushed from room to room, wondering where her servants were, and then I heard laughter coming from the garden courtyard. Before I got there, Sorcha swept through the archway, wine goblets in her hands, smiling over her shoulder at someone outside. When she turned and saw me, her mouth opened in surprise.

"Fallon!" she exclaimed. "What—"

"He's dead!" I blurted. "Sorcha . . . Caesar's dead!"

She froze. The goblets shattered on the mosaic beneath her feet.

We stood there, staring at each other, and I couldn't even think of how to tell her what had happened. It was like Caesar's torn and bloodied body lay on the floor between us and I couldn't step around it.

But then I heard a sound—a convulsive intake of breath—and we both turned to see Cleopatra standing there. Her kohl-rimmed eyes were huge in her face, but the rest of her looked tiny. Childlike. I'd never thought of her as small before. The lapis and carnelian stones set in the necklace around her throat winked in the lamplight as she struggled for a breath.

"Your Highness—"

"You'll excuse me, Sorcha," she said abruptly, turning to Sennefer, her chief steward, who was suddenly at her side as if he'd sensed he was needed. "I . . . excuse me."

In a flurry of striped linen and jangling bracelets, Sennefer swooped down on his mistress, wrapped her in the protective cocoon of his flowing robes, and whisked her through the archway to the gardens. Wordlessly, they swept past Cai and Elka, who'd followed in my wake while Quint and Acheron had stayed in the yard.

"I'm sorry," I said to Sorcha. "I didn't see the queen there when I . . ."

She shook her head. "No," she said. "It's not your fault. Fallon—what in the name of the Morrigan has happened? Was there an accident?"

I could see in her eyes that she knew there hadn't been. But I also knew that, whatever she imagined had happened to Caesar, it wasn't anywhere near as bad as the truth of it. I didn't even know where to begin, so Cai stepped forward and told her the bald facts of the assassination as he knew them. As he did so, Charon came in from the garden to join us. His dark eyes focused on Cai, unblinking, as he waited for him to finish, and then he asked, "What state was the capital in when you left?"

"Quiet," Cai said. "Streets empty, windows and doors shuttered and locked. They wouldn't even show themselves to take away the body. The vigiles have gone to ground, and the legions are hunkered in their barracks, likely trying to decide whose side they're on. I think everyone else is too damned afraid to leave their houses. But it won't stay that way for long."

Suddenly Kronos came striding in, covered in sweat and road dust. "It didn't," he said. "That was an uneasy peace short-lived." He nodded at me, deep relief in his eyes. "I'm damned glad you're safe."

"You too," I said.

"They hadn't shut the gates?" Cai asked.

Kronos shook his head. "No one around to give the order. I imagine they have now, or will soon. But for who knows how long."

So Aquila and his people could still be a threat, I thought.

"An impromptu memorial was gathering momentum as I left the city," Kronos continued. "A handful of slaves from Caesar's own house finally came and took the body away. But before I left, there was a mob brewing in the Forum, and certain *senators*"—he spat the word—"decided, in their collective wisdom, to send that treacherous, weak-kneed fool Brutus out to gentle them."

"But he was one of the assassins!" I exclaimed.

"That he was." Kronos spat in disgust. "But he pleaded with the crowd, telling them what they did was all for the love of Rome. To save the poor downtrodden plebs from the ravages of a self-proclaimed emperor and tyrant."

"Did they listen?" Sorcha asked.

"Oh, aye," Kronos grunted, a narrow grin twisting his mouth. "Right up until the moment Marc Antony entreated for a chance to speak too."

Charon grunted in grim amusement, as if he suspected what had happened next, and said, "And?"

"He's a sorcerer, that one." Kronos shook his head. "Under the guise of praising Caesar's murderers, he managed to whip the crowd into a frenzy against them."

That didn't actually surprise me. Back home, there were bards who could speak a tale that, under the pretense of "honoring" a chief or a freeman, would drip poison from a honeyed tongue in order to exact another man's revenge. I thought about how sly Antony had been at the party and did not doubt he could give any one of those bards a stiff challenge.

"And the conspirators?" Cai asked.

"Most of 'em—the ones he mentioned by name, at least—are running for their lives or hiding behind high walls. If they've any sense. The crowd had already taken to building bonfires and throwing rocks."

"And Aquila?" I asked.

"No sign of him that I could see." Kronos shrugged.

"He's like the runt of the pack that hangs back while the other jackals bring down the lion," Cai said, "then sneaks in to steal the choicest piece of meat and runs away unnoticed."

"He's gone to gather other jackals," I said directly to Sorcha. Then I took a breath and told them all about the mutilated practice dummies we'd seen in the Theatrum

Pompeii. When I was finished, I turned back to my sister. Her lips were pressed together in a thin, bloodless line. "They were Aquila's men, with Aquila's grievances. He'll take his revenge out on the ludus. You know it. He'll lay siege to this place if he has to. And in the chaos and the void left in Caesar's wake, there will be no one to come to our aid. "

She nodded. "We don't have much time. Gather the girls."

I hesitated. Unwilling, suddenly, to take that step.

Elka looked back and forth between the two of us. "What are we going to do?" she asked, frowning. "You're not actually thinking of leaving the ludus again, are you?" She turned to me. "*Are* we?"

The walls of the Ludus Achillea were high and hard to climb. But they wouldn't hold forever. And if we were caught behind them, without Caesar, Aquila could afford to be patient. The thought of it hit me like a fist to my heart. After everything that had happened—everything we'd all fought so very hard for—the home we'd built was nothing more than sticks and stones standing in the way of a deluge. Without Caesar's protection . . . we would be swept away.

I turned away from Elka, unable to answer. Across the courtyard, I saw Sennefer backing out the doorway of Cleopatra's quarters, his hands raised in a placating gesture. I heard the slam of the door and saw his shoulders slump, and I remembered suddenly the conversation I'd had with the queen's chief steward the last time I'd seen him, when he'd led me down to the boat the queen had given me on the night we'd retaken the ludus from Aquila.

"*If the great general topples,*" he'd said, "*then Cleopatra will have no friend here in the land of the Romans. They hate women. They hate powerful women. They hate her, most of all.*"

He'd been expecting this day to come all along. I wondered if Cleopatra had. Up until that moment, I'd only thought of getting her somewhere safe. But I suddenly realized there *was* nowhere safe. Nowhere within the bounds of the Republic, at least. Not for her. Maybe not for any of us. I looked around at the faces of those gathered there: my sister, Kronos, Elka, Charon and Quint, Cai . . .

All of them stood there, waiting to hear what *I* would say.

Even Sorcha deferred to me in that moment in a way that she never had before. We'd come so far together in such a short time—since that day when she'd bought me at a slave auction for far too much money, so she could save my life. Now it was my turn to try to save someone else's.

"We can't just abandon the ludus and run," I said. "If we must go—and I know, I'm sorry, Elka, but we *must*—we can't just all scatter to the ends of the world like leaves on the wind. I say we do it on our own terms. And I say we do it for a worthy cause."

"And that would be?"

"Saving Cleopatra."

Sorcha's eyes went wide, her glance darting out to the garden, to where Sennefer had taken up a position squatting on his haunches, his voluminous striped robes tucked around him and the naked blade of a curved sword resting across his knees, outside the queen's door.

"They'll kill her if they get their hands on her," I said. "Just like they killed Caesar. Unless *we* protect her. All of us, together."

Elka's frown disappeared, and she took a deep breath and nodded. "Well, there's nothing more to argue beyond that then, is there?" she said, the matter—to her mind—decided beyond doubt. "I'll help round up the others."

My sister's gaze drifted around the room, taking in all of us, one by one, and then settled on Charon's face.

He nodded before she uttered a word and said, "Cosa. Less than two days' journey if we push it. There will be ships there that will take us to Alexandria."

"Are any of those ships yours?" I asked him.

"No," he said. "But there will be traders there I know. We'll ask for passage."

"And if they say no?" I said.

"We'll ask again. Less politely."

Sorcha nodded at me and Elka. "Gather the girls," she said. "Tell them to pack essentials only. But we travel equipped. We leave at first light, before sunrise."

"And the ludus itself?" I asked, a painfully tight knot in my throat.

"Burn it. Burn it to the ground," she said, and swept past me out of the room.

XI

AFTER ELKA AND I told the others what was happening and to get what sleep they could before the coming morn, I went to seek out Cleopatra before I retired to my own bed one last time. By then, I knew, Sorcha would've told the queen what had happened to her lord, but I still felt the need to speak to her myself. *I* was the one who'd seen it happen. I owed it to Cleopatra to speak to her directly. And I dreaded having to do it. I think, in truth, I half expected her to put a knife in my guts for not having been able to stop Caesar's murderers from doing the same to him. I'm not sure I would have blamed her.

I found Cleopatra still in the guest quarters Sorcha kept for her. I knew she was in there because, outside, Sennefer remained squatting by the door in the darkness with his sword. And because, inside, I could hear the sound of things shattering.

The queen's chief steward and I exchanged wordless glances as I pushed open the door and stepped carefully over the threshold. A dozen lamps were lit, throwing enough light for me to see the room and its lone occupant clearly. The sight of the queen of Aegypt in mourning was shocking—not at all what I was expecting. I suppose I should have been used to that where Cleopatra was concerned. I had, of course, expected passionate emotions from her. Just not the particular manner in which she chose to express them. I'd expected her—with her flair for dramatics—to be overcome with grief, perhaps tearing at her hair or rending her garments. But Cleopatra was the furthest thing from distraught. Instead, she stood in the middle of the room: regal, composed . . . and methodically picking up every breakable item within arm's reach, one at a time, only to hurl whatever it was at the far wall.

There was already a substantial pile of glass and pottery shards at the base of the mural painted there, which bore the stains of a multitude of cosmetic pigments and the wine of, I guessed, *several* amphorae. I watched silently for a moment as she went about her business, calmly wreaking material carnage, until finally she sensed my presence.

She turned to look over her shoulder, beckoning me to enter with a wave of her hand, and I bit my cheek at the sight of her face. Cleopatra's expression remained utterly impassive, but the thick black lines of kohl that were always so meticulously and artfully applied around her lovely eyes had mixed with tears and run in dark rivulets down her face, spattering the front of the elegant linen sheath she wore with ugly black blots. I shivered, remembering the dripping paint of the grotesque eyes on the practice dummy in the arena.

"Majesty," I choked out, swallowing hard against the knot in my throat and bowing my head to hide my dismay.

Wordlessly, she shifted her attention back to her breakables.

I hovered there in the doorway, wondering if I shouldn't just turn around and leave the queen alone. I wondered if I should attempt some kind of . . . what? Comfort? Commiseration? I had, truthfully, no idea. The most powerful woman in the world had just lost her great love—the most powerful man in the world—to hideous violence. I had no idea what she was feeling.

Except, perhaps, pure, incandescent, ice-cold *rage* . . .

"I would have every last one of them strung up in the desert to be flayed alive by sandstorms," I heard her say as she picked up a blue glass perfume bottle and hurled it at the wall. It smashed into a thousand pieces, filling the room with a heady waft of cypress and lotus blossom. She picked up a pot of cheek rouge next. "I would carve out their eyes with my own golden knife and feed them to the vultures, one by one." Another smash, another stain on the wall.

I didn't know if she was speaking to me, or to the air, or to the gods themselves. But it sounded as if she had been uttering these variations of a death curse with each bauble or bit of crockery sacrificed.

"I would fill their mouths with scorpions and seal their lips with molten lead." She picked up a hand mirror made of solid polished silver and, with one last heave, launched it at the wall. When it made a dull thud and only cracked off a chunk of plaster instead of shattering, Cleopatra sighed—a sound halfway between disappointment and exhaustion—and sank down on the couch, her fury seemingly spent. For the moment, at least.

She turned and beckoned me forward again with a wave of her hand.

Before joining her, I searched a side table and found the one small wine jug she hadn't obliterated in her rage and two exquisite, lapis-inlaid goblets. I poured out two measures, handing one to the queen, then sat on the couch opposite hers and waited.

She took a sip and nodded thanks.

"Tell me, Fallon." She gazed down at the dark kohl stains on the dress she wore, plucking at them as if she couldn't quite figure out how they got there. "Did he die honorably?"

Very honorably, I wanted to say. *He went down fighting like the conqueror he was, wresting a blade from the hands of his assailants and drawing more blood than he spilled . . .*

Except I couldn't. I owed her the truth, however ugly and horrid it was.

"No," I said. "There was no honor in it, Majesty. It was cheap and it was dirty and Caesar stood no chance. Sheer numbers took your lord. His attackers were like a pack of hyenas on a lion, and you are right to curse the heads of every single one of the filthy curs responsible."

She nodded. "Thank you. I wanted to know the truth before everyone tells me how valiant my lord was in the moments before they cut him down." She drank from the cup I'd given her. "Did you recognize any of them? Caesar's murderers?"

I hesitated. In truth, I'd be hard-pressed to identify a single senator at a triumphal parade even if they wore plaques hanging from their necks with their names written on them. I told Cleopatra as much, apologetically. But then I also told her of how I *had* recognized Pontius Aquila—and how he'd slithered out of the shadows like a snake after the terrible deed was done.

She wasn't the least bit surprised.

But then I remembered one other thing. One other *face*.

"Marcus Junius Brutus . . ."

Cleopatra repeated the name after me, pronouncing each syllable like an invocation of his impending doom. I told her what Kronos had reported. About Brutus's impromptu funeral orations—and Antony's rabble-rousing rebuttal—and how it had inflamed the mob and resulted in the direct opposite reaction the conspirators had been hoping for. That almost brought a smile to her face. I picked up the little wine jug and refilled the queen's goblet.

"I still find it hard to believe," I said, "that a man like Brutus would have anything to do with this kind of perfidy." I shook my head. "He is, by every account, an honorable man."

"Caesar certainly thought so," Cleopatra said flatly. "Brutus was dear to him. Almost like a son."

"I would have expected it more from a creature like Antony."

But she wagged a finger at me saying, "*Honorable* men, Fallon, are often the ones who are easiest to manipulate. All you have to do is turn their sense of justice against their better judgment." She laughed bitterly. "As for Antony, he is a politician and a survivor. He has his own dearly held vices and he doesn't need to participate in anyone else's. In fact, to do so would probably just get in his way—Antony worships Antony alone. It's one of the things I admire about him."

I was silent for a moment. Then I said, "You know we have to leave soon?"

"Yes, I know," she sighed. "I must flee the Republic like a guilty thief and disappear into the night. Sennefer has already descended upon me like a flock of pecking hens and told me of this plan of yours and Sorcha's." A wan grin touched her lips. "Thank you, Fallon, for having a care for this poor bedraggled queen."

"You are hardly that."

"Don't flatter, dear. I looked into that mirror before I threw it at the wall." She shook her head, and the golden beads woven into her hair flickered like sparks. "Sennefer also told me we'll be traveling light. I thought, since I won't be bringing any of this with me . . ." She waved a hand at the shattered remains of her usual complement of worldly comforts. Then she tossed back the rest of her wine and hurled the goblet to the floor.

"My feelings exactly, my queen," I said, and followed her example.

I didn't tell her that my ludus sisters and I planned to do exactly the same thing—for whatever that was worth. None of us had much to lose. What I *did* want to tell her in that moment was how sorry I was for her loss, but I bit my tongue on those words too. I would not shame her in that moment with sympathy or softness she clearly didn't need. No. What Cleopatra needed most from me just then was strength, swords, and safe passage. And she would have them. From me and from my sisters of the Ludus Achillea. Because it wouldn't be long before there was nothing else for us in the world but that—a mission and a purpose. And none of *us* wanted sympathy either.

I stood.

"Send in Sennefer, won't you?" Cleopatra said before I left, wiping the edge of her little finger under her eye. She glared at the black smudge left on her fingertip in disgust. "And my women. I know we only have until daybreak. But I'm not going anywhere until I look like the goddess I am. The goddess Caesar loved. I'm sure there must still be one pot of eyepaint left intact, at least . . ."

I promised her we'd find some elsewhere if there wasn't. Then I bowed and took my leave of the queen of Aegypt, my sandals crunching on a sea of broken, glittering glass as I went. The sky was clear and full of bright stars that night, and as I lay awake on the cot in my ludus cell for the last time, moonlight spilled over me. I closed my eyes and imagined that same light pouring like tears over the stone steps of the Theatrum Pompeii in Rome, unable to wash away the black stain of Julius Caesar's blood.

XII

"THIS PLACE WAS just starting to feel like home," Kallista said, slipping the halter off one of the draft horses and giving him a slap on the neck. She watched as he wandered away to nibble on a patch of clover growing beneath an olive tree.

"I know," Selene, her Amazon sister, nodded, leading a pair of chariot ponies into the field. "I'll miss the baths most of all, I think."

"They have baths in Aegypt," I said. "Even better ones."

She frowned at me, clearly skeptical.

"And home isn't where you are," I continued. "It's who you're with."

Kallista thought about that for a moment, her expression serious, then shrugged. "It's just more adventure, I suppose," she said, looking over at Selene. "And that is what we told Areto we wanted when she agreed to let us leave Corsica, isn't it?"

"Exactly." I nodded far more enthusiastically than I felt.

What I felt, really, was nothing but heartache. We'd only just rebuilt the stables. And now, here we were in the hour before we were to leave, leading the ludus draft horses and chariot ponies—and even Tempest, the mighty ox—out into the field in front of the main gate of the ludus, where we turned them loose to fend for themselves. The ponies whickered softly to each other in the purple predawn gloom. The cantankerous old donkey was the last of the animals to go. I led him a ways out into the field beyond the walls and slipped the halter off his head. Then I slapped him on the rump and turned to walk away. I didn't get very far before I glanced back over my shoulder and saw him standing there, glaring at me reproachfully.

"Go," I said. "Go on!"

Instead, he trotted a few steps toward me and butted my chest with his long, homely nose. I felt tears spring to my eyes. I reached up to scratch his ear, and he let me—without even trying to bite, which was a rarity—and shook his head, braying loudly, lips pulled back from his long yellow teeth. Then he turned and, tail lifted high like a gamboling foal, trotted off in the direction of the far hills without once looking back.

I watched him go.

He would be fine, I knew. They all would—caught and cared for by the nearby farms and villas—but they wouldn't be ours. We hurried back to finish our last tasks before leaving.

"We're taking three wagons," Sorcha told me when I joined her in the main yard, "each harnessed to a double team of horses. And five saddled horses to act as outriders and armed escort."

"I'll ride," I said. "If you want me to."

"I do." She nodded. "Along with Caius and Quint. Who else?"

"Hestia is a seasoned rider," I suggested.

"Agreed."

Acheron, passing by, stopped in front of us. "If you need another rider, I was born into a family of horse thieves," he said.

I'd told Sorcha who Acheron's brother was the night before. We'd agreed to keep the means of Ixion's death a secret between us. I'd also told her how he'd come to Cai's aid in the arena. She tilted her head and looked at him. "Were you, now?" she asked.

He shrugged. "I was stealing ponies before I was five. Long before I found myself good, honorable work as a gladiator. There's not much that can knock me off a horse's back, lady."

It was decided then. Acheron would be our fifth rider.

"Ajani and Elka can each take up a defensive position in the first and third wagons," Sorcha continued. "And Kallista and her Amazons can act as bodyguard to the queen in the middle one. They are to keep Cleopatra surrounded and safe. At any cost. Impress that upon them, Fallon. *Any* cost."

I nodded, knowing full well that they'd commit to that whether I impressed it upon them or not. They were Amazons. They'd die by their own hands if they outlived their queen. And Cleopatra was their queen now.

Across the yard I saw some of Sennefer's men escorting the ludus staff toward the lake gate. "Where are they going?" I asked Sorcha.

"The queen has insisted that the Achillea staff—cooks, body slaves, blacksmiths, house servants—everyone is to be ferried across Lake Sabatinus to the estate she was occupying in Caesar's absence," she said. "She's given instructions that they be taken in hand by the estate manager and found suitable employment."

"I'm glad of it," I said.

Sorcha nodded. "She is a good woman. A good friend."

But I could see her heart breaking a little as she watched them go. The staff at the Ludus Achillea—servants and slaves both—had been unfailingly honorable in their service, and when she'd brought them together to tell them what was happening, not a single voice was raised in opposition. None of them had forgotten what it was like when Pontius Aquila had taken the ludus by force. And it would soon be reduced to ashes and blackened stone walls, anyway.

What I hadn't expected was that Heron, our ludus physician, would be going along with the staff—and not with us. Again. The last time we'd fled the ludus, he's stayed behind because of Lydia, to treat her injuries. Three months ago, she'd succumbed to them—or rather, to the damages wrought on her mind—drowning herself in Lake Sabatinus one night after Heron had gone to bed. I wasn't certain the physician didn't blame himself for it. Still, it hadn't occurred to me he wouldn't come with us. His refusal to prompted an argument from me when I found him in the herb garden we'd planted where Tartarus had once stood.

He forestalled my ire with a raised hand. "Fallon," he said, "I'm not a warrior. I'm not young. And I'm not needed."

"But—"

"You have more than enough to worry about without dragging along a fussy old man who cannot fight his own battles." He shook his head and went back to gathering the last of the medicinal plants the garden would ever yield, perfuming the air around us with a bittersweet tang. "Neferet is one of you," he continued. "She can take care of the girls and herself at the same time. Miss me if you will—I will miss all of you with all of my heart—but go with my blessings."

It felt like losing another part of myself. Everything was falling away, and I couldn't stop it. But I also couldn't blame him for his choice. So instead, I hugged him hard and let him go. When I got back to the stables, Elka and Vorya were splashing lamp oil from large storage skins on the floors of the empty stalls. Gratia and Ajani followed close behind with torches.

"It's a strange thing, isn't it?" Vorya said, coming up to stand beside me as the first flames caught and began to lick greedily at the piles of straw and fodder. "To come together and build something—something real and right—and then have it all taken from you in an instant. By people you've never even met and have nothing to do with."

"We'll still be together," I said, but I heard the hitch in my voice as the stable post I'd used for practice ever since arriving at the ludus—carving marks into it with my blades like notches on a druid seer stone—began to smolder. "We'll still be sisters. We'll still have . . ."

"Purpose?" Vorya said.

"I was going to say 'each other.'" I turned so the others could hear me when I said, "But you're right, Vorya. Our purpose *is* each other."

How I hope that's not just a hollow platitude, I thought bitterly.

But when Ajani threw her torch into the flames, she turned her back on the fire and walked toward me, wordlessly holding out her hands for me to take. I reached out, and she gave my fingers a tight squeeze, her expression serene. That gesture, and the simple fact that my friends hadn't all just packed up and left on the barge along with the ludus staff . . . maybe it wasn't *all* falling apart. Maybe the platitudes—like that one, and the ones I'd given Kallista and Selene—carried a kind of truth in them. Maybe home really *was* who you were with, not where.

"It's just a stable post, after all," I muttered.

Ajani glanced at me sideways but didn't ask me what I meant by that.

Elka came to stand with us for a moment as Gratia whirled her torch above her head and lobbed it high into the rafters of the barn. The smoke began to rise into the stillness of the sky. Elka put an arm over Vorya's shoulder; the expressions on both their faces remained stony. *Varini mettle at work*, I thought. I remembered the conversation I'd had with Elka when we'd first met and become fugitives on the run from Charon and his slavers. About how her tribe, if they decided to move somewhere else— because of war or famine or the whim of a Varini chief— would burn their houses before they left. I'd thought at the time that it was a ridiculous idea. Wasteful. I'd only ever done a similar thing out of sheer emotion. In a fit of despair, I'd thrown my most prized possessions into the fire on the night my father had denied me my place in his war band.

When I'd asked Elka what the Varini reasoning was, she'd answered, "*There is only forward. Only tomorrow. No yesterday, no going back. And nothing of value is left behind, so nothing is truly lost.*"

She'd also said, rather more pragmatically, "*You don't leave a freshly made bed behind for your enemy to sleep in.*"

That conversation still echoed in my head as, together, we turned and strode to the barracks building where the others waited for us. So we could perform our one last act of rebellion. Of fierce independence. Rome could not have us. Rome—whatever it was to become in the dawning days—*would* not have us.

It didn't take any of us long.

Outside my cell, I could hear the others starting to gather in the corridor, but I still stood at the foot of my cot with my trunk open and the few things I would take with me laid out on top of a scant pile of clothing— tunics and breeches, nothing fancy. No stolas or pallas— I likely wouldn't need such things where I was going, and I wouldn't miss wearing the finery of a Roman lady. It had never suited me anyway. I was already wearing my armor, and my sword belt hung from my hips. My best warm cloak was fastened at my neck, and I'd laced up my best pair of boots tight around my ankles.

The rest was . . . sentimental. Small, but meaningful. A pair of silver brooches Sorcha had presented me with after I'd won a hard bout. A fine iron dagger that was a gift from Heron, the Sekhemet pendant Cleopatra had given me, my new oath lamp . . . the key to my cell in Tartarus.

Beside a stack of letters and drawings Cai had sent when he'd been on campaign, there was a neat pile of wax-sealed courier tubes containing the letters I'd sent to him at the Ludus Flaminius. Letters he'd never read and sent back to me unopened. I frowned down at them, wondering, and then gathered them all up and dumped them back into the trunk. With everything that had happened, I'd forgotten to ask Cai why he'd returned them.

But it no longer mattered. That time apart had been hard on us both, and it seemed silly—petty, even—to bring it up now. I had Cai himself back—the letters could burn.

From the missives he'd sent me, I chose only one: the almost lifelike picture he had sketched of his hand. I rolled it carefully into a bronze tube and tucked it into the bottom of a canvas traveling pack. Then I shoved everything else I was taking in after it and yanked the straps tight. I took down the skin of lamp oil that hung on a peg by my washstand and splashed it on the floor and on my neatly made bed. Before I left, I remembered one last thing I needed to take: a small, sealed ebony wood box that sat on my windowsill and contained only a handful of earth.

I tucked that into my traveling pack too, and stepped out into the hall to join my ludus sisters. We exchanged silent glances. And then, as if it was some kind of ritual we'd rehearsed and enacted time and again, we each took a torch down from the iron brackets that hung on the corridor walls beside the doors to our rooms.

Like silent, cloaked statues of the warriors we'd become in this place, we stood. As one, we threw the torches into the cells, turned our backs, and strode in a line out of the ludus barracks and into the chill predawn air, leaving nothing but growing red light and the sounds of crackling flames behind us.

Not one of us looked back.

I thought, for a moment, that Gratia might have been on the verge of tears. But when I turned to her, I realized the glint in her eye was something else entirely. I tracked her gaze and saw that she was staring intently at where Acheron was lifting Cleopatra's cumbersome trunks into a wagon—all bulging muscles and heaving chest, his copper braids tossing like the mane of a stallion. When Gratia noticed me looking at her, she shrugged and said, "What?"

"Nothing . . ." I shrugged. "I just thought you might be . . . upset?"

"About leaving here?"

"Yes."

She shook her head. "I'll be all right. A place is just a place. I've got you lot for company, and I'm sure I can find *some*thing new and interesting to occupy myself with until we get settled somewhere else . . ." And then, grinning in a somewhat predatory fashion, she loped across the yard to go lift heavy things and make Acheron nervous.

I was about to follow with the others when I saw Charon standing at the head of the path leading to the smallest of the ludus's carefully manicured garden court-yards, all of which would soon be nothing more than ash and blackened stumps. As we approached, he nodded his head.

I turned to Elka. "Go on," I said. "We'll follow in a moment."

"Don't take too long," she said. "Fire's catching. If the wind shifts, this place will serve you for a funeral pyre just as well as it did for a training ground."

"You're not getting rid of me that easily," I said.

She snorted and punched me in the shoulder, then hurried to catch up with the others. I turned back to Charon, and he led me a little way down the path into the garden, to where there was a stone bench set beneath a fig tree. The tree's graceful, spreading branches were just beginning to unfurl pale green buds overhead, not even close to blooming.

It was only March.

"I wanted to speak to you for a moment, without the others around," Charon said. His eyes narrowed, and he frowned as he looked at me. "Fallon . . . are you all right?"

"I don't know." I shrugged, staring up hopelessly at the tree and telling myself the stinging in my eyes was from the smoke. "I don't really know what that is anymore. We're leaving—again—and this time it's for good. Because there won't be anything to come back to, even if we wanted to. And at the same time, I don't know why that wounds me so, because I feel like all I've managed to do with my time here in this place has been . . . meaningless."

Charon shook his head. "You're wrong about that."

"Am I?" I looked at him, wondering if that was what he really thought. "Everyone still calls me Victrix. They tell me I'm some kind of hero or leader or something. And yet it feels to me like all I've done is somehow master the art of triumphantly snatching defeat from the jaws of victory."

"This isn't over yet, Fallon," he said. "For any of you."

I laughed a little. "Not over? Isn't the world ending?"

"For Rome, for a while . . . maybe." He ran a hand over his beard, seriously considering the question. "Not for long. Never that. The wheel turns. And for you and your sisters? I think it's just beginning. I can't say whether that's a thing to be hoped for or feared. But I *know* you. And you don't let a little thing like ended worlds stop you." He turned and walked away from me, over toward the stone bench. "Because of that, I wanted to give you something," Charon said, reaching for a box that lay on the ground beside the bench. "Before we leave this place."

It was the same garden where he'd gifted me my first real set of armor. The one I'd worn on the circuit, when I'd first started out on my journey to become Caesar's Victrix. And now Caesar was dead. And what was I? I wasn't being dramatic with the former slave master. I really *didn't* know. But Charon seemed to think *he* might. And so, just like on the day that he'd presented me with my gladiatrix armor, he had a gift for me. This time, the box was made of wood, not wicker, and it was long and slender.

Just the right size to hold a sword.

I found myself frowning in wonder as he lifted the lid . . . and then everything went a bit blurry. I blinked, wiping at my eyes. I couldn't even lie anymore and tell myself it was just the smoke as two fat tears spilled down my cheeks. Charon gestured to the sword belt I wore and the single blade hanging from my left hip.

"It was starting to look a little lonely without its fellow," he said.

"Charon, I . . ." I didn't know what to say as I reached for the leather-wrapped hilt. The thing was glorious. Perfectly balanced, expertly crafted and honed, polished to a gleaming sheen. And an identical match to my other dimachaerus blade. Well, *almost* identical. As my fingers tightened around the grip and I brought it close to my face, devouring the lines and shape of it with my eyes, I saw that the blade was marked with a symbol just like my old sword—no. *Not* just like my old sword . . . I lifted my other hand and traced the inscribed shape on the iron. Similar to the triple-raven marking of the Morrigan, but different. Not three ravens . . . but a single eagle. The symbol of Caesar's legions—of Rome's finest warriors—only it was rendered in the twisting, fantastical style of the Celtic tribes.

"I hope you don't think that presumptuous," Charon said as I ran my fingertip over the design. "Or distasteful. I simply wanted to pay homage to your . . . dual nature, shall we say."

"No," I murmured, feeling the shape of the thing beneath my fingertip. "No, it's . . . it feels *right*. Somehow."

It did. In the same way that it had felt right for me to keep the key to my Tartarus prison cell. Something hated and hurtful but endured. Overcome. Rome—and Caesar—had shaped me. Become part of me. I found it strange how Charon always seemed so eerily insightful where my character was concerned. I told him so, but he shook his head.

"It's a by-product of the trade, Fallon," he said ruefully. "That's all. I'm not so much insightful as I am—I *was*—simply awash in a sea of human experience, generally in its rawest, most wretched expression. I have seen far too much of the inner workings of the soul laid bare to be able to ignore it now. Especially from someone with a pure one. Like you."

I looked at him, tilting my head, as if that would help me make more sense of this man who was—at the very heart of it—the chief architect of so much of the last two years of my life. Perhaps one day, I thought, but not today. I handed Charon back the box and spun the eagle blade in my palm, sheathing it in the empty scabbard at my right hip. The eagle and the raven. Rome . . . and home.

I nodded and said, "Thank you."

Then together we hurried to join the others, so we could leave the Ludus Achillea before the fires burned it to the ground around our ears. Back in the main courtyard, the gates stood wide open and there were only two sentries left up on the walls to watch for dust clouds. Once we were on the road to Cosa, they would go their own ways with fat, coin-filled purses.

Cai was helping harness and load the wagons with the few things we would take from the place. Mostly weapons. He came over to stand with me for a moment, taking my hands in his and squeezing them as if he sensed my uncertainty and could pour all of the strength and surety I needed into me through that touch.

"Are we dismantling our home for nothing?" I asked. "What happens if Aquila doesn't come here?"

"Rome is at war with itself, Fallon," he said. "And you are warriors. Do not think that this place will remain untouched by the strife of powerful men."

I thought back to the mutilated practice dummies in the arena in Rome and knew he was right. To try to convince myself otherwise was nothing more than dangerous folly.

"Even if Aquila doesn't?" Cai continued. "Someone else will. Maybe someone worse than Aquila."

"There isn't anyone worse than him."

"My father was."

I looked up into his face and realized that Cai had already resolved himself to leave behind everything he'd ever had too. His father's vast fortune, the city he'd called home, and the legion he'd pledged life and loyalty to. We were about to head toward the port of Cosa and ships. But it felt as if, once on those ships, we'd be setting a course toward the edge of the world and out into the abyss. And at the end of it all, Cai might be the only thing I'd have left to hang on to. But as our eyes met, and I saw the shadow of his father haunting his gaze, I wondered if he'd rather not just let go himself and drown. I wasn't about to let that happen. Not after everything we'd already been through.

"You heard what Caesar said." I squeezed his hands back just as hard. "The son is not the father. And you are the *best* of men, Caius Varro. In spite of him."

He tried to smile, but I knew, without him saying it, that he held the elder Varro responsible in large part for what was happening to us. To the ludus. And because he *was* his father's son, he would have to bear the burden of that guilt too, until such time as he could atone for those dread wrongs. It was his Roman way.

As his gaze dropped away from mine, I saw a tiny frown tick between Cai's brows. He let go of my hand to touch a fingertip to the pommel of my new sword. I reached down and drew it from its scabbard, handing it to him so he could take a closer look.

"From Charon. I think he still feels bad for stealing me away from home," I said with a casual shrug. "And for threatening to kill me. And for almost *getting* me killed. More than once . . ."

Cai shook his head. "I think he believes in you."

"Whatever it is I've become."

"A wandering hero, of course." He leaned down and kissed me on the forehead. "Like in the old epic stories. Odysseus or Achilles."

With one more kiss, and a last fleeting smile, Cai went to finish packing the wagon so we could leave on our adventure. Behind me, the flames continued to grow, casting their light on the faces of my friends as we gathered together beneath the main gate. I looked up at the carved image of Achilles and the Amazon warrior queen Penthesilea frozen in time on the lintel stone over the ludus gate that Senator Varro had given Sorcha as a gift. The figures, poised on the brink of deadly battle in the heat of the Trojan War, were already darkening with smoke.

I knew something of those stories Cai spoke of. They always started with leaving home. And finished with coming back to a place where peace and harmony were restored. But we weren't leaving anything to come back *to*. How, then, could we have a happy ending?

Or any kind of ending at all?

XIII

WE MADE IT as far as the Tarquin Valley on the first leg of
the journey, just as the sun was sinking into his watery bed,
far out over the Mare Nostrum. The sky in the east was
already dark, and I could see the pinpricks of stars fading
into view. An eerie glow behind the dark hills heralded the
rising of the moon.

Down across the rolling hills that swept toward the
coast, we could see the winking lights of the town of
Tarquinii. With the breeze wafting inland, I could smell
the salt marshes. I had been here once before—there was a
fledgling ludus nearby that some of us had fought in tour-
naments at—but the town itself was a tumbledown place.
I'd been told it had started out as an Etruscan settlement
that had been largely abandoned over time. The evidence
of its ancient roots was everywhere, especially in the vast,
crumbling necropolis—a city of the dead—that surrounded

the town itself, sprawling and spreading up into the surrounding hills like a creeping leprosy.

In the distance, wolves howled at the moon as it crept up over the horizon, bloated and blue, casting deep shadows in the gullies between the rolling hills. We pulled the wagons off the road and hid them behind the walls of a stone courtyard that must have once been a mortuary garden for a person of some importance. A shiver traced up and down my spine. But as unsettling and forlorn as the Tarquinii necropolis was, it had the advantage of being utterly deserted after nightfall. Or so we hoped.

"Reminds me of that night in Alesia," Elka said, rubbing her arms against a sudden shiver of gooseflesh. "This place is full of ghosts."

I felt it too.

Cai and Quintus took first watch. Acheron went with them, tracing a wide berth around the wagon where Sennefer was helping Cleopatra step down. I think he was still a bit flummoxed to find himself in the presence of royalty—especially her particularly robust manifestation of royalty—and more female gladiators than he'd even known existed. Most of whom (Gratia's mildly terrifying flirtations notwithstanding) regarded him with curious, skeptical, *warning* glances. Acheron might have been with us, but he wasn't one of us. Not yet. Still, I was glad to have another proficient fighter along for the journey. Even as I prayed to the Morrigan that we would have no opportunity to call upon those skills.

"No fires," Cai said before he went to find a vantage point where he could settle himself to watch for any movement beyond our little encampment.

I looked over to see Sennefer flush almost instantly to purple. Turning back to Cai, I raised an eyebrow and nodded my head at the queen's steward about to launch into a full-blown flap.

Cai sighed. "*One* fire," he amended the order. "A small one. In there."

He pointed to a tomb that was half tumbled down but still provided a decent amount of shelter from wind and prying eyes. I gestured for Sennefer to escort Cleopatra inside and led the way, sword drawn in case we weren't the only ones—human or animal—who'd thought to take refuge there that night.

Being inside the tomb was like standing inside the shell of a cracked egg. The roof had been split open, and the night sky showed through the wide, jagged crack. Painted figures of men and women, long-faded and peeling away from the plaster, strode around a border near the top of the wall or reclined indolently on couches. Above that, where the wall arched toward the ceiling, a pair of fierce, spotted leopards sat facing each other. Guardians of the place, it seemed. I hoped they wouldn't mind us intruding just long enough to spend a single watchful night.

In the most sheltered corner, Sennefer produced tools from one of the many pouches on his embroidered belt, and in almost no time at all, he'd conjured a neat, small, smokeless fire with admirable efficiency. I watched as he stripped off his cloak and folded it into a thick pad for the queen to sit upon. Cleopatra sank gracefully down onto it, arranging the folds of her own cloak artfully around her, as if the cold stone floor of the ancient tomb was one of the gilded couches on her pleasure barge. I admired her composure.

Sorcha sank down beside her, and the queen reached over to squeeze my sister's hand, a silent gesture that somehow managed to convey friendship, strength, and gratitude all at the same time. Had it been anyone else, I might have felt a sting of sisterly jealousy for how close the two of them were. As it was, I was just grateful that, for all the years I had missed her so desperately, Sorcha had been able to rely on at least one true, deep friendship in a world that had never really stopped seeing her as a barbarian. Saving Cleopatra had been the right thing to do, I thought.

As the little fire began to warm the chamber, the rest of our group drifted inside and, one by one, found a space to lay down a cloak. We would sleep close by each other tonight, surrounded by the tumbled shelter of the ruins.

"Who built this place?" Lysa wondered out loud, gazing up at the painted leopards.

"The Etruscans," Kronos said, hunkering down in front of a gap in the stone wall where he could keep another watch out. "It's ancient. Older even than Rome, they say."

"You mean Rome isn't the first, last, and everything of all the whole wide world?" Gratia said with a sarcastic snort.

Some of the other girls grinned at that, but I couldn't help wondering if Rome wouldn't one day lie in runs, just like this place. A vanished city, a fallen empire, a forgotten people . . .

I sank down on my haunches across the fire from Cleopatra and Sorcha. "Apologies for the rough conditions, Majesty," I said, stretching out my fingers to the warmth of the flames.

"Nonsense." Cleopatra waved away my apology with one hand. "I'm not some delicate blossom."

When a full goblet of wine suddenly appeared in that same hand—Sennefer was nothing if not a master of his queen's creature comforts—Cleopatra took a moment, and a sip, and then she fixed her gaze upon me like one of the bards around my father's fire would when I was little and they had a story to tell me.

"When I was a girl," the queen said in a voice full of memory, "my father took me on an excursion out into the desert, past the Valley of the Kings to a place deep in the canyons. We spent three days there, sleeping under the stars, beneath the cliffs of Deir el-Bahari, in the shadow of Djeser-Djeseru—the great mortuary temple of my mighty ancestress, the Pharaoh Hatshepsut."

"Ancestress?" For a moment, I thought my Latin had failed me, and I blinked at her in confusion. "A pharaoh?

Forgive me, Your Majesty, but I was under the impression that only the . . . well, only *men* were allowed to take the title of pharaoh."

"They called Hatshepsut 'She Who Is King,'" Cleopatra explained. "But you're right. It was a long time ago, in an age when women were considered inferior." Her eyes shone with a hard light, like a freshly sharpened blade. I knew perfectly well her own views on such things. "So the mighty Hatshepsut," she continued, "declared herself the *son* of the great god Ra, tied on a ceremonial beard and a golden phallus, and ascended the throne. None dared gainsay her. She ruled wisely and well, and Aegypt flourished under her benevolent and generous kingship."

I glanced over my shoulder to see Elka gaping at Cleopatra, clearly impressed by the strength of Hatshepsut's character.

"You girls . . ." Cleopatra waved a hand at where our ludus sisters were scattered about, hunkering down to prepare for a night of fitful, anxious sleep. "You are, in a way, just as much her daughters as I am. You are her heirs in spirit."

"My queen." Neferet spoke up from where she'd been listening. "If you don't mind me asking, what do you mean by that?"

Cleopatra grinned at the girl who hailed from her own country. "I don't mind at all. And you, my dear, are a perfect example."

"I am?"

"You are the physician to this company, are you not?"

Neferet frowned, but once she realized that Cleopatra's question wasn't a mocking one, she nodded. "Yes. I am."

"And you are a woman?"

Antonia leaned forward and answered for her. "She is."

Neferet elbowed her and, blushing, said to the queen, "I am."

"A woman and a physician—not a midwife nor an herb witch—a *physician*." Cleopatra's mouth bent upward. "A vocation reserved solely for men."

She gazed around at the lot of us, an expression of deep satisfaction on her face. Most of the girls had stopped what they were doing by that point and had gathered near to hear what the queen had to say. She and Sorcha shared a glance and a grin as we all leaned in, rapt. The queen of Aegypt's voice was low and musical drifting through the ancient vault, the flickering shadows seeming to make the figures on the walls dance above our heads.

"All of you," Cleopatra continued. "*All* of you are extraordinary young women. Never doubt that, or what you have accomplished. You have all walked fearlessly into a place that, before you, was a kind of temple reserved for men only. You took oaths that, before you, only men took. You fought and hurt, and some of you even died . . . but you won glory in ways only men did. And you did it all with the grace of women."

"And the occasional kick to the stones of the nearest man," Elka said.

Cleopatra's bright laughter echoed off the broken stones of the old tomb. But after a moment, she grew serious. Almost solemn. By the light of the tiny campfire, her face glowed golden, as if lit from within by some divine flame, and her dark eyes were large and luminous and seemed to take all of us in at a glance.

"When Hatshepsut died," she said, "the pharaoh who came after her tried to have all memory of her erased. He smashed all the sphinxes with faces carved in her likeness. He defaced the walls of her great temple and had her image chiseled from the stone, her *cartouche*—her very name—malleted to dust. And yet, her legend and her legacy persist down through the ages. You all have left your home behind, and your arena. And that wounds. Deeply. You think you will be forgotten. You will not. You will find your place, you will find your purpose. And you will inspire the warriors—the *women* warriors—who will come after *you*."

A kind of hallowed silence descended on us then, with the only sound the crackling of the fire and an owl hooting somewhere in the distance.

And then Antonia leaned forward, her eyes glinting, and said, "Is it true you had yourself rolled up in a carpet and smuggled past the praetorian guards into Caesar's chambers?"

The rest of us might have been a bit shocked by Antonia's audacity, but Cleopatra just grinned and said, "That . . . was Sennefer's idea."

"And you all thought I was such a stick in the Nile mud." He sniffed, clearly pleased at having his cleverness acknowledged, and produced a small bowl of figs for his mistress to nibble at.

"If you want something bad enough," Cleopatra said, settling back on one elbow and looking every bit a queen among the ruins, "then don't let anything—or anyone—stand in your way. And always enlist those clever, helpful friends who stand by your side. You are each other's greatest assets, ladies. Never forget that."

I suspected I knew what Cleopatra was doing in that moment, and I was grateful for it. Throughout the day's travel, everyone had been fretful and on edge, riding into absolute uncertainty. We knew—all of us, I think—the essence of what she was saying. But hearing someone like her say it . . . it made a difference. The air of unease that had settled like a fog around us began to lift and fade. There was murmuring and quiet laughter now among the girls as they bedded down for the night.

I went and laid down my cloak near Elka and Vorya, across from Hestia and Ajani, who sat cross-legged on hers, staring up at the sky through the gaping hole in the vaulting roof, watching the stars.

"What do you think wrecked this place?" Ajani wondered aloud.

Vorya glanced up and grunted. "Earthquake, probably."

"I've only ever heard of those," Ajani said. "Never been through one."

"Be glad of that," Hestia said. "When I was small, an earthquake brought down a mountainside and wiped out half my village."

"What causes them?"

Hestia shrugged. "They say that's what happens when Hades gets angry."

"Well then," Elka said, "let's not anger him."

Ajani lifted an eyebrow at her. "What do you think would anger the god of the dead?" she asked.

Vorya answered for her. "Not killing anyone within reach who richly deserves it," she said with a knife-edge grin.

Elka and Vorya both laughed, sharing the same cheerfully grim sense of humor that was, I'd learned, a characteristic of the Varini tribes. I probably would have laughed too, except I was wondering just how long it would be before we'd find ourselves in that very likely situation.

In fairly short order, Vorya was curled into a ball like a sleeping pup and Elka had flopped down on the ground, the edge of her cloak tugged over her shoulder. Within moments, both of them were snoring gently. Ajani stayed where she was, sitting staring at the sky, and I . . . I was restless and thinking of Cai and the coming morn and wondering about everything.

"I'm going to go take a few hours of watch," I told Ajani quietly. "I'm too wide awake to sleep."

"Be careful," she said.

"As a fox in an open field."

"Don't forget to look up." She pointed at the star-spattered indigo sky. "That's where the hunting owl comes from."

She wasn't wrong.

I saw the horse first, tethered to a tree at the edge of the necropolis. But I heard the whine of the arrow coming from above me. And the only thing that saved me in that moment was Charon. His shoulder hit me just beneath my rib cage, knocking me from my feet and the breath from my lungs. I landed on a bare patch of earth with the bulk of his frame pinning me to the ground. Another whine and a second arrow punched into the dirt beside my head. I heaved Charon off me, and we both scrambled for cover behind a low stone wall.

"What are you doing out here?" I whispered frantically.

"Same thing you are," he grunted at me through clenched teeth.

I peered at him through the deep shadows cast by the moon and saw that his face was rigid with pain. He had one hand pressed to his flank—blood seeping between his fingers where the first arrow had found its mark. Another missile sang through the air, and I ducked belatedly.

"Do you have anything I could—"

"Here."

Charon had a throwing knife, drawn from a sheath in his boot, and I had anger and fear-fueled aim. He handed me the blade. I waited for the gleam of moonlight on the pale wood of a drawn bow, and I threw. I was rewarded with a grunt of pain, the clatter of an arrow shot far wide, and—after a long moment of silence—the scrabble of feet on gravel. Then hoofbeats receding into the distance. I sank back down to the ground and expelled a shaky breath. Then I turned to Charon, who still lay sprawled awkwardly. The arrow had pierced his side, mid-back, and come out the front, lodging in his flesh. The iron head stuck obscenely out from beneath his ribs, and the black-feathered fletching quivered with each breath he took.

I swallowed the panic welling up my throat and said, "I'll get Neferet—"

"No." His hand, clamped hard on my wrist, had lost none of its strength. His fingers were like iron bands. "Just . . . snap the shaft and pull the damned thing out. It's only a flesh wound."

I gaped at him. "Flesh wound or no, you'll still need cleaning and dressing, and I'm not the one to do it."

"Then find Quintus," he said, wincing. "He'll have a field kit in his legion pack, and he'll know how to dress a wound." Then he looked at me, his dark eyes serious. "Fallon . . . there is only a thin, fragile shell of confidence holding our company together. Weakness—any weakness—can crack that shell. You need every one of those girls to have the confidence and the commitment that we can do this thing. Or they'll start to fall away. You'll lose them. You don't want that."

I understood his logic—I'd once kept a wound hidden from Cai and the others for similar reasons—and so I couldn't really argue that particular point. Still, I shook my head. "I don't want to lose them to arrow fire, either," I said. "Them or—oddly enough—you."

"You're not about to get rid of me that easily," he said with a grin. "And if it was any more than one lone assailant, we wouldn't be having this conversation. Places like this are havens for bandits and outlaws. Whoever that was likely thought we were no more than defenseless travelers and decided to take advantage of an opportunity. When they realized that we were no easy prey—nice throw, by the way—well, you heard the hoofbeats. They're probably long gone by now. And I doubt they'll be coming back anytime soon."

I grudgingly left him there alone for the brief while it took me to track down Quint and tell him what had happened. I pointed out where Charon was and went to go find Cai. Regardless of what I'd promised Charon, I wasn't keeping this a secret from Cai. I would never again keep anything secret from him. It was a promise we'd made each other. Cai found me first, leaping soundlessly down from atop a stone crypt shrouded in wild grapevines. He landed in front of me in a crouch with his sword drawn.

"Fallon?" He stepped toward me, a frown of concern on his face. "What is it? What's happened?"

"We've had company," I said. "Charon's hurt. Quint's gone to help him, but I think you should come too."

Cai followed as I crouched low and made my way back through the necropolis.

"Where's Acheron?" I asked as we took cover behind a stand of cypress, scanning the terrain for any movement before a last dash across a stretch of open ground.

"He's positioned himself farther down the hill, toward the town," Cai said. "Making sure we don't get any late-night visitors come to pay ancestral respects."

"Good." I nodded. "One surprise tonight was too many."

Quint had his kit out and had already sawed through the arrow shaft with a small, serrated blade by the time we got there. By the light of the moon, I could see a sheen of sweat on Charon's brow, but he lay there, propped on one elbow, as if he reclined on a dining couch in the triclinium of a rich Roman villa. He even managed a sardonic smile.

"Quint?" I asked.

"It's field medicine I know," he answered. "That's all."

"It's enough," Charon said. "Stop furrowing your brow—all of you—you're going to give me a headache."

"Do you want something to bite down on?" Quint asked.

"Are you offering a finger?" Charon snapped, getting impatient with the feathered end of the shaft still protruding from his flank. "Pull the damned thing out."

I knelt in front of my erstwhile slaver and held out a hand. Wordlessly, Charon took hold of my wrist and braced himself as Quint put a knee against his spine and took a breath. Then, without so much as a warning count, he gave the thing a swift, smooth pull . . . and it was out. Charon gasped, and his head dropped forward for a moment. I helped lift the material of his tunic so that Quint could bind the wounds and saw that there was a small, neat red hole on the front of Charon's torso, just under his rib cage. And surprisingly little blood. The edges of the wound seemed to have drawn together, even as I applied an antiseptic salve of honey and yarrow from the small clay pot in Quint's field kit.

"Told you," Charon grunted as I stepped back out of the way so Quint could pack the wounds and bandage-wrap them. "And no word of this to anyone beyond us four." Quint and Cai frowned at each other, but then Charon explained his reasoning, the way he had to me, and they both agreed. They were soldiers. They understood the perils of shaky morale and the effect it could have.

"All right," I said. "We won't tell anyone else you got *shot*. But I want Sorcha to at least know about the *shooter*."

Charon raised an eyebrow at me. "Because . . . ?"

"Because that was no lone bandit like you thought it might be," I said. "That was a scout. For Aquila. His people . . . I think they're hunting us."

Quint chewed on the inside of his cheek, frowning as he listened. "What makes you think that?" he asked.

I held up the feathered end of the arrow Quint had pulled from Charon's flesh. There was a tiny mark whittled into the shaft below where the fletching was attached. A carving of an eye—only circular and feathered around the edges, like the keen eye of a hawk.

"It's Tanis's mark," I said. The name of the girl who'd once been a trusted Achillea gladiatrix was a bitter taste on my tongue. "Ajani taught her arrow-crafting—I've seen this mark dozens of times, usually at the center of a practice target."

Charon plucked the arrow shaft from my fingers and examined it closely, his gaze keen in spite of the pain. After a moment, he handed the shaft back and frowned up at me. "You think she's still with him?" he asked. "With Aquila?"

I shrugged, knowing full well she was. "She had nowhere else to go after we retook the ludus," I said. "She was alone. Friendless—"

"She declared herself his creature," Cai said, his mouth a hard, unforgiving line, "when she bartered her bow in service for her freedom."

"Or, maybe, her life," I said, wondering about this new, cold steel in him as he met my gaze. "And, let's not forget, she thinks I betrayed her."

Cai shook his head. "You didn't—"

"I *did*," I countered. "I didn't have much of a choice, but I did."

We stared at each other, waging a battle of wills that I wasn't sure I fully understood in that moment. And then Cai exhaled sharply and turned away from me, saying, "Well, there's no sense arguing that particular point at the moment—especially not if she's still lurking around somewhere. I think you two"—he looked at Charon and Quint—"should get back to camp. Tell the others about our archer friend, and make sure they're on their guard and ready to go at first light."

I nodded in agreement. "I'll take over watch until dawn."

Quint held out a hand to help Charon stand as Cai turned to me. "I'll watch with you," he said.

As they picked their way through the tumble of grave ruins, I saw Charon was moving only a little awkwardly.

But when he stumbled on a bit of uneven ground and briefly put a hand to his side, I hissed, feeling it in the scar I bore beneath my own ribs.

"It's my fault," I said, shaking my head. "She was aiming at me—and he knocked me out of the way."

"That *doesn't* make it your fault," Cai said, his tone emphatic. Almost angry. "That makes it the fault of the one who shot the arrow."

I turned and blinked at him. An uneasy tension had been building between us since I'd gone to visit him in the Ludus Flaminius. I didn't understand it, but I could feel it—like the uncomfortable pressure of a deep bruise forming beneath your skin before you can even see it.

"Tanis. Yes," I said. "*Also* my fault."

I might have sounded mulish and irrational to him in that moment, but I simply couldn't shake the image of Tanis on her knees in the rain and the mud that night we escaped the Ludus Achillea, crying out for me not to leave her as I galloped away. And maybe it was because we were sitting in the middle of a graveyard, but suddenly all of the friends—and enemies—I'd lost came back to stand in a circle around me, like the statues in my dreams. The Fury. Meriel. Leander. Nyx . . . Nyx, who would've stabbed me through the heart and walked away whistling if she could have. I'd lost them all, one way or another. And yet, Tanis was the one I couldn't seem to shake . . .

Cai put a hand on my shoulder and turned me to face him.

He held my gaze with his own steady, unblinking one, and I saw a roil of emotion churning behind his eyes. "Listen to me, Fallon," he said, his voice low and insistent. "If you'd gone back for her that night, they would have caught you and killed you. You know that."

"I do know, Cai," I said. "I really do. But . . . that's the thing, isn't it? At least I would have gone back for her. Instead, I saved myself. She's *not* wrong in thinking I betrayed her. Tanis was terrified and alone, and I left her. After all my grand, hollow words about how we were a family, together, I failed her. If she's become a monster . . . I helped make her one."

"You also *saved* her life. Or have you forgotten that?"

I knew what he was talking about. Cleopatra's nautical spectacle, when I'd cut Tanis down from the ship rigging after she'd fallen from the yardarm and become trapped.

I shook my head. "It's not the same thing. The *naumachia* wasn't real peril. It was a game. She probably wouldn't have—"

"Stop! Fallon, just . . . *stop*. You have to stop shouldering everyone else's failings. It's a noble impulse, but . . ." He shook his head, his eyes burning into mine. "It's also dangerous hubris."

I blinked at him, startled and speechless. And suddenly angry. For him to attribute my feelings of guilt—of remorse—to that kind of . . . of *arrogance* . . . "You don't know what you're talking about," I said, and started to get up to walk away.

He grabbed me by the wrist. Not hard, but not a grip I was about to easily break. "I do," he said. "And I'm not finished. Fallon, you have to learn to let people make their own mistakes and dig their own way out of the holes they fall in. Or not. You have to stop trying to rescue everyone at the expense of your own self."

I shook my head. "That's *not* what I do—"

"Then why weren't you free and home and back with your people, living the life you always thought you were destined to live, in the weeks following Caesar's Triumphs?" he said. "Why haven't you ever accepted any of the offers of freedom set in front of you? I know why. Because you want to help people. So you stay. You do it for your sister. For your friends. You even did it for Nyx."

"I—"

"You've done it for me." His grip on my wrist loosened, but he didn't let go. "And now you're doing it for the queen of a far-off land you never even knew existed just a few years ago."

When I looked at him, I could see the deep wells of compassion in his gaze. But I also saw the glint of implacable purpose. There, in the midst of a moonwashed city of the dead, ancient shadows lingering to hear our words, Cai was going to serve me the truth about me as he saw it, whether I wanted to listen to him or not.

"Sorcha chose to serve Caesar," he continued. "The ludus girls—no fault of their own—were slaves before you ever met them. Cleopatra is a career politician and a master manipulator and knew perfectly well what she was getting into with Caesar . . . And *I* didn't wind up in the Ludus Flaminius because of you, Fallon. I got there all on my own. I don't blame you, and I refuse to let you blame yourself. That's too easy—for both of us." He let out a sigh of frustration. "We keep trying to treat each other as equals, and truthfully, we're not very good at it. But I'll be dead and damned if I'm going to let that be the thin end of the wedge that will one day drive us apart. I'm trying to change that. I'm trying to make you see—I'm trying to see for *myself*—that you can love someone and honor them and be their equal and *not* have to blame yourself for every bad thing that happens to them."

"What about all the blood on my hands, Cai?" I asked. "And all the other blood spilled because I made a wrong choice? What if one day it's Elka's, or Ajani's, or . . . what if one day it's *yours*?"

To my surprise, he smiled at that. Gently.

"My fate is mine," he said, letting go of my wrist so he could take both my hands in his and hold them tightly to his chest. "I want nothing more than to *share* it with you . . . but it's mine. And I will not let you tear yourself to pieces if and when my end comes. Because it will be *my* end, Fallon."

I didn't even have words to tell Cai the dread that filled me at the barest thought of such a thing. As we sat there, my throat began to close and the sting of unshed tears burned behind my eyes. My mind tumbled back into the past, back to a different love, a different end . . . and Cai saw it happen. Like he could read my memories as clearly as if I'd written them out the way he could, with strokes of a charcoal stick on a papyrus scroll. I closed my eyes.

But he just squeezed my hands even harder and said, "I'm *not* Maelgwyn Ironhand, Fallon. And I'm not going anywhere anytime soon."

I sucked in a sharp breath and opened my eyes at the sound of that name in his mouth, but the smile—sad and lovely and wonderful—never left Cai's lips. And his eyes never lost their compassion.

"You've been carrying his shadow on your back since before the day I first met you," he said. "And sometimes . . . sometimes, I admit, it's hard. There were times when I thought I could almost see him in your eyes."

"I . . . I didn't know that."

"In the days after we retook the ludus—after Aeddan died—it was worse." Cai's gaze faltered then, and he looked down at where our hands were clasped so tightly together between us. "For obvious reasons, of course— they were brothers, and they both loved you—and I wasn't surprised, but . . . I hated seeing you hurt. And I hated *them* because of it. I hated dead men."

I waited for him to look back up at me, searching his gaze when he did.

"Is that why you didn't even try to argue when Caesar banished you to the Ludus Flaminius?" I asked. "Because you had to get away from me and my ghosts?"

"No." He shook his head adamantly. "Oh, my dear heart, no. Leaving you was the last thing I ever wanted to do. After a while I realized that I couldn't hate them for having done the same thing I had: falling in love with you. Although, I will admit . . . it's not so easy sometimes living up to a ghost—but no. It was my *own* ghost that drove me there."

"Your father."

He nodded. "He tried to convince me that what he did was out of care for me. And there were moments—even after I put a sword through his guts—that I wanted so desperately to believe him."

"We have that in common," I said, remembering how my own father had been willing to bind me to a loveless marriage to keep me safe. What he thought of as safe, at least.

"I know," Cai said. "And it's cost us both dearly because we loved them and we honored them and we both thought—somehow—that we were blameful for their actions. But we weren't. We *aren't*. Not for anyone else. You don't have to carry around ghosts and guilt anymore, Fallon. And neither do I. Those were their choices, not yours. And not mine."

A stray night breeze picked up a strand of Cai's long hair from around the side of his face and teased it across his brow. I untangled the fingers of my right hand from his and reached up to brush the hair back from his face. With that touch, a spark ignited in his gaze. He turned his head and leaned into the palm of my hand. His lips found my wrist, and he kissed the place where my pulse beat in time with my heart. When his hands came up to pull me closer, I heard myself draw a shaking breath.

"You've never—*ever*—had anything to live up to, Caius Varro," I whispered. "Or anyone. Not with me."

Cai's head stayed dipped beneath mine as his mouth moved from my wrist to the inside of my elbow, and I shivered as he kissed the soft skin there, tipping my own head back so that I could see the stars overhead. My eyes drifted closed, and my free arm wrapped around Cai's back. My fingers traced up the twin columns of muscle along his spine, until I reached the collar of his tunic and could slip my hand beneath to feel the warmth of his skin.

"This is dangerous," I whispered.

"Horribly," he murmured, not stopping.

"Foolish . . ."

"Irresponsible . . ."

I could feel the scars on his shoulder, like runes carved on stone. My head began to swim dizzyingly as my heart beat faster. "Tanis could still be near . . ." I murmured as Cai's head lifted and he shifted his attention to my neck, kissing me just below the point of my jaw.

"We're not talking about Tanis any more tonight," he said, his voice gone husky. His hands moved up under my hair, fingers kneading the muscles at the back of my neck until I thought I might actually melt. "And anyway . . ." His teeth caught at my earlobe, sending little sparks of lightning shooting through me. "You said she rode off . . ."

"I did." My head tipped all the way back.

Cai's kisses traveled in a trail of fire down the front of my neck to the hollow at the base of my throat. "And you also said," he murmured against my skin, "you thought you might have wounded her . . ."

"I did . . ."

I fell slowly backward until I felt the moss-covered ground beneath my shoulders, and Cai leaned over me, blocking out the moon, his hair hanging forward over his face. But not enough to hide the gleam of hunger in his eyes.

"She's a coward," he said, the weight of him pressing down on me. "And she's lost the element of surprise." His breath was hot on my cheek as he lowered his face down toward mine again.

"I thought we weren't talking about her . . ." I gasped.

"We're not. Don't worry. She won't be back."

"Exactly . . ."

He made a sound like a low rumble of thunder in the back of his throat as my fingernails pressed hard into his skin, and I seriously considered adding to his collection of scars.

"Wait . . ." I dragged my nails across his shoulder blades, decision made. "How can you be so sure?"

He gasped, spine arching, and said, "Call it a soldier's instinct."

"You're not a soldier anymore."

"And you're not a slave." He paused to look me in the eyes, and I could almost feel the heat of that gaze on my face. "I'm no longer a patrician, and even if you are still a princess . . ."

"I'm not." I grinned up at him. "I can assure you."

"And we are together, alone, just us. With a roof of stars over our head and hours left until dawn. Just Fallon and Cai. For the first and—the way things are going—maybe last time for a long while . . . and I intend to take full advantage of that."

I closed my eyes, drowning in a kind of bliss I'd never really known before as his hands traced the contours of my waist and hips, up the sides of my ribs. I felt his fingers tugging at the lacing on the front of my tunic. I lifted a hand to help with the knots and opened my eyes . . .

And froze.

A pair of wide yellow eyes, glowing in the moonlight, stared down at us from less than three arms' lengths away.

"Cai . . ." I whispered.

He didn't seem to hear me.

"*Cai* . . ."

"Fallon? What—"

"Shh!"

I nodded my chin up, without taking my eyes off the large gray wolf that stared back at me and huffed out a breath of blue mist through quivering nostrils. I could feel Cai's arm muscles tense and heard the scrape of stone on stone as he picked up a rock. The wolf tilted his head and let out a low warning whine. Cai tossed the rock—not even attempting to hit the creature, more just to send a warning back—and the beast huffed again and backed up on shifting paws. Then he yawned, as if bored by a pair of silly lovestruck humans, and loped away with his tongue hanging out the side of his mouth.

Cai sat up, frowning. "I think he was laughing at us."

"If he was, he had every right to do so," I said ruefully, sitting up on my elbows and trying to catch back some of the breath Cai had stolen from me. "Some night watch we are. If a *wolf* can get that close . . ."

Cai picked up the fletched end of Tanis's arrow shaft from where it lay in the ground and held it up between us.

"Then a jackal might too."

I shifted up onto my knees, plucking the broken arrow from Cai's fingers and sighing. "I swear . . . if I even spot a jackal at a distance when we get to Alexandria . . ." I threw the shaft into the weeds.

"I wouldn't worry," Cai said, standing and stretching and holding out a hand to help me do the same. "All the jackals there are in the temples, guarding the gates to the underworld. All we have to do is stay alive, and they won't bother with us."

"Why does that sound like a task easier said than done?" I asked.

In the near distance, the wolf howled. But if it was in answer to my question, I couldn't understand what he was trying to tell me.

XIV

WE WERE MORE than half a day out from Tarquinii without any further trouble and only fifteen or so miles away from Cosa when Charon, driving the lead wagon, called a brief halt before we reached our destination. I kept glancing at him surreptitiously as we stopped and dismounted to ease our cramped muscles and water the horses. He was a bit on the pale side, but his features weren't drawn in pain, and—more to the point—Sorcha didn't seem to think there was anything amiss. And she'd been sitting up beside him on the driver's bench the whole time we'd been on the move.

I breathed a sigh of relief that, in light of the conversation—not to say argument—Cai and I'd had in the night that I wouldn't have another guilty bruise to add to my tender conscience.

I wiped the sweat from my brow and nodded thanks to Acheron, dismounting as he came to take my horse over to picket with the others while we rested. There was a flat, scrubby patch of ground at the edge of the road and a little tumbling brook running through the field beyond. It was clearly a place that had been used as a way station by countless travelers before us and a good spot to check the horses' hooves for any stones or bruising, as well as to feed and water them. A cluster of elm trees offered a welcome bit of shelter—a windbreak for Cleopatra to rest out of the reach of an incessant chill breeze that had dogged our journey all morning and into the afternoon. But the queen refused to take her ease until she'd helped Damya and Gratia set out a small feast of meat and cheese and bread from the Achillea larders for everyone to refresh themselves. I shook my head in wonder as Sorcha came to stand beside me.

"Look at her," I said, nodding my chin in the queen's direction.

"Still fresh as a lily." Sorcha grinned wryly. "I know."

"How does she do that?"

Sorcha shrugged. "She's a daughter of the gods. How else?"

I shook my head in wonder, gazing around at the rest of our company, who were uniformly road-dusty and bedraggled . . . and, unfortunately, destined to stay that way.

"Sorcha . . ."

She turned sharply at the tone of my voice.

I lifted an arm and pointed wordlessly in the direction we'd just come from. At the cluster of black dots on the horizon to the south of us. Moving fast.

"Pack everything back up," she said.

I didn't even need the warning the Morrigan whispered in my ear. I *knew* what was coming. Sorcha knew too. Without another word, we both took off sprinting, Sorcha toward Cleopatra and me toward Antonia and Neferet, who'd flopped down on the ground not far from me, resting tired backs and legs.

"We have to go," I said, reaching down to pull Neferet to her feet. "Now."

Antonia frowned up at me, and I hooked a thumb over my shoulder. "Riders approaching," I said. "Fast."

"How do we know they're after us?" Neferet asked, squinting into the distance. "This is the main road north—"

"They are. Believe me." There was, of course, every chance that the riders were simply fellow travelers on the road. Merchants or citizens, maybe traveling fast—as we were—to get away from the turmoil in the capital. But I wasn't willing to take the risk.

"But how would they have known which direction we went in the first place?" Antonia wondered, shading her eyes from the sun. "We could have gone anywhere—"

"Just get to the wagons," I said, and hurried to round up the others.

The answer to Antonia's question was that anyone traveling north up the Via Clodia from Rome would have seen the smoke from the Ludus Achillea from a good long distance. Anyone looking for *us* would have been watching the road going south. When we didn't pass that way, it would have been easy to deduce that our path was either west to Cosa or overland to the east costal port of Ancona on the Mare Adriaticum. The road east was harder going and would have slowed us down, but the rugged terrain also would have offered more places to hide from pursuit. I wondered, in that moment, if maybe we shouldn't have gone that way. Maybe I'd missed a trick. Maybe when Charon had said Cosa, I should have argued . . .

And then I remembered what Cai and I had talked about only a few hours earlier. It hadn't been my decision alone to make. It had been mine and Sorcha's and, well, everyone's, really. Cleopatra's most of all. And *she* trusted me. They all did. Maybe it was time I started trusting myself . . .

No, I thought. *Maybe it's time you started trusting others.*

My friends. My sisters and comrades.

We were better than this—than *them*. Better than Aquila's thugs and traitors and fanatics. We were the queen of Aegypt's gladiatrix guard, and we would defend her with our honor and our lives.

From where he was taking care of the animals with Acheron and Quint, Cai saw me hurrying and loped over to meet me. "Fallon?" he called.

"Riders," I answered back.

He glanced behind me, into the far distance down the road, and his mouth set in a hard line. Then he spun on his heel and headed back toward the horses. "Get the wagons hitched back up," he called to Quint as he went. "On the double."

"What's going on?" Acheron asked as I ran toward my own mount.

"Company's coming," I said over my shoulder, not stopping. "Fast."

Elka and Ajani didn't even bother to ask when I told them to pack up. Neither did Cleopatra. Sennefer just sighed gustily and began gathering up the repast his mistress had just laid out. It took us very little time to get everyone ready and moving again.

I reached my horse and tightened the girth strap on his saddle again. He whinnied at me in protest, and I apologized for the brevity of the break. Then I vaulted into the saddle, shortening the reins until he danced in a half circle and pawed impatiently at the ground. The rest of the company was back aboard the wagons and ready to go, and they all looked to me for orders. I swallowed my uncertainly, raising my voice so they could all hear.

"Whatever happens, no stopping. No slowing," I said. I took a deep breath in before I finished. "No going back for the fallen."

Sitting beside Charon in the lead wagon, Sorcha gave me a firm nod. Elka raised an eyebrow at me but kept silent. She knew as well as I did that if we lost anyone on that road, then we'd lose them for good.

The road was wide enough at that point that those of us who were mounted on horseback could still ride flanking the three wagons. So Hestia and Acheron took up outrider positions on the left flank of the caravan, while Quint and I took up corresponding positions on the right. Cai rode lead, far enough out to warn of any danger up ahead. It wasn't long before we came to a bend in the road that led us into a twisty, shallow valley. The hills closed in, hiding us from the sight of our pursuers. But it also hid our pursuers from us. For a tense few miles, I had no idea if they were still following or how fast. But soon enough, the hills receded and the Roman road unwound itself again, cutting arrow-straight across the middle of a landscape that was shaped almost like a bowl—like a vast meadow cradled in a ring of hills.

It reminded me of an arena.

One carved from the land by the gods themselves.

As we rode, I kept glancing over my shoulder. It wasn't long before the first of the riders emerged from the valley bend behind us. Closer than they had been. Much closer. Dressed in the signature black cloaks and armor of Pontius Aquila's Dis acolytes, and riding flat out.

"They've picked up speed," I called to Cai, who'd dropped back to ride beside me. "They'll overtake us before we get to the next mile marker."

"Let's move!" He put his heels to his mount and gave the horse his head.

Cai thundered ahead of the caravan, and I signaled to Charon as I rode up beside the lead cart. He lashed the horses, urging them on to greater speed. Damya and Gratia, driving the other two wagons, followed his lead. But with three wagons loaded down with passengers and gear, we were never going to outrun our pursuers. When they got close enough, the arrows began to fly.

Tanis . . .

The Ludus Achillea's wayward archer. From galloping horseback, she couldn't aim with any great accuracy, but Tanis could still manage to keep Ajani and Elka pinned down, unable to return much fire as the first of their riders to reach us pounded up to bracket the rear wagon. I was far enough out that I saw it all as one of them reached for the side to pull himself aboard. Kronos lunged to grapple with the man, but the wagon was bucking all over the road and the rider managed to grab Kronos by the wrists. He almost pulled him right off the back of the cart, but Ajani lurched to her feet and smashed the rider over the head with the short curved bow she carried, wielding it like a club.

The man tumbled instantly from the back of his horse, dead or unconscious, and Ajani's bow was broken in two. In that moment, another rider grabbed hold of Vorya. He clutched at her tunic as Vorya raised her sword to strike, but she couldn't get any solid footing in the lurching wagon. As a wheel hit a rut, she fell forward, and there was nothing to stop her . . .

Nothing but the rider's blade, thrust to the hilt between Vorya's ribs.

"*No!*" I screamed out in denial as her eyes went wide and the rider wrenched his bloody sword from her flesh. "*Vorya!*"

She fell in a kind of graceful arc, like a dancer, and then hit the ground with such violence that her body bounced and contorted, tumbling beneath the hooves of another attacker's horse. Nephele, who'd been beside her in the cart, lunged for the man who'd killed Vorya and, with a cry of pure rage, thrust her dagger straight through his eye. The man screamed and fell, arms and legs bent and twisting, and Ceto and Lysa—the two newest girls from the ludus, who'd only just taken the oath a month earlier—leaped forward to grab Nephele before her momentum tumbled her from the wagon too.

Choking on rage and road dust, I heard the whine of another arrow. It arced just above Lysa's head as the girls slammed themselves flat to the floor of the careening cart. Up front on the bench seat, Gratia hunched her shoulders up around her ears and bent low over the reins, driving with grim determination as another shot grazed the rump of one of her horses. We needed to be able to return arrow fire or Tanis would just pick us off one by one, but Ajani had packed her longbow for travel and stowed it in the forward cart, with some of the other gear. It might as well have been left back at the ludus for all the good it did there.

I hauled hard on the reins of my horse and veered sharply toward the last wagon, shouting, "Ajani—to me! I'll get you to your other bow!"

Ajani scrambled and clambered over the other girls in the wagon bed to get to me, and I maneuvered in as tightly as I could between the spinning wheels of the cart. Without hesitation, she threw herself over the side boards and onto the back of my mount, wrapping her arms around my waist and holding tight. We peeled away at a sharp angle as Kore and Thalassa lurched over Ceto and Lysa, howling war cries. There were two more attackers climbing up the back of the wagon, and the pair of Cretan gladiatrices fell upon them with raw ferocity.

I glanced over my shoulder and saw the rest of the Dis riders closing the gap on our band. Three of them broke left and thundered past our last wagon, angling to overtake the lead one. But they abruptly changed tack when Acheron appeared across from me, galloping madly.

"Protect the queen!" he shouted frantically, gesturing to where she was hunkered down in the middle wagon, hidden from sight by a circle of six Amazons laden with weapons. "Protect Cleopatra!"

I immediately wished he'd kept his mouth shut.

If the Dis riders had believed it was just a pack of Caesar's worthless gladiatrices they were after, there might have been a slim chance they would have given up the chase if we'd made things too hard on them. That was no longer even a remote possibility. Not when the great Aegyptian whore rode in a wagon just within their grasp.

I didn't have time to explain that to Acheron.

I had to get Ajani her bow.

And the Dis riders had plainly gotten his unintended message anyway.

They tried to surround Cleopatra's cart as Damya, up on the driver's bench, shouted curses. Up ahead, the hills had begun to encroach again. We were heading toward another steep-sided valley. I lashed my horse faster and pulled up beside the lead cart, and Ajani flung herself aboard, grasping at Devana's and Anat's hands for help. Neferet was already digging in one of the travel trunks for

Ajani's bow and quiver, with Antonia—her scythe blade strapped to her arm—there to watch her back. Neferet found the longbow, and I left them to it, dropping back to help Cai and Quint protect the middle wagon with its precious royal occupant.

Kallista and her Amazon sisters stuck to the queen like bees on honey, shielding her from all angles with their own flesh, but that left only Elka—up on her knees on the driver's bench beside Damya—to fend off the attackers. As I came abreast of one of the Dis riders, Elka brought the shaft of her spear crashing down on his helmeted head. The rider dropped sideways off his mount, and the horse veered into mine, nearly throwing me.

An arrow sang past my ear.

And then another. The second one punched through the large muscle of Damya's upper right arm, drawing a bright arc of blood and a full-throated roar of pain. Quint saw the hit and pulled his horse alongside the driver's bench.

"Move over!" he shouted to Damya.

She slid out of the way, handing him the reins with her left hand.

"Ajani!" I called. "We need cover fire! Any day now!"

She ignored me, concentrating on stringing her weapon and setting her quiver. When one of the cart's wheels hit a stone and sent her arrows clattering, Devana and Anat scrambled to gather them for her.

And then suddenly, she was up on her feet, legs braced wide . . .

Firing in rapid succession . . .

Cries of pain announced that we suddenly had a bit of breathing space. The hills in front of us folded sharply upward, and the road would soon be restricted to the width of a single wagon. I shot another glance over my shoulder and saw Tanis angle off, racing toward a steep path that led up into the hills instead of through the narrow valley. I waved an arm at Hestia, who pulled hard on her reins and sent her mount galloping after her.

"Acheron!" I shouted. "Follow Hestia—and *stop those arrows!*"

If Tanis were to achieve a high vantage from which to shoot, we were in a lot of trouble. A lot *more* trouble. But for the moment, we had Ajani. She pegged another two riders and sent them flying off the backs of their horses . . . but there was one who still managed to slip through. The rider put a whip and his heels to his horse and shot past me, angling toward the lead wagon, overtaking it and pulling abreast of the horses. Slashing at the beasts with his sword from the back of his own mount did little good, though— he couldn't get close enough to inflict more than superficial wounds, and the animals knew enough to know that they were under attack, and they would run full out until they were either mortally wounded or dropped from exhaustion. So he turned his attention, instead, to their reins.

I spat a curse and lashed my lathered horse to greater speed. If the bastard managed to cut the reins or cut the horses loose altogether, we were lost. The road was far too narrow at that point for the following wagons to even steer around a crash. One horse down or disabled would mean a catastrophic pileup, and all would be lost. But it wasn't an easy feat to just cut the reins. He would have to lean so far out over the back of the yoked, galloping pair that a single misstep from either horse would throw him under the wagon. In fact, anyone sane wouldn't have attempted what he was trying to do. But Aquila's Sons of Dis were fanatics, so sanity wasn't really an issue.

Apparently, it wasn't really one for *me* either . . .

As Sorcha helpfully pointed out, shouting, "Fallon, stop! You're mad!"

Maybe, but I wasn't about to stop. I galloped up beside the rider hacking at the reins and flung myself from the back of my horse onto his—knocking him from his saddle. I almost fell with him but managed to grip the mane of his horse, winding my fingers tight in the horsehair as, beneath me, the Dis rider grappled desperately, clutching the side of the saddle girth strap with one hand and the harness of the wagon horse with the other. Both animals were panicked and running full out, but the rider clung on grimly, hanging faceup between the two beasts and kicking his feet, trying to hook them onto the harness.

I heard myself snarl, looking down on him as I righted myself in his vacated saddle. We locked eyes for a brief moment, and I saw the maniacal hatred in his gaze, unmitigated by fear . . .

I lifted my knee and drove the heel of my boot down into his face.

His scream as he lost his grip and fell was brief, truncated mid-cry when the wagon wheels ran him over. But even though he hadn't managed to sever the reins, he had managed to pull them free from Charon's grip. I looked down and saw that the reins were trailing uselessly on the ground between the galloping beasts. Without a firm hand guiding them both, the horses were running wild, and it was only a matter of time before, in their panicked state, a swerve or a misstep ended in bone-crushing disaster. Charon was leaning out over the front boards of the wagon, reaching for all he was worth, arm outstretched and fingers splayed wide, but he wasn't even close.

The wagon was runaway, and there was no stopping it.

My own horse pounded along behind the mount I'd appropriated, running full out even though he was riderless, because there was nowhere else to go but forward. Soon there would be no room for the horse I was on. The only thing for me to do was to switch mounts again—this time to the yoked wagon horse running beside me. The steep walls of the pass soared up on either side, closer and closer. I hitched my legs up under me and leaped—

Just as two more arrows split the air.

The first missed. The second laid a fiery kiss along the top of my shoulder, the razor-sharp point slicing through the fabric of both my cloak and my tunic and carving a searing gash in my flesh. The sudden bloom of pain made me twist midair and overshoot my target. I slewed across the draft horse's broad withers and barely managed to grasp a handful of harness before tumbling off the other side and down between the two galloping beasts.

"Morrigan's teeth!" I swore, hanging half upside down, with a clear view of Tanis on horseback, galloping along the top of the valley ridge high above. "Damn it, Hestia! Where *are* you . . ."

I snarled through my teeth, kicking my feet as I struggled to right myself. After that, there wasn't much I could do but hang on. Draft horses didn't exactly respond to the pressure of a rider's knee and heel.

"Macha . . ." I ground out the first of the three sacred names of the Morrigan, my jaw clenched to keep my teeth from rattling out of my head. "Macha, Nemain . . . Badb Catha . . ." I despaired of the goddess hearing me over the thunder of hooves and wheels. "Hear me, my goddess . . . Help me save my friends. Send me your strength . . . Send me help! Take my blood, take anything you want from me . . . Raven of Battles . . . *help me!*"

My grip was failing. In another moment I would fall. The horses would falter. All would be lost . . .

And then, the Morrigan answered my prayer.

XV

"FALLON!"

I twisted and looked over my other shoulder to see that Sorcha had thrown a leg out over the front boards of the wagon. Charon was shouting at her to stop, but she ignored him and edged out onto the yoke pole that ran between the horses.

"Fallon!" she called to me again. "Stay where you are! I'm coming out . . ."

I didn't have much choice *but* to stay where I was, crouched and clinging to the back of the wagon horse like a burr. My hair, torn from my braid by the wind, whipped into my eyes, and blood was running down my arm from the arrow crease on my shoulder. Sorcha was coming to save me, but the last time my sister had tried anything like the risky stunt she was about to attempt, it had been performing the Morrigan's Flight in the Circus Maximus for the entertainment of the masses rather than the life and death of her friends. And she'd failed. Fallen. The chariot wheels had rolled over her, and she'd never completely recovered from her injuries.

No, I thought. *When I prayed for help from the Morrigan, this is* not *what I meant.*

But the Morrigan sent what help she saw fit. That was not for me to decide. I had asked . . . and this was her answer.

Sorcha . . .

The cloak she wore whirled madly around her, catching at her limbs, and she reached up and tore it from her throat. The wind caught it and spun it up into the sky like a great bird, wings spread wide. Her face a rigid grimace of fierce concentration, Sorcha edged farther out onto the rattling yoke pole. She tilted her head, squinting with her bad eye as if she were having trouble judging the distance between her outstretched foot and the pole. I held my breath. She was Sorcha. My warrior sister. Legend of my tribe and hero of the sands of Rome's arenas. The accident had been a fluke. Sorcha didn't even need her eyes, I told myself, she could do this blindfolded. And I almost believed it.

So did she.

She made it almost all the way out to the yoke that tethered the two galloping horses together when suddenly the far horse stumbled—a small misstep, barely a jostle—and Charon cried out in alarm. Sorcha's arms circled madly in the air as she tried to right herself and she toppled, falling between the two horses, and slamming the side of her head—*hard*—on the edge of the wooden yoke . . .

Her panicked scream cut short the instant she realized I had her.

And I wasn't about to let go.

I could feel the cords of muscle and tendons in Sorcha's wrist beneath the vise-clamp of my fingers as I held on to her with every ounce of strength I possessed. Sorcha's legs kicked and swung wildly through the air until she managed to gain a precarious foothold again. She steadied herself and looked over at me. Blood from a deep gash at her hairline painted half her face red, running into her dim eye, but she flashed a tight grin.

"There's a bit of rust on the old sword . . ." she panted.

"But it still has an edge," I finished for her, grinning back, my face full of horse mane and my own wild hair. "The Morrigan be praised."

"I'm going to hand you the reins," she said. "Be ready . . ."

I let go of her wrist, and she dropped into a crouch on the yoke pole. The lathered flanks of the galloping horses, so close on either side of her, heaved like the bellows in a blacksmith's forge. Teeth gritted, jaw muscles clenched, Sorcha leaned down, fingers splayed and reaching for the trailing reins. Sweat ran from her skin like rain. Her first attempt fell short. So did the second. Then . . . with a cry torn from the center of her chest, she made one last, desperate grab—

Success!

Sorcha flung her arm out, whipping the outside rein up around my horse's neck, and I caught it, grasping frantically at the leather with sweat-slick fingers. She threw me the inside rein next, and I hauled them up short—gradually, carefully—even as the horse, sensing a guiding hand on the reins again, instinctively, exhaustedly, began to slow. The second horse followed his lead.

The wagon slowed, finally, to a halt.

I looked back to see that the rest of the Dis riders had retreated. Their numbers were diminished by Ajani's arrow fire, and the narrow valley was no place to stage an attack. With any luck, I thought, we could make it the rest of the way to Cosa before they had a chance to regroup.

The wagon horses stamped and snorted as Cai galloped up beside us, pulling his horse to a rearing stop, then catching me around the waist as I leaned from the back of the wagon horse and fell into his arms. On the other side of the wagon, Charon swung himself down from the driver's bench and ran to help Sorcha extricate herself from the tangle of harnesses and horses.

"The queen . . ." I gasped into Cai's chest. "Take me to her."

He wheeled his mount, and we cantered back over to the middle cart, dismounting to assess any damage or injuries and hoping for the best. My contingent of Amazons remained mostly intact. Kallista sported a blossoming purple bruise along her jawline, and Selene had blood in her hair and at the corner of her mouth, but the other four seemed fine as they clambered to their feet, still surrounding their charge with a protective wall of Amazonian wrath.

At the center of their circle, Sennefer stirred and drew back the voluminous robes he'd thrown like a shield over the queen. Cleopatra sat on the floor of the cart with her knees drawn up to her chin and her arms wrapped over her head. Freed from Sennefer's protective encumbrance, she stood—slowly, but without the assistance of all the hands reaching out to help—her eyes glittering like shards of onyx.

The arrows had stopped raining down, and I silently blessed Hestia and Acheron, as Cai held out an arm to help the queen down from the cart. Cleopatra accepted his help, stepping daintily to the road. She was about to nod her thanks when a heavy groaning sound came from the far side of the wagon. Her wide eyes met mine, and I gestured to stay where she was and circled around to see what had made the noise.

I looked down to see that one of the Dis riders had, it seemed, gotten his cloak caught on the hinge of the wagon's back board and been dragged for some way behind it. The man lay upon the ground, covered in scrapes and road dust, his arm bent at an unnatural angle beneath him, but otherwise he appeared relatively unharmed. He glared up at me, eyes clouded with pain, chest heaving. When his gaze suddenly shifted, I realized that Cleopatra had followed me and was standing at my side.

"Majesty—"

She lifted a hand to silence me.

Then she walked up to him, her gait purposeful but unhurried, her azure blue cloak flowing majestically in her wake. I watched as she drew a small, jeweled dagger from her belt and cut the fabric of the rider's cloak, releasing him. He slumped to the ground and she crouched before him, lifting the man's head up by his hair.

"You know who I am?" she asked.

The man nodded.

"Good," she said. "Then tell your dark god when you meet him that it was I who sent you to his realm." Then the queen of Aegypt calmly slit the man's throat from ear to ear.

A thunderous silence descended upon us all as Cleopatra stood, sidestepped the blood spreading in a pool beneath the body, and handed her dagger to Sennefer so he could wipe the blade clean. As she made her way back to the wagon, he knelt and used the dead man's cloak to do so. Then he spat on the corpse and, smoothing a crease from his flowing robes, turned to follow after his queen. Cai watched the two of them climb back into the wagon and then turned to me, a rueful expression on his face.

"I understand her anger," he said to me in a low murmur, "but we could have at least gotten some information out of him *before* she cut his throat."

I sighed, nodding in agreement, but it was a rather moot point.

There was nothing for us to do but carry on and hope the message left behind by the queen might deter any of his friends who decided to continue the hunt. Cai and I doubled up on his mount—mine had bolted and was nowhere to be seen, nor was there time to go back to look—and we moved out in short order, continuing on our way toward Cosa.

We brought up the rear while the rest of the cara-van rumbled along ahead of us, with Quint riding point. After Cleopatra's execution of the Dis rider, we'd wasted no time tending to wounds beyond rudimentary ban-daging and washing the blood from Sorcha's face with water from one of the skins we'd hastily filled. There would be opportunity enough for Neferet to work her medical magic later, hopefully. Once we were on board a ship and safely away from the shores of Italia.

Cai's arms were wrapped around me, and it was tempting to just lean back against his chest and close my eyes as we rode, but I couldn't relax. Not yet. "I'm start-ing to worry about Hestia," I said. "And—"

I was about to say "Acheron," but then I heard him, hallooing us from a distance. I twisted in the saddle to see him riding down a steep path from the top of the ridge of hills. He was covered in dust and leading Hestia's mount—her riderless mount—and there were blood-stains on Acheron's hands and arms. I felt my guts grow cold. His expression was grim, and there was a black-feathered arrow shoved through his belt. Cai pulled his horse to a stop, and we waited until he'd caught up to us.

"I'm sorry," Acheron said, and pulled the arrow from his belt, holding it out to me. The iron point was stained with blood. "They got too far ahead of me. When I caught up . . ."

The arrow in his hand was like a poisonous viper, and I shrank from it. "Where is Tanis?" was all I could ask. "The archer—where is she?"

He just shook his head.

"*You lose some along the way*," Charon had once said to me. It was after Meriel had fallen, saving me from Nyx's sword. Now calm, steady, capable Hestia was lost. And wry, wintry, methodically dangerous Vorya. I was losing too many.

"What happened?" Cai asked, when I couldn't.

"I found the girl—Hestia, was it?—on the ground," Acheron said. "With this arrow through her heart. No sign of the archer. I took the time to pile what rocks I could find over her. You know. To discourage scavengers . . ." He looked at me, an expression of helplessness in his eyes. "I'm sorry, Victrix."

I nodded, wondering . . . was Hestia's sacrifice part of the price the Morrigan demanded of my prayer? What more would she ask me to pay? I dismounted and reached for the black-feathered arrow Acheron held. He gave it to me, and I snapped it in two over my knee, hurling its pieces into the scrub with a snarled curse.

I mounted up on Hestia's horse and turned to Cai. "Let's get out of here," I said.

We arrived in Cosa to an eerily calm market square. The port settlement, nestled in the harbor below the actual town, was one of those hardscrabble places where every-one kept to themselves, avoiding too much familiarity or even, in most cases, simple eye contact. What I knew of its history was that, never hugely popular due to its relative proximity to Ostia, Cosa had, some twenty years earlier, endured a string of bad luck: an earthquake, a full-scale pirate sacking, and a plague of vermin. It showed. While the forbidding structures of temples loomed over the town from a high hill, down along the shoreline most of the houses and shops were squat, ugly, makeshift structures that looked like they might blow over in a good stiff breeze. The whole place smelled of rancid fish sauce.

The place, Cai told me, was a den of thieves and scoundrels. Perfect for making bargains with very few questions asked. The folk of the town came and went about their business, eyes averted, browsing the stalls and ignoring our wagons. As if it were just any other day, I thought, and not the beginning of the end of the Republic as they knew it. News, it seemed, had yet to really travel as far north as this little seaside settlement. I did notice one or two groups of men—soldiers or men with the bearing of ex-legionnaires—huddled in clusters of urgent conversation.

But word clearly hadn't filtered out to the general citizenry, and that was cause for relief. Because even here, the plebs had heard of the Aegyptian queen and her sorceress's sway over Julius Caesar. Word of his death wouldn't take long to spark the kind of gossipy tinder that could light a bonfire of fear. Or worse, avarice. With her hood pulled far up over her face, Cleopatra was as anonymous as any of us, but for her kohl-rimmed eyes, which stared out from the shadows of her cowl with an intensity a blind man could feel. I sent up silent prayers to the Morrigan and Minerva and Sekhemet that we could just get her aboard a ship without incident.

We rolled through the rutted streets of the town, and I felt like there were eyes watching us from every shadowed doorway. I rode beside the queen's wagon, where Elka had taken over the reins. She glanced over at me.

"If this all goes south," she said in a low voice, "I say we just get out of Her Majesty's way and let her unleash all that wrath she's carrying around. This place wouldn't stand a chance."

I laughed a little, but she wasn't wrong. I still had the image of the queen cutting that man's throat in the forefront of my mind. Cleopatra was no wilting lily, that was certain. And I'd heard tales of the terrible things her unfettered anger had wrought in her own country from time to time.

I nudged my horse into a trot and pulled up beside the lead wagon as we reached a shabby wharf that still boasted more than a half dozen vessels at berth of varying shapes and sizes, plus a few more out in the harbor, coming and going. Our caravan rumbled to a stop, and Charon and I exchanged a glance as I dismounted and he swung himself down from the driver's bench. Sorcha was in no shape to accompany him, not with her head wrapped in a linen bandage from Neferet's surgeon's bag, and we decided that—for appearance's sake—the men should stay guarding the wagons while Charon conducted business. That way we could hopefully maintain the illusion of Charon's slave trader origins, while in reality trying to secure passage for some fifteen gladiatrices, six Amazons, two ex-legionnaires, a fugitive gladiator, a eunuch, and the queen of Aegypt.

"Shall we?" Charon said, gesturing to the docks.

I loosened my swords in their scabbards beneath my cloak, while I adopted a deferential attitude to him, walking slightly behind as if he owned me. But, as it happened, we didn't actually have to fight our way onto a ship. Thanks to Charon's artful persuasion—his "asking politely"—there was a shipmaster in Cosa who was happy to take us aboard for passage. Well, perhaps "happy" was too strong a word.

From where I stood meekly behind him, I craned my neck so that I could hear what passed between Charon and the captain of the large, low-slung merchant galley that was moored directly in front of us. She had the look of a fast vessel, and I'd felt a surge of optimism as we approached. All I had to do was stand by and wait for Charon to work his devious magic. Most of which seemed to consist of him being rather upfront with the captain.

To a point . . .

"You know me, Darius," Charon was saying. "I deal straight."

"Aye," the man he'd called Darius grunted. "Straighter'n most for all you're a slaver."

Charon let that go without comment. "Will you allow me and mine the use of your ship and crew?" he asked. "We need transport out of Italia."

Darius sniffed, rubbing at his ear and seeming to con-template the request. I could tell he smelled the money in it, in spite of Charon's deceptively casual demeanor. "Where're you headed?" he asked.

"South. Beyond that, I'll tell you when we're cast off and well away."

Darius's eyes narrowed, but I could tell the scent of *denarii* was strong in his nostrils. "When?" he asked.

"With the next tide."

"But that's"—Darius glanced from Charon to the har-bor and back again—"within the hour!"

"So it is."

"Too soon." The shipmaster shook his head. "No. No . . . Not enough time. We've no extra provisions laid in. No food, no water—"

"Then it'll be a hungry trip," Charon cut him short. "But worth your effort. *More* than worth it, I promise you."

Darius's calloused fingers departed his ear and roamed over his head, scratching at the back of his neck and then the scruff on his chin as he chewed over Charon's extraor-dinary request, thinking. "Well, we could put in at Ostia, I suppose—"

"No. No coastal Italia ports of call until Messana."

"Wh-what?" the master sputtered. "No coastal ports? You mean sail by way of Sardinia? That'll double our trav-eling time! At least! You're mad. I'll have a mutiny on my hands—"

"Listen to me"—Charon clamped a hand on Darius's shoulder—"and listen well, old friend. At the end of this journey you will be handsomely paid. I promise you that. Far beyond what you're expecting. And you'd be wise to leave these lands for a while yourself, regardless. I've friends in Ephesus and Carthage—and elsewhere—who'd be happy to trade with you. Half my own fleet is docked at Lepsis Magna right now. I can write letters, make introductions . . . Believe me when I tell you that the Romans are soon to be a bit too occupied with backstabbing and bloodletting to care much about trade."

Darius said nothing for a long moment. When he spoke again his tone was carefully neutral—a tone I suspected most men would adopt when speaking of Caesar for the next little while, until loyalties were known. "So it's true then," he said. "The great tyrant's dead."

Charon nodded. "And we must look to our own interests."

"I heard a whisper on the wind only an hour or so gone," Darius murmured, shaking his head, "but I just assumed it was rumor. Idle gossip. Maybe a bit of wishful wondering . . ."

"Do we have a deal?" Charon asked.

Darius frowned deeply, and for a long moment, I thought he would say no. But after a bit of negotiating, an agreement was inevitably reached. The negotiations included a hefty price per head and the wagons and horses we'd ridden in on. Which really wasn't a problem. We wouldn't be needing them again. Satisfied with the price he would receive, Darius turned his attention over Charon's shoulder to the wagons—and their occupants.

"Is that what this is, then?" Darius asked. "You're off to sell a pack of girls?"

"Never mind the girls," Charon said. "Can we go aboard? Time is of the essence . . ."

"You'll have to wait while we finish unloading what cargo we shipped in with." Darius waved toward the sparsely populated southern end of the wharf. "You can wait out of the way until that's done."

Charon visibly reined in his impatience and said, "Be quick about it, then. Before the tide or my mind changes."

XVI

I COULDN'T KEEP the anxious fluttering in my chest from moving up into my throat as we waited and waited and the tide rose higher and higher. Soon it would begin to turn, racing with the afternoon sun back out to sea, and we needed to go with it. The last time I'd been on a dock, waiting for the moment to board and cast off, I'd been ambushed.

And Meriel had died.

I paced and fidgeted and finally hunkered down in the lee of Cleopatra's wagon and pulled a whetstone from the pouch at my belt. I figured, to pass the time, I'd sharpen one of the already perfectly sharp weapons I bore.

"I hate boats," Elka sighed, sliding down to crouch beside me.

I snorted and was about to point out just how much fun we'd had during Cleopatra's naumachia, but it suddenly became clear that the dock where we waited was far less deserted than any of us had thought. This time when

Tanis struck, relentless as a toothache, there was no warning from the Morrigan.

No whisper in my ear . . .

But I heard the arrow's hiss and ducked as the black-fletched shaft sank with a thud into the side board of the wagon, just beside my head. Elka and I exchanged a surprised glance as another one clattered off the iron wheel hub and grazed my thigh. Cai's horse screamed a warning whinny and reared violently, throwing him from the saddle to land hard on the uneven cobbles. Quint shouted his name and leaped from his own saddle to help. Everyone in the other carts ducked for cover, and Elka and I scrambled up into Cleopatra's wagon, diving flat behind the high wooden sides.

At first, I wasn't sure where the arrow fire was coming from—the missiles seemed to have more than one trajectory—but Ajani knew.

"There!" she said, pointing. "She's on the roof and running. She can target us from different vantages. So long as she has arrows, she can keep us pinned down. And if I know her mind, she has a *lot* of arrows."

"Wonderful," I muttered.

I doubted very much that Tanis was alone. If I were her, I thought, I wouldn't risk attacking us single-handedly. Rather, I guessed she'd doubled back after murdering Hestia and losing Acheron, and gathered the remaining members of her Dis fellows. They could be waiting for us anywhere. In any doorway, any alley . . .

"Ajani, can you—"

She shook her head, her brow creased in frustration. "My quiver's near empty," she said. "And she has all the cover. We're fish in a fountain waiting to be speared here. Someone's got to draw her off."

I scanned the faces of the Amazon girls who still clustered around Cleopatra in the wagon bed, keeping her hidden behind the relative safety of her stacks of traveling trunks. Three of them, including Selene, were tall. Too tall for what I had in mind—Tanis had seen the queen enough times at the Ludus Achillea to be familiar with Cleopatra's build. Two were less than my height, but broad-shouldered. And then there was Kallista. Wiry, lean-muscled, and fleet-footed, about the right height . . .

"Majesty," I said, crawling over to where Cleopatra crouched, "can you take off your cloak without too much difficulty?"

She was the only one of our little traveling band who wore a cloak dyed a shade of rich azure blue. The rest of us wore dun colors or undyed wool. She blinked at me with her wide, dark eyes and then nodded.

"Kallista?" I said, turning to her.

She nodded, already guessing what I had in mind, and reached up to the plain bronze brooch that held her own cloak around her neck, unfastening it with nimble fingers. Then she took the queen's cloak and shrugged it up around her shoulders, fastening the brooch and tugging it closed in front, pulling the deep cowl up over her head to hide her face and hair.

"Ready?" I asked when she was done.

She looked at me, eyes shining with a kind of frantic excitement. "Ready."

"Don't take any chances," I said. And then amended that to: "Don't take any *unnecessary* chances. I'll be right behind you—'chasing' you—and I'll have your back if you get into any real trouble. We just need to buy enough time for Charon's captain to finish stowing his cargo and for everyone to get aboard. All right?"

She nodded again, grinning, and reached up to grip the sides of the wagon.

"Good," I said, squeezing her shoulder hard and then letting go. "The Morrigan guide your feet. Now go!"

Nimble as a fawn, Kallista leaped, vaulting over the side of the cart and landing in a neat crouch on the cobbles. Then *I* did what Acheron had done back on the road—the thing that had drawn so much unwanted attention down upon the queen in the first place.

I raised my voice and shouted, "My queen! No!"

Kallista played her part to perfection, shouting back at me in Greek, her voice tinged with what sounded like unbridled panic. Greek was a language Kallista had learned from her father—Quint's older brother—on Corsica, and it was one that Cleopatra was not only fluent in but spoke frequently.

"Majesty!" I shouted as made a desperate grab for her—missing, intentionally, by inches. "Come back! It's not safe!"

Then she ran. The azure cloak spread wide behind her, like a brilliant slash of sunlit sky streaming through the dreary gray shabbiness of Cosa, Kallista pelted down a side alley, faster than I'd ever seen anyone run. In an instant, she was out of sight, leaping over a low wall like a gazelle and disappearing down an alley.

"Tell Charon to get everyone on board that ship," I said to Elka. *"Now."*

Then I vaulted over the wagon side, sprinting madly after my runaway "queen." Kallista was clever. She'd paused just out of sight, waiting for me to catch up. Then, at the first opportunity, she took a hard right, heading down a twisting narrow alley that angled east through the city *away* from the docks. I followed her long enough to make sure Tanis had taken the bait. When I heard the sound of sandals on clay roof tiles above me and the slap of a bow-string—followed by the clatter of an arrow missing its target—I knew our ruse had worked.

But I also knew the kind of peril I'd put Kallista in. I'd have to hurry.

Tanis was fairly adept at dealing damage from a distance. Up close . . . not as adept. It was something the other girls at the ludus had teased her about, and *that* was one of the things, I suspected, that had contributed to her turning against us when all the other girls who'd remained Aquila's captives hadn't. It was a regret I harbored in my heart but one I still planned to use against her. I just had to get close enough. With all of Tanis's concentration focused so narrowly on trying to put an arrow through "Cleopatra's" blue cloak, I dropped back in my pursuit—not half because I could barely keep up with Kallista myself—and let Tanis get ahead of me on the rooftops. While she could track Kallista from on high, I could track *her* by following the trail of broken roof tiles her passage had knocked into the streets.

I drew a few black glares, but no Cosan tried to stop me as I ran through the winding, narrow alleys. When I sensed Tanis had come to a stop on the roof of a smithy just ahead of me, I circled around to the other side of the squat, ugly building and found a stack of crates I could use to climb up to the roof. The clanging from the blacksmith's hammer within and the column of smoke belching upward from the forge fires helped hide my approach.

Tanis had another arrow nocked and ready to fire.

She pulled the bowstring taut beside her ear . . .

And I hurled myself at her, hitting her with my shoulder, hard in the center of her back. She arched like her bow with a grunt of pain, and the arrow shot harmlessly skyward. Then together we tumbled off the roof into the street below. As I landed, I gave thanks to the Morrigan that Cosa maintained its streets in such poor condition. We hit soft-packed dirt instead of unforgiving paving stones. Tanis's arrows spilled from the quiver on her back, scattering into the ruts and gutters, and she landed heavily on her bow. I heard the sharp snap of the wood as it cracked in two.

I was back on my feet before she had a chance to get up on her hands and knees, and I delivered a swift kick to her ribs. The breath left her lungs with a pained grunt, and she curled in on herself, rolling away from me. I followed, and all of the fear and frustration of the last few days—Vorya dead, Hestia dead, our home gone forever—it just poured out of me. With a snarl like a lioness, I lurched toward Tanis and grabbed her by the front of her tunic. I hauled her to her feet and drove my fist into her face. Her head snapped back, and blood flew in a thin arc from her mouth. She staggered a few steps, barely raising her hands to defend herself, but a fiery red mist descended like a curtain before my eyes, and I hit her again. And again. And then I drew my sword—the new one Charon had given me, with the eagle symbol on it—and, grabbing a handful of her tunic again, I drew back my arm and leveled the blade at her throat. I was breathing so heavily my chest was heaving and my throat burned.

I'd never felt such raw fury. Not even in the arena.

Tanis's face, so close to mine, was a mess of blood, tears, and dirt . . . and fresh bruises blossoming in the shape of my knuckles. There was both fear and defiance in her gaze. I couldn't tell if there was any regret. But I did see something that I wasn't expecting: bravery.

She lifted her chin and stared down the length of my sword, directly into my eyes. "Go on," she said through a mouthful of blood and spittle. "Make an end of it."

Every muscle in my arm was on fire to do just that. Holding myself back in that moment felt like holding back someone else. Someone with a raging thirst for vengeance. For retribution . . .

"What's wrong, Fallon?" Tanis asked, her mouth twisting around my name in a grimace of pure, acrid wretchedness. "You left me behind to die that night, but you won't kill me yourself?"

And I saw, in that moment, that what Tanis hated wasn't me. It wasn't the girls who'd been her sisters. It was her own self. I felt a sudden welling up of shame in my breast. And pity . . .

"No." I shook my head and took a weary step back, letting go of her tunic and dropping my sword arm down to my side. "I won't kill you, Tanis."

She laughed bitterly. "I'm not even worthy of *that* in your eyes?"

"You want to embrace Death so badly?" I snapped. "You'll have to seek him out without my help. I'm sure your new master will point you down the right road. But beware. The grave isn't an ending for him. It's a beginning. Think long on how you really wish to spend eternity, Tanis. Now get out of my sight before I change my mind."

Her eyes narrowed—as if she didn't quite believe that I would just let her walk away—and she wiped the back of her hand across her mouth, smearing the blood that had gathered at the corner of her lips across her cheek.

"Go!" I shouted, and sheathed my blade.

Like a deer suddenly released from the spell of the Huntress, she spun on her heel and bounded away from me down the twisted alley, disappearing in an instant. Unless Tanis could find herself a brand-new bow somewhere in the rag-end shops of Cosa before we sailed, I thought, she would trouble me and my friends no further.

But it seemed that, blinded by my own anger, I'd somehow forgotten she hadn't ridden into town alone. Because when I took to my own heels—heading back to the wharf, cutting through a narrow alley to emerge in the open square that served as the town forum—I almost ran straight into the black-cloaked back of one of the Dis riders.

He must have tethered his mount somewhere and was now prowling the streets looking for the fugitive queen of Aegypt. In my dirt-stained cloak, with my weapons hidden and my hair tucked back under my cowl, I very likely could have passed for just a regular citizen from Cosa but for the fact that I gasped audibly when I saw him standing there, like a shard of darkness in the middle of the town square. He spun around and looked down at me. I staggered back a few steps as he drew a wickedly curved sica blade from the sheath at his hip and, without pausing for thought, slashed at my head.

I cursed my telltale reaction and dropped to my knees, throwing myself forward into a diving roll that took me beneath his blade and past his reach. I was a bit surprised that no one in the square even blinked an eye at the seemingly random attempted beheading in their midst. When I lurched to my feet and started to run—spinning a stout older woman carrying a basket of bread loaves into the path of the Dis assassin and shouldering aside a pair of merchants—I earned a smattering of shouted curses, but that was the extent of the general reaction. How often did this sort of thing occur in a place like Cosa, I wondered as I dodged a laden mule and ducked past a fishmonger's stall. Everyone seemed so utterly unruffled by it. Not that it mattered. I just hoped it meant my pursuer was unlikely to receive any help from the local populace in catching me.

Unfortunately, he didn't need their help. He had a partner.

And his partner was right on Kallista's heels.

I saw the blue blaze of her cloak out of the corner of my eye and headed in that direction just as another shard of darkness—a second Dis assassin—stepped out of a doorway right in front of me, axe held high and poised to throw at her fleeing back. I shouted to draw his attention, and he turned to see me running straight for him. He swung his axe, expecting I would dodge to his left—the only space available in the narrow lane—but instead, I ducked right, and as the momentum of his axe swing shifted his body on an angle, I bounced off his armored chest, spun myself around, and kept on running after Kallista . . .

Right into a blind alley.

A dead end.

She stood there, a look of blank disbelief on her face. As if there had to be an escape path there *some*where . . . I glanced around wildly. There wasn't. Just three doors, two of them boarded up, the last with a dilapidated wooden sign above advertising a public bathhouse. We were caught. Cornered. The first Dis assassin appeared then at the far end of the alley and joined his partner, the two of them moving languidly toward us, supremely confident that they'd run their quarry to ground. I could tell by the look in their eyes, they meant to enjoy what came next.

"I wish I had my fire chain," Kallista murmured.

"I wish you did too," I said as I stepped in front of her and drew my swords . . .

And then there was a shout.

The azure flutter of the queen's cloak flashed past again—*behind* our assailants, who'd turned to look and now frowned at each other in confusion. I blinked and glanced back at Kallista, not trusting my own eyes either. But when my *ears* reported back the slap-slap-slap of dainty sandals pelting down the lane, I swore under my breath.

That, I thought, *is the* real *Cleopatra*.

And she was playing decoy for *us*!

I grabbed Kallista by the wrist and shouldered open the bathhouse door, shoving her through ahead of me and slamming the door shut. Outside, I could hear our assailants cursing in confusion.

"Which one is the bloody queen?" one of them asked.

"Damned if I know—pick one and go!" snarled the other. "Catch the bitch!"

There was a feeble bar lock with rusty brackets on the door that wouldn't hold long if our pursuer got even halfway serious about opening it. I slammed it shut anyway, and together Kallista and I pelted through the dressing vestibule and into a dimly lit steam-filled chamber with a vaulted ceiling. Ghost-pale bodies, mostly naked, were splayed about on stone benches, and I did my best to ignore them, mumbling apologies for the intrusion, as Kallista and I made our way toward a shaft of diffuse light at the end of a corridor. We burst through an archway into a small courtyard open to the sky with a colonnade surrounding a pool filled with brackish-looking green water. Like almost everything else in Cosa, it smelled like fish sauce. A half dozen bathers floated about, as oblivious to the stench as to me and Kallista running around the perimeter of the pool, boots slipping on the algae-slick tiles.

"Here!" I stopped near the far corner, where the level of the colonnade roof was at its lowest, and sheathed my blades.

It was too high to jump to without help, so I cupped my hands to give Kallista a boost. She didn't hesitate, just took a run, planted her foot in my hands, and vaulted onto the roof, disappearing from view. I heard angry shouting coming from inside the bathhouse and the sound of clay oil pots shattering. I glanced around, looking desperately for something I could use to climb on. There was nothing. I swallowed anxiously, knowing I was trapped . . .

"Fallon!"

I glanced up, astonished when I saw—not Kallista, but a pair of gleaming hazel eyes. Cai's face staring down at me. Wordlessly, he thrust his hands toward me, and I grabbed hold. His arm muscles went taut, and with a jump from me and a heave of his shoulders, I was on the roof. I rolled over on the cracked and crumbling tiles, gasping for breath.

"You!" shouted a voice from below. "Haul your pasty carcass over here so I can climb on your back or I'll cut your heart out and sink it in that swamp you call a bath!"

Cai and I exchanged a glance and scrambled to get down off the roof to the alley behind the bathhouse, where

Kallista waited for us. I leaped down beside her and told her to strip off the cloak she wore. Cai followed, landing in a crouch beside me. When he stood, he turned to glare at me with equal parts frustration and relief, with maybe a little bit of anger thrown in. I realized that I hadn't exactly had the opportunity to convey my hastily formulated plan to him. When "Cleopatra" and I had both suddenly bolted from the caravan, he must have thought the queen—or I, or *both*—had gone mad. And then when the *actual* Cleopatra had followed our lead . . .

"The queen!" I gasped. "She's—"

"A lunatic," Cai said. "You're both . . ." He shook his head, sharing his glare with Kallista. "All *three* of you . . . utter lunatics. You know that? Mad."

"Actually, Kallista and I are just dangerously reckless and desperate," I said. "Cleopatra . . . ? *She's* definitely mad."

"Hsst."

I frowned at Cai. "What?"

"What?" He frowned back.

"Did you hiss at me?"

"I don't think so . . ."

I looked at Kallista, who shrugged.

"Hssst."

I glanced around, blinking, and peered into the deep shadows beneath a gloomy taberna portico across the street—where the queen of Aegypt stood, draped in a drab brown woolen cloak that looked unbearably itchy, even from that distance.

She read my expression with uncanny accuracy as I ran toward her and shrugged her shoulders under the thing, saying, "It's nowhere near as itchy as that damned carpet Sennefer smuggled me into Caesar's chamber in. I pilfered it from a laundry line in a yard the next street over, but I left behind an earring in payment."

I lifted an edge of the homespun fabric and saw that she still wore her azure cloak beneath—which she must have donned after I'd gone chasing after her decoy. Before she'd become her decoy's decoy. "You packed two of the same cloak?" I asked. "I thought we were traveling light."

"I might be a fugitive on the run," she said, bright-eyed and flushed from dashing around the town, "but I'm still a queen, sweet girl. I never travel with only one of anything. For me, this *is* traveling light."

"Majesty . . ." Cai said. "Respectfully, what in Hades are you doing here?"

"You've all been risking—and *losing*—your lives for me," she said. "I decided enough was enough and I should lend a hand to help save my own skin. I practiced the athletic arts as a girl. And besides . . . I'm the daughter of the gods. Isis and Osiris protect me." She said that last as if there was no shred of doubt in her mind. And I really don't think there was.

"Sennefer?" I asked. "He must be—"

"Torn between hopping mad and nervous wreck, I'd imagine." She grinned wickedly and shrugged. Then she looked back and forth between me and Cai and Kallista.

"You should probably return me to him before he does himself any permanent damage."

Back at the wharf, the very last of our gear was being loaded up the ramp onto the ship as the four of us came pelting out from between two warehouses, staggering on board moments before the ship's captain gave the order to shove off. Sennefer came bounding across the deck, a blooming flush deepening his already deeply tanned face, eyes watery and hands fluttering like startled birds at the sight of his precious queen returned to him undamaged.

I grinned at Kallista and leaned on Cai, catching my breath as the ship drifted gracefully out into the middle of the harbor, sails unfurling. We were safe. At last. The sun had gained in strength throughout the day, finally burning through a layer of high, thin cloud cover as we hit the open seas and, one by one, the girls started to shed their cloaks, revealing the lean-muscled bodies—and abundant weaponry—that had been concealed beneath.

Darius, the captain, looked around, mouth agape, as it slowly dawned on him that we were not exactly Charon's "cargo." There was nothing about any of us that resembled slaves. Not anymore.

"I don't know why you were so polite securing passage," I heard him say to Charon. "With *this* lot? You could have just commandeered my ship without so much as a 'by your leave.'"

"What are we but savages, Darius, without the conventions of commerce?" Charon grinned. "Of course, had you said *no* . . ."

"Right . . ." Darius looked at him sideways. "And where, exactly, was it you said you were bound for?"

"I didn't." Charon turned to Cleopatra with a deferential nod. "Your Highness?"

The queen stepped forward and pushed the deep cowl of the homespun cloak off her face. "Alexandria, Master Darius," she said, smiling sweetly as he went pale as milk and looked as though he might collapse to the deck. "In Aegypt. My home."

XVII

SOMETHING WAS WRONG.

I could tell by the way Charon was clutching at the rigging rope, white-knuckled, and leaning heavily on the rail. It was just over a week since we'd set out on our sea journey, and the morning had dawned bright and clear. The Mare Nostrum that day was almost without any chop, the water as smooth as any sailor could ask for. But Charon looked as if he was having a hard time standing upright. I'd never seen him without sea legs on the water, and I almost made a joke about it—about him finally succumbing to seasickness—but when I approached, I was struck by the pallor of his skin. And then I saw that his left arm was hidden beneath his cloak, and I could tell by the way the fabric draped that he had it wrapped around his torso. When I looked at the deck beneath his feet, I saw the drops of blood spattering the wood beside his boot.

"Charon . . ." I said. "Your arrow wound—"

"It's nothing." He glanced at me.

"I'll get Neferet—"

"No!"

He reached out to clutch at me as I turned to go find our physician. "I don't want anyone else to know about this," he said.

I looked at him through narrowed eyes, wondering what exactly he was trying to hide. "That's what you said the night it happened. I kept quiet then, but . . ."

"All right." He shook his head. "I don't want *Sorcha* to know about this." He let go of me and winced, putting a hand to his side again.

"I'm sorry, Charon," I said with a sigh. "I never meant to drag you into this kind of situation."

"Oh well." He laughed a little. "It's my own fault, really, for kidnapping you in the first place."

I bit my lip. "It's bad, isn't it?"

He shook his head. "No. No . . . it's healing."

I glanced down at the fresh blood spatters on the deck, then back up at him.

"For the most part," he amended. "Slowly." He scuffed at the stains with the toe of his boot, then he raised his gaze to mine, his dark eyes serious. "Fallon . . . promise me you won't tell Sorcha."

"Why Sorcha specifically?" I asked, lifting an eyebrow at him.

He grinned, but it was almost bashful. "I just don't want her to worry."

I may have gasped a little. "You and Sorcha—"

"Are in . . . conversation," he said and cleared his throat, shrugging. "For the last few months now, really. And often late into the night. She is a balm on my battered slave trader's heart."

"Ye gods." I snorted, rolling my eyes before he could wax romantic. "And it's all *my* fault."

"It is that." He laughed again, and this time it didn't seem to pain him as much. "Don't forget it was your sword—the one *you* helped me save from that sinking ship—that carved out this destiny for us both." The laughter faded to a quiet smile. "Thank you."

"Be good to her, Charon," I said. "Something tells me she has needed you as much as you have needed her."

He nodded. But then the smile disappeared from his face altogether, and he sighed. "I don't deserve this," he said. "I'm not . . . I'm not a *good* man, Fallon. And what I did to you—to so many people—was deplorable. Unforgivable." A fleeting, troubled frown shadowed his brow and then was gone. "But if the truth of it were known, I would probably do most of it again, given a choice, because that is how I have lived my life and I have done well by it. So I won't apologize, because an apology would be meaningless."

I half unsheathed the sword he'd given me before we left the ludus. "What was this meant to be, then?" I asked.

He quirked an eyebrow at me, and his customary grin twitched back into place. "I am your patron, remember? Perhaps it was meant to be . . . an investment."

"I'm not so sure it was a wise one, then," I said, gesturing to the wide expanse of ocean all around us. "As I am, sadly, without an arena in which to display your generous patronage. And I doubt I'll ever see the inside of one again."

He shrugged. "You never know. Arenas come in all shapes and sizes. And as I said then: Your journey is not over, and you may yet find more use for your martial skills." He sniffed and drew himself upright. "No, Fallon, that"—he gestured to the sword—"what that *really* is is a thank-you. You have given me the opportunity to become, if not a good man, maybe at least a better man before I die."

He gripped my shoulder for a moment and then walked back toward the ship's stern, proud and upright, as arrogant as ever. But maybe just a little bit humbled by experience. A little bit more human. I watched him go and then went to seek out Elka. There was something I needed to say to her that I'd been avoiding for days. Since we boarded, really.

She sat alone on the deck near the bow, with her knees drawn up and her back resting against the curve of the ship's side. Her eyes were closed and her face tipped skyward, bathed in sunlight. The sea air lifted stray strands of her long blonde hair; she'd left it loose instead of plaited into her usual long, tight braids. For the first time, I could see what Quint had been talking about when he'd called her a "divine nymph." Any trace of her customary fierceness, the haughty ice maiden warrior, was nowhere to be seen. She was just a girl on a ship in the middle of the sea. We all were. And some of us were missing. One of those had belonged to the same tribe as Elka.

I sank down beside her, and for a while we just sat there, not speaking. Eventually, she rolled her head toward me and opened her eyes, waiting for me to say what was on my mind.

"I'm sorry for the loss of your kinswoman," I said. "For the loss of our sisters. For Hestia too."

Elka snorted. "Vorya was Varini," she said with a dismissive wave of her hand. "She would probably laugh at your sorrow and tell you that she's gone to drink the All-Father's finest mead in his hall of heroes." She shrugged. "I don't know Hestia's customs or where her soul will wander in death, but I have sent a prayer to the All-Father and asked him to welcome her too, should she pass that way. You should envy them, little fox, not weep for them."

"Right." I nodded. "And so I shall. Just as soon as I finish weeping."

"*Ja.* Me too . . ."

Elka put her head on my shoulder. I put an arm around her and pretended not to notice when her tears dropped onto my tunic.

The journey to Alexandria would take us a little less than a month, slower than I would have liked, but then . . . I don't know why I was in such a great hurry. We had escaped our pursuers. Still, I glanced behind us out to

sea so often it became almost a habit. When we eventually put in at the port of Messana on the island of Sicilia to
take on supplies of food and fresh water, I was a bundle of
raw nerves the entire time. It had been decided that none
of us from the ludus would go ashore while we waited
for the provisions to be loaded. Even though the odds of
any of Aquila's assassins having caught up with us were
long, I would not bet against them. None of us would. Cai
and Quint, though, took the opportunity to go ashore and
gather what news they could of Rome and the Republic in
the wake of Caesar's assassination. The news was war.

"I don't know what they expected," Acheron said,
shaking his head.

"Not what they got," Cai said.

He wiped the sweat from his face and sank down onto
a stool beneath the striped canvas awning Darius's sailors
had rigged up midship to shade us while we were docked
in Messana.

"Certainly not what they'll get in the coming days,"
Cai continued. "Which may very well be the death of the
Republic and a return to the days when Rome was an
empire. The very thing they so feared under Caesar. Fools.
They thought they would be hailed as heroes. Now Rome
is half on fire and half hiding behind doors, and the only
thing keeping the Republic from tearing itself straight
down the middle seems to be some kind of compromise
between Marc Antony and the senate."

"It won't last." Quint said, dipping a ladle into the
water barrel on deck and pouring it over the back of his

neck for relief from the sun's heat, which had grown steadily ever since we'd left Cosa. "There'll be full-blown civil war before long. It's inevitable."

"Weren't they, though?" Acheron asked. "Heroes? I mean . . . Caesar *was* a tyrant, wasn't he?"

Cai tilted his head and looked at his fellow ex-gladiator. "Most great leaders are, in one fashion or another," he said. "As tyrants go, Caesar was less monstrous than some."

"Tell that to most any Gaul," Acheron said. "Tell it to the Romans who never wanted a king. Tell that to Fallon's people." He nodded at me.

"What do you know of her people?" Quint asked, seemingly genuinely curious. I admit I was too.

"Enough." Acheron shrugged. "I had a cell at the Ludus Flaminius next to that painted fool Yoreth for long enough that some of his constant whining stuck. Didn't *you* ever want Caesar dead, lass?" he asked me.

The bluntness of his assessment took me aback, but yes. Of *course* I'd wanted Caesar dead. For most of my life growing up, truth be told. Right up until the moment when I'd met the man face-to-face.

"You sound like one of them, Acheron," Quint said with a thin smile. "Like a bloody Optimate."

"Eh? Oh no." Acheron blinked at him. "Not me. Let the big men have at it. I've got more important things to do with my life." He grinned a wide grin and held his arms out, gesturing to all of us. "Thanks to you lot, I have a destiny. I'm on my way to Aegypt. Always wanted to see that great sprawling sand heap—"

His mouth snapped shut all of a sudden, and I turned to see that Cleopatra had joined us beneath the awning and had been standing there for who knows how long, listening to us discuss matters that were so very much bigger than us. Not her, though. I wondered what she was thinking.

"Your, er, your pardon, Majesty . . ." Acheron stammered an apology, still flummoxed any time the queen was within sight. "I . . . uh . . ."

She raised an eyebrow, but after a moment, she graciously inclined her head and said, "There *is* rather a lot of sand."

I bit the inside of my cheek to keep from laughing out loud. Less than two years earlier, I'd been the daughter of a king. Serene in the knowledge that one day, after I'd attained my rightful status as a celebrated warrior, I would have become a queen of my people. I shook my head at the very thought. The girl I'd been then probably would have become the kind of queen who would have had the Cantii at war with half a dozen other tribes inside of a month.

But a leader, I now knew, wasn't just the hand that held a sword the best. Even in small things, beneath her glittering veneer of willful arrogance and wild abandon, Cleopatra was a statesman. A diplomat and a queen, with the temperament and training to rule her people wisely.

Even in the shadow of a brawling, bullying juggernaut like Rome. Especially since she was a woman.

I understood why she and Sorcha had become such great friends.

And I understood why men were powerless in her presence.

I shook my head and excused myself, leaving the boys on deck to hover around the queen like bees around a blossom, and went below to see my sister. Sorcha had not been up on deck very often since we began the journey, and I was growing increasingly worried about her. I understood, in that light, why Charon was reluctant to let her know about his own difficulties—he wanted her to focus on healing herself. Neferet had been attending to her, giving her potions to ease the searing headaches that made even the dimmest light unbearable. She'd also begun to administer poultices to Sorcha's head wound when she'd noticed a degree of swelling around the stiches she'd sewn there immediately after we'd left Cosa.

She was there with my sister when I climbed down into the cool darkness belowdecks, holding a bowl that Sorcha weakly vomited the latest potion dose into before collapsing back onto the makeshift bed we'd arranged for her. Antonia was there too, waiting at the bottom of the ladder, and she stopped me, holding out an arm. Once we were beyond reach of our enemies, she'd switched back to wearing the plain leather sheath on her truncated limb. I looked down at it and thought to myself, *Neferet healed Antonia. She will do the same for my sister.* It would just take time. And a good long stretch spent on dry land.

"Maybe best to just let her rest, Fallon," Antonia said quietly. "Nef's been trying to make her comfortable, but she's very restless—"

"Fallon!" Sorcha called out, her voice reedy and thin. "Is that you? Are you there?"

"Here, Sorcha. I'm right here . . ."

I went and sat on the edge of her cot. She looked at me, squinting and twisting her head so she could see me clearly with her good eye. She looked gaunt in the light of the tallow lamp that burned on a nearby crate, and the bandage wrapped around her head was stained with blood and tar-sticky unguents.

"Look at you. Your hair's a mess," she said, reaching up to smooth down the strands that the sea wind had been playing with all afternoon. "Where's Clota? Have her brush it out and give you a proper plait before supper."

I blinked at her, confused, and then looked at Neferet. Her small face was lined with concern, and she shook her head at me.

"You've been off in the vale again all day and look like a wild pony . . ." Sorcha kept fretfully stroking my hair. "And light the lamps, will you? It's so dark in here . . ."

I took Sorcha's hand and squeezed it between my own until she relaxed, sinking back into the cloak that was bundled behind her head like a pillow with a ragged sigh. After a few moments, she seemed to drift off into a doze. I placed her hand gently on her chest and stood, beckoning Neferet away from where she lay.

"Clota is my father's bondswoman," I said. "She took care of us after our mother died."

Neferet nodded. "Sorcha's confused. She has been for a while now."

"Is it the draughts you're giving her?"

"I don't think so. She barely keeps enough of them down," Neferet said. "I'm no expert, but I think she's aggravated her old injury from the chariot accident long ago. There may be a pressure point—like a kind of bruise—on the inside of her head, but . . ." She shrugged, a look of frustration on her face. "I don't even think Heron was skilled at remedying such a thing. There are doctors in Aegypt, though, who might be. Heron told me about them. They call them trepanners, and they are surgeons of the brain. They have tools to drill holes in the cranium—that's the skull—and . . ."

She stopped when she looked up and saw my expression. I felt as though I might empty the contents of my stomach too, if she didn't stop talking.

"Um." She shrugged. "I just meant . . . perhaps they can help."

"I'm sure they can," I murmured, swallowing thickly.

Then I mustered an encouraging smile and climbed the ladder topside. Truthfully, I wasn't sure. But I *was* sure that hovering over Neferet in the hold of the ship while she did her very best to make my sister well again wasn't going to help.

The days continued to pass in a kind of waking dream. Mornings broke, blue and gold, evenings shaded to russet and purple, and the white eye of the sun glared balefully down on us from a mostly cloudless sky as we traveled ever southward across the sea. Sometimes we could see land, sometimes only waves. Boredom came and went, mitigated by practice drills and deck chores and storytelling. Usually in the form of a circle of Cleopatra's admirers listening as she regaled them with more tales of her land and people. One afternoon, when I was done filing the burrs from my blades after a bout with Cai, I wandered over to hear what the queen was saying, leaning on the ship rail as she spoke again about her lady pharaoh ancestress.

"Did I ever tell you girls how Hatshepsut led her armies into battle against the Kushite hordes," the queen said, "riding at the head of her troops in her golden war chariot, drawn by snow-white horses, fighting brave as any man?"

"Did she still have to wear the golden"—Devana waved her hand vaguely in the direction of her nether regions—"you know . . ."

Cleopatra laughed. "No, I shouldn't think so," she said. "She was pharaoh by then, and that probably would have gotten in the way. But her troops accepted her as their general and revered her as their commander."

"Because she was good, or because they didn't have a choice?" I asked.

I hadn't meant to be that blunt, but the rest of the girls grew instantly silent and exchanged a few laden glances. Cleopatra turned to me, her dark eyes glittering. For a moment, I thought she was angry. But then she held out a hand and beckoned me to come and stand beside her. She took my hands and held them up between us, her smooth thumbs pressing into the calluses on my palms, built up over countless hours of practice with my swords.

"*Both*," she said, her grip on my hands like iron. "Because she *made* herself one thing, she *became* the other in their eyes. Many a weak king has fallen in battle in my land—and not always with a wound on the *front* of his divine body, if you take my meaning. Destiny is not something that is given. It's something you prove yourself worthy of taking. Hatshepsut would still have been Hatshepsut if she hadn't done what she'd done. She just wouldn't have been pharaoh. You would still be Fallon even if you'd never proven yourself Victrix. That wasn't something mighty Caesar simply bestowed upon you. It was something you earned from his hand." She looked around at the gathered girls. "That goes for all of you."

I felt the tension in my shoulders release as she clapped my hands together and let them go. The girls all began to chatter among themselves, and I joined in as it led to several rounds of regaling ourselves with the deeds we'd performed both in and out of the arena that—Cleopatra was damned well right—we'd *earned* the right to boast of. Even if just to each other.

"And then when Damya sat on that Tarquin retiarius," Nephele was saying, snorting with laughter, "in the middle of the arena and refused to let her up until she'd agreed to trade helmets!"

"It's a nice helmet," Damya said. "I still have it. Very comfortable."

"Poor thing'd still be there if she hadn't said yes!"

Damya shrugged. "She was pretty comfortable too."

The deck was rolling with laughter when I looked out over the sea to the east and saw the jagged shapes of mountains rising up in the distance.

"What place is that?" I asked.

"Home . . ."

I turned to see Kore and Thalassa beside me, leaning out over the ship's rail. Both of them were staring intently at the white sand beaches skirting rugged hills climbing upward to mountains in the distance.

"Is that Crete?" I said to Kore, who'd been the one to speak.

She nodded. "The Island of the Sacred Bull."

"Would you ever want to go back there?" I asked. "To live?"

"Oh . . ." Thalassa shook her head vigorously. "No. No, no . . . Kore didn't mean 'home' in a *good* way."

Kore snorted at her fellow Cretan's reaction and glanced at me sideways. "Remember the story?" she said. "Daedalus and Icarus built wings to *escape* that place."

"I'd build wings to keep us from ever having to go back, if I had to," Thalassa said with a shudder. "I would not step foot into *that* arena again."

"What do you mean?"

"You think the *Roman* arena is bad?" Kore scoffed. "You never leave the ring of Knossos, and you never win your

way out. You're just another sacrifice to the Bull God waiting to happen. Day after day, you go and face the horns.
Until you die. And they *all* die, eventually. We were lucky
enough to have a troupe master who was also a vile, roaring drunk."

"That's lucky?" I said.

"He owed the local wine seller so much money that he
had to sell us off before the bull's horns claimed us." She
grinned. "But because of that—because we had the audacity to leave the ring of blood *alive*—we were considered a
disgrace and shunned by our countrymen."

"I'm sorry." I shook my head. "I had no idea."

"Pff." Thalassa waved a hand dismissively in the direction of the island brooding on the horizon. "There are other
fields of battle where we can earn our glory. And have at
least a *chance* of keeping our lives while we do."

"Tell me again why you two thought it was a good idea
for *us* to practice flying over angry bulls, when it all sounds
so delightfully lethal?" Elka called up from where she sat
cross-legged on the deck with the other girls.

Kore grinned down at her. "At least we didn't sharpen
Tempest's horns like they do in Knossos."

"And you *were* really quite good at it," Thalassa said.
"Nice height. Good form—"

Elka frowned fiercely. "There's *no* flying in the oath."

"Maybe there should be," Ajani said. "We've done
almost everything else."

"Burned, bound, beaten . . ." Damya counted off on her
blunt fingertips.

"Don't forget shot with an arrow," Ceto pointed at the bandage Damya sported around her upper arm.

Damya shrugged. "Haven't been killed by the sword. Yet."

"Give it time," Gratia said cheerfully, punching her good shoulder.

"*Lots* of time," Lysa, the youngest of us, said. "I hope."

I hoped so too.

XVIII

IT WAS IN the deep black watches of middle night when our ship finally approached the Great Harbor of the city of Alexandria. Almost everyone on board, except for the sailors on watch, was asleep. But slumber eluded me that night, and so it was I who first saw the fire on the horizon, blazing like the eye of some distant, fiery giant in the south. Beautiful and terrifying . . .

"The lighthouse of Alexandria," Cai's voice whispered in my ear.

Apparently I wasn't the only one who couldn't sleep that night.

"I've seen it once before," he continued, wrapping his arms around me, "when I was a very small boy and my father brought me here."

"A lighthouse?" I asked, leaning into the warmth of him. "What is that?"

"It's a tower—a great stone tower reaching up into the sky, almost as tall as a hundred men standing on each other's shoulders, at the mouth of the harbor, and it shines with a great blazing fire at night to warn approaching ships of the shallows and rocks."

"What god built such a thing?" I asked, my voice soft with awe. Even in Rome I'd never seen anything as massive as what he'd just described.

"No god," Cai said. "Men. The Aegyptians are master builders, the architects of many wondrous things. Now that you're here, you'll be able to visit them. The pyramids. The mighty Sphinx . . . Djeser-Djeseru, the temple the queen spoke of."

As Cai spoke, I felt a cold knot of something like dread tighten in my stomach. But I didn't quite know why. It all sounded very exciting. The chance to see such marvels as I never—not in my wildest imaginings—even dreamed of when I was a girl. A girl growing up in a village made of stone and thatch, peat smoke and spring water and mist, surrounded by the majesty of nothing more than soaring forests and dappled glades, the songs of wolves and the call of the ravens . . .

And now I was in Aegypt.

Were there even ravens here, in the desert? I wondered, suddenly panicking. What if there weren't? How would the Morrigan find me to watch over me? The Sekhemet pendant Cleopatra had gifted me lay heavy and cold on my breast. A goddess to be honored and feared and

worshipped, but not *my* goddess . . . Suddenly, in the darkness lit only by the distant gleam of godfire conjured by
men, the weight of the last handful of weeks rose up like
a rogue wave on the Mare Nostrum and crashed over me.
I felt my shoulder heave with a shuddering breath and
the wetness of tears on my cheeks. Cai wrapped his arms
tighter around me and held me until I could manage to
speak without sobbing.

I turned around to face him, and he smiled gently
down on me, his eyes, reflecting the lighthouse fire's
glow, full of concern. "What is it, Fallon?" he asked in a
whisper.

"I've never felt so far from home," I said, my voice
small in the night.

"You've never *been* so far from home." He brushed at
the tear tracks on my cheeks with his thumbs. "I think it's
probably normal to feel that way."

"Except I don't even know where home is anymore. I
don't know this place we're going to, but I don't think I
will find it there."

I kept thinking how Kore and Thalassa had first
answered "home" when I'd asked them what the island
of Crete was called. But then they'd vehemently denied
ever wanting to go back there. All the girls of the Ludus
Achillea were wanderers now, our only tribe each other,
so it shouldn't have bothered me *where* I was . . . but it did.
The thought of waking in the morning and looking out on
the shores of a place so fundamentally alien terrified me.

It was as if I'd already passed over into the Otherworld only to find myself somewhere *other* than the Blessed Isles.

The city of Alexandria was like a fever dream. Drenched in the kind of heat that sears your lungs and slides over your skin like a knife blade, awash in colors so bright the murals and statues seemed to pulse with the vibrancy of their hues. It was a place of wonder. Of mystery and magic. A portal to another realm I'd never even imagined existed. When the sun rose that morning and we sailed into the Great Harbor of Alexandria, the lighthouse was something that my mind had an even harder time comprehending than it had in the darkness. I couldn't tear my eyes from it. I had to crane and arch my back, looking up, as we sailed beneath its shadow. It was colossal. Constructed of three tapering tiers of limestone, pale and gleaming in the sun and pointing skyward like an accusing finger that would pierce the vault of the heavens themselves. The lighthouse stood on an island called Pharos, connected to the mainland by a long narrow causeway that formed the western arm of the Great Harbor. The structure, built to house a fiery beacon, was topped with a statue of the great god Zeus, clutching a fistful of thunderbolts and gazing down at the ships that came and went far below.

"I didn't think it possible for men to build such things," Elka said, her jaw hanging open as she shaded her eyes to gaze up at it.

"Alexandria is full of such marvels," Cleopatra informed us with a smile that spoke of pure joy at her homecoming. "Once we are settled in my house, I'll take you over to the mainland and show you girls such sights," she said, "that you will think yourselves in the land of the gods."

Even from far out in the harbor, I could see the distant golden gleam of desert sands. Shimmering azure waves kissed the shore where clusters of date palms waved their green-spiked fans in the breeze from off the sea, and the buildings and temples and gardens sparkled like a jeweled mosaic. I wanted to see it all. But first, before setting foot in the city of gods, we were to experience the home of a goddess. For that is what Cleopatra truly was, here in her own realm. She almost shone like gold herself in the sunlight that burned my skin but only seemed to caress hers.

Darius was only allowed to pilot his ship a certain distance from the island of Antirhodos, where the queen kept her primary residence. And so we weighed anchor some ways out and waited to be ferried over from our galley, along with what scant few possessions we'd managed to bring along. A fleet of reed skiffs transported us to the crescent-shaped island with its gleaming palace rising up from the middle of the harbor like a mirage.

The skiffs were piloted by muscular men with heads completely shaved except for a braided sidelock over one ear, wearing curved swords on their hips, belted on over the briefest of loincloths. More than one of the girls went wide-eyed at the sight of them, but I thought Gratia's eyes might actually fall out of her head when they appeared. *Fickle thing*, I thought to myself, grinning, and wondered if she'd grown weary of leering at Acheron's muscles and scars. To be fair, the boatmen were uniformly handsome—almost as if they'd been handpicked to match, like a set of expensive glassware—each one sun-browned and oiled, dark-eyed and smiling enigmatically at us, a strange bedraggled gaggle of the queen's guests. We waited until every last one of us had stepped from the skiffs onto the pristine docks, unsure of what to do next or where to go. Then the queen of Aegypt spun on the heel of her golden sandal and threw her arms wide.

"Ladies of the Ludus Achillea, worthy lords, my friends and generous saviors," Cleopatra said with a wide smile as an army of house slaves suddenly appeared, hurrying toward us with Sennefer at their head. "Welcome to my house."

That's what she called it. "House." I was the daughter of a king. I had walked the halls of Julius Caesar's estate and the marble corridors of residences belonging to some of Rome's richest families. And yet, I suddenly began to seriously question my understanding of the word "house." The docks were on the eastern end of the island, and a grand causeway of sixty towering red granite columns led from them to the palace itself. We ascended the shallow steps through the cool shadows of a breezeway and out into a sprawling courtyard resplendent with palm trees and fish ponds and fountains. It felt like a dream.

"You could fit my entire village in this courtyard," Ajani murmured, blinking at the opulence. "With room for the cattle. All of them."

Slaves with trays of cool sweet wine and a vast array of sugared confections circulated among us, and I remembered, with a grin, just how much a ludus full of hungry gladiatrices could devour in a very short time. I glanced around, looking for Sorcha, and saw her sitting beneath a striped silk awning with Charon at her side. I headed toward her but was almost run down by a charging toddler in a bright white tunic edged with gold, squealing, "Mama! Mama!" in Greek.

"Ptolemy!" Cleopatra exclaimed with delight, crouching down and opening her arms for the little boy to run into. She embraced him tightly, and for a moment, I saw the alabaster mask of the queen slip to reveal the woman beneath. The little boy was her son. Hers and Caesar's. The last thing she had of him, I thought, and infinitely precious, if her expression was anything to judge by. She took the child's chubby hands in hers and spoke to him, tugging the little baby sidelock that hung over his ear straight and smoothing the creases from his tunic, and it seemed that the rest of the world just disappeared for her. The chaos of a courtyard full of warrior girls faded into the mist. She was home, with her son, and I was suddenly so very glad that we'd been the ones to get her there.

"Together again at long last. But the sacrifices we've made getting her here pierce the heart," I heard Sorcha say, and turned to find her standing beside me, pale and drawn but steady, her gaze fixed on her dear friend, the queen. "I know."

I almost wondered how she'd known exactly what I'd been thinking, but she was Sorcha. She knew me almost as well as I knew myself.

Cleopatra turned and looked over her shoulder at Sorcha, and they shared a long, silent glance. Then two women draped in pleated linen gowns appeared and stood waiting. Sorcha nodded and turned to me, reaching out to take my hand.

"The queen's physician waits to see me," she said, her fingers spasming weakly as she squeezed mine. I clutched at her, but she just lifted a hand to my cheek and smiled. "They'll take care of me, Fallon," she said. "Let them."

I bit my lip. "I never should have . . ."

"What?" she asked. "Suggested we rescue my dearest friend from death or imprisonment or . . . whatever it is that they would have done to Cleopatra back in Rome if those Optimate bastards had gotten their hands on her?"

"I know." I shook my head. "I do know. It's just . . . I've already lost friends and—"

"I'll be *fine*. Aegypt has regained her queen," Sorcha said. "More importantly . . . Ptolemy has regained his mother."

She nodded back at where the queen had her son in her lap, and he was laughing with such pure joy, his little arms wrapped around Cleopatra's neck, that it eased the tightness in my chest a bit.

"The gods give and take life as it pleases them, little sister," Sorcha continued. "If sometimes we take matters into our own hands, I don't think that's a bad thing. And even as I grieve their loss, I honor our ludus sisters. I don't think there's any one of us who wouldn't have made the same sacrifices for each other as Vorya or Hestia did." She waved at the little prince as he looked over at us. "Or for *that*."

At his mother's urging, Ptolemy waved back. Shyly.

I smiled and waved too, thinking that, if he was anything like his parents, he wouldn't remain shy for very long. Sorcha let go of my hand then and disappeared into the palace with the waiting women. I watched her go and then turned to see Charon gazing after her, the shadow of a frown on his brow and Neferet at his elbow, murmuring words into his ear that I couldn't hear. Words that only made the shadows on his brow grow darker.

I had barely stepped foot over the threshold of the room I'd been given when a smiling, cheerfully insistent matron with an elaborately braided wig and eyes rimmed heavily in kohl appeared to escort me to the bathing house, where I was to "refresh and rejuvenate from my long journey." Apparently, I hadn't been exaggerating when I'd told Kallista and Selene about the sumptuousness of the baths in Aegypt surpassing the ones at the Ludus Achillea. In a land hot enough to make sweating an almost constant pastime, where the sand tended to leave behind a fine, shimmering grit clinging to that sweat, well . . . they took bathing seriously.

The guest baths of the palace seemed almost like a temple to me. There was no *frigidarium*—the cold plunge pool the Romans were so fond of—and Elka almost cheered at that omission. There were several individual tubs, each with its own personal attendant. We were directed to sit waist-deep in the heady scented water sprinkled with flower petals while more fragrant water was poured over our heads. We were scrubbed to glowing with brushes, and our hair was washed with perfumed solutions and combed tangle-free. Musicians perched on a raised dais at the center of the tub room and played soothing melodies on lyres and sistra. The columns were painted like lotus flowers, and gossamer curtains floated like mist in the slightest breezes caused by fan bearers moving the air with gilded fans on long poles.

After the tubs, it was into the large pool to splash about, and then on to massage tables where honey and goat's milk was kneaded into our skin. I started to seriously wonder if maybe I *had* passed through to the Otherworld . . . and Aegypt *was* the Blessed Isles.

When I finally left the baths, toweled dry, and wrapped myself in a length of fine linen, I padded back to my room. It was larger than my whole house back in Durovernum. Ten times the size of my cell at the Ludus Achillea. I could stretch out on the middle of the bed and my hands and feet

wouldn't even touch the four corners. The walls of most
of the rooms were covered with elaborate painted murals,
filled with stylized, elegant figures of gods and royals
striding in stately processions, and surrounded by incom-
prehensible symbols that Cai told me were called "hiero-
glyphics"—the written language of the Aegyptians. I'd
barely begun to learn Latin letters and was suddenly very
glad that I'd grown up in a tribe that saw no use for such
things. I couldn't imagine the time it would have taken to
learn such complex mysteries, but I was sure it would have
conflicted unhappily with the hours I'd spent running
through the forests and sparring with Mael and Sorcha.

"You know there's a library here in Alexandria," Cai
had said, grinning, when I'd told him as much. "A great,
huge building solely devoted to the collection of scrolls
and tablets and all manner of writing. It's so big, it's almost
a city itself."

"I'm not sure I believe you," I said, gazing at him
narrowly.

"We'll go there one day," he said. "You'll see."

I sighed and rolled over onto my stomach on the ridiculous bed, staring at the god with the strange beard and the
green-painted skin on the wall. A city within the city. Just
the thought of it overwhelmed me. Alexandria, just outside
my window and across the harbor, already loomed large in
my mind, strange and forbidding and, I feared, ultimately
unknowable.

"Are you brooding?" Ajani said, popping her head in
through my door. "You're brooding again, aren't you?"

"What? No!"

"Yes, you are," she said, floating a little ways into the room, wrapped in a bright orange gown, her limbs and neck and ears dripping with gold and amber jewelry that made her look like a living torch. "Well, stop it. Your dress *and* your army of dressers—I swear, there's an *army* of them—will be around any minute to start winding you up in linens like one of their mummies. So prepare yourself for the ordeal. I'll see you at supper. Good luck!"

And then she was gone.

I sat up, blinking, and not a moment later, the "army" arrived, with their siege engines of fabric and jewels and belts and sandals . . . and they began their delicate, strategic assault on my appearance. The gossamer gown they dressed me in was a shade of green so pale and pretty it was like moonlight shining through a new leaf. Threads of silver were woven through the material and made it sparkle in the light of the multitude of lamps. My hair was dressed up with a thin silver band, and silver and amethyst gleamed at my throat and wrists and around my waist.

Thoroughly transformed, I made my way to the great hall where, one by one, we all gathered, drifting into the room like butterflies in a flower garden, a riot of color and sparkle. I saw that they'd draped Elka in sky blue again, the color that seemed to suit her best. She rolled her eyes when she saw me.

"Good thing we clean up all right," she said. "I mean, if they're going to keep fancying us up like this . . ."

I remembered the *first* time anyone had "fancied us up." Right before Charon had sold us to my sister at the slave auctions in Rome. I glanced around, wondering where the two of them were . . . and then I saw them. And smiled. My fears from earlier that day vanished like smoke on a breeze. Charon was handsomely attired in a long, sweeping robe dyed a shade of midnight blue with wide sleeves and a broad, wrapped sash around his waist. With his beard trimmed and his dark hair swept back from his brow, he somehow looked more lordly and more roguish, at the same time. But he stood there proudly with Sorcha on his arm, and for a moment, I almost didn't recognize her. The silvery, diaphanous gown she wore shifted and flowed like a cloud of mist all around her. At her throat, she wore a wide, jeweled collar, and instead of having her hair dressed up, she wore a wig in the Aegyptian style. Hundreds of tiny ebony braids, set with gold beads that shimmered and gleamed, swept past her shoulders and covered her forehead in a fringe, hiding the bandage that I knew must still be there, even after her visit to the Aegyptian doctors. Her eyes sparkled so brightly it was like looking up at a starry sky. They were rimmed with thick ebony kohl, and her lips and cheeks were dusted with carnelian and gold dust. But the most beautiful thing my sister wore that night was the smile on her face. And it shone mostly on the man at her side.

I shook my head, wondering that the Morrigan had seen fit to set Sorcha's feet—and mine and Charon's too— on such a strange, tangled, intertwined path. It was like one of the tortuous designs the tribes worked into our jewelry and art: knotted and twisted but ultimately—if one looked long enough—a thing of beauty.

"That frown clashes with your circlet," Elka said, nudging me with a sharp elbow. "Stop thinking so much, little fox. We're here for a party. A party thrown by the queen of Aegypt in *our* honor. If my wicked old mother could only see me now. I wonder what she'd think."

"That she sold you for too low a price."

Elka's wintery gaze flashed fiercely, and she nodded once. "*Ja*," she said. "Joke's on her."

Ajani wandered up to join us then, but her gaze shifted in the middle of a greeting, and her eyes went wide. "Oh . . ." she said. "Oh my . . ."

"What?" Elka asked.

"Would you look at that," Ajani said, smiling as she nodded toward the main entrance to the hall.

I turned and saw Gratia standing there. She was draped in a turquoise gown that was pleated in such a way that it flowed like a waterfall whenever she took a step. Her hair was loose about her shoulders, held back off her face with peacock-feather embellished combs, and Cleopatra's women had dusted shimmering powder over her eyelids and rouged her lips. I didn't think I'd ever seen Gratia in anything other than a practice tunic and armor. As she walked toward us, I couldn't stop staring in a combination of astonishment and frank admiration. Neither could Elka and Ajani.

"What?" she growled, glowering at us.

"I never realized how blue your eyes are," Ajani said.

"Nobody ever really looks past my fists long enough to notice," she said, raising them up in front of her face.

I reached up and grabbed her by the wrists. "You look spectacular," I said, and gave her a kiss on the cheek.

"Pff." She gave me a little shove. "Go find your ex-decurion to play at kissing with. *I'm* going to go find Devana and arm wrestle her for a crack at those boatmen."

Elka snorted in amusement and said, "I think there might have been enough for both of you."

Gratia grinned at her. "I guess we'll find out!"

And then she floated off, ethereal and dangerous all at once, and I shook my head in quiet amazement as I watched her go. But Gratia wasn't the only one to draw stares and loosen jaws that night. When our menfolk finally appeared, some of the ludus girls actually whistled at them. Kronos arrived first, draped handsomely in a flowing robe that made him look more like a statesman and less like the hard-bitten ex-legionnaire fight master he was. But then Cai, Acheron, and Quint strode into the hall together. And I knew that I wasn't the only one to feel a fluttering in my chest. Beside me, Elka made a little strangled sound in the back of her throat and grabbed a goblet off the tray of a passing slave.

The boys had divested themselves of anything remotely Roman-looking that night, and all three of them were dressed after the Aegyptian fashion. Cai was bare-chested, wearing sandals that strapped up to just below his knees and a pleated linen kilt, secured around his waist with a silver-and-coral-studded leather belt. He wore a wide, jeweled pectoral collar that rested on his shoulders in the shape of an eagle, wings outspread. His hair was brushed back from his face, and he was clean-shaven, looking freshly scrubbed and oiled from the baths. Quint and Acheron were dressed similarly, with subtle variations to their collars. Acheron's coppery braids fell about his shoulders, freshly dressed with blue and gold faience beads. Quint's military-short haircut was a bit jarring, perhaps, along with all the rest. But it was clear that the one person in the room whose opinion mattered to him couldn't have cared less. Of course, I wasn't sure Elka's gaze had actually managed to drift above the bare legion-conditioned contours of his chest . . .

When Quint strode over to her and offered his elbow, asking her to accompany him on a stroll through one of the two perfumed gardens open to the night sky beyond the pillars on either side of the hall, she nodded—devoid of any wry retort in the moment—and handed me her goblet without looking my way. Without looking *any* way but Quint's. I glanced over to see Kallista struggling mightily not to giggle with delight at her uncle, and I felt the same way myself about my friend. It was nothing short of wondrous to see the two of them—each so self-possessed on their own—reduce one another to blushing and stammering.

"An ass," Cai sighed, suddenly there at my side.

"But a loyal ass," I said, grinning, remembering how Cai had first described his second-in-command. A small part of me wondered what Quintus would be second of now here in Aegypt—indeed, wondered what *any* of us would be—but I pushed away the thought.

"And a smitten one," Cai said. Then he looked at me and took a step back, his gaze traveling the length of me from head to foot. "He's not the only one, either . . ."

"Not the only ass?" I asked playfully, hoping to distract from the heat that had crept up my face in a blush.

"You are a goddess, Fallon," Cai said in a low murmur, ignoring my diversion. There was heat of another kind, flaring like kindled embers, behind his eyes.

I held on to Elka's cup with numb fingers, unable to put it down because my brain and body seemed to have completely divided themselves from each other and I suddenly found myself incapable of the simplest of tasks. The great hall of the queen's palace seemed to grow dim and distant all around me until the only thing I could focus on was Cai. He smiled—that slow, secret smile of his—and plucked the goblet from my fingers. I honestly have no idea what he did with it or where he put it. I only knew that one moment I was standing there surrounded by a glittering crowd of Aegyptian dignitaries and warrior girls turned princesses, and the next Cai was leading me out into the moonlight—into the garden *not* currently occupied by Elka and Quint—his hand wrapped around mine, warm and strong, both our palms calloused from the sword.

The music and laughter carried on behind us, and the delectable smells of roasting fish and fowl slowly gave way to the scents of night-blooming flowers that perfumed the air. A pair of black granite sphinxes—with the body of a lion and the face of a man that bore a strong resemblance to Cleopatra herself—rested gracefully, watchfully on top of marble pedestals beneath the spreading branches of a flowering tree I couldn't identify.

"I wonder if that's her father," Cai said, gazing up at the serene, regal features.

"I think it must be," I said. "You can almost feel his spirit guarding this place, keeping his daughter safe . . ."

Cai looked at me and smiled. "Cleopatra, it seems, has many guardians."

We turned from the statues and strolled deeper into the shadows beneath the trees. The night air was soft and beguiling, as different from the air of the day as moonlight was from sunlight.

"What's bothering you?" Cai asked me.

"Why would you think something is bothering me?"

"Your hand," he said, and held our clasped hands up between us. "You always tighten your grip too much right before a big fight."

I looked down at his fingers. They'd gone a bit pale where I gripped them and pink at the ends. I sighed and smiled up at him, loosening my clenched fist. "I don't know what I'm expecting," I said. "There's nothing for me to fight here."

"And isn't that just a little bit nice, for a change?" he asked.

I nodded. It was. And yet . . .

"You did what you set out to do," he said. "Cleopatra is safe. Home. And you, Fallon ferch Virico . . . you're free."

"So are *you*," I said, smiling up at him. "Whatever shall we do with ourselves and all this idle time on our hands, here in this strange and sandy land?"

His gaze went a bit smoldery then. "I have a few ideas," he said, leaning down to lay a kiss in the hollow of my collarbone.

A horn sounded from inside the palace hall, calling us to the tables to feast.

Cai sighed. "Once all the festivities are out of the way, that is," he said.

Not *quite* completely free, it seemed. But together nonetheless, Cai had reminded me. And we would stay that way.

"Remember what I told you that night at my father's house," he said. "If you want me to, I will lie beside you under thatch, under marble and glass, under stars in the middle of a desert . . ."

"I *do* remember," I said, grinning a bit wickedly at him. "I never really thought you meant that last one. All that *sand* . . ."

He grinned back. "We don't actually have to go out into the dunes, you know."

"Oh good . . ."

He dipped his head back down and began nuzzling my other shoulder, sending shivers up and down my spine. "Unless, of course, you want to . . ."

"If you're that hungry," Elka's voice suddenly drifted over to us from beneath an archway, "supper is served. And we're not allowed to start eating until everyone is sitting. Apparently."

I could tell from her tone that, having been likewise summoned from *her* garden stroll, Elka was torn between her love of food . . . and her blooming affection for Quint. That in itself was a drastic change in how I was familiar with the world working. But it was one I could get used to. And as Cai led me back toward the lights of the dining hall, I told myself that I could get used to all the rest too. Eventually. So long as he was with me to look up at those stars.

XIX

TO BE COMPLETELY fair, I wasn't the only one having a wee bit of trouble finding solid footing in the sands of Cleopatra's glorious kingdom.

"There's no such *thing* as a female gladiator in this realm," I lamented to Sorcha one early morning as I sat with her in the courtyard off her rooms, enjoying the cool shade before the heat of the day took hold.

"Of course not," Sorcha said, sipping from a delicate blue glass cup. She made a face and put the cup down. Even from a distance, I could smell the pungent herbs of the medicinal tincture. "It's still a novelty even in Rome. Or, at least, it was until you and your band of war maidens made it so wildly popular."

"*My* band of war maidens, Lady Achillea?"

She gave me a wan smile. "*Our* band, then."

I snorted. "There are gladiatorial *arenas* scattered through this realm," I said, "but those are mostly in rough-and-tumble outpost cities. Maybe we could build one here in Alexandria. Maybe Cleopatra would dedicate it to Hatshepsut . . ."

I rattled on for a bit, and Sorcha made encouraging, noncommittal noises until a slender girl appeared, bringing a tray of dates and cold fowl for Sorcha to eat. She offered to bring me a tray as well, but I had no appetite. I wondered where Charon was—he was rarely away from Sorcha's side as she convalesced—but didn't bring it up. I'd promised Cai I would try to stop fretting over everyone and everything at the expense of my own serenity, but it was a hard thing to do. I was finally free of Pontius Aquila. Free of Caesar. A world away and without anything— without any*one*—left to fight. I should have been at peace. I wasn't. I left my sister to her breakfast and went in search of my fellow war maidens.

The longer we were in Aegypt, the more it became evident I wasn't the only one feeling uneasy. Most of the ludus girls spent a great deal of time those days prowling like wolves on the hunt through the halls and gardens of the palace on Antirhodos, and no one seemed quite able to figure out what to do with the whole restless pack of us. Eventually, for our amusement—or perhaps just to get us out of her hair while she reacquainted herself with matters of state after her long absence—Cleopatra instructed one of her generals to take us out on excursions to the garrison on the outskirts of the city of Alexandria and show us what it was like to be a soldier of Aegypt. We spent days watching drills and participating in target shooting and chariot racing and sharing and comparing techniques, and it felt so good to be able to stretch our muscles and hit things. And people.

The queen's personal guard were very accommodating in that respect.

Initially, I think they'd indulged us out of nothing more than duty to their queen. But I was also proud to see that, once we actually started to drill with them, it didn't take long before the men began to take us seriously. And Cai and Quint stood on the sidelines with "told you so" expressions on their faces.

Of course, not all the girls were quite so keen to dive back into the rigors of fight training. Unsurprisingly, we lost Neferet to the Great Library on the second day, and Antonia and Acheron eventually had to go fetch her to bring her back to our accommodations long after the sun had set. And then, one day, our entire contingent of Amazons decided to go exploring in the sprawling ancient city, taking along Kronos to act as their guide and chaperone. They returned to the palace that night starry-eyed and chattering of wonders and bearing a little woven basket full of multicolored glass-bead necklaces, which they gave out to the rest of us, to the delight of all the girls over supper.

The one they'd chosen for me was green and gold, with deep red carnelian stones as accents. It was beautiful and cool against my throat, it complimented my eyes and my skin tone and my hair . . . and it felt so strange to wear. It reminded me of all the bits of delicate finery—torcs and bangles and circlets—that I'd worn growing up in Durovernum as a girl. As a princess. I'd been away from that life for little more than two years, and yet it seemed so alien to me. I'd grown so accustomed to tunics and armor and a leather hair tie and nothing else. Nothing other than weapons. Dressed in delicate linen sheaths, I felt naked. Awkward and vulnerable.

Restless . . .

And then, late one evening, Cleopatra summoned me to her private chambers. Moonlight spilled in through the open ceiling of an elegant room with walls dressed in thin sheets of beaten silver inscribed with placid scenes of fishing and hunting, farming and sailing, all along the banks of the River Nile.

"In three months' time," the queen said, noticing the direction of my gaze, "the Inundation will begin. Every year the goddess Isis sheds tears for the death of her brother-husband Osiris, and the sacred Nile overflows its banks with the deluge of her sorrow. It is a time of mourning and of thanksgiving both, for those waters bring the rich soil to the fields and make our crops grow. So we honor his sacrifice, and her sorrow, in a celebration that lasts two weeks."

I looked over to see her watching me over the rim of a goblet.

"I wonder," she continued, "will you still be here to dance and feast with us then?"

I laughed, confused. "Majesty, where else would I go?"

"The world is wide, Fallon," she said.

I frowned, thinking about that, and shrugged. "Sorcha once told me that one day she'd take me to Athens—"

"Sorcha is your sister," the queen interrupted me. "*Not* your chaperone. She has her own destiny and you have yours, and one day those roads will diverge."

I blinked at her, startled by the sharpness of her words.

Her expression softened, and she smiled at me. "I simply meant that you are a woman grown now, Fallon," she said. "With a life of your own. You've been following in your dear sister's footsteps—whether you meant to or not—since you were a child. You have the chance now to take your freedom and find your *own* road and see where it leads you in the wide world. Greece, Hispania, Thrace, Carthage . . . wherever you'd like to go. I would give you money and means. Whatever you need."

I sat there, silent, lost for any kind of answer.

"Or," the queen continued, "you can stay here. And I will give you a place and position of honor in my guard, if that is what you want. What *you* want, Fallon."

"I . . ."

"You do not know what you want."

"Yes." I shook my head. "I mean, no. I don't. I don't *know*."

She sighed and gave me a sympathetic smile. "Might I make a suggestion?"

"Please, Majesty."

"A night spent in the temple of Sekhemet."

I blinked at her. "Will that help?"

"I think it might."

She dismissed me then, without further enlightenment. As I left the queen's chambers and made my way back to my own room, I thought I saw a shadow moving in the gardens that bordered the breezeway. But when I stopped to look, I saw only the silhouettes of date palms swaying in the night breeze. It could have been any one of Cleopatra's guards or slaves or even one of my own sisters. But the hackles on the back of my neck lifted, and I wondered if Sekhemet had not already begun stalking me, to prey upon or protect me. And I wished, with all my heart, that I could still hear the voice of the Morrigan whispering in my heart.

But the goddess had been silent, and I wondered if she had abandoned me after my demands of her on the road to Cosa. I wondered if she'd finally turned her face from me forever.

"Where are you going?" Elka asked. Again. It was a question she asked of me a lot. And I rarely had a satisfactory answer.

"I told you," I sighed. "I'm not supposed to tell you."

It wasn't that I didn't want to tell her. It was just that a priest from the temple of Sekhemet in Alexandria had sought me out after the morning meal that day and told me—in private—that the queen had made arrangements with his order and I was to be granted a private communing with the goddess. That night. And I was to tell no one. For reasons that weren't quite clear to me other than that the goddess herself was . . . private. Secretive.

What did I know? Other than that I was a rudderless ship on an unknown sea and I needed some kind of . . . pilot, landmark, *some*thing to point me in the right direction. So I heeded the priest's admonitions to keep my temple visit a secret and didn't tell Elka where I was going. I didn't even tell Cai.

"I'll be back in the morning," I said to Elka. "Try not to wreck the palace while I'm gone?"

She crossed her arms and raised an eyebrow, watching as I stepped onto the reed skiff, accompanied by the priest—a tall man with a shaved head and soulful brown eyes named Intef—and the boatman pushed off, working the single oar with practiced strokes to take me to the mainland. Out of sight of Elka back on the palace dock, I reached into the little pouch I wore on my belt and took out the lioness amulet Cleopatra had given me. I usually kept it tucked away there, along with my whetstone and Tartarus key. I stared at it for a moment, at the wise eyes of the goddess, and then clasped it around my neck. The queen had given it to me for protection, but I silently placed more trust in the swords I wore on my hips for that.

The air in Alexandria was perfumed with waves of spice and sweetness, rolling over one another, heady in my nostrils and hot-soft on my skin—which had gone from rosy to freckled after all the hours I'd spent out in the sun. The priest led me silently through the streets of the city, laid out in an orderly grid of wide, swept avenues, lined with temples and shops and the houses of the wealthy, decorated with the fantastical statues of Aegyptian gods, half-human and half-animal, striding boldly or standing serenely in little garden squares kept lush and green with water carried from the sacred River Nile.

The late afternoon was mellowing to evening when we reached the southwest quadrant of the city and the temple of the lioness. Inside Sekhemet's sanctuary, I found a place of peace and shadows. Ponds crowned with lotus flowers floating on emerald lily pads sparkled beneath the dappled shade of thorny-branched trees called myrrh. Inside the temple proper, there was a central chamber guarded by double doors, dressed in sheets of beaten silver like Cleopatra's rooms back in the palace. Instead of pastoral scenes, though, they were inscribed with scenes of war and carnage on one side and peace and plenty on the other.

Inside, there was a large main sanctuary surrounded by nooks and niches fitted with shrines and altars, private alcoves for worship, and public space for ritual. Double rows of stately columns marched toward a far dais, where a larger-than-life figure of the goddess Sekhemet was carved in black granite. She was seated overlooking a shallow bronze brazier filled with smoking coals in front of a long rectangular reflecting pool. The center of the sanctum roof was open to the sky, and I could imagine the stars reflecting back off the still, dark surface of the water at night. I thought about how beautiful that would be and then remembered I would find out soon enough.

Intef, my guide, led me to a temple anteroom and turned me over to a handful of priestesses. One of them pressed a cup into my hand and bid me drink. Then they took me to another room, instructed me to bathe, and once I was done, they brushed out my hair so that it hung loose down my back and gave me a linen garment to wear. It was simple and fell just to my mid-thigh, almost like a gladiatrix tunic, but it fastened with a single shoulder clasp carved of amber and was open on the side.

Back in the anteroom, I buckled my sword belt back on over the tunic to keep it closed, but Intef stepped forward and stopped me with a gentle, apologetic smile, gesturing to my weapons. I hesitated for a moment and then drew the twin swords from their sheaths, handing them over. He took them reverently and placed them in a cubbyhole with the clothes I'd worn there. Wishing me an auspicious night, he bowed himself out. I still wasn't entirely certain what I was supposed to accomplish.

And no one seemed inclined to tell me, either.

They just led me back out to the goddess chamber, where a sleeping pallet made of woven reeds had been laid out on the floor at the feet of the Sekhemet statue. On either side, incense burned in braziers suspended from tall standing metal poles—a subtle, beguiling fragrance that made my head begin to swim a little.

"We will lock the doors," the chief priestess, a regal older woman with long, expressive hands, informed me in heavily accented Latin. "No one will disturb you. Tonight is to be shared between you and the goddess. And whomever she sees fit to send to you."

"Whomever she *sends* me?" I frowned, not understanding. "But if the doors—"

She smiled. "In the morning all will be clear."

The priestesses drifted out of the temple, and I heard
the low thrum of bars sliding across the doors. The clank
of a heavy key turning. They had not only locked the
world *out*, they'd locked me *in*. I sighed and sat down
cross-legged on the reed mat in front of the granite statue
of the goddess. She was seated, human hands resting on
her lap, lioness eyes staring serenely over my head into
the unknown. I tried to clear my mind and ignore the
rumbling in my stomach that made me wish there was
something in it other than the honeyed mead they'd given
me to drink when I'd first arrived . . .

I was asleep before I even realized that I'd closed my
eyes and lain down.

At least, I *thought* I was asleep. At first.

But then light, crimson and flickering, bloomed in the
darkness, filtering through my closed eyelids. I sat up and
turned to see a figure swathed and hooded in a voluminous white robe standing in front of Sekhemet's statue,
stoking the embers in the brazier before the altar. A priest
of the temple, I thought. Until he turned and sat on the
steps of the statue with a weary sigh and pushed the cowl
back from his face. In the light from the glowing brazier, I
recognized the profile.

Gaius Julius Caesar.

A long way from home.

"Oh," he said in answer to my unvoiced thought, "so much farther away than you can imagine."

It wasn't the first time I'd had a conversation with someone who wasn't there. Only this time, I knew I really was talking to a dead man. I'd seen him killed with my own eyes. Not that it made things any less awkward.

"Did you know Arviragus still lives?" I asked, without even a proper greeting. Then cursed myself for my rudeness. Caesar didn't seem to notice.

"Ha." He looked up at the stars overhead—which were brighter than I'd ever seen them—and chuckled. "Is *that* why the old rogue wasn't there to greet me? I confess, I wondered. So many of the others were . . . Pompeii Magnus, Crassus, Cato . . . My beloved daughter, Julia . . ." His gaze drifted down from the sky to my face, and I saw stars reflected in his eyes. "This is very far from *your* green home too, my Victrix."

"Yes, well." I shrugged. "Someone had to get Cleopatra out of Rome after . . . well. After."

"Indeed."

A silence drifted down between us, and I wished I had some wine to offer him. Something. I realized in that moment that I actually missed my old dictator. My conqueror. The man who'd made me a shooting star in the arena of the Circus Maximus.

"Did you ever wonder, Fallon, why I crossed the sea to step my foot upon your shores?" he asked.

"I thought it was because invading far-off lands played well for the plebs back in Rome." As much as I missed him, it seemed I was still not wholly forgiving of him.

He raised an amused eyebrow at me. "So cynical." He tutted. "And after such a short time too."

I raised an eyebrow back at him.

"All right." He shrugged and adjusted the folds of his pristine, purple-striped toga. Not a dagger slash to be seen in it anywhere. Not a spot of blood. "You're not wrong. Do you know why else?"

"Gold? Lumber? Slaves?"

"Pearls."

I blinked at him. Pearls? It was true that the Island of the Mighty was rich with them, harvested from the rivers in the north and traded between the tribes. So rich in fact that, unlike the Romans and Aegyptians, who considered them a symbol of high status, we sometimes decorated our saddles and armor and children's dolls with them.

"I found the richest pearl of all there . . ." Caesar continued. "Your sister."

I thought about Sorcha's pearl-studded breastplate, which Caesar had enshrined in his temple of Venus. She'd been wearing it when she'd ridden out from Durovernum to meet the legions on the field of battle. The night she didn't come home. Spoils of war.

He laughed when I mentioned it and said, "Yes, well. The *real* ones were lovely too."

"You know you never actually conquered us," I said, comfortable with making such a statement to the ghost of a man when I never would have dared with the man himself. "You *know* that . . ."

He shrugged noncommittally.

"But you *could* have returned," I pressed. "Planted your golden eagles in the soil of Prydain and left them there."

He nodded. "Aye. I could have."

I looked at him through narrowed eyes, hearing in the tone of his voice something I would have never suspected of mighty Caesar. Reluctance. "You could have," I said, "but you didn't."

He shook his head and rose to his feet, picking up the poker to stoke the brazier coals to brighter fire. "No, Fallon," he said. "I didn't. And I wouldn't have, even if I'd lived to be an old man. I made the decision to leave that destiny for another. For one who comes after me."

"Why?"

He held the poker out in front of him like a sword and grinned at me. "Because there need always be worlds left to conquer."

"Even for you?"

"For me. For Rome." He sat down on the step again, his gaze drifting past me, past the marble columns that ringed us round. His eyes searched the distance beyond the temple. "There must always be that which is beyond one's grasp. Else what is there to strive for?"

This from a man who had put the stamp of his foot down on the soil of countries I hadn't even known existed growing up. I shook my head and sighed. "I don't know if I'll ever fully understand the Roman mind."

He laughed. "That's because you don't need to. And it would poison your own mind if you did. You are a pure creature, Fallon. A pearl of great price. I envy you that. And I wonder sometimes . . ."

"Wonder what, my lord?"

"What you would have become had you stayed where you were, running wild through your forests and fields."

"I would have become what I am still, Caesar," I said. "What I have always been. A Cantii warrior."

"Indeed . . ."

He looked at me with almost fatherly affection, and I felt a twist in my heart that he was dead and I'd been able to do absolutely nothing to alter that fact. And then I felt another, sharper twist that I should feel that way for him.

"A remarkable girl from a remarkable people," he said. "It would not surprise me if one day your little island became an empire to be reckoned with all on its own."

My little island? With my father, the king. Ruling—just like all the other kings back home—from the hearth of a stone hut, lord over herds of cows and squabbling chieftains. I shook my head. I had seen Rome now, and I had seen Aegypt, and I had seen the magnificent cities and the bustling towns in between. A Prydain *empire*? Great Caesar's ghost was dreaming.

And so was I.

But dreamers wake. And I woke then too.

The brazier was cold. Dark.

Useless, I thought. The goddess hadn't sent me a destiny or a direction. She'd sent me a vision of a dead man with delusions. I was no closer to knowing what to do or where to go than I had been before I'd come to this place. I pushed myself up to one elbow on the reed mat and stared up at the stone visage of the lion-headed goddess reproachfully. Not even the Morrigan was so cryptic in her messages—if a message it had even been.

I sighed in the darkness lit only by torches hanging on the lotus columns. Perhaps it was my own fault. Maybe I'd done something wrong. Or maybe the goddess only spoke to her own people. I rolled up onto my knees and looked down into the black mirror of the reflecting pool. I saw only the moon above and a bounty of stars framing my own face. For a moment.

And then I saw something else.

The glint of torchlight on a dagger blade raised high over my head . . .

And Acheron's face, smiling triumphantly, over my shoulder.

XX

I GASPED AND lunged forward, diving into the temple's reflecting pool as the blade descended. I felt the wind of the slash between my shoulder blades in the instant before the water closed over me. Beneath the surface, I kicked for all I was worth, knifing through the water toward the far end of the pool. Faster, I hoped, than Acheron could run.

But he wasn't running.

I swam the full length of the pool and scrambled to hoist myself up out of the water. But when I turned around, I saw that Acheron was still at the other end of the temple, lounging in the lap of the Sekhemet statue, spinning the dagger he carried in his hand like a top. I ducked behind a lotus pillar and pressed myself against it, my tunic dripping wet and clinging to me. My hands went automatically to the scabbards at my sides . . . and found them empty.

"Where are you going to go, Victrix?" he called. "They've locked you in for the night, and no one knows you're here. No one but me."

The shadow in the palace garden, I remembered suddenly. After Cleopatra had summoned me and told me to seek out the goddess, I thought I'd seen something. Someone.

"You were in the queen's garden last night."

"I was," he said. "I was going to kill *her*, you see. But I can always get around to that later. Because no one will suspect I was the one who killed *you* first. No one knows you're here." He laughed. "Not even your precious soldier boy."

Acheron was an assassin, I thought. And I'd brought him right into Cleopatra's house. I cursed myself for being a fool. And then I told myself I could stop being one any time now, as that might help me figure a way out of what was clearly a bad situation.

One that became instantly, infinitely worse in that moment.

I heard the scuff of a sandal and spun around in time to see the jackal god Anubis himself swinging a sword at my head. With a terrified yelp I dropped into a crouch as splinters of stone, chiseled from the pillar by the blow from his blade, cut my cheek. I lurched past my assailant and scurried into one of the smaller altar spaces, ducking behind a stone plinth and trying not to pant with fear. Acheron wasn't alone. He had the Aegyptian god of the dead with him!

The adversary of the goddess Sekhemet herself . . .

But then, when I risked a glance around the corner of the plinth I hid behind, I saw it wasn't a god at all. It was a man in a jackal mask. Like the corpse-hook-bearing attendants of the arenas in Rome.

But that made no sense. What was one of *them* doing here?

What if I was still dreaming?

That had to be it. Not a dream, but a nightmare.

But whether it was or wasn't, I needed time to figure out my next move. Time and darkness. There was a lit torch in a sconce on a pillar just above me. I reached up and knocked it loose, throwing it into the middle of the reflecting pool and casting that corner of the temple, at least, into darkness. Acheron laughed as the smoke from the doused flames curled up toward the stars overhead.

"What are you going to do in the dark?" he called out. "They took your weapons. And you, stupid girl, you let them. Sekhemet is a goddess of bloodshed and battle. She would never have relinquished hers so readily. You shouldn't have either."

He had a point. I couldn't imagine the Morrigan ever demanding unarmed worship—the very notion seemed counterintuitive for a battle goddess. Maybe it had been some kind of test—one I'd clearly failed—and now this was the consequence of that failure.

"Do you know what made me a good gladiator, Victrix?" Acheron's voice floated through the dim air. "Do you?"

When I kept silent, he answered his own question.

"I like to watch men suffer," he said, and laughed.

By the sound of his voice, I could tell he was still over near the statue. I didn't know where Acheron's accomplice was, but I took a chance and made a dash for another lotus pillar at my end of the pool and threw that torch into the pool as well. I heard a grunt of annoyance from somewhere off to my right. The jackal man was near . . .

"Like I watched your soft-hearted decurion suffer," Acheron continued, "every time the letter-bearers came round to the Ludus Flaminius . . . with no scrolls addressed to poor Caius Varro."

No scrolls? But I'd sent letters weekly. "One of the advantages of being the lanista's trusted lackey. I got myself assigned to mail duty and amassed quite a little collection of love tokens meant for some of the other lads."

"You *bastard* . . ." I hissed.

The anger that bloomed in my chest was almost enough to make me step out into the open to confront him. But that's what his taunts were designed to do. I knew that. So I darted, instead, for the next pillar over and snuffed out another torch.

"I even thought about keeping those scrolls of yours tucked away instead of sending them back to you . . ." He laughed again, and it was an ugly sound. "Almost opened one up once or twice just to amuse myself—see what kind of sweet words I was keeping away from Varro's pretty eyes—but it was actually better imagining how *you* felt every time one returned to your hands, the seal unbroken."

"Why do you hate me so much, Acheron?" I asked, creeping around an altar covered in offerings—small stones carved in the shape of the scarab beetle, a sacred symbol to the Aegyptians. I whispered an apology to Sekhemet and scooped up a few of them in my hand. "Why *did* you? We'd never even met—"

"A man doesn't suffer once he's dead," Acheron snapped, his voice turning hard and cold. "And *you*, Victrix, killed the one man in all this world I wanted to suffer the most. Didn't you? Blood of my blood spilled by your hand."

Ixion . . .

His brother.

I'd cut that evil bastard's throat at the Ludus Achillea, and Acheron knew it. He'd known all along that Ixion was dead, and somehow he knew that *I* was the one who'd killed him. *But how?*

"Acheron," I said, "I'm sorry—"

"No, you're not!" he cut my apology short with a snarl. "And why should you be? I should know better than anyone—Ixion was a soulless monster. You think I got all these scars in the arena? No . . . he was a monster, and you cut his throat. And that was a far cleaner death than he deserved."

I could tell by the sound of his voice that he was moving, stealthily, silently . . . unlike his jackal accomplice, he must have taken off his sandals. His casual, languid pose over by the statue had been a feint, but I listened keenly to his voice and knew he was on the move.

Hunting me . . .

"I don't understand," I called out, intent on keeping him talking. "Ixion tortured you growing up together and you're *angry* he's dead? He—"

"Taught me!"

I heard his hand slam against stone. He was over near one of the small altars. I froze, doused another torch, and then scurried, mouse quiet, in the opposite direction I'd been moving.

"He toughened me up," Acheron continued. "I'm not angry, Victrix. I just really, *really* wanted to be the one to kill him. Now? I'll just have to settle for killing you instead. But you know what? The beauty of it is . . . *that* will still serve my god, Dis, and my master, Pontius Aquila, just fine."

There it was. *That* was how Acheron knew I'd killed his brother. Because when Pontius Aquila had found Ixion's body, he'd just assumed—correctly—that it had been me who'd killed him. And Acheron was Aquila's man. He had been from the beginning.

His reasons for hating me were legion.

"Fate's a funny old thing," he continued, his voice tracking to my right. "I almost thought that idiot Yoreth had you convinced to let *him* out of his cell so he could join your noble little band. But he was so stupid you probably would have guessed his allegiance before you reached the gate out of the city."

Yoreth too? My own countryman . . .

"You're *both* Sons of Dis?" I could hear the horror in my voice.

I also heard a whispery snicker ten—maybe fifteen—paces to my left. The jackal man, it seemed, was enjoying my distress. Enough to forget himself for an instant.

"Most of us in there were." Acheron's voice was closer. Softer. "The arena is a place of sacred death, Victrix. You . . . you *girls* don't understand that—you never could—but we men of the arena? The true gladiators? We embrace it. Revel in it. Your soldier boy is lucky to have survived as long as he did. I'll have to remedy that too."

"But you stood with him in the arena. You—"

"Once I saw you in the stands at the theatrum games," he continued, "I thought, well . . . honey catches flies and all that. How best to get close to Caesar's Victrix? Get close to her son-of-a-whore lover. And then, of all the great good fortune, you yourself rescued me. Welcomed me into your little band. And when I found out you lot were sailing—with the great bitch queen herself, no less—to Aegypt? The very land where the Sons of Dis were born. Where there are temples dedicated to our great dark lord. I *told* you I had a destiny . . ."

He was moving again, off to my right, circling behind. The jackal man was still to my left . . .

They were trying to box me in. I looked up to see that the moon had drifted far enough past the temple that her light no longer shone down through the open roof. The goddess's face no longer reflected in the mirror pool . . .

"You know . . . no one ever expected those soft-handed senators to carry out the deed and kill Caesar," he continued, clearly reveling in the opportunity to flaunt his own cleverness. "Truthfully, I never really thought the tyrant *could* fall. But he did. Praise Dis Pater . . ."

I took a chance and peered around the pillar I hid behind. Acheron was standing, facing the other direction. The last of the light glimmered on the blade in his fist—and on its reflection—and I saw it clearly. I felt all the blood in my body rush from my head to my feet. I felt as if I might faint, but I couldn't tear my eyes from the red stone in the hilt of the weapon . . . and the rust-brown stains on the blade. It was the same knife Aquila had dipped in Caesar's blood.

I wondered if his ghost was still near, watching . . .

But how? I wondered. *How did Acheron come by that blade?*

And then I remembered when we'd been trying to leave the city after Caesar's murder . . . and Acheron had been the one to lead the Dis gladiators away from the gate. Once out of sight, they, in turn, could lead him to Aquila. Who'd given Acheron the dagger and his orders.

Orders to stay with us.

To ingratiate himself with our company. To wait for an opportunity.

And now I knew, too, how Hestia had really died.

A fire that blazed hot for vengeance kindled to life in my chest. I made a dash for the last lit torch and lobbed it into the pool, plunging the temple into absolute blackness.

"And I also knew," Acheron continued, "that even with Caesar dead, Aquila was still never going to give up his quest for *your* soul, sweet gladiatrix. One way or another, he is going to have it. And now? I'll be the one to deliver it to him . . . *Hah!*"

I heard him strike stone with steel in the place where I'd been standing only a moment earlier. Except that, in the darkness, I'd silently slipped back into the pool, careful not to make so much as a ripple on the water.

I heard him whispering, "Where is she, Intef?"

There was an answering murmur.

Intef. The priest who'd brought me to the temple from the palace. The one who'd taken my swords. That explained, at least, how Acheron had gotten in through the locked doors. And it gave me some idea of just how deep the corruption of the Sons of Dis ran here in Aegypt. At least as deep as in Rome.

I still clutched the scarab pebbles I'd taken from the altar, and I threw one into a far corner. It made a clattering sound, and I could hear them move off in that direction. When they couldn't find me there, Acheron started talking again, taunting me in hopes I'd give away my position.

"Of course, your countryman Yoreth will get his reward too," he called out. "Don't worry about that, Victrix. He's on his way back home now. Well, back to *your* home, that is. With Aquila and a whole regiment of Dis mercenaries. I imagine once the walls of your little village fall, he'll probably make himself right at home in the cozy house that used to be yours . . ."

Home . . . No . . .

A wave of fear and fury washed over me at his words. I tried hard to ignore the sensation, concentrating instead on just the sound of his voice. I threw another scarab over near the private devotee shrines and heard the scrabble of Intef's sandals—and then a muffled curse as the priest slammed his shin on one of the low altars.

"Do you hear me, Victrix?" Acheron continued, his tone growing angrier. "I'll join them once I'm through with you here. I'll put my feet up by your dear old papa's great roaring fire. And I'll toast to his severed head hanging on the doorpost. Isn't that the way you barbarians like to celebrate a victory? That's what Yoreth always said . . . I'll drink your old man's beer and laugh while the Collector and his loyal Sons gather up all your pretty warrior friends and neighbors and send them packing back to his ludus. Endless, peerless fodder for Pontius Aquila's munera."

The water of the reflecting pool was warm, but I suddenly felt ice cold.

"Are there any more like you back home?" I remembered that vile, drunken senator at Octavia's party had asked me.

There were. Of course there were.

So very many pearls to gather.

And that was where Pontius Aquila had gone. I didn't think that was what Caesar had meant when he'd told me—when his shade had told me—that he'd leave the conquest of the Island of the Mighty to others. But without Caesar to stop him—without *anyone* to stop him—the Collector had gone to enrich his collection. If he couldn't have me, he would take my folk . . . and he would make them suffer. As Acheron had said: fodder for his munera.

I have to do something, I thought.

But first, I had to survive the night.

Suddenly, a torch flared in the darkness. Intef knew where everything was in the temple. He must have found an unlit torch to thrust into the dying coals of the brazier at the far end of the pool. He scuttled around, setting fire to offerings and braziers and anything else that would produce any amount of light. I had only moments to act before he or Acheron found me. I slipped silently back out of the pool at the far end. The water that ran from my limbs made no sound as it pooled on the thick woven rugs laid on the tiled floor. I remained undetected, but I was weaponless—Intef had seen to that, stowing my blades safely out of my reach in the anteroom and leaving me with only empty scabbards and a whetstone in my belt pouch.

As sullen orange light from the flames began to fill the temple, I reached into the pouch. Without blades to sharpen, the whetstone was basically useless—the most I could do was keep it in my fist to hit my assailants if one came close enough—but at least that was something. But then, as my fingers closed around it, my knuckles brushed something colder than stone . . .

Acheron found me in the same moment as I found the jagged iron key his brother, Ixion, had turned in the lock of my Tartarus prison cell. One of the few things I'd carried with me from the Ludus Achillea when we'd left. As Acheron's hand descended with bruising force on my shoulder, spinning me around, my fingers closed on the heavy iron key, on its ugly clawlike contours. A hideous grin split Acheron's face as he lifted Pontius Aquila's bloodstained blade high above me . . .

I lunged upward, the Tartarus key clutched in my fist like a dagger.

And I drove it straight through his eye.

With a cry of agony he dropped Aquila's knife, and it clattered across the tile floor. Acheron clutched weakly for the key jutting obscenely out from his eye socket before toppling backward and hitting the surface of the reflecting pool with a splash like a thunderclap. His copper-hued braids floated out like river weeds, and I dropped to my knees at the water's edge, watching as his body sank in a swirling red cloud to the bottom.

The breath left my lungs in a sob of relief, but then I looked up to see Intef standing only ten paces away from me, a smoking torch held tightly in one fist and a curved sword held in the other. His features were still hidden from me by the jackal mask he wore, but I heard him snarl like an animal as he took a step forward.

His second step faltered.

And as a sword's point seemed to suddenly sprout like a flower from the center of his naked chest, he fell to his knees in front of me. As he pitched forward onto his face, I looked up to see Cai standing there, a second blade in his hand, staring down impassively at the dead priest like an avenging god.

"Cai!" I screamed. I leaped up and ran to him.

"Fallon . . ." He wrapped his arms around me so tightly that for a moment I couldn't breathe.

When he let me go, I looked back and forth from him to the dead priest at our feet. There was something sticking out from beneath his body. Something shiny . . . I reached down and picked up the silver feather. The symbol of the Sons of Dis. It used to terrify me. But now? Now it just filled me with anger. And determination to put an end to the evil that had wrought it. I tucked it into my belt pouch, in place of the Tartarus key.

"How did you find me?" I asked quietly.

"I didn't. I followed him." He nodded at the body in the water. "Acheron skulked out of the palace not long after you left with this creature." He nudged dead Intef with his foot.

"Why? Why did you follow?"

"Remember what Caesar said about blind trust?" Cai smiled ruefully. "Apparently his advice somewhat belatedly stuck with me. I never fully trusted Acheron. And I've never trusted a priest—of any kind."

"He's not a real priest," I said. "At least, not one of Sekhemet's. He's one of the Sons of Dis. They both are. Were . . . Acheron has been working for Aquila all this time. I think he murdered Hestia."

Cai shook his head in disgust. "Then I'm glad to be suspicious in this case," he said. "Although, to be fair, Quint's smelled something off about him for a few days now too. And when we saw him heading for the docks on Antirhodos—when Elka had already complained to Quint about you heading off into the city on your own with that priest as your guide—well, we got curious."

"Are they here?" I asked.

Cai nodded. "The two of them are outside now, watching our backs. I'm sorry it took me so long to get to you. The doors were locked, and I had to find a high window that opened into a temple storeroom. It was a tight squeeze."

He smiled at me, and I was suddenly overwhelmed with gratitude for the friends I had somehow managed to be deserving of. Cai took my hand and turned to go, but I pulled him back.

"Cai," I said, "Acheron intercepted letters I sent to you. He returned them all to me unopened. To torment us both. I wanted you to know. In case you thought . . ."

Cai's smile vanished and his eyes flashed with anger. And something else. He *had* thought—as I had—that we'd stopped communicating for all those months. That I hadn't wanted to see or hear from him . . . I could tell by the look in his eyes.

But all he said was, "After all your hard work learning Latin? For that alone, Acheron needed to die."

I squeezed his arm and then let go, stepping over to the edge of the pool before we left the temple. For a long moment, I gazed down at Acheron. The scars on his chest and arms gleamed white in the water, and a faint, distant wash of pity brushed fleetingly over my heart. The Tartarus key was, in a way, his brother Ixion's last act of brutality against him.

I knelt down and picked up the dagger with its bloodstained blade.

Caesar's blood.

"Cleopatra might want this," I said. Then I bowed my head to the statue of Sekhemet the lioness and walked with Cai out of the temple room. I never once looked back.

XXI

THE SKY IN the east was beginning to glow with sunfire, and the predawn shadows were shades of deep purple and blue between the pillars that led from the docks on Antirhodos to the palace of the queen of Aegypt. Sekhemet hadn't sent me a cryptic vision after all. She'd sent me a singular message, simple and straightforward. It hadn't come from Caesar—that had been my *own* dream, perhaps, something I'd carried into the temple with me. No, it had come from Acheron.

And that message was: *Go home, Fallon. You're needed.*

But first, I had to speak to Sorcha.

I was almost running through the halls by the time I reached the wing where Sorcha had her rooms. The torches burning in the halls there guttered and smoked, untended, and the only slaves I encountered hid their faces from me as I passed. Usually the palace was buzzing like a hive in the hour before daybreak, but on that morning, there was an eerie quiet blanketing the place. I started to run.

Cai and Elka both called out my name, but I didn't stop.

Something was wrong. Terribly wrong—I could feel it in my bones . . .

"Sorcha!" I called as I ran. *"Sorcha!"*

I turned the last corner, into the short hall that led to a door emblazoned with a life-size painting of Isis. Charon was there, standing in front of it. Waiting for me. He looked like he hadn't slept in days. It occurred to me that I hadn't seen him very much over the past week and then only at a distance. As I went to go past him into my sister's chamber, he put out a hand and stopped me.

"Fallon—"

"Get out of my way, Charon."

"No." He didn't move. "Fallon, you have to listen to me. She doesn't want to see you right now."

"Why not?"

His dark eyes locked on mine, and I almost couldn't hold his gaze for all the soul-searing pain I saw there. "All right," he said. "She doesn't want *you* to see *her* right now. Not like this."

"Like what, Charon?" I snapped. "Let me past—"

"No!" He took a step to block my way.

I shoved him back against the door, out of my way. It was a hard shove—I was angry—but it wasn't hard enough to make him double over in agony. Or cough up blood. Both of which he did in that moment.

"Charon, what . . ."

I stared at him in horror as he reached up inside the embroidered sleeve of his robe and withdrew a cloth that was already stained red-brown in places. Many places. With an expression that was more irritation than concern, he dabbed at the corner of his mouth.

"Why didn't you tell me?" I asked quietly.

"Because you would have told *her*."

How would that have made a difference? I wondered. How could Sorcha not have known just by *looking* at him that . . .

"You're dying." The words clawed at my throat. "Aren't you? The wound never healed and you—"

"I'm *happy*," he said. "For the first time in my life."

He glared at me from under his brows, daring me to argue his assertion, as Cai and Elka caught up and joined us in our tense standoff. Elka made a small, distressed noise when she saw Charon's condition. There was nothing I could do for him in that moment. I took another step toward the door.

"I promised her I would keep you away," Charon said to me, ignoring the others.

"I have to see her," I said. "I have to speak with her."

"I—"

"*Please*, Charon."

Maybe it was the "please" that did it—a word not many people used when dealing with a slave trader—or maybe it was just that he simply didn't have any strength left himself to stop me. But his shoulders slumped, and he took a step back and let me pass.

I stepped into the room, and the smell of blood—fresh and stale both—assaulted my nostrils. Inside her chamber it was a contained whirlwind of chaos, centered around the bed on the raised platform. Slaves hurried back and forth with basins and cloths and incense burners, waving fans to rid the room of the stench of sickness and a fog of pungent medicinal smells. Cleopatra was there in a simple sleeping sheath, sitting tense and upright in a backless chair surrounded by a handful of her women. Her hair was held back from her face by a plain linen band, and her face was bare of her usual cosmetics. Her gaze on my sister was focused, unblinking, and her cheeks were dry.

Neferet's weren't. When she saw me, she ran to me.

My friend, my ludus sister, was weeping and trying desperately not to.

"I'm so sorry, Fallon," she said.

"Is she . . ." I swallowed hard, trying to speak past the fist that seemed jammed in my throat. "Is . . ."

There was a man there, bald, wearing a floor-length linen kilt belted around his waist and no shirt or pectoral collar. He was skinny, his chest showing the ridged bones of his rib cage, and he was spattered up to his elbows in blood. Sorcha's blood, welling from an incision he'd already made on her scalp.

"Her injuries are grave," Neferet explained in answer to my unfinished question. "Old and new, the damage to the inside of her skull has been compounded. And it's worsening. Blood has been collecting, pooling there—like a bruise, like I told you—pressing on her brain. The physicians have been keeping her pain-free with poppy draughts, but last evening, she began having seizures."

While I was in a temple. Talking to phantoms.

My brave, glorious sister . . .

"What is that man doing?" I asked quietly. I was trying hard not to shake.

"He's trying to release the pressure."

"He's . . ." I couldn't say the words. But I knew then that he was the kind of surgeon Neferet had told me about on the boat, when Sorcha had been ill and confused. He was cutting a hole in my sister's skull.

Neferet laid a hand—very gently—on my arm. "Maybe we should wait outside."

I hesitated, but then Sorcha moaned like an animal, and the sound of the bone saw was like someone filing the burrs from a sword blade with a dull, rusty rasp. The smell of burning, though, was what finally drove me from the room. Outside in the corridor I collapsed against Cai. Charon had told him what was happening—I thankfully didn't need to—and he led me outside to sit on a garden bench while the sun rose, gilding the waves out in the Great Harbor of Alexandria.

"I have to speak to her," I kept saying. "I have to tell her. We have to go home. She has to come with me. I can't . . . I can't do this . . . I . . ."

He didn't try to comfort me with empty promises about how she would be all right. About how we would go triumphantly home together. He just wrapped his arms around me as I shook. I don't know how long we sat there.

It must have been an hour. Maybe two. I suppose it could have been a day or two and I don't know that I would have noticed the difference. But eventually Cleopatra herself came out to find me. To tell me Sorcha was dead, I thought.

But instead, she said, "She wishes to see you now."

Then she held out her hand and led me back into Sorcha's room.

I could still smell the blood. And the burning. But faintly. A waft of cedar incense perfumed the air, masking most of the odor, and the room itself was pristine and orderly. The bed linens were crisp and tucked neatly around the limp figure lying there, with Charon sitting close beside, holding her hand.

They had shaved my sister's head, and there was a small square bandage covering half of her forehead, just above her left eye. And the white of that eye was crimson. But other than that, she looked surprisingly well. Pale but smiling, her head cushioned on a thick pillow. I remembered how her eyes had shone so brightly at the banquet. How relaxed and happy she'd seemed. How serene and untroubled in the days since. I knew now that it must have been the Aegyptian medicines, the draughts of poppy wine they had been giving her.

"Fallon?"

"I'm here, Sorcha."

"See?" she said. "Not dead yet. You were worried for nothing."

"I wasn't worried." I tried to smile, but it felt like the muscles of my face were frozen stiff. "I always thought you would die in battle. I mean, I already thought you had. Now I just assume you're unkillable. And you'll be well again soon. I know it. You have to get well, Sorcha. There's a battle still to fight, you and me, together. Aquila has gone to Prydain, and Father—"

"Fallon." She tried to quiet my babbling. *"Fallon."*

"I . . ."

"Dear little sister." She could still smile at me.

It wasn't fair, I thought. She was always so much better at things than me . . .

"There's something you need to understand," she said. "I'm not *you*, Fallon. And I'm not who you've always imagined me to be, either. You think I am this questing, heroic soul. Always searching, never resting. That isn't you looking through a window and seeing *me*, but you looking at a mirror . . . and seeing yourself." She reached for my hand and drew me nearer. "When we were young, I always knew you would be the one to achieve greatness. I was restless when I was young. Now? All I *want* is to rest. And I can do that now. Now that I have known happiness. Now that I know you will carry on for both of us. Wherever you go . . . whatever you do . . ."

Through the pain in my heart I searched my soul to see if I could find the truth in what she said. I thought back to the moments when I'd made Sorcha put on *my* armor to go back into the arena to fight Nyx in my place. I remembered how uncertain she'd seemed . . . and how—maybe—I might have convinced myself at the time that it was only because she'd been too long away from the fight. Looking back on that moment now, I wondered. Maybe Sorcha really wasn't the warrior queen I'd always imagined her to be. Maybe I would have to be content with her as just a queen. Maybe even just my sister.

"You should rest," Charon said to her, softly.

She turned her head slightly and said, "In a moment, love."

The room went blurry from the tears that filled my eyes.

"Fallon . . ." Sorcha let go of my hand and waved in the direction of a trunk set against one wall of her room. "Go. Open it."

I stood and crossed the room. When I lifted the lid of the trunk, I saw that it contained all of Sorcha's things that she'd brought with her on our journey from the Ludus Achillea. There wasn't much. But underneath a folded cloak, there was the thing I knew she wanted me to see. Her armor. The breastplate—the one studded with river pearls from Prydain that Caesar had installed as a spoil of war, displayed in his temple of Venus Genetrix. I lifted it gently, reverently, out of the trunk and held it up in front of me so I could look at it. There was a scar on the leather from a sword blade where it covered the ribs on one side and another scar on the back piece. But other than that, it was in beautiful condition. The leather oiled and supple, the bronze buckles and fittings polished to gleaming, and the multitude of pearls glowing with an ethereal shine.

"The one in the temple is a fake." Sorcha's laugh was a thready whisper. "A cleverly made replica."

"Does . . . I mean, *did* Caesar know?"

"It was his idea," she said. "He gave that one back to me and said that his pearl collection should stay together. I never really knew what he meant by that . . ."

I knew.

"Wear it home, my sister," Sorcha said, her voice growing fainter. "Lead the war band. *Your* war band. Like I once did . . ."

I crossed back over to her side. "I can't do this alone."

"You are the furthest thing from that."

"I can't do it without *you*."

"I'm not going anywhere," she said. "Not really. I've always been with you. Too much, I think. But know that I always will be."

"Aren't you afraid?"

She rolled her head back and forth a little on the pillow. "Caesar once told me that he didn't understand those who feared death," she said. "It will come when it comes, he said. To everyone. Even to him."

"He fought against them. His murderers . . ."

"Well, not being afraid to die isn't the same as not wanting to live." She smiled, and her expression grew distant. "I had a dream last night. I saw a raven in the sky. Biggest one I'd ever seen. Beautiful. Only . . . it had the wings of an eagle. Isn't that strange?"

I looked at Charon and he looked at me.

I wondered if he'd ever told Sorcha about the mark on the second sword he'd had made for me. But he shook his head, a small, bemused frown on his face.

"I'm thirsty," Sorcha murmured.

I looked around, but when they'd cleaned up the room, they hadn't left a water pitcher behind. Charon went to stand, but I shook my head. "Stay with her," I said. "I'll go."

When I returned to the room, Charon was sitting on the bed with Sorcha curled up beside him, her body curved around his and her head resting in his lap. He had his arm laid across her shoulder, and their fingers were woven together. And he was smiling gently, staring at the ceiling and lost in thought or a memory or . . .

"Charon?"

When he didn't answer me, I set the tray down on a table and walked slowly over to them. There was only a small trickle of blood at the corner of Charon's mouth, a thin crimson line that disappeared into his beard. And Sorcha looked for all the world as if she were asleep. Dreaming a wonderful dream . . .

I reached over and closed Charon's dark, empty eyes.

And then my knees gave out. I laid my head down on the bed and I wept for them both.

XXII

I DON'T REMEMBER returning to my own chambers after they found me there, still kneeling at the side of Sorcha's bed. I only remember waking up in mine, wondering where I was. What had happened . . . Then it all came crashing back to me.

My sister was gone.

And I was going home. Alone.

"I'll gather the others, then, and we can tell them what's going on," Elka was saying. "I mean, I know you'll want to leave as soon as . . . well, as soon as we can."

I stood staring out the window at the lighthouse in the Great Harbor. Elka hadn't left my room since I'd woken up. She been there when I had. Cai, she'd told me, was making . . . arrangements. On my behalf. So I wouldn't have to. I loved him for that. I don't think I would have been able to sit down with Cleopatra in that moment to plan for Charon and my sister's funerary monument. I think that would have broken me beyond repair.

"How long a journey is it, do you think, from here all the way back to your island? I would think that we'd go overland from Massilia. We can get carts again, and Quint will know the fastest routes—"

"Elka." I turned to face her. "I'm not asking the others to come with me."

"Sorry?"

"And I think it's probably for the best if you stay here too," I said. "You and Quint."

"What in the world are you talking about?" She looked at me as if I'd suddenly just started to speak Aegyptian.

"You'll have a life here," I said. "Just look at this place. It's a palace. We never imagined such a place existed when we were back at the Ludus Achillea. It's like a kind of dream. You'll be happy and you'll be rich. All of you. I *have* to go, but the rest of you can stay here and be happy."

Elka pulled no punches. She stared at me, unblinking, and said, "Maybe you've been hit on the head just like your sister, *ja*?"

A wave of cold anger washed over me. "What did you say?" I asked quietly.

"It would explain your loss of memory," she answered, just as quietly.

"I don't know what you're talking about."

"Really." She crossed her arms over her chest. "You don't remember when you told us that if we're together we keep our purpose?"

"Elka—"

"*My* purpose isn't to live in a palace guarding a queen who isn't mine, in a land that never even knows the glory of a midwinter frost."

"This isn't your fight. Durovernum's not your home."

"But it's yours. And that makes it mine. Together, remember? Or have you forsaken me as your sister?"

I glared at her flatly. "My blood sister is staying here. In a tomb."

She nodded. "Yes. She is. Laid to rest there by the woman she called friend above all others, beside the man she—finally, it must be said, because she was just as damnably stubborn as you—the man she *finally* realized she loved. Sorcha doesn't need her gladiatrices anymore. I thought you still did. We still need *you*, little fox."

"Damn it, Elka!" I snapped in frustration. "We're not shackled together by the ankle anymore. I won't be responsible for dragging you to the end of the world just so you can die for the sake of a backwater kingdom I never should have left in the first place! I don't want that on my soul. Can't you make a life for your*self*?"

She took a step back. The look on her face was like I'd slapped her. Hard.

"No," she said. "No, I can't. Not like you. I don't have a den left to return to, little fox. None of us do. You know, I think your sister was wrong. You aren't searching. You're running. You started running that night back in Durovernum and you never stopped. One day, you'll run right off the edge of the world. It would be a great pity if there was no one there to catch you and bring you back."

I didn't know how to explain. How to make her see. "I'm not running," I said. "I just have to get word to my father about Aquila. That's *all*. I don't even know for certain that Acheron wasn't lying."

"And what if he wasn't?" she countered. "What if Aquila and his mercenaries are already there? What will you—*you*, all by *yourself*—do then? Tell me that."

"I'll figure something out—"

She threw her hand in the air in frustration. "For the love of your own grim goddess, Fallon!" she exclaimed. "*Think* for a second, will you? Just one second. You already have your own war band. Those girls would die for you and—"

"*That's* the whole damned problem, Elka!" I rounded on her, anger and fear and sorrow—everything, really— crashed down on me in that moment, and hot, stinging tears sprang to my eyes. "Meriel *did* die. Leander died. Vorya died. Hestia died. My own sister died. All because *I* wanted to save Sorcha. Because *I* wanted to save the queen. Not *our* queen, as you yourself have already pointed out, but a queen nonetheless and so therefore deserving of saving. Right? Of sacrifice. Who in all the world am I to decide that one woman's life is worth more than another's? Several others'?"

"That's arrogant."

"I know—"

"No." She cut me off with the sharpness of her tone. "That's not what I meant. What I meant was, it's arrogant of *you* to think that you made the decision *for* us. That we didn't all—each one of us—decide for ourselves to stay or go every time. To fight or not. To flee or not. I've even heard you claim responsibility for Tanis and her catastrophically bad judgment, and I, for one, would appreciate not being loaded into the same sack as *that* one, thanks very much."

I stared at her, taken aback by the scolding. It was starting to sound very much like the argument I'd had with Cai back in the Tarquin necropolis. Was I *really* that girl? Was that who I'd become?

"You're a noble warrior and a steady friend," Elka continued, shaking her head. "You also think too much, second-guess yourself, and carry everyone else's grief and guilt. Well, I'm here to tell you, Fallon ferch Virico, that we have strong enough arms and backs to carry our own. And to help you carry yours. *If* we decide we want to. And it is *we* who decide."

She took a breath and looked at me. Her pale blue eyes held wisdom beyond her years. And compassion. But there was also a scorching honesty there. And I knew, in that moment, that how much she valued our bond— forged from everything we'd been through together—was not above how much Elka valued herself. She sighed and picked up her spear. "You didn't load any one of us onto a boat—either time—at sword-point, Fallon. So please, stop acting like you did and try accepting the bare face of friendship with all its beauty and flaws. Or don't. Just let me know what you decide."

And then she was gone. Leaving me standing there alone in the middle of my opulent palace bedroom, feeling like I had at Octavia's party when Elka had cut the scarf that held us tethered together. The tension was suddenly gone, but I was left woefully unbalanced.

Ajani came to find me not too long after. I thought it was to lecture me some more, but no. It was Ajani. I could only wish to achieve a fraction of her serenity one day— but I didn't think I'd ever live so long. Certainly not if I kept acting the way I had been, she seemed to agree. At the very least, Elka might just kill me.

"You're angry and you're scared because you've lost your sister," Ajani was saying. "Elka's angry and scared for the very same reason."

"I don't—"

"She thinks she's about to lose you, Fallon."

"She doesn't *need* me. She has Quint."

"And you have Cai, but that's hardly the point." She sighed dramatically and rolled her eyes skyward. "Sadly, *I'm* like the old maiden sister who winds up stuck with both of you."

I flopped down on the bed and gazed up at the painted ceiling. "Aren't you all getting tired of me dragging you to the ends of the world on my ridiculous fool's quests?" I asked. "Just because I can't seem to keep myself and my family out of trouble, why should the rest of you all have to suffer as well?"

"Because Elka's right. We swore an oath."

"To the ludus. And that doesn't even exist anymore."

"To each other. So that *we* may continue to."

Her patient argument was wearing away at my stubborn—not to say irrational—refusals. But I wasn't ready to give in. Not quite. "Neferet is Aegyptian," I said. "She'll stay here. Which means so will Antonia."

Ajani shrugged philosophically. "If they do, it's because *they* have already found their true home in each other's hearts. And because Neferet *really* hates the cold."

"And you?"

"I don't mind a chilly evening here and there."

I gave her a stern look, and she matched it.

Then she dropped her gaze to where her long, nimble fingers interlaced in her lap and said, "Truthfully? I've been asked to stay here and captain the queen's palace archers."

I gaped at her, astonished.

"The invitation came from Queen Cleopatra herself," she continued. "I would be first in command, with my own regiment. It is a great honor."

"Ajani! That's . . . Of course you must—"

"So I *very* politely declined."

"What?" I blinked at her, not understanding. "You *what*? Why?"

She looked back up at me, and there was that wise, *amused* glint in her eye that I was so familiar with. "You don't think I'd let the lot of you go charging off on another of your 'ridiculous fool's quests' by yourselves, do you?" She laughed. "You and Elka wouldn't last a week without me. That's what I told the queen. Upon reflection, she agreed and graciously rescinded the offer. I'm coming with you. To the very ends of your strange green island, if I must. If you'll have me."

I really had nothing more to say to that.

Nothing except, "I'd be honored."

Ajani nodded, acknowledging my return to my senses.

I sighed. "Let's go find Elka, then, and let her gloat over my apology."

Ajani put an arm around me. "I can think of nothing she'd want more."

Five days later, I stood on the docks of Antirhodos, waiting for the ship that would take me and my friends back across the Mare Nostrum to Massilia. It was barely daybreak, but I hadn't been able to sleep a moment longer, and I was up before most of the palace had even begun to stir. That was where Cai found me as the rising sun's rays gilded the tops of the waves ruffling the surface of the harbor. I could feel time racing against me, slipping faster and faster through my grasping fingertips the way the hours and days had flowed inexorably through Heron's *clepsydra*—the Greek water clock the physician had kept in his infirmary back at the Ludus Achillea. How much of a head start did Pontius Aquila have? It was the question I kept asking myself over and over. Just sailing across the sea to Massilia from Alexandria—we would have to go by way of Carthage to avoid putting into port in Italia—would likely take a solid month.

"After Massilia," Cai had informed me, "we'll be traveling overland until we reach the north coast of Gaul in another month, plus a few days maybe."

I knew from my own travels in Charon's slave galley that, from there, it would be less than a day's journey across the waters my people had never thought to give a name but that the Romans called Mare Britannicum. We would sail past the sacred white cliffs, up the River Dwr . . . home.

Sorcha, I thought, in her heart, hadn't ever really forgiven herself for not returning home. To me and to our father. For living a life that, as much as it was unexpected and unasked for and so completely beyond what she'd grown up anticipating as her fate, had suited her . . . at the expense of others. In much the same way Charon had. I knew that. And I forgave both of them.

The same way I forgave myself for taking so long to return.

And now that I'd decided I would, I'd be lying to say that there wasn't a flutter of excitement in my belly at the prospect of breathing in the green and gold scents of the forests I'd grown up in. Regardless of the reason I was going back . . . I really *was* going back. The blood sang in my veins at the notion, in discord with the constant hiss of worry in the back of my mind at what I would find when I finally got there. I stalked back and forth on the wharf, scanning the ships in the Great Harbor impatiently, wondering which one Cleopatra had commissioned for our use. Cai perched on a bollard, watching me pace like one of the caged lions trained to fight the bestiarii in the Circus Maximus. "Caesar used to speak of Prydain to us sometimes," he said. "Back when we were on campaign in Hispania."

"You pronounced it right," I said over my shoulder. "Caesar never could quite manage it."

"Well, even if he called it Britannia, it was still fascinating to hear him speak of it," Cai said. "There was always a sense of . . . I don't know . . . *wonder* in his voice. A sense that the land, even though he'd been there and seen it with his own eyes, felt the ground under his feet and breathed its air . . . I always got the impression that the place remained a mystery to him. I think he felt—although I'm sure he never would have spoken such a thing aloud—that the island was unconquerable. Or perhaps 'unknowable' is a better way of putting it."

I recalled the last conversation I'd had with Caesar— with Caesar's shade—in the temple of Sekhemet. Maybe it hadn't been my imagination. Maybe he really had felt that way. A shiver traced up my spine. Then I thought of the pearl-studded breastplate I would wear on my—hopefully triumphant—return to defeat one of Caesar's enemies on the soil of my tribe and smiled a little. Somehow, I suspected he would appreciate the irony.

"I have to admit," Cai continued, shaking his head a little, "charging headlong into a place that mighty Caesar found intimidating is, well . . . what's the Cantii word for 'terrifying'?"

"Cai . . ." I stopped my pacing and walked over to stand before him. Even though every word hurt, I still looked at him and said, "You don't have to do this. You don't have to come with me. Prydain might be my destiny, but that doesn't mean it has to be yours. It is a place beyond the ends of your world. And I will understand if you do not want to do this thing."

I'd learned from my experience with Elka that I needed to give him a choice—*not* an ultimatum—but I still found myself holding my breath, wondering if there was a chance he would choose to stay . . .

He looked at me for a long moment, then said, "Do you want me to come with you?"

I nodded. "With all of my heart."

He kissed me and said, "Then it will take the strength of one of your terrifying Cantii gods to tear me from your side."

I wrapped my arms around his neck and whispered in his ear, "Don't give them any ideas."

We'd taken five day to prepare. Most of the girls had gone into the city to purchase things they thought they might need on the journey with money Cleopatra gave them for the purpose. Unsurprisingly, most of those things were weapons and armor. There was a focused purposefulness to our preparations that had made those five days seem less like an eternity, but now that the day had finally come, I was almost leaping out of my skin with impatience.

I tried not to let it show as I stood before Cleopatra one last time. But as anxious as I was to leave, I couldn't help but feel a strange hesitation. Almost as though we were leaving her behind, alone and vulnerable. I knew that wasn't true. Cleopatra had whole armies at her disposal and more wealth than almost any other ruler in the world. She had Ptolemy, her son. She didn't need us. Me . . .

She was wise enough to know that and to know what I needed too.

In that moment? Apparently, a dagger pointed at my heart.

"Look at this blade," she said, drawing from her belt the dagger that she'd used to kill the Dis rider on the way to Cosa. It was the finest of Aegyptian craftsmanship—a perfect blend of decorative and deadly. She smiled at me and placed the tip of the blade against my breastbone. "It's just like you, Fallon. It's beautiful. Meticulously crafted and sharpened, honed to a keen edge . . . and it doesn't quite know what to do with itself unless it's trying to stab something."

She spun the dagger in her hand and resheathed it.

"I *know* what you're thinking," she said. "War will come to this land one day. Once the Romans settle their disputes, or decide they need my wealth to do so, or just plain need to keep themselves occupied. And you're right. But that day is not tomorrow. Or next year. Nor, I dare say, will it be the year after. It may not even come in my lifetime, although I doubt that. And I will be here waiting when it does. But *you* . . ." She looped her arm through mine and walked with me through the garden, out toward the forest of red granite pillars that led back down to the docks, where I'd spent the daybreak pacing. "You have better things to do with your time than wander the halls of my palace or the streets of Alexandria, as marvelous as both may be. You and your sister gladiatrices and your Amazons . . . you are warrior maids, and you were meant for a different purpose. A different path. And the last few years of your life have, well, meticulously crafted and sharpened you. Honed you to a fine edge. Like my dagger. Now. Go find something to stab at, won't you?"

"I will, Your Majesty."

"Good." She turned toward me and took my face in her hands, her eyes glittering like gemstones. "And I pity whomever that walking target turns out to be. Now, away with you."

"Thank you, Majesty—"

"Oh! One little thing before you leave . . ." The queen put a finger to her carmined lips, as if she'd just remember something. "Do you recall me telling you how Hatshepsut led her armies into battle against the Kushite hordes, riding at the head of her troops in her golden war chariot?"

"I remember well," I said, smiling at her endless fondness for stories of her exceptional ancestress. "That must have been a magnificent sight to see, Your Majesty."

"Of course it was," she said. "Sorcha used to tell me that *your* people value the horse—and the chariot—almost above all else. Is that true?"

I nodded. "It is."

"Marvelous!" She clapped her hands together. "I do so like picking out appropriate gifts . . ."

She turned and gestured with one elegant hand, and there, moving in a stately line up the grand causeway, driven by lean young men in linen kilts, I saw eight of the finest snow-white horses drawing four of the swiftest-looking chariots I'd ever seen. I gasped and felt a surge of passionate longing drawn up from the very deep depths of my horse-loving Cantii soul. Horses, ridden or driven, were the great love of my people. And *these* horses were like the semidivine ancestors of the shaggy, fierce, neat-footed beasts of the island.

"I didn't have time to have the chariots gilded," she said. "But my commander of cavalry tells me they are perfectly serviceable."

"They're . . . *beautiful*," I said, hardly daring to believe my eyes. "Perfect."

"I hope you don't mind," the queen continued, "but I had Sennefer make arrangements with my admirals for a horse transport ship rather than a plain old galley for you and your sisters to travel across the sea—and for a crew from the royal stables to accompany you and care for the animals until you get to Massilia. You're on your own after that, as they'll return here on the ship once the animals are safely landed. But I did so want you to have something to remember me by."

"I can hardly think how in the wide world I would ever forget you, my queen," I said, as I blinked at the tears on my lashes and the world around me shattered into glittering rainbow shards.

I reached up around my neck and unclasped the necklace she'd given me on the night we retook the ludus from Pontius Aquila. Sorcha's ludus. Lady Achillea's own little kingdom, while it had lasted.

"Will you bury this with her, Majesty?" I asked. "I want her to have something of me. And I will have my own goddess, the Morrigan, to guide me once we reach my shores."

Cleopatra reached for the pendant, her own lashes suddenly sparkling in the sun, and said, "Of course, my very dear girl."

She turned to Sennefer, who had appeared at her side, and gave him the amulet. He took it reverentially, and it disappeared into one of the many folds or pockets or pouches he had hidden in his robes.

Then he tilted his head to me and said, "A thousand thousand thanks, Lady Fallon, for your service to my mistress. My soul owes you a debt unpayable in a single lifetime."

"Oh no, please." I shook my head. "Don't say that, Sennefer. You are a dear man, but I won't have your shade following me around in the afterlife, pouring my wine and opening doors for me. I release you from any debt on your soul."

I'd been joking, but he actually looked relieved at that.

"Thank you, lady." He rolled his kohl-rimmed eyes at Cleopatra. "I imagine my shade will be worn exceedingly thin by then."

The queen raised a sculpted eyebrow at him.

"For I expect it to be a very long time," he continued smoothly, "before the reed boat ferries you to the eternal peace of Aaru."

I grinned. "That's what I'm planning for."

"The gods guide you."

"And you, Sennefer."

He sighed. "Only if my lady lets them."

I left them and went to check on the rest of my friends, surprised to see Neferet and Antonia at the foot of the gang-plank, standing beside a stack of luggage.

"I thought you two were staying here," I said, frowning when I saw that both of them were packed for travel.

Antonia just shrugged and nodded at Neferet. "Where she goes, I go."

I looked at Neferet. "You hate the cold."

"Yes. But I want to talk to druids," Neferet said matter-of-factly. "About their healing magic. And Antonia promised she would find the thickest cloak ever woven for me, and fur-lined boots. I'll brave the cold for druids. And for you."

"Thank you, Neferet—"

She put up a hand. "Mostly druids. Don't get misty on me, Fallon."

"I wouldn't dream of it." I shook my head. "As it happens, I know where one of the druiddyn lives. And I also know a woman in Durovernum who weaves the most extraordinary cloaks."

"And boots?"

"I'll scour the kingdom."

She nodded, very seriously, and then dropped to her knee to go through her bags and do a gear check. Again.

"It's the fourth time she's done that," Antonia said. "This hour."

She looked down at Neferet with an expression of patient exasperation and absolute adoration. Neferet might not have been able to keep Sorcha from journeying to the Blessed Isle,

I thought, but she'd kept Antonia in this world long enough for them to become the world for each other. And that, in itself, was more than a wonder. Now she wanted to learn from the druids. If she continued on her path, I suspected, Neferet might just save us all one day with her skills. One way or another.

XXIII

THIRTY DAYS. WE would be in Massilia within thirty days of leaving the Great Harbor at Alexandria. Depending entirely, of course, on the changeable moods of Neptune, the great trident-wielding god of the Mare Nostrum. It was a fast ship. There was time. That's what I kept telling myself.

There was time . . . There had to be.

We put in at Lepsis Magna and Carthage and smaller scattered ports of call in between, sailing west and then north, and as the days passed, I had to admit—even if only to myself—that it was strange being on a sea voyage without Charon. I kept glancing toward the bow rail to see if he was standing there. Every time we made port, I wanted to ask him questions about the people and places—and, mostly, how to keep from getting in trouble—but, of course, he wasn't there.

He was with my sister.

That ache—that emptiness—went deeper, of course. And yet, in a way, it was so familiar to me I could almost ignore it. After all, I'd spent years of my life, growing up, doing just that. For the first few days after Sorcha's death, back in Cleopatra's palace on Antirhodos, I'd feared that I might fall into a black despair, having found my sister again only to lose her. But, instead, I decided that the time I'd spent with her once I had found her again had been a gift. She'd been right when she'd said she was still with me. She always had been, really, and now I knew she always would be.

And I could finally tell our father all about her.

I only hoped that he would understand.

Both her disappearance . . . and my own. Not that it mattered whether he understood or not, I supposed, until such time as we—my friends and I—made sure that his kingdom was safe from Pontius Aquila and his Sons of Dis and the treacherous Coritani. Once we'd done that, then Virico could accept me, reject me, or cast me out altogether. First, we had a job to do.

And, thanks to Cleopatra, we had the means to accomplish it in high style.

After we'd left her shores, I wondered if the queen might not have propitiated her own gods for our safe passage on the sea. The weather stayed mild and the waves calm. And our equine charges were better behaved than most people I'd ever traveled with. They were housed in specially built stalls belowdecks equipped with slings that loosely cradled them beneath their bellies to support the animals and keep them from falling with the movement of the waves. The chariots had been stowed securely, and the rest of the cargo hold had been stocked with abundant feed. Whenever we made port, some of the horse boys walked and watered them while the others mucked out the stalls with impressive efficiency. I was told by the ship's captain that the court of Aegypt had been in the business of providing horse troops to other lands for generations and had somewhat perfected the methods of transporting them. As far as such things could be perfected, at least.

I spent a great deal of time with the horses on the journey, down in the hold with Cai, the two of us grooming them or just sitting with them. He and I would make a nest of the loose hay and our cloaks and curl up together, telling the horses—and each other—stories. It made the journey fly by on swifter wings. And it helped take my mind off the prospect of what we would find once we reached our ultimate destination. While we were down in the hold, at least. Up on deck, it was a different story. The horizon and our next port always seemed too far away. I drilled every morning and every afternoon with the girls, but the constant fear that Aquila'd had too much of a head start on us gnawed at my nerves, even as I imagined his head rolling on the ground at my feet.

"If Durovernum and the Cantii really are his target," Cai said, when he and Quint caught me pacing the deck after a drill session one late afternoon, "and not just any of the Prydain tribes he thinks might provide him with easy pickings, then Aquila would not only have had to gather what forces and resources he had in Rome, he also would've had to secure passage and travel to Britannia . . ."

It was a variation on the same thing he'd been telling me for days. The same thing I'd been telling myself. I was still having a hard time listening to either of us. Making myself believe.

"Once there, as I understand it, he would then have to convene with these Coritani chiefs. And you've already told me they're a prickly lot, yes?"

I nodded. They were.

"Right. Well. Assuming they're even interested in any plan of Aquila's to storm Durovernum—and they don't just kill him outright for being a meddling foreigner—they, in turn, will have to gather *their* forces. Also correct?"

I nodded again.

Cai took both my hands in his and made me look at him. "That, in itself, could take weeks. We have *time*, Fallon."

Quint was in absolute agreement that the military logistics—even for what was essentially nothing more than a large-scale slave raid on my home—were complicated. "Now, see, the legions are a smooth-running machine that have entire contingents to deal with all that stuff. But both of us"—he hooked a thumb at Cai—"have had experience dealing with auxiliary troops and barbarian mercenaries and, by Juno's perfect teeth, it's a nightmare! A true wonder *any*thing ever gets conquered in those situations."

"You have a problem with 'barbarians'?" Elka asked sweetly.

Cai interjected before Quint could get himself into trouble.

"Even if Aquila does get there before we do," he said to me, "your people aren't just going to march out of their front gates with their hands in the air in surrender. Look how long Arviragus held out against Caesar's finest legions at the siege of Alesia. And Pontius Aquila will only have mercenaries and whomever he gathers from this rival tribe of yours. Virico might not even need us!"

He'd told me variations of the same thing probably a hundred times by that point, so much so that Elka was mouthing his words along with him and rolling her eyes. And I knew that it was true enough. We might very well be marching to rescue a town secure in its own military might. Virico Lugotorix might not even open his gates for us. I said as much.

"Well, that would be irony, I suppose," Cai said, his mouth twisting in wry grin. "But, either way, we won't know until we arrive . . . Fallon?"

He put a hand on my shoulder as I stared out at the setting sun. The day had been long. All the days in Aegypt under the unblinking white eye of the desert sun had been so, but as we traveled north, afternoons seemed to be taking longer and longer to become evening. I had lost track of the turning of the year's wheel living in lands where the seasons weren't so very different from each other. But suddenly a horrible realization crashed down on me.

"Fallon." Cai's fingers tightened on my shoulder. "Are you all right?"

I shook my head. *"Your people aren't just going to march out of their front gates with their hands in the air in surrender,"* Cai had said. No . . . but they might very well go dancing into the fields beyond the walls of Durovernum with no weapons ready to grasp in those hands . . .

"*Litha*," I said, the word sticking in my throat gone suddenly dry with fear. "Midsummer."

Cai and Quint exchanged confused glances, and Elka frowned at me.

I looked back and forth between them. "We're approaching the longest day of the year."

"The solstice?" Quint asked. "What of it?"

"That's when Aquila will attack," I said.

Cai let go of my shoulder. "Tell me."

"I don't know what you Romans do or how you celebrate the . . . the . . ."

"Solstice."

"Yes. Solstice." I tried to keep my voice steady against the rising tide of dread I felt in my heart. "But at home . . . it is a time of plenty and a celebration of peace. For all the tribes. It is our custom to leave our towns and go out into the fields to celebrate. We build bonfires and we sing and dance and feast. And we leave our weapons behind, laid at the foot of our beds."

"And Yoreth knows that," Cai said.

"Yes."

Quint nodded. "She's right. That's when they'll attack."

I looked back and forth between him and Cai and saw the soldiers in them in that moment. The soldier's resolve to make it to the field of battle, even if they had to kill themselves to do it. Cai smiled at me—an expression of grim anticipation.

"Well then," he said. "We'd best not dawdle when we make port at Massilia."

Once we did make port at Massilia, our journey would take us on a trek overland through the forests and fields of Gaul, north to the port of Gesoriacum. It was the very first place I'd set foot on land after I'd been stolen from Durovernum by Charon's slavers and taken across the sea . . . the beginning of *my* journey, all those endless days past, to the Forum in Rome, where I was sold to a school for female gladiators. We would, in essence, be replicating that endless, horrid trek in reverse, starting from Massilia—hopefully without Alesian bandit encounters this time—and I was sure Elka was probably thinking the same thoughts as me.

About where we'd started. And how far we'd come . . .

In Massilia, we bid our Aegyptian crew safe travel home and parted ways. The next day I waited, consumed with impatience and counting the hours, while Kronos acquired wagons for transport and together all the girls packed them up and were waiting while Cai and Quint went on a last errand into the city. When they returned to where we'd camped in the fields north of Massilia's walls, I felt a shock of displaced memory shiver through me.

"I know," Cai said, lifting the decurion's helmet off his head.

His hair beneath was back to a military-short cut, and he was clean-shaven again. He looked almost exactly the way he had the first day I'd met him. It felt for an instant as if the thread of my destiny was spooling in reverse, winding backward . . .

"We figured it would be easier going north if our company travels under what looks like military escort," Cai explained. "For one thing, it'll be faster, with access to better roads and amenities. For another, it will likely preempt any casual trouble we might encounter along the way." He gestured to the legion regalia that fit him like a skin he'd always worn. "There's an officer at the garrison here who was loyal to Caesar and a friend to me."

"And he stole you a set of armor?" I raised an eyebrow.

"More like 'liberated,'" Quint said, grinning. "Cai's, uh, discharge from the legions didn't sit right with the old boy. He was happy to help."

"Now I'm *really* going to have some explaining to do when I see my father again," I said. "You were almost starting to look like a proper Celt."

Cai reached for me and put his hands on my waist, pulling me close. "You can present me as your captive, if that would make things easier . . ."

Quint rolled his eyes, and I reluctantly shrugged out of Cai's embrace.

"Tempting," I said. "But my tribe doesn't take prisoners of war. Only their heads."

Cai's mouth opened then shut, and he took a step back, glancing at me sideways. I was half joking—the Cantii, in fact, took both—but I could see that I'd given Cai a moment's pause over what to expect when the moment came and I introduced him to my father, the king. *If* that moment came. If we weren't too late . . .

"You've nothing to worry about," I said airily, trying to convince myself that *I* didn't. "If he doesn't like you, he'll just marry me off to another chieftain."

I heard Elka snort with amusement and turned to see her and Kronos walking over from where they'd been doing a last check on the chariot harnesses. "Because things worked out *so* well the last time your father did that," she said.

I grinned at her and shook my head. She shrugged and grinned back. Some things really *had* worked out all right the last time. Most things. Not the least of which was my friendship with the tall blonde Varini girl.

"What news of Rome?" she asked Quint.

"Well, it seems as though they've stopped setting bits of it on fire, at least," Quint said.

"But Antony and Brutus still might just set the rest of the world ablaze," Cai added, shrugging off the legion marching pack from his shoulders. "With Octavian's help."

"Caesar's nephew?" Kronos asked,

"Aye." Cai nodded. "Headed back to Rome from his studies overseas."

Quint laughed harshly. "The very moment he got the news, no doubt, the young upstart. And, of course, he's now claiming his rightful place as mighty Caesar's heir." He shook his head in wan disgust. "They're all busy massing armies, and they'll go at it tooth and claw until one of them winds up on top of the heap of bodies. It's going to be a bloody free-for-all. Not quite the dignified return to the Republic's glory days that the Optimates were hoping for."

I was utterly without sympathy. "I hope they all choke on it," I said. "Now let's get as far away from that nest of vipers as we can."

"Gladly," Cai said. "I could use a bit of clean bloodshed in the service of a noble cause, for a change."

A short time later, our entire company was mounted up and ready to go. We had all four of the chariots harnessed to go along with the wagons and would take turns driving. The horses themselves were champing at their bits for the exercise after all of that time spent in the ship's hold. I stood in the lead chariot with Cai as he slapped the reins, urging the Aegyptian horses forward, and we moved out, leaving Massilia and the Mare Nostrum—and Rome and Romans—behind us in a cloud of dust.

Time played tricks on my mind as we traveled. It took another month to reach the north coast of Gaul, and the days alternated between flying and crawling. And then, early one evening, we crested a hill and emerged from beneath a canopy of ancient oak trees at the edge of a field. In the near distance, I could see the walls of Gesoriacum— and smell the salt tang of the sea beyond. I felt my heart beat faster with hope.

That hope was dashed as the sun sank below the hills to the west of us, and instead of the gates of the town closing for the night, they stayed open to let the people of Gesoriacum out into the fields beyond the town . . .

To celebrate the eve of the summer solstice.

The distant strains of laughter and music that accompanied the flickering lanterns filled my heart with a cold, cruel dread.

"Oh no," I whispered, leaning on the trunk of a tree to keep from collapsing to my knees. "Litha . . ."

"What is it, Fallon?" Cai peered at me with concern. "What's wrong?"

"We're too late." The bark of the tree was still warm beneath my palm, heated by the sun throughout the longest day of the year. "Tonight. It's midsummer eve *tonight*."

The celebration was a small one compared to those back home, but slowly the lantern bearers came together, and I saw the flicker of flames grow as piles of driftwood gathered for the bonfires were lit. Torches, lanterns, fires, and stars, they all blurred as the tears spilled down my cheeks at the thought of my own folk making merry, defenseless and unsuspecting . . .

"I thought we still had time. A day or two, at least . . ."

We'd pushed the horses and our own bodies at a punishing pace to get here—to get to this place. And now I stood here, on the wrong side of a narrow strip of sea. And on the morrow, Pontius Aquila and his Sons of Dis would, in all likelihood, attack my home and kill my folk, unsuspecting as they lay asleep in the fields after a night of celebration. While the war band I was bringing to help was stuck crossing that narrow strip of sea. My stomach turned, and I felt as if I might be sick.

I could feel the whole caravan, all of my friends, gathering at my back. They knew as well as I did what the lights in the field meant. A hand descended on my shoulder, and I turned to see Elka standing at my side.

"What was it you told Charon when we were on our way to Corsica to rescue Sorcha?" she asked.

I blinked at her, not remembering what I'd said, or even that I'd told her.

"'Even if we're too late for rescue,'" she said, quoting my own words back to me, "'we'll still be right on time for revenge.' *Ja?*"

Gratia stepped up beside her. "Elka's right. There's nothing we can do now if we're late. Not from here. So we make the best of the situation when we get there. And in the meantime?" She nodded at where the town revelers had begun to dance and sing to the music of pipes and handheld drums. "I say we join the party."

Elka grinned savagely. "Feasting before fighting. Best idea I've heard in a long time."

"That's because feasting involves food," Ajani said.

The whole of our company laughed at that. I wanted to scream.

"Fallon," Cai said softly into my ear. "You've been racing toward the moment *when* you will face your enemy. But tonight you must decide *how* you will face them. Show these girls that you're not afraid of what you will find on the other side of the water."

He was right, of course. They all were.

There was nothing I could do in that moment but hope, by the grace of the Morrigan, that Aquila's mercenaries had been delayed. Even if they hadn't, I had to trust that the royal war band of the Cantii were still made of the iron and fire I'd known as a girl and could hold their own. At least until we got there. In the meantime, Gratia had a point: after months of grueling travel halfway across the world, I owed my own war band a celebration.

It didn't take us very long to ready ourselves for the feast. It wasn't as if we'd brought trunks full of the finery Cleopatra's army of dressers had bestowed upon us back in Alexandria. We made do with decorating ourselves from pots of woad war paint and taking each other's hair down and weaving simple circlets of wildflowers to wear. But when it came to leaving our weapons behind—as was customary during the rites of Litha—our Amazon contingent balked. Kallista and her fierce sisters would rather sever a limb than walk into a crowd of strangers weaponless.

"All right," I sighed. "You can bring your fire chains—in a *ceremonial* capacity only."

The rest of us piled our blades together, leaving them with Kronos—who'd declined to come with us, saying he didn't dance and would rather spend a quiet night guarding the wagons instead. Then we set out from beneath the canopy of the forest and into the fields to join the folk of the town. The Amazon fire chains painted patterns of flame in the purple dusk air as they led our company down toward the bonfires, heralding our arrival with the kind of showy spectacle the gladiatrices of the Ludus Achillea were used to presenting. The people of Gesoriacum might have been startled at our sudden appearance, but they soon welcomed us and drew us into their dancing. Later, we shared what food and drink we had left over from our journey.

That was the sacred way of Litha.

I even managed to forget for a while—with Cai's help—my fears about reaching our ultimate destination. Cai took my hand and drew me beyond the circle of firelight. Once we were far enough away from the crowd, he stopped and turned to face me. His mouth bent into a slow smile as he reached into the leather scrip that hung from the belt at his waist and drew forth a circle of iron. My old slave collar. The night I'd finally agreed to have the cursed thing removed, I'd given it to Cai as a promise—that one day, when I was finally able to buy my freedom from Caesar on my own terms, I would come to him. As an equal.

"There's no longer a contract for you to buy," Cai said. "And you're about to reclaim your royal birthright . . ."

"And you've waited long enough for us to truly be together," I said.

"I would wait for you until the stars went dim and the sun and moon drowned themselves in the ocean never to rise again, Fallon ferch Virico," he said. "But there's a man on the other side of the sea whose blessing I'm going to need . . ."

"You'll need to prove your worth in battle, you know." I grinned at him. "And you'll need a chieftain's torc." I plucked the slave collar from his grasp and held it up between us. "The first torc a warrior of my tribe ever wears is always one that has been forged from a battle-damaged blade. It symbolizes turning something broken into something beautiful. Something new . . ."

"You were never broken," he said. "And you've always been beautiful. But I would wear a torc made from that iron proudly if your father would have it so. If *you* would have it so."

Cai might have been right when he said I was never broken. Not completely. But I'd come close. So close. And he'd been there time after time to keep me from shattering completely—like he was doing this very night. I slipped the collar back into the scrip on his belt and smiled up at him. Then, in the darkness beneath the stars and moon, he kissed me. He kissed me until it felt as though he would steal every last wisp of breath from my body. I wrapped my arms around his neck and kissed him back just as hard. The earth beneath our feet tilted on its axis, and we sank down into the cool, long grass. The dew sparkled gemlike in the light of the bonfires, cooling my heated skin, and I had never felt as free in all my life as I did in that moment. So untethered to worry or want or thoughts of what might happen next.

The Morrigan guided my swords. Cai carried my soul. In the morning I would rise to meet my destiny, whatever it would be.

But that night was mine to cherish.

At the very break of day, we rose from our grassy beds and entered the town walls of the port of Gesoriacum. The fields were dotted with the smoldering remains of bonfires and scattered sleeping bodies wrapped in cloaks and each other's arms. But if I'd been worried that a night spent drinking and dancing and getting very little rest would in any way dull the senses of my companions, there was no such worry now. There was a sense of fierce anticipation, of barely leashed excitement, among the girls.

"Finally!" I heard Ceto say to Lysa as I passed by on my way to the wagons. "We're going to fight—*really* fight—and not just each other."

"I thought after the ludus fell that I'd never see a real battle," Lysa agreed, sighing contentedly, as if speaking about a lover returning home after too long.

I whispered a prayer to the Morrigan that they both felt the same way in the aftermath of what was to come.

We sold the carts and draft horses in town. Prydain was a land largely without roads. The tracks through field and forest would accommodate a chariot easily enough, but for the rest, the way to Durovernum once we landed would be made on foot. We used the money to hire transport across the narrow sea to Prydain. Most of the commerce done in that town was trade back and forth across the water, and we managed to find a trader with both a ship and a live-stock barge. It certainly wasn't the luxurious accommodations our Aegyptian beasts had grown used to crossing the Mare Nostrum, but it would do for less than a day's journey, port to port.

The captain of the boats was a northman, stolid and competent-seeming, with a weathered, experienced crew on both vessels. "We leave within the hour," he said. "And if the gods will it and the weather holds, you'll step foot on the Island of the Mighty not very much after midday."

I glanced at the horizon. That much, at least, seemed to be in our favor. There wasn't a cloud in sight, and only a slight, freshening breeze that lifted my hair as I went to speak to the pair of boys who would be manning the barge carrying the chariot horses. They were from the Iceni tribe—friends to the Cantii, holding territory to the north-east of my own folk—and mostly hired for their expertise with horse and cattle. But because the Iceni lands were on the coast, they were also seasoned sailors and had made the crossing on merchant ships and transport barges count-less times.

"Were there others who've crossed in the last while?" I asked, speaking to them in their own language. "Men? Recently . . . maybe dressed in black—"

They started nodding and said that, indeed, there had been a man with a black cloak and very bad manners who'd wanted to be taken up the east coast as far as the Wash—a large natural harbor controlled by the Coritani.

"What are they saying?" Cai asked, frowning.

I told him and then turned to question the lads further.

"They say their master doesn't trade with the Coritani, though," I relayed to Cai. "Not since they started trans-porting human livestock . . ."

"Slaves?"

I nodded, listening. "But the man in black found other passage with a less scrupulous trader, and he and his men went on their way."

"When?" Cai asked.

The boy shrugged.

"Two weeks, maybe," I relayed. "He's not exactly precise on the passage of time."

As with most of the tribes of Prydain, things took as long as they took, or as short. You got to your destination when you did, or you didn't. It used to be that way for me. But now I'd never been more starkly aware of the passage of time. I couldn't get anything more precise from the two Iceni lads, though, and they were far too interested in the horses to pay me very much more attention. So instead, I told Cai to gather everyone together, and we went over what I knew of what to expect on the other side of the crossing—which wasn't all that much.

The girls gathered around, crouched in a wide circle on the beach as I drew a simple map in the sand. "We will land here," I said, pointing to the north-curving line I'd made. "Just east past the sacred white cliffs, at the mouth of the River Dwr. Then it's a simple matter of following the river until we wind up at Durovernum. My home. There are docks on the river about a mile south of the actual town, so we should be able to disembark without being seen, and we'll make our approach from the west, following a track to the farmsteads there. That way we'll hopefully avoid detection if Aquila is already at the town walls. Because he"—I continued the coastal line I'd drawn up from the line marking the river—"will have traveled up the coast to here." I pointed to the curve that marked the Wash. "Once he gathered his warriors, he would have had to travel south. Through Catuvellauni territory."

"Isn't that risky for him?" Kronos asked.

"At any other time of year. But in the days leading up to the midsummer celebrations, there is much traveling between the towns and territories . . . Aquila and his Coritani mercenaries could have easily moved through Catuvellauni lands without rousing suspicion." I was distantly pleased to hear that there was no tremor in my voice at the thought of Aquila already scratching like a rabid dog at the gates of my home. "If any of my tribe manage to escape back inside the walls of the town, then the Coritani will simply camp out in front of the gates and wait them out."

Cai nodded, scratching at his chin. "If that's the situation, we'll need to alert those inside the wall that we're there before we attack. Once they know they have help, we can come at Aquila from both sides—Virico from the front, us in a surprise attack from the rear—and we can wipe the bastard out before he really even knows what's hit him."

"And you can do that?" Quint asked. "Get inside to speak with the king?"

I smiled, confident in that, at least. "There are hidden places where the walls can be climbed. Don't worry. I've been sneaking in and out of Durovernum since I could toddle about upright," I said. "I'll get us into my father's great hall, even if I have to grow the Morrigan's own wings to fly there."

XXIV

THE SEA WAS rippled glass and the sky a cloudless vault of pale blue. A breeze from the east had the boat captain's beard drifting over his shoulder as he muttered and paced, eyeing the birds that swooped and dove overhead as the barge boys loaded Cleopatra's gift horses onto the barge and secured the chariots on the ship. We boarded the galley and stowed our gear, settling in for the next several hours of open-water passage as the ship nudged her way into the channel, trailing the transport barge in her wake.

Kallista came up to stand beside me in the bow, her freckled cheeks flushed with excitement. "Now I'll finally get to see *your* island," she said, grinning. "I feel just like one of my ancestor queens, traveling the breadth of the wide world to find new lands."

She leaned out over the very front of the ship's bow, hair streaming out behind her, and I heard Quint sigh. I looked over my shoulder at him where he stood, arms crossed, gazing at the niece he hadn't even known he'd had less than a year ago.

"She's just like my brother," he said, and I could almost see the memories chasing through his mind. "Always looking over the next hill, running to catch the horizon . . . I owe you a great debt, Fallon."

"Owe *me*?" I said, blinking at him. "For what?"

"If it weren't for you and your mad quests," he said, "I never would have met that girl." He looked over at Elka, and his expression shifted from proud uncle to smitten soldier. "Or *that* one."

"You're a good friend, Quintus," I said. "And if it hadn't been for you teaching us those legion shield techniques, we wouldn't have survived that particular mad quest. You owe me nothing."

"Yeah, well, I still plan to make myself useful to the Legio Achillea on this mission," he said, recalling the name Cai had given us during our fight with the Amazons on Corsica. "If nothing else," he continued, nodding at Elka, "it'll make me look good."

I shook my head, smiling, as he loped off to go find Cai. He was near the stern speaking to the sailors whose duty on that voyage was mostly keeping an eye on the barge towlines as we made the crossing. The barge had no sails or oars of its own and was entirely dependent on the galley to move across the waves. I knew that the tides could sometimes be treacherous on that stretch of water—I'd heard the traders who'd plied their wares speak of it, growing up—but not that day, I thought. The sky overhead was filled with wheeling gulls, and the water sparkled with the silver flash of schools of fish. It was a perfect day for a crossing.

Right up until the very moment that it wasn't.

We'd been on the sea for hours, the sun climbing steadily higher into a sky slowly hazing to overcast, when a thin, faint line of white on the horizon heralded the appearance of the sacred white cliffs of the Island of the Mighty. *Finally . . .*

"Look!" I grabbed for Ajani's arm, pointing feverishly. She had the keenest sight of any of us, and I needed to know that I wasn't imagining things.

"What?" Ajani squinted. "Where?"

"There . . . you see? The line of white . . ."

She was silent, squinting in the direction I pointed for so long I was starting to doubt my own eyes. But then she smiled and said, "I see it."

Prydain didn't need a towering great lighthouse to let ships know they were near its shores, I thought. The shores themselves were enough for that. I felt a great heavy weight lift from my heart in that moment, and I breathed deeply, as if I could smell the forests and fields of home on the wind— but, of course, we were still too far out for that. I glanced over my shoulder to see where Cai was, to show him his first glimpse of Prydain . . .

And the weight that had lifted from me came crashing back down.

The sky to the south of us was a black rampart of clouds.

The storm wall looked as though it had been built by the hands of an angry god, and it was moving swiftly toward us, flickering tongues of lightning down into the sea. The storm's approach was so rapid—and I'd been so focused on catching sight of home—that I hadn't even noticed the change in the day. But suddenly I could *feel* it. A tingling along my arms and the chill of the shifting wind. The sails overhead balked at the change, and the mast creaked. The sailors began hurrying across the deck, hauling on ropes and calling to each other in loud, insistent voices.

In the blink of an eye, the waves began to gather in peaks and troughs, iron gray and angry, and a stiff gale whipped the foam from them and drove it into our faces like rain. The clouds rolled in, and the ceiling of the world lowered down upon us until we could barely tell sea from sky. Then the rain began in earnest. We were so close. So *very* close to home. I peered so hard into the darkness in front of us, it felt like I could almost draw the sacred white cliffs closer through sheer force of will . . .

A flash of lightning shattered the chaotic gloom, and there they were—a ghostly white curtain drifting ever closer—then the thunderclap that followed almost knocked me flat to the deck.

"Hang on to something!" the captain shouted as the ship heaved to one side.

We all scrambled for ropes and handholds—anything to keep from plunging over the sides. I saw Damya wrap an arm around Nephele to keep her from being swept into the sea as a rogue wave swamped the stern. Over the howling chaos I heard the whinnying of the chariot horses and the shouts of the barge boys.

The white cliffs loomed up in front of us, and suddenly they seemed far more forbidding than welcoming. But it was what was behind us that was the real threat. The heavy hemp tow ropes for the transport barge had gone slack, sinking beneath the surface of the waves as the storm drove the vessel hard toward the galley. I watched, horrified, as the craft suddenly lifted high on a cresting wave, the front end rising to tower above the deck of our ship like some kind of leviathan out of a legend—a sea monster from the depths—hanging suspended in the air above us for an eternity before it came crashing down.

"Quint!" Cai shouted. "Look out!"

Elka and I both screamed warnings as Cai lunged forward to tackle his friend out of the way as the nose of the barge descended, clipping the galley and smashing off a chunk of the stern rail, sending split and splintered planks flying. The rigging that tethered the two vessels together knotted in a hopeless tangle, and if it wasn't cut loose—fast—both would flounder. Through the lashing, blinding rain, I could just make out Cai and Quint dragging themselves across the deck toward the stern. I called Cai's name, but I doubted he could hear me over the crashing of waves and thunder. The only other thing *I* could hear was the high-pitched screaming of the panicked animals picketed on the deck of the barge. My heart pounded in my chest at the thought of those beautiful creatures—Cleopatra's gift to me—lost to the raging sea.

I struggled against the heeling of the deck and dragged myself along the rail toward the stern, where the sailors were furiously hacking at the tangled rigging. Damya and Gratia had joined them, wielding axes like foresters to cut through the heavy ropes. Most of the rest of the girls were just desperately trying not to get washed overboard.

Then I saw Cai stripping off his armor and throwing it to the deck.

"What are you doing?" I screamed at him.

"We've got to cut the horses free!" he shouted back.

"Cai—no!"

He grabbed me by the shoulders. His face was less than a handsbreadth from mine and I could still barely hear him. "The barge is sinking, and the horses won't stand a chance if it goes down and they're still tethered! They can swim but not if they're still tied down . . ."

I hesitated, and he dropped a swift kiss on my forehead before sprinting away. "Quint!" he called.

"Right behind you!" Quint called back.

The two of them together took a running leap off the stern of the ship.

"*Cai!*"

But he was already gone.

Another wave rose up and swamped the deck, knocking me off my feet, and suddenly Elka was there beside me, helping me to stand.

"I don't know about you," she yelled over the storm, "but I'm not letting *them* grab all the glory of a dramatic rescue!" I could see in her eyes that glory was hardly the issue. She was terrified for Quint. Like I was for Cai.

"We'd best go help them," I yelled back. "They're use-less without us!"

By that time, more of the girls had made their way to the stern to help hack the ship free with axes and swords. Kallista and Selene had heard us and staggered over.

"We'll come too," Kallista said. Then she rolled her eyes at me. "He's my uncle—I'm honor bound to make sure nothing happens to him."

"We can swim like fish!" Selene said, already stripping off her boots. "It'll be fun!"

The captain shouted for everyone to brace themselves again, and the ship heeled sharply over. I hung on with grim determination, arms wrapped around a bollard, until the ship slowly righted itself. In the blackness between bursts of day-bright lightning, afterimages of the ship flashed before my eyes.

Just the ship. Not the barge.

The barge, when I finally reached the stern rail and stared out over the water into the rain and waves, was nowhere to be seen. Cai and Quint, the horses, the Iceni boys . . . they were all gone. Swallowed by the storm as if they'd never been . . .

"*There . . .*" Ajani's sharp gaze pierced the curtains of rain, and she thrust out her arm. The barge floated, half-swamped, just to the west of us.

"Come on!" Elka shouted.

I looked over to see the other girls—the ones not actively engaged in cutting loose the sinking barge lines—gathering all the spare lengths of rope and any-thing that would float and hauling it all to the side. Anything for the barge boys to grab on to once they went into the water.

Elka looked at me and, with a sharp nod, the two of us took a run at the railing as our ship crested another wave and dove high and long through the air. The shock of the cold water hit me like a giant fist, driving the breath from my body, as a gray wave closed over my head. Beneath the surface, it seemed almost calm for a moment. With my eyes open, I could see the dark shape of the barge. And I could see that it was breaking apart. Sinking . . .

Elka was just off to my right, and the two of us swam for all we were worth. I couldn't see Kallista or Selene. By the time I reached the side of the barge, my arms and legs were like lead from the drag of the water and my skin felt raw from the lashing of the wind-driven rain. The side of the barge had sunk so low that it was easy enough to pull myself up on deck. I hauled myself to my feet on the slick planks and saw Kallista struggling to do the same. Staggering over, I grabbed her hand and pulled her up. Elka and Selene were already working on sawing through two of the tether ropes, ducking and dancing on the sea-slick deck to stay clear of flailing hooves.

"Fallon!" Cai hollered. "What in Hades are you doing here?"

"Helping you rescue my presents from the queen of Aegypt!" I hollered back.

"Your 'presents' aren't making it easy!"

The horse he was trying to cut free kept snapping at him. I glanced around the deck and saw a stack of empty feed bags that somehow hadn't been washed overboard. I threw him one.

"Put that over his head—cover his eyes—it'll calm him down . . ."

As much as anything could be calm in that chaos.

I worked my way down the line of picketed horses, thrusting the feed bags into the hands of Quint and Elka, the two barge boys, and Kallista and Selene with similar instructions. Then I got to work on the rope of the horse at the end of the line, just as the waves began to wash over the deck stern to bow, swirling up to my knees. As the last strand of rope parted beneath my blade, I felt my stomach float up toward my chest, and the barge sank completely beneath the surface, a sea monster sinking gracefully back down to its watery bed.

I expected to sink too. Sink and drown. But my momentary surge of panic vanished as the horse I'd freed suddenly began to swim—as if it had been born from the ocean depths and not the sands of the Aegyptian deserts. Strong, graceful legs churning, the creature lifted his head, and I reached over to pull the feed bag away. Then I threw my leg over his back and hung on, riding him all the way to shore. For a brief, giddy moment, I couldn't help but think back to the very first bath I'd had back in Rome and the elaborate murals painted on the ceiling of the bathhouse. Scenes of frolicking sea nymphs and demigods riding the cresting waves on the backs of fish-tailed horses . . .

I wiped the water from my eyes and looked to see a whole line of us—eight sea-horses all with riders—borne toward the beaches beneath the towering cliffs of home.

As swiftly as it had descended, the storm moved on, lessening dramatically even before we reached land. The thunderheads swept past, racing east to vent their fury on others, leaving behind sweeps of silvery waves and pale streaks of sunlight filtering down through left-behind clouds. In the wake of the diminishing thunder, the sea was still high and the waves curled in rolling breakers that crashed on the beach, like galloping lines of white horses, suddenly made flesh and blood as we reached the beach and the chariot horses cantered up through the surf and onto the sand. They snorted and shook out manes and tails ribboned with seaweed, pawing at the ground as if to reassure themselves that they were on solid footing again.

My fingers were numb with cold, and I had to struggle to unclench them from gripping my horse's mane so I could slide off his back. Once I did, I found that my legs didn't really work either, and I collapsed in a heap on the damp, shushing sands. That was the state Cai found me in. He staggered over, deathly cold, lips pale, and limbs shivering, but alive. Gloriously, giddily alive. He sank to his knees in front of me and flopped an arm around my neck.

I reached up and ruffled his short, sopping wet hair, grinning at him. "You're just lucky you were right about horses from the desert knowing how to swim," I said.

Then I threw my arms around him and we huddled there in the swirling surf, in the lee of the towering white cliffs, clinging to each other. The sun's rays poured down through the remnants of clouds, illuminating a world washed and gleaming, made pristine by the wind and the rain. The waves rolled gently to shore beneath the soaring cliffs that shone in the sunlight.

"Will you two stop nuzzling each other and come on?" Elka called finally. "We still have a battle to fight!"

I looked over to see her standing with one arm wrapped around Quint's waist. Kallista and Selene and the barge lads were gathering the horses together. I turned back to look out to sea and saw the galley heading east, toward the harbor at the mouth of the River Dwr. I could barely make out the tiny figures at the railing waving at us. I waved back, and we started to walk.

We trekked along the beach beneath the cliffs until we made it to the port village at the mouth of the River Dwr—our original intended destination—and met back up with the galley captain so we could return his barge lads to him and pick up the rest of our friends and our gear. Along the beach I only saw two or three long wooden planks, torn from the hull of the sunken barge, that lay washed up on shore, nudged gently by the surf. That was all. It was as if the sea had devoured the thing whole.

"I've never lost a vessel in a crossing before," the captain told me.

"Never lose one again," I told him back.

"The gods look kindly on you, lady," he said. "You rescued my boys."

"I think they were looking kindly on all of us today," I said.

I kept quiet about whatever god it might have been that sent the storm in the first place. I needed all the goodwill I could get. Then I gave him all of the money I had left from what Cleopatra had given me for our journey and asked him to share some of it out between the barge lads. Once the chariots were ready, we shouldered the rest of our gear in traveling packs and set off, following the road inland that ran beside the River Dwr.

"We should leave the main road," I told them. "There's a cart track that leads west, away from the river and into the forest. It comes out the other end just a stone's throw from the walls of the town, in a place called the Forgotten Vale—a long clearing hidden away and surrounded by woods. It should make a good staging area for us, and it's on the opposite side of Durovernum from the main gates. No one goes there."

Almost no one, I thought. It was the place where Mael and I always used to escape to growing up, whenever we'd wanted to be alone.

Cai nodded in agreement.

"Quint"—he slapped him on the shoulder—"scout ahead. Make sure we don't run across any surprises along the way to this vale of Fallon's. Use your signal whistle if you run into trouble."

Quint nodded and jumped down from his chariot, tossing the reins to Elka, who took his place. I climbed up behind Cai in one of the other chariots, and we started out again at a cautious pace, some of the girls riding, others jogging along behind the chariots. Kronos brought up the rear, ever watchful and armed with a small horn to alert us if we were attacked from behind. Along the way, we passed a few dwellings—small farms and craftsmen's huts—set back from the track, all of them seemingly deserted. Of course they would be. Everyone had gone to the festival the night before. As we got closer to Durovernum, I started watching the skyline above the trees.

"There," I said quietly, tapping Cai on the shoulder. He pulled up on the chariot reins, and we slowed. We could see smoke trails rising from beyond the tops of the oaks. More than just the cooking fires of the town, it seemed to me that there was smoke rising from what must have been campfires in the field beyond. Campfires—not bonfires. Those would have burnt out in the night.

"They beat us here," I said, feeling my heart beat faster. Pontius Aquila was at the gates of my home.

"Here, yes." Cai nodded. "But they haven't taken the town, or there wouldn't still be fires in the fields—"

"Shh!" I clapped a hand over his mouth. Something was moving through the trees directly ahead of us. Cai signaled to the others to move into the woods as he and I hid behind the thicket of a yew tree, waiting. When the bearded man burst through the thicket and stumbled onto the path, I had to grab frantically for Cai before he leaped out and ran him through.

"Olun!" I cried, rushing forward from our hiding place.

It was my father's chief druid. And he was hurt.

His beard had been black threaded with silver when I'd climbed over the walls of Durovernum for the very last time. Now the silver threads were streaks, and the lines around his eyes were carved deep with worry or weariness. Made deeper in that moment with pain. He'd exchanged his usual robes of undyed wool for a shorter tunic and trousers, and his left arm hung swaying from his shoulder, the sleeve dyed crimson with blood from a wound just beneath his collarbone.

He stumbled forward and sank to his knees on the path.

"Olun—it's me!" I put my hands on his chest to keep him from falling on his face. "It's Fallon . . . I've come home . . ."

He looked into my eyes, and the haze of pain vanished like a mist. I saw in him the sharp intelligence he'd always had. The shrewdness and arrogance and—surprisingly—a hint of something like gratitude. Directed at me or at the gods, I wasn't sure. But then he smiled and nodded. As if things suddenly made sense to his druiddyn mind.

"Fallon," he said, panting for breath. "I didn't expect it to be you. But . . . now I understand. The path . . . You will save your father from the Roman. Just like your sister, Sorcha, before you did . . ."

When I was little, Olun had prophesied that I would follow in my sister's footsteps. I'd thought that path had ended when Sorcha had died. But Olun seemed to think it still stretched out ahead of me. Sorcha had gone into battle and rescued Virico from Caesar. Could I do the same and save him from Pontius Aquila?

"Olun," I said. "Father—is he all right? Does he still live?"

"Aye." The old druid nodded, sinking back onto one elbow in the dirt. "The bastards hit us at dawn ... but Virico has never let his war band leave their swords behind for a Litha feast. They carry their blades into the field in secret."

"What?" I gaped at him, shocked to my core that my father would order his warriors to commit such a blatant trespass against the sacred laws. Shocked as I was, I was also secretly proud.

Olun grinned at me, clearly not disapproving of my father's decision in any way, even if it offended the gods themselves. "The old fox won't go anywhere disadvantaged ever again. Not since seeing the inside of Caesar's camp."

So much for those chiefs who thought my father weak, I thought.

"We fought long enough to get most of our folk back inside the walls. But they outnumber us. Filthy Romans."

He spat on the ground, and Cai winced.

"Filthy Coritani."

He spat again. His spittle was webbed with blood.

"Get Neferet," I said to Cai. "She wanted to meet a druid? Here's her chance to make an excellent first impression."

"You didn't, by chance, bring a war band with you, did you?" Olun asked.

I grinned at him, watching his face as, one by one, my friends caught up with us on the path. Once Neferet got a good look at Olun's wounds, she determined that they weren't enough to kill him—but he also wasn't going anywhere anytime soon.

"I'll have to treat him where he lies," she said. "Moving him risks a collapse of his lung into his chest cavity."

Teeth clenched in pain, Olun raised an eyebrow at her as she swiftly and efficiently went about treating him . . . and then began to offer her suggestions for medicinal herbs—some of them within arm's reach—that could be of help with stanching the flow of blood. Neferet was clearly delighted to have him as her patient. In between bouts of their professional chatter, I gleaned what insights I could from him.

When Quint circled back from scouting ahead, he jogged to a halt beside me and stood blinking down at the wounded druid. "Huh," he grunted. "Missed that one . . ."

Cai shook his head at his friend. "Any more on the trail?" he asked.

Quint glanced at me. "Uh. Just . . . bodies," he said. "Not many, but . . ."

I felt my jaw tighten. Pontius Aquila would pay dearly for every soul of my tribe he'd taken. I looked down at Neferet.

"Go," she said. "Leave Antonia to keep watch for us, and I'll take care of your druid."

I nodded. "Come when you can. We'll likely have need of you before the sun sets."

I didn't like the thought of leaving anyone behind. But I *did* relish the thought of any of Aquila's people stumbling on Antonia and her crescent blade unawares. She saluted me with the weapon and took up a position where she could see both ends of the path, coming and going.

The rest of us moved on. Cai checked any bodies we passed for signs of life so that I wouldn't have to. It wasn't long before the trees directly ahead of us thinned and I caught my first glimpse of the Forgotten Vale. I ignored the fist squeezing my heart at the thought of revisiting the long green meadow where Mael and I had raced our chariot day after day and I'd first accomplished the Morrigan's Flight. There would be time for reminiscences later. I hoped. Instead, I told Cai to keep going and gather the girls to wait in the vale. I'd meet him there after I'd scouted the place where I planned to go over the wall.

So I could tell my father that I was home. That I'd brought help. That I would lend him my war band—my Legio Achillea—and together we would triumph over our enemies.

XXV

"HOPELESS!" I SNARLED. "By the gods . . . useless! There's nothing—no way in this world for me to get over the damned walls! Not unless I grow wings and—"

"Fallon—stop. Stop pacing and talk to me!" Cai reached out a hand and pulled me to a halt. "What's the matter? What did you see?"

"It's all different. Everything. Cai, it's hopeless!"

"Different how? What do you mean?"

"I mean I can't get *in*. I can't go home. There's no way."

There had never been a time in my life when I hadn't been able to scramble over the earthworks at a little hidden place near where the forest encroached on the western edge of Durovernum. You had to know it was there, and you had to know how to navigate the stones and branches, but I'd done it since I was a girl, and that was where I'd gone first to scout out my way into the town. But when I got there, everything was different. From my hiding place in a thicket two hundred paces from the wall, I could see that the overhanging trees had been cleared and the ramparts built up. Topped with jagged stone and sharpened stakes, surrounded by a bank and ditch. Durovernum was less a fort now than a fortress. The walls around Durovernum had never been so high. They'd never had to be. But now they were, and because of it, we were in danger of being defeated by the very people we were trying to help.

No sending a message through.

No getting close.

With Aquila and his Coritani camped in full view of the gates of the town, I didn't stand a chance at getting inside that way, either. My father would not even know it was me before his sentries shot me dead on the ground if I approached. And that was only if Aquila's people didn't get to me first. And if my war band and I attacked Aquila's gang of thugs without the help of my father's warriors, we'd be torn to pieces by their superior numbers before the Cantii even realized we were on their side and opened the gates.

"What has happened to my home?" I wondered aloud.

"War," Quint said with a helpless shrug. "What you're telling us means that over the last two years, your people have probably been attacked. More than once. And your father decided to do something about it. Your town hasn't fallen, which means it isn't weak. But someone seems to think it might be weak enough. If they just keep at it."

Virico Lugotorix had always been a just and brave man. A thoughtful king instead of a raider or a warmonger. Some had called him a weak king because he'd been taken prisoner by Caesar's legions and returned home afterward rather than taking his own life in shame. I'd even wondered at his valor when he refused to give me my rightful status in his royal war band and had, instead, tried to marry me off. My betrothal to Aeddan—Mael's brother, the son of the king of the Trinovante tribe—had been meant to seal a bond between our people and form an unbreakable alliance. My stomach dropped as I realized what my running away—what *my* disappearance—had done to him politically. I'd learned a lot about that sort of thing during my time in Rome. And now I knew it meant that my father had been denied that vital alliance. He'd been isolated.

He likely still was. No one would be coming to his aid against Aquila.

No one except us.

And I had no way of letting him know that.

Cai and Quint put their heads together to try to figure out a strategy that would get us around the impasse as the girls hunkered down to eat and check weapons and wait for their marching orders—if we could even get that far. In a fog of frustration I left them all to it. I picked up my traveling pack and walked to the far end of the vale, toward the old, forgotten grave barrow, with its lone standing stone at the end of the clearing. When I got close enough, I saw there was another mound there, beside the ancient one. Smaller. Covered in new growth that had yet to cloak its contours completely in soft green.

"Maelgwyn . . ." His name caught on the sob stuck in my throat.

So they had buried him here. I somehow knew they would.

I walked up to stand before the mound, then dropped to my knees and shrugged the straps of my traveling pack off my shoulders. Yanking open the drawstring, I dug around inside and found the small, smooth ebony box that held a handful of earth from a graveyard in Italia, near the Ludus Achillea.

Earth from Aeddan's grave.

The memory of holding Aeddan's hand as he sighed out his last breath—the arrow that had pierced his chest one that had been meant for me—crashed over me like a wave left over from the storm on the sea. I'd told him, as the light had left his eyes, to greet his brother, Maelgwyn, in the Otherworld for me. Mael, whom Aeddan had killed. Because of me. One more soul gone over to the Blessed Isles because of *me*.

One more meal of blood for the Morrigan to feast upon . . .

I pulled the raven-marked sword from its scabbard on my hip and jammed it into the loamy turf of Maelgwyn Ironhand's grave barrow, using it as a spade to dig a hole. When it was deeper than it needed to be, I emptied the dirt from the little box into the hole and shoveled the earth back in.

"Is it enough?" I called out, thrusting the empty box up toward the empty sky, the empty, ravenless trees. The place where my goddess should have been but wasn't. "Will it ever be enough? Was Sorcha not even enough for you? Or will you take my friends and my father too? Everyone

who's ever fought with me and everyone who's ever fought
for *you* because they fought with me . . . All while I listened
to *your* voice whispering in my ear . . . I don't hear you now,
Carrion Eater."

The grass under my knees was still wet with rain left
behind by the storm, but the earth of the grave barrow
beneath felt warm.

"Durovernum will fall without help," I said, my own
voice a harsh mockery of a raven's cry. "Help that I cannot
give them if you do not show me the way!"

Silence spun out in the wake of my plea.

Emptiness.

I stood and turned my back on the barrow and stalked
back to Cai and Quint. They both bore looks of hopeless frustration on their faces. There was no remedy that they had
found. No way around the wall my father had built. With
a cry of rage, I threw the empty ebony box into the trees.
There was a mad flapping of black wings, and a whole flock
of ravens burst into the sky. I watched them disappear . . .

And then I heard Quint say, "Hang on . . ."

His arm lifted, and I looked in the direction he was
pointing. At the copse of yew trees where the ravens had
been hidden. At first I didn't see it. And then I did . . .
machines. Wooden machines, tucked in behind a screen of
bushes. And the smile on Quint's face was that of a man
who'd just seen a marvel. He jogged over to the edge of the
trees, Cai following in his wake, and was almost bouncing
with excitement by the time I reached them. Elka and Ajani
joined us at the same time, curious.

"Catapults," Quint said, rubbing his hands together with unbridled glee. "*Those* are catapults . . . and *I* have an idea . . ."

"Wait," Elka said, taking a step toward the trees, peering cautiously as if there weren't manmade contraptions but rather dragons lurking there. "What are they doing here?"

I wondered the same thing myself. But Cai and Quint were already pushing through the trees to investigate, and they had a theory. *This* was the reason my father had built up the walls.

"These siege engines," Cai mused, "were doubtless left behind by Caesar's legions."

"Right. After they 'conquered' our lands." I couldn't keep the sarcasm from my tone.

Cai pretended not to hear it. "Exactly," he said.

"I'm guessing one of the other tribes decided to try their hand at putting our war machines to work for their own ends," Quint said.

I thought about that. "Most likely the Catuvellauni," I said. "They're a brawling, marauding lot with a long-honored favorite pastime of attacking the Cantii. But they're also lazy. They don't really like to put too much effort into warring. Cuts into their beer drinking."

"Do they still work?" Ajani asked. "The catapults, I mean?"

"Oh, aye!" Quint nodded, circling the mechanisms, kicking at the wooden wheels and cogs and tugging on the heavy ropes. "A bit creaky, but yeah. They'd work. Just . . . it looks as though they likely abandoned them when they realized it's far more fun *flinging* the stones than it is *finding* them."

Elka frowned at him, and Cai took up the explanation while Quint continued to poke and prod at the fittings on the machines.

"A catapult without something to hurl is useless," Cai said. "The Catuvellauni were likely far more interested in actually fighting your people and stealing their cattle than they were in having to quarry boulders or peck around the surrounding fields, looking for decent-sized rocks to load the machines with. If they're as easily distracted as you say, they probably got frustrated after heaving over the first few shots and then gave up."

"Right!" Quint jogged back over to us, a man with a look of focused purpose. "They're not legion. We are. We don't give up." He turned to me. "And neither do *you*."

"I don't want to heave great stones at my own father's house, Quint," I said. "That's not the way to get his attention."

He shook his head. "Not what I had in mind," he said, and his gaze drifted over to where Elka stood. A smile tugged at the corner of his mouth. "Elka . . . ?"

"What?" she asked, suddenly wary.

I couldn't blame her.

"You're not bound to your old ludus oath anymore, are you?" he said.

She glanced back and forth from him to me to Cai and back to Quint and said, even more warily, "No . . ."

"Good!" His smile grew larger. "Then you can just make up another one that *does* include flying."

This is madness, I thought, as I scrambled up onto the platform of the wood-and-rope contraption meant for rocks, not girls. *If human beings were meant to fly, surely the gods would have given us wings . . .*

And then, suddenly—shockingly—I remembered what Sorcha had said to me in her room in Cleopatra's palace just before she died. She'd told me that she'd dreamed of a raven flying through the sky . . . on the wings of an eagle. I'd thought, at the time, that perhaps she was talking about my swords. But now I understood. I was the Morrigan's raven. And the wings she'd sent me—the catapults left behind in the Forgotten Vale—had been built by Romans.

I was Sorcha's dream.

I'd even said it myself back in Gesoriacum: *"I'll get us into my father's great hall, even if I have to grow the Morrigan's own wings to fly there."*

Of course, I hadn't meant it quite so *literally*. But it seemed that all of the prophecies—intended or not—were converging upon me. I thought about Olun on the path. And about the path he'd seen for me. I thought about Sorcha. I wished with all my heart she were with me in that moment. Then I realized . . . she *was*. She would never leave me. She was my sister.

And I was her Morrigan's Flight.

But this time, I would not soar alone in the sky.

I'd volunteered to take flight all on my own, but my other sisters—my sister gladiatrices—would hear nothing of it. There were, they said, five siege engines. So there were going to be five girls going over the wall. Quint had checked and double-checked the machines. He'd test-fired them all, without loading them, and declared them ideal for his intended purpose: launching me and four other girls over the walls of Durovernum. Kore and Thalassa had volunteered almost immediately, citing, of course, their experience with bull-leaping on Crete. And Ajani and Elka weren't about to let me go without them. The catapults were small. Portable, but still relatively powerful. And Quint assured us they would easily propel us over the wall without actually killing or wounding us in the process. He hoped.

"Just . . . uh, go limp," he'd said. "Tuck your head in. That sort of thing . . ."

We dragged the things, like lumbering behemoths, to a section of the wall that had no sentries to startle or, more importantly, shoot at us. And it was in sight of our target. We'd decided that we would take aim as best we could—as best Quint, with his engineering experience, could—at the great broad expanse that was the roof of my father's great hall, rising up above the walls of the town. It was a perfect target: a gentle slope of thick thatch, it would cushion our landing. Hopefully. As I settled myself onto the wooden platform in a loose, ready crouch, Kronos stood with his arms crossed over his broad chest, shaking his head. But there was also the barest hint of a smile tugging at the corner of his mouth, which made me feel the tiniest bit better about our impending act of lunacy. He actually thought it would work. And Kronos wasn't what I would call an optimist on the best of days.

Cai and I had worked out the details and timing of what would happen once we were successfully inside the town, based on my best guesses as to how my father and his chiefs might react to my sudden reappearance. Cai would either receive a signal from me within an hour's time, or he wouldn't. We had come up with contingencies either way.

I wore my sister's pearl-studded breastplate and had my twin swords sheathed at my sides. Elka gripped her spear tightly. And Ajani had her bow held in front of her, with a quiver stuffed full of arrows on her back—tied down and secured for flight. I glanced over at Kore and Thalassa on one side of me and Elka and Ajani on the other. All of us were coiled and ready, and grinning fiercely with anticipation . . . and just a little bit of terror.

"Let's fly!" I called. And I gave Quint the signal to loose.

The force of the catapult's propulsion was like nothing I'd ever felt before—a bone-jarring, sudden thrust upward—followed by the sheer exhilaration of flying through the air, borne aloft like a bird. I heard Thalassa utter a brief squeal and saw Elka's mouth open in a silent cry.

I don't know if I made any sound.

All I could hear close by was the wind rushing past my ears as I flew in the moments before we hit the roof with enough force that the thatch caught us, softened our landings, and then . . . collapsed inward. Suddenly the world all around me went from day-bright sky to peat-smoky darkness as the five of us descended into the middle of my father's great feast hall.

Where he happened to be conducting a meeting of his war chiefs.

I landed at Virico's feet in a pile of thatch with a thud that knocked the wind from my lungs and lay there, groaning for a moment in the stunned silence that descended on the hall. That silence was broken a moment later, as Elka yelped and rolled out of the edge of the fire that was crackling in the central hearth. By the time I lifted my head to look around, I saw Ajani was already up on her feet, crouched in a wary stance, folded protectively around her bow and surrounded by a circle of gape-mouthed Cantii warriors, all of them bristling with swords.

"Father!" I gasped, struggling to my feet and fumbling at the chinstrap of my helmet, clawing the thing off my head so he could see my face. "It's me—Fallon!"

As I lurched to my feet, Kore and Thalassa were stamping the smoldering embers from Elka's tunic hem and helping her to stand too. I turned and looked up to see my father rising slowly from his seat, his gaze fastened on my face, eyes wide and his expression one of naked disbelief. To him, I was a ghost.

"Father, it's me—I've come home . . ." I said. Then I realized I was speaking Latin. I tried again, in the language of my tribe. "I'm here. Home. Father—"

That was as far as I got before he lunged for me.

He hauled me in to his chest, and his great long arms wrapped around me so tightly I couldn't breathe as he lifted me off my feet in a crushing embrace. If I hadn't been wearing Sorcha's armor, I think he might have broken a rib or two. I'm fairly certain my friends thought I was being attacked, until the moment he uttered my name, muffled by the embrace and hindered by the emotions that choked his throat closed.

"Fallon . . ." He set me down, finally, on my feet and pushed me to arm's length, peering into my face. "My girl . . . It's really *you* . . ."

I nodded, my own throat squeezed tight, and looked up at him, tears blurring my vision. Virico's great thick mane of auburn hair had gone iron gray in my absence. There was still a sprinkling of red in his beard, but that too was frosted a dark silver. His face, like Olun's, was more lined than it had been. The planes of his cheeks and the angle of his forehead more pronounced. But he was still tall and unbowed and strong and my father. I'd feared he would be angry, unforgiving . . . but his eyes were full of love.

And, perhaps understandably, confusion.

"These are my friends," I said, turning to gesture to my gladiatrix sisters. "Elka and Ajani, Kore and Thalassa . . ." The girls each nodded politely in turn. "I know I should have asked you first before inviting them in . . ."

Virico glanced upward to the holes our arrival had torn in his roof.

"Or perhaps used the door," he said.

Then he turned to his chiefs and gestured for them to lower their weapons.

"How?" he asked, first, gesturing to the roof. My father had a pragmatic mind, and all of the other questions he had could wait their logical turn. First things first. How had his daughter and her companions come to be flying over—and crashing into—his house?

"There were catapults," I said. "Siege engines in a field near the vale . . ."

He nodded. I could see that he knew of the catapults, and I suspected Quint and Cai had been right about Catuvellauni raids prompting higher walls.

"We loaded them with, um, well . . . with ourselves instead of stones. It's . . . a thing we've been practicing . . . sort of." I looked back and forth between the other girls. "It's . . . Oh, Da . . . it's such a long story. All of it."

Virico smiled and turned to a woman standing off to one side. She was staring at me with a wide, incredulous grin on her face and tears in her eyes.

"Clota," he said, "would you be so kind as to fetch five mugs? These girls look thirsty. And I think they have a tale to tell us." Then he turned back to me, and I saw his gaze focus on the armor I wore. Sorcha's armor. He reached out a hand as if he would touch it to make certain it was real. But stopped himself mid-gesture. "And I, for one, would open my ears to hear it."

We only had an hour until I'd told Cai I'd signal him, and so I tried to be brief. But it took a while to tell even half of the whole story. For one thing, Elka and Ajani kept interjecting breathlessly, and every time they did I had to keep switching back and forth from Latin to the Cantii tongue for those of the chiefs who'd never bothered to learn the language of the traders beyond what would get them the best price on an amphora of wine or a bolt of cloth for their wife. Eventually, I managed to convey a goodly portion—or the salient parts, at least—of what had transpired in my life over the last two years.

"So . . . you see . . . the enemy at your gates was really *my* enemy first," I concluded. "I'm so sorry."

"In only two short years you managed to acquire a dire, vengeful adversary," my father said, a glint of grim amusement in his eyes. "That was industrious of you, daughter."

"I like your father," Elka whispered in my ear.

I elbowed her in the ribs.

"He's not getting away with his atrocities," I told Virico. "Not this time. We've suffered enough at his hands. He took our home, our friends, and our lives in the arena. Things we fought hard to build—things Sorcha fought for . . . You would have been so proud of her, Father."

I could tell from his face that the news of what had happened to her had both healed a wound in him and torn a new one open at the same time. "I always have been," he said, his voice rough. "Of both of you, Fallon. So proud. And now, it seems, you will have the opportunity to show me what, exactly, you learned from your sister at this . . . what did you call it? This Ludus Achillea."

As his men and women prepared for the coming battle, my father took me aside.

"I wronged you, Fallon," he said.

I shook my head, even though I had myself believed that same thing for a very long time. "For the right reasons," I said.

"I should have let you join the war band."

I nodded, grinning. "It would have saved me having to go out and find one on my own. But then again, the one I found . . . I wouldn't trade for all the wide world."

I glanced over to where Ajani and Elka were showing off their weapons to some of the younger warriors. "What do you think? How did I fare?"

"I think I have the cleverest war leader for a daughter that Lugh and the Morrigan ever made," Virico said. "And I think I'm a fool for not having seen it."

"Wait until you meet the others—and see the horses and chariots Cleopatra gave me! Wait until you meet Cai and . . . uh. Cai is . . . another story. A good one. One for the bards to sing of . . . I promise . . ."

He looked at me, more than a little mystified. Then he shook his head and said, "Fallon . . . I . . . Can you ever forgive me?"

I reached out and took his hand. "Will you let me fight beside you, Father?"

"No."

He wrapped his great large hand around mine.

"I would ask that *you* let me fight beside you and your friends."

For a moment, I couldn't speak. I took a deep breath in. "You'd do such a thing?" I asked.

"With great pride."

"Then there is nothing to forgive."

His eyes glittered. "Will you do me the honor then, my warrior daughter, of helping me with my armor?"

"Of course."

"Good." He nodded. "Then let's go get the bastards. Together."

XXVI

"KEEP MY CHARIOT ready," I had told Cai in the moments before I'd climbed up onto the catapult. "Ajani will send up a signal when we're ready, and the moment you see movement at the gate—"

"I'll be there."

"Cai, I—"

He'd put a finger to my lips, a fierce spark flashing in his eyes. "Tell me when it's over," he said. "After we win."

Now I stood there before the gates of Durovernum, beside my warrior father, with blue woad painted on my cheeks and my raven sword in my hand and a shield from my father's own wall strapped on my arm. I kept my eagle sword sheathed. I would need one hand free to grip the chariot when Cai came for me.

Virico looked at me and nodded. I, in turn, nodded at Ajani. She drew back the string on her bow and loosed a flaming arrow high into the sky, trailing a black-and-red ribbon of smoke. My father's sentries sounded the carnyx horns, and the gates of the town swung outward, like a great beast opening its jaws in a mighty yawn.

Aquila had maybe a hundred and fifty warriors with him, all told. Not many, but enough. Just enough to overrun Durovernum and take whatever defeated Cantii warriors he wanted as slaves for his munera. Enough to destroy my home. At least, that's what he thought. The front ranks were all dressed in the garb of the Sons of Dis— black armor, black cloaks, helmets with black crests—and the rest were a tattooed and largely armorless collection of Coritani berserker warriors. Fierce, yes, but undisciplined. In between them and us were a few bodies—theirs and ours—scattered in the field, left behind after Aquila's despicable surprise attack. And I knew that somewhere, behind their ranks, there would also be prisoners.

I strode forward, just far enough out so that Aquila and his warriors would see me standing there, apart. I waited until I could feel all of their eyes on me, and then I drew the silver feather from the pouch at my belt. The one the priest had dropped in the temple of Sekhemet when Acheron had tried to kill me. I held it up high over my head so that it shone in the late afternoon sunlight. I saw a black-cloaked figure take a few long steps forward.

Steps that faltered when he realized who it was . . . and what I held.

"Pontius Aquila!" I cried out in my loudest voice. "Your assassin failed and is no more. Acheron is dead! Just like the Sons of Dis will be before this day's sun sets."

I hurled the silver feather into the air, and it spun, glittering, end over end to land somewhere in the grass between us. It would be lost in the coming battle, I knew. Trampled in the mud and twisted. It would be broken like his hideous order would be broken.

"He met his end in the temple of Sekhemet," I continued. "Just as you will meet yours here, on the field of battle, in the temple of the Morrigan. There will be no jackal men to drag your corpse away today. We will leave it to the sky for the ravens and the earth for the wolves and the worms. And you will do no more collecting."

I saw the black-cloaked figure turn from me and huddle with his warriors. They were more than a match for my father's war band, and they knew it. What they didn't know was that, just beyond the margins of the fields, a small but highly motivated band of exceptionally trained gladiatrices, Amazons, and ex-legionnaires waited patiently to enter the fray. And more than a match became substantially less of a surety when suddenly faced with fighting on two fronts. Particularly when one of those fronts was equipped with chariots given to them by a queen who also happened to be the daughter of gods.

The carnyx brayed again, and a sound echoed back from beneath the cover of the trees at the edge of the field. It started as a far-off murmur, swelled to a rumble, and then became a roar as the Legio Achillea came thundering out from between the oaks to attack the left flank of Pontius Aquila's mercenaries. Simultaneously, my father gave his warriors the command to attack, and they streamed out of the gates, curving around to attack our enemy's right flank. Kore and Thalassa went with them, woad-painted and howling war cries, as if the Cantii were their own fierce folk.

I waited at the gate with my father, along with Elka and Ajani, for the brief seconds it took for our four chariots to arrive. When Cai—in full Roman decurion regalia *and* war paint on his cheeks—pulled to a halt in front of me, he greeted my father with a legion salute and a brisk, "My lord king!" as I leaped into the swift cart. Elka jumped up behind Quint, whose cart was supplied with a full complement of spears. Ajani stepped up behind Kronos, and Gratia made room for my father with a fierce grin.

"Never driven a king before, sir," she said over her shoulder as Virico Lugotorix stepped up into her chariot. "I'll try to avoid too many bumps!"

My father laughed and slapped her on the shoulder. Then we all wheeled away and joined the fight. The storm had turned the ground soft, and where Aquila's people were, their feet churned it to mud. But the high, narrow wheels of the Aegyptian chariots and the lightning-swift hooves of the horses skimmed over the grass as we harried their flanks and made them turn outward to face us. My father's own charioteers followed our lead, driving Cantii archers around the perimeter of the field while the rest of his war band engaged hand-to-hand.

Aquila, unsurprisingly, huddled right in the middle of a thick clot of his Dis warriors, as protected as he could be, dressed in a ceremonial polished black-scale mail tunic that looked as though it had never seen a moment's battle. Cai maneuvered our chariot with clever, steady hands, but we couldn't get close. Every black-cloaked warrior I cut away with my blade seemed to just make a hole for another to step into his place. Until, finally, I saw a gap. Narrow—too narrow for a chariot—and suddenly I was down on the ground and running.

Cai shouted for me to stop, but I didn't. I couldn't.

Pontius Aquila would die that day, and he would die by *my* hand.

But just before I reached him, there was suddenly another warrior standing in my way. He wore no black armor, but fought barefoot and shirtless . . . and I recognized the tattoos on his arm even before I looked up at his face.

"Yoreth." I spat his name as our eyes locked.

A vicious grin split his features.

I remembered how he'd howled, promising vengeance one day, as I'd left him behind at the Ludus Flaminius to rot. He clearly remembered it too.

A heartbeat, then two, passed . . . and he ran at me. He no longer fought with the trident he'd used in the arena— just a long, wicked-bladed spear. His first thrust tagged my thigh, just below the straps of my battle kilt—a long, shallow cut—and I stumbled in the muddy grass and fell to one knee with a grunt of pain. I blocked his next blow with my shield, but as I staggered up to regain my feet, he lunged forward with a long dagger drawn from his belt. Yoreth thrust it toward my sword-hand side, and we locked up blades, hilt to hilt.

His snarl was a feral thing, and there was battle madness in his eyes.

I head-butted him with the brim of my helmet, and it barely fazed him. With blood running down both cheeks from the gash on his forehead, he pressed me backward, back down into the mud. I ground my teeth together, straining to push him back, but my grip on my sword was slipping . . .

And then, suddenly, the iron point of an arrowhead burst through the skin at the front of his neck. I recoiled as he gagged once, a horrid, harrowing sound, and blood poured from his mouth. His eyes rolled backward in his head, and he fell face-first to the ground before me.

Ajani! I thought, springing back up to my feet. But then I saw the fletching on the arrow shaft lodged in the back of Yoreth's neck. The feathers were black. I glanced around and saw Tanis, surrounded by Dis warriors, firing arrows—not at us, not at *my* war band, but at her own. In the chaos of the melee, no one really seemed to notice. At least, they hadn't up until that moment. The two of us locked eyes for an instant, and she gave me a small smile.

Then she turned and calmly nocked another arrow and shot another Coritani berserker that was giving Devana some trouble at the edge of the fray. I wasn't the only one who noticed that time. In the next instant, Tanis was down on hands and knees from a blow to the back of her head. I shouted her name, but my cry was swallowed up in the din of the fight. I ducked under a wide, wild blow from a Coritani and slashed at his flank, pushing past to get into a pocket of breathing space. The warrior who'd taken Tanis down had his sword raised for a killing blow.

I had no choice and no chance to think twice—I would not fail her again—and I threw my sword at him. It spun end over end, and the blade caught him right at the join between his neck and shoulder. Not a lethal blow, but enough to make him scream and drop his own sword. It gave Tanis just enough time to draw another arrow from the quiver on her hip, and, spinning on one knee, she thrust it up into his torso, underneath his rib cage. She glanced back over her shoulder at me and nodded sharply in thanks. I nodded back and then turned away when I heard someone shouting my name over the din.

Cai swung his chariot in a tight turn and, as he raced past, hollered for me to get back on board. I took a running leap and swung myself up behind him as he slapped the reins and the horses surged forward. I drew my eagle sword from its scabbard. The tide of battle was beginning to turn. But not fast enough. Elka and Quint were just off to our left, wreaking havoc with spear and sword.

"Quint!" I shouted. "Now!"

He nodded at me and, lifting his legion signal whistle to his lips, blew three sharp blasts on it. At the edge of the clearing, the leaves of the trees began to glow red. While my gladiatrix sisters and I fought on the field, my band of Amazons had circled around in stealth to free Aquila's captives. Perhaps, in hindsight, it hadn't been the wisest thing for Aquila to do—taking only prisoners he thought would fight fiercely and well in his munera back in Rome.

Because those men and women, once freed, fought just as fiercely and well on the battlefield that day. Led by Kallista and her sisters, the daughters of Amazons, wielding their fire chains with mesmerizing, deadly grace.

The rout of Aquila's forces began in earnest.

Like peeling an onion, with our blades we stripped away the warriors that surrounded him, protecting him, until the moment when he stood there, alone in a field where others still fought around him. His own sword was unbloodied, clenched white-knuckled in his hand. I signaled Cai to stop the chariot. Off to my right, I saw Virico signal Gratia to do the same.

I stepped down onto the muddy grass and walked toward the man who'd haunted my days in Rome. The man who'd stood gloating in the shadows while Caesar fell. A coward and a villain. A madman . . .

"You only exist because of me," he snarled at me, flecks of foam spittle spraying from his mouth. "You think Caesar cared for you? You were a tool. I would have made you a talisman. Divine. A name to conjure with. Now I'll just kill you where you stand and leave this fetid island to sink under the weight of its own barbarism."

I snorted. "You really don't know when you're beaten, do you?"

"Defeating this rabble isn't the same as defeating me, girl." He lifted his sword and widened his stance.

"Know this, Roman," my father said, striding over to stand within striking distance on Aquila's other side. "If my daughter falls, you will have to face me."

"Is that supposed to be a threat, old man?" Aquila sneered, turning the full force of his venomous attention on Virico. "I know you. I know what you are. You're a coward and a captive and—"

I took three steps forward, and thrust my sword up under the polished black scales of his pristine ceremonial armor, stabbing him through the heart while he ranted.

Pontius Aquila had never been an honorable enemy. And it was my absolute pleasure to visit a dishonorable death upon him. He'd thought I would adhere to the rules of the gladiatorial arena. Face him in honorable single combat. I was more than happy to prove him wrong. We weren't in an arena. And he'd insulted my father, the king. As he flailed weakly at the hilt of my eagle sword, sticking grotesquely out from between his ribs, I looked Pontius Aquila right in his black eyes.

"He is my father. He is a king. He and Caesar are the reasons *I* am Victrix."

Aquila sagged to his knees, still staring up at me in disbelief.

"And you?" I continued. "You are nothing. Nothing except a reason for me to finally come home."

In the wake of Aquila's death, the Coritani lost interest in any further fighting almost instantly. They'd already gambled much on the Roman Tribune's promises to them and let their hatred of the Cantii sway them to a cause that really wasn't even theirs in the first place. But with the Collector dead, so were their hopes of rich purses and Cantii slaves to sell. The easy pickings they'd been promised were nothing of the sort. I could see them start to turn tail with the idea of heading for other unsuspecting prey. I knew the Coritani. They would pillage and kill all the way back to their own lands if we gave them the chance. We didn't. The handful who survived melted into the surrounding forest, leaving the Sons of Dis—what was left of them—to be surrounded and cut down by my father's war band.

In the end, there was only one black-clad warrior left standing in that whole field. And that was because she'd saved my life. In the aftermath of the battle, with the sun sinking low behind the trees and my war band ranged in a loose circle around us, Tanis walked haltingly up to me, my lost raven sword—the one I'd thrown at her assailant— dangling loosely in her hand.

She stopped and held my sword out to me, hilt-first. "I didn't kill Hestia."

I reached for the blade, nodding thanks.

"I didn't kill any of ours," she continued. "I mean . . . any of yours."

"I know," I said, glancing at Ajani. "I thought about it after Cosa, and I realized . . . you're a much better shot than that."

Ajani tilted her head at Tanis, and a small smile lifted the corner of her mouth. Tanis stood there for a long moment, just staring at us, then Gratia stepped down from the chariot she'd been driving and walked slowly over to her. I felt my muscles tense. Gratia had never allowed Tanis much slack back at the Ludus Achillea. A lot of the girls hadn't. I waited to see what she would do, half expecting she would hurl a punch at Tanis. Or maybe worse.

Her hand came up and fell heavily on Tanis's shoulder. "Welcome back, little archer," she said. "We've missed you."

Tanis bit her lip, and Gratia wrapped her in a punishing bear hug as the rest of us let loose a thunderous cheer that echoed off the oaks of the Island of the Mighty.

XXVII

DESTINY, CLEOPATRA HAD once told me, *is not something that is given. It's something you prove yourself worthy of taking.*

I thought about that as I lit the lamps that hung from the rafters of my roundhouse, wondering if she would appreciate the manner in which I'd proved myself worthy. I suspected she would. In truth, I suspected that she would have had a good long laugh over it.

The last lamp I lit was the one Sorcha had given me to replace my oath lamp back at the ludus. Flickering light and shadow played along the walls and floors, picked out the colors of the pillows and rugs covering the sleeping platform, and reflected off the wavy bronze mirror that hung on one wall. No one had moved a thing in the little house since I'd left. My father had forbade it. The remains of my fire-tarnished dagger and torc were still sitting in the brazier, and even the stain on the rug from where Aeddan had dropped the amphora of wine that night was still there.

I tidied those things up and aired the place out before inviting Cai in later that night. There had been a feast, of course. A celebration. A *lot* of flirting between my father's war band and mine.

Now there was only the song of a night bird drifting in through the tiny window. Lamplight, peace, my own bed, and Caius Antonius Varro in my arms.

"Your Forgotten Vale reminds me of the Circus Maximus," Cai said quietly, staring up into the shadows beneath the thatched roof. "The shape of it. You know . . . the way you girls fought today, I don't think you're going to have to worry about tribal raids for some time to come, do you?"

I grinned. "Probably not. Word gets around . . ."

"Exactly," he said. "So I was thinking. Maybe we could turn the Forgotten Vale into something. Something other than a place of sadness and fading memories."

"You mean, something like . . . an arena?" I said.

"Why not?" he said, rising up on one elbow so he could look into my eyes. "A place where you could still compete. Race those wondrous chariots. Continue to hone your skills and teach new warriors . . . Invite the tribes to *friendly* competitions . . . Turn the grave barrows into a proper monument to honor the fallen. To *not* forget them. Maybe hold your own Triumphs one day."

I smiled at him.

Our own Triumphs . . .

The words sounded like a distant carnyx calling me and all my sisters to arms . . . and I liked the sound of that.

Acknowledgments

Bringing Fallon and Company's adventures to a close in *The Triumphant* feels, well, triumphant. This girl—this story—has been with me for a very long time and I feel indescribably lucky to have had the opportunity to bring her, and it, to life through this series. With a little (a LOT) of help and hard work and love and support and prodigious bloodshed (maybe not that last one) from my own war band.

Jessica Regel, as always, gets my first fist-to-the-heart salute. She is a fierce and fearsome agent and would look fabulous holding a spear. Thanks also, once again, to the wonderful crew at Foundry Literary + Media and to Dana Spector at CAA. Ave, guys!

Likewise, my other Jessica—editrix extraordinaire Jessica Harriton—would absolutely rock a weaponized ensemble. Something shiny with a wicked-sharp edge! I am so grateful to her, and to Ben Schrank, and to the entire amazing Razorbill team, for helping me shape this story and make it shine and get it out into the world. This entire experience has been nothing short of wonderful. Laurel wreaths and battle hugs all around! That goes double for Elyse Marshall and Samantha Devotta, my wondrous warrior publicists. And triple for the design team who cloaked my words in such stunningly beautiful images. Fallon and the girls have never looked better!

Also, I still owe Tiffany Liao and Hadley Dyer deep debts of gratitude. All roads may very well lead to Rome, but you still need someone to grab you by the hair and throw you in the back of the chariot first or you're never gonna get there. Thanks for that, guys.

Love and gratitude, always and forever, to my family—especially my mom and brother—for believing in me and not bugging me every time I curled up in a corner to read a book about long-dead civilizations.

For my readers and fans, all I can say is it has been an honor and a privilege to have gone on this journey with you guys. You both humble and inspire me.

And finally, as always, to John. There's no flying in the Oath. Until there is.